Last time, she almost killed them all.

Now, a band of heroes risk their lives.

To prevent ultimate evil from laying the lands to waste, five friends must infiltrate the very heart of darkness and take on the most maniacal demon in the Abyss. . . .

**The Queen of the Demonweb Pits!**

Praise for Paul Kidd's *Descent into the Depths of the Earth* . . .

". . . a fantastic piece of work, a fast-paced, witty, and by turns downright silly romp. Kidd has succeeded in giving structure to a near-structureless adventure and in filling the depths of the earth with larger-than-life characters. If you thought Dirty Harry was a mean cop, wait until you see the Justicar at work."

—*Black Gate* Magazine

Praise for Paul Kidd . . .

"You may already be a winner!"

—*Reader's Digest*

# GREYHAWK

# Queen of the Demonweb Pits

## Paul Kidd

# QUEEN OF THE DEMONWEB PITS
## ©2001 Wizards of the Coast, Inc.

Distributed in the United States by Holtzbrinck Publishing. Distributed in Canada by Fenn Ltd.

Distributed to the hobby, toy, and comic trade in the United States and Canada by regional distributors.

Distributed worldwide by Wizards of the Coast, Inc. and regional distributors.

Cover art by Justin Sweet
Map by Todd Gamble
First Printing: October 2001
Library of Congress Catalog Card Number:

9 8 7 6 5 4 3 2 1

ISBN: 0-7869-1903-5
UK ISBN: 0-7869-2671-6
620-T21903

U.S., CANADA,
ASIA, PACIFIC, & LATIN AMERICA
Wizards of the Coast, Inc.
P.O. Box 707
Renton, WA 98057-0707
+1-800-324-6496

EUROPEAN HEADQUARTERS
Wizards of the Coast, Belgium
P.B. 2031
2600 Berchem
Belgium
+32-70-23-32-77

Visit our web site at www.wizards.com/

For Tim Baverstock, master of puns, intrepid tourist, and without whom none of this could have been written!
(Love you long time, GI-san!)

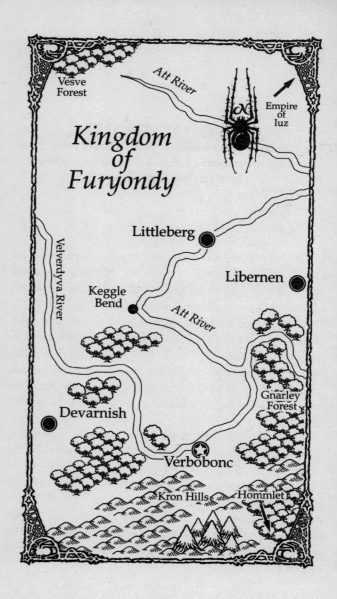

# The Beginning . . .

## CY 583

This time, it had all gone wrong.

Deep in the heart of conquered territory, a resistance war raged. Harsh, pitiless, and savage, a war without rest, without honor, without glory. A war where small bands of men made the minions of Iuz pay for their deeds in blood.

The hordes of Iuz had swept over villages, towns, and cities, obliterating those who fled from them. Men, women, children, and animals had been butchered, then raised as rotting, shambling legions of the damned. Iuz had stormed forward with his undead monsters, slaughtering everything in his path, but in the lands behind him, he had unknowingly left a cancer that gnawed at his heart.

The roving bands of freedom fighters were good at slaughter. They had been formed from the hard, silent men of the wilds, the rangers who had failed to protect the borders and the sacred wilderness, the men who had been guardians but who had been helpless against the demon hordes. The armies of Iuz had come—demons and rotting corpses covered by vast clouds of carrion flies—leaving the once-fertile lands covered in slime and ash. The armies had moved on, and behind them a scattered handful of rangers rose to fight.

They were few, and they were terrible. The homeless warriors tore into Iuz's supply columns, slaughtered his couriers, and assassinated his scouts. Blades killed sentries in the night. Wells were poisoned and roads strewn with traps. Soon it took entire regiments to escort a single messenger, and supply columns were convoyed by legions of guards. Iuz stripped troops from the conquering armies to try to stamp out the enemies within, and still the killers struck. They fought endlessly, viciously, with infinite cunning and utterly without mercy. Leaving nothing but corpses in their wake, they mutilated even their own dead to render them useless to Iuz's necromancers. They had failed to protect their own people—and now they paid for it with their suicidal struggle.

The tide had finally turned against them. Iuz had abandoned his plans of conquest to hunt for the roving bands of freedom fighters. Half their numbers had died in a few short weeks. The rest fought with ten times the fury, morning, noon, and night.

Iuz turned inward, pruning his conquering armies of men, and the humans, elves, and dwarves from the surrounding nations began to hammer the demons back, step by step. Iuz had lost the war. Exhausted, harried, and dying man by man, the freedom fighters continued to fight, knowing they had won. They had paid their debt.

These were the last days of the war, a time when a man could lay low and know that the horror soon would pass. But for some, the fight and slaughter had been sweet. There was a *power* that came with action, an intensity that became a drug, intoxicating and addictive.

Of all the war band leaders, the most savage, the most daring, was Recca—swordmaster and last lord of the grass elves. He had taught the art of the blade for three hundred years, taking only the most dedicated, most cunning, and most perfect students. His blade struck faster than thought, and he moved through a fight as if it were a dance. His sword, jet black with a wolf skull pommel, was sharp enough to carve a war-horse in two.

As Iuz's war ground to an end, Recca had eleven followers remaining—rangers and battle-mages hardened in this thankless war. He also had a single student, an apprentice as unlike him as iron was to silk: brooding, massive, humorless, a man who no longer had a name.

Recca was charismatic, a cavalier, dapper and sly, cunning and adored. He had taken on this apprentice because the boy looked like he had the devotion to listen and learn. Recca had taught the boy to fight, to track, to hunt, and above all to think. They had been companions through many long, silent missions— teacher and student, leader and learner. The apprentice's devotion was based on a strange sense of honor that he cherished deep inside his soul. Recca despaired of ever teaching the boy proper practicality.

Master and apprentice lay in the heather, side by side. Recca's armor, though bearing scrapes and scratches from many battles, still had a worn flamboyance about it, and his steel helmet was fashioned like a screaming eagle. Next to his master, the apprentice was in gear rugged, tested, and unadorned. Where Recca was thin and rakishly handsome with amber eyes and golden hair as soft as silk, his apprentice, almost invisible in the weeds beside him, was huge and unappealing. When they'd first met, Recca had thought the boy too big and too powerful to move in stealth, yet the human was always somehow silent as a cat. No, not a cat, a bear—dark, terrifying, and immense.

The war had taught the boy failure, hate, and emptiness. He had a stark brilliance with the sword, which Recca found annoying. No flamboyance, no style—merely a brutal, unforgiving efficiency. Recca's reputation had been founded on his brilliance, his merciless speed, and his raffish charisma. But in dark times, men looked to tireless, efficient men for comfort. Men like Recca's apprentice.

With the turning of the war, decent targets had become fewer and fewer. The only troops of Iuz to be seen were armies in retreat, and the small band of freedom fighters could do little but harry their scouts.

But here, all of a sudden, a mistake had been made. A general was bringing troops to build field fortifications. Besides the general, there would be officers and officials—and they were guarded only by shambling, rotting zombies armed with shovels and stakes. There were no abyssal bats, no demons. A general of Iuz would fall, the greatest coup achieved by any band through the entire war. Recca's reputation would be immortalized.

The war was ending, and it was time to look to the future. A new generation would be searching for heroes—for kings. As the hero of the resistance, Recca's name would ring upon a hundred thousand tongues. . . .

Recca thought the new attack would be easy, but his apprentice failed to agree. The big human studied the scattered parties of zombies digging ditches and hauling rocks. He looked at the general's tents and the few guards set on hills and ridgelines, and he drew back into cover.

"Withdraw." His voice was bass—quiet, grim, definite. "It's a trap."

The elf rolled to look at his apprentice and raised one brow. "And we know this *how?*"

"It smells wrong."

"What? Have you become part man, part hell hound?" Recca slid an amused sidewise glance at his apprentice. "The problem with humans is that they cannot accept being clever! There is a superiority that comes with intelligence and training. I have trained you superbly. Every movement you make is properly honed." Recca smiled. "Remember—evil may have cunning, but it never has wit or style."

If the apprentice had been a bear, he would have growled. The big man made to speak, but Recca had already slithered back down from the ridge to give orders to his men.

They collected there under cover—painted men, camouflaged and almost invisible. Eleven of them sat and listened, trusting their leader to give shape to their lives. Recca looked about the empty wilderness and filled his mind with images of his victory—his glory.

"They're coming! More Iuz vermin to kill! A general, and without an escort in sight!" The elven warlord infected his men with his confidence. "We'll slaughter a general!"

An Iuz general. The only demonic warlord to be slain in this war, and his head would fall to Recca! Recca parted the weeds and showed his men his plan for victory.

"They're fortifying this valley. That means their army is coming, so we must work fast." Recca looked the scene over with all the care of a true artist at work. "They'll survey this ridge. This is the obvious point to use as the crest of their line. So we hide, and when the general comes, we fight. I want you all to attack the workers in one group. This will draw attention to your position. I will then slay their general. We flee down the gully, here into the trees, so lay traps to kill the pursuit—usual mix. Rendezvous at broken pine an hour after dusk." He slapped his men on the shoulders and bade them go. "Good hunting!"

The apprentice did not leave. He hovered, huge and unsmiling, beside his teacher. He never smiled, never laughed, and never tired. His sword jutted through his belt, always poised for a lightning-draw.

"I will cover your back, Master Recca."

"I do not need you." The elf rested one hand languidly on his sword—the black sword of the swordmaster of the elves. "My blade and I have work to do."

The apprentice was unmoved. "Then I will make sure you are free to do it."

The apprentice led the way into the best possible cover—not the obvious place to hide, it was a place in which only a ranger could disappear. He used his sword to slit a thin carpet of the dead, dry grass, and he slid beneath it, disappearing totally from view. Unwilling to follow a mere student's lead, Recca stood proud and alone on the hilltop until prudence dictated that he hide at last.

Soon, shambling footfalls sounded on the turf. The undead servants came to build their master's wall. With them came their overlords—a general, his scribes, and advisors—all feeling perfectly safe so far behind their lines. Soon the sounds of the attack came—rangers' war cries and the sounds of spells. Recca saw his target standing and staring at the commotion. The elf rose in silence, sliding forward to strike from behind—

And then everything went wrong.

Eleven of Recca's men engaged the undead in battle, and the air rang to the sound of piercing screams. Shambling, rotting corpses on the hillside split open as shapes inside the dead flesh exploded into the air. The zombies burst and took shape as filth-spattered, howling monsters with dead grey skin, fangs, and claws. Carnivorous and mad with rage, they flung themselves on the freedom fighters, fighting in a frenzy of speed.

*Wights!*

Recca swiped with his sword, but his target was merely an illusion—a spell sent by an enemy that mocked him. From within the enemy tents, more shapes exploded into the sky—abyssal bats and huge rotting demons, skull-headed and spewing acid as they flew. A blast of fluid ploughed through Recca's men, turning three into skeletons and scattering the others.

A laughing toadlike demon lurched up the hillside toward Recca. The huge demon was covered in pustules and bristled with fangs. It struck sparks from the boulders with its claws. Towering over the elf, the demon leaped and capered on the hill, bellowing in lust and glee.

As the monster drew near, three of the wights attacked Recca. He spun past one, cut, spun, cut again. The sole surviving monster threw itself at him. Recca ran and jumped, twirling like an acrobat. He landed behind his prey, lanced backward with his sword, and felt it strike home. He jerked his blade free, turned, and decapitated his enemy in a single blinding stroke.

Behind him, he heard a blade striking with incredible speed— once, twice, thrice—strokes that hit home with massive force. Recca saw his apprentice standing, smeared with soil and dust. Two wights lay dead at his feet, each one almost sheared in two. Seeing the abyssal bats and wights charging into the other men, Recca turned and lunged toward the valley with its gully and its traps.

"Retreat!" Recca bellowed. *"Now!"*

Recca ran. He sped as only a grass elf could—the swiftest runners of the Flanaess. Amongst thick brush and boulders too thick for the titanic bats to penetrate, Recca ducked past traps, reached safety, and then looked back up the hill.

His apprentice had obeyed him, running with the heavy, lumbering stride of a big man. He reached the boulders, turned, and saw his comrades fighting not far away. There were now only five survivors, but they were making for the gully, and the enemy had left themselves open to attack. The apprentice flicked an eye over the fight, then moved forward.

"Master, I'll go left. You can hit from behind once they see me charge."

Recca looked at the fight and sheathed his blade. "No."

His apprentice stared, his eyes searching Recca for an answer, unable to comprehend. "Why?"

Honor! Men like Recca and his marauding rangers could not afford the luxury of honor. Survival was a practical art, and only survivors returned to fight and kill and win. Recca raked his apprentice with a glance that despaired of the human's petty intellect.

"You suffer from an overdeveloped sense of justice."

"We can save them!"

*"We can't save them!"* Recca shoved his apprentice onward. "We've lost, so we go while we still can, and we live to avenge them!"

The apprentice stared, shocked and lost. "They did what you asked them to!"

"Because they were sworn to!" Recca's voice rose in anger at his student looming over him in the gully. "People are tools! You leave them when you're done with them!"

Recca turned to go. His student watched him leave, turned . . . then charged.

He was young, but he had a violence in him that could detonate mountains. The big man burst through the weeds and ploughed his sword through an abyssal bat, cleaving off its wing. The bat screamed and spurted out a column of acid. The apprentice dived and rolled, and the acid missed him, blasting a second bat off its feet. The huge man lifted a hand, and a spell made grass burst into life and grapple a bat to the ground. He stabbed down with his sword in one swift blow—and two bats were dead and down.

The other rangers fled, fighting their way back to the gully. Wights sprang like javelins from the grass, but the apprentice cut them down, sheltering injured comrades as they helped each other walk. He fought as he had never fought before—swift, punishing, and precise. He was death. Swift, pitiless, and unyielding. Recca watched his student fight, and he simply stared.

His apprentice was holding them back. He was holding them! If survivors returned with tales of Recca fleeing the battle, his ambitions of leadership would be dead. Recca snarled and charged into the fight. He spun in a spectacular acrobatic flip over the enemy, spinning to cut a shapeshifter through the spine.

Far beyond its warriors, the toad demon watched the fight. The beast reared, its great yellow gut swelling as it roared in challenge. It was a demon none would dare to fight except a swordmaster. Recca sped away from the combat and ran at his chosen foe. He gave an ululating scream, feeling the glory of the eagle in his veins. He was Recca, he was a blademaster, and he was invincible!

The demon had a sword of its own, but the monster never bothered to draw. It blinked out of sight. Recca stopped, looking wildly about, then staggered as something tore into his back. The demon stood behind him, bawling with joy. Recca spun and cut, but the monster had gone, and again claws ripped him from behind, tearing through his armor and gouging his flesh. Recca lurched, lashed out—then had the sword smashed from his grasp. The demon croaked, its throat pouch puffing. Recca dragged a dagger from his belt and blundered forward, screeching in hatred as the demon laughed.

The demon struck, punching through armor, ripping Recca's heart out of his chest. The elf collapsed to his knees, staring in horror. The demon held the heart above its head, screaming in victory—and then suddenly it fell back with a roar. A sword hacked at the creature. The demon dodged, only to be caught by a kick from a massive boot. The demon staggered, and suddenly Recca's apprentice was there, huge with rage.

The toad flickered out of sight. The apprentice whirled and swung, but the screaming monster had appeared behind him. It caught the human's sword and snapped the blade in two. Snarling, the apprentice turned and tore the black blade out of Recca's dying grasp. He cut, the blow fast and vicious, but the demon disappeared an instant before the blade struck home.

The apprentice reversed and jammed his sword behind him, striking the demon as it reappeared. Black, steaming blood burst from the fat toad's guts. The monster screamed, wrenched free, then flashed out of sight again. Whirling, the apprentice brought his sword down in a massive blow aimed at empty air behind him.

The demon flickered back into view, and the blow smashed the demon in two, plowing through skull and chest.

Other monsters backed away as the bisected monster fell aside. The warrior bellowed, and his enemies fled into the gloom.

Somehow, Recca still lived. He lived long enough to see his apprentice win the fight that he had failed.

\* \* \* \* \*

The apprentice worked in silence. Stone-faced, he hacked off Recca's hand and foot to prevent the corpse being animated as a weapon. He buried the body in the same shallow scrape of dirt that had hidden him before the attack. He placed the heads of Recca's kills at his head and feet. He made no prayers, for the gods were a mockery who enslaved the weak.

Recca was gone. It was as if the swordmaster had been judged and found wanting. The apprentice took Recca's sword to honor him, letting the blade go on to do its work.

It was growing dark. There were wounded survivors to get to safety, and soon the monsters would return. The apprentice—a warrior who had no name—took one last glance at his master's final battlefield. He looked once, turned his back, and left the place behind.

## CY 589

*"Bastards!"*

Three malformed slaves hopped back through a palace door, only to be blown apart, their guts and bones spattering on the walls. Demonic servitors dared not flee. They abased themselves, utterly cowed, as their dark mistress stormed by.

Lolth the Demon Queen, Mistress of Spiders, Queen of the Drow, Dark Empress of abyssal hordes was not pleased. A throne of skulls, a lake of blood, a palace lined with the screaming bodies of the damned . . . all the pleasures of being a demon queen had turned dull and pale. Orgiastic rites lacked flavor. Torturing victims seemed a pointless bore. Even breeding mutant spider legions had become a total waste of time.

Lolth stormed into her rooms, flung herself onto her couch of living flesh, and *seethed*.

The world of Oerth had caused her absolute humiliation. Her major temple there had been destroyed. Her drow priesthood had been decimated. Hundreds of years of careful planning had been blown apart in a matter of hours. Primal energy had exploded through a magical gate, destroying Lolth's underground temple, her high priestesses and acolytes, and the flower of the drow nobility. Caves had cracked, and the vast underground city that her minions had labored upon was now buried beneath untold megatons of rock. Worst of all, Lolth's body upon that world had been destroyed—a good body, a powerful body, a titanic spider so huge it made kings and demons tremble. All gone. All burned to ash!

The shame of it! Her enemies had made her drunk on faerie wine, mocking her pure magnificence! She was now the laughing stock of the Abyss, with tanar'ri lords sending presents of wine and hangover cures to her palace day after day! Lolth flopped listlessly and muttered. She detonated minions and brooded endlessly. Fury and frustration made her universe seem dim and tasteless.

Oerth . . .

The place preyed on her night and day. There were other worlds, other campaigns. She had armies of evil conquering continents all across the planes. Oerth was a nothing. A speck! A tiny bauble amongst a universe of treasures—

Yet it had mocked her! It had humiliated Lolth the beautiful, the perfect! It had dared to laugh at the majesty of the Spider Queen!

Lolth's bedroom was in a palace, and the palace was mounted inside a mechanical spider fortress a hundred feet tall. The juggernaut strode through the nexus of the planes, moving from world to world as Lolth supervised her minions and their military campaigns. Lying face down on her couch, Lolth felt the fortress rock beneath her as it walked, her lithe elven face dire and seething with hate. She had eyes of fire, a skin of jet, and pure silver hair that cascaded to the floor. Her sleek body sprawled on her couch, her fingers drumming as she watched a bronze clock ticking the minutes away.

The clock sounded a deep, dark chime, and Lolth jerked upright, naked and careless. Amorphous handmaidens slithered to open the doors and usher in her waiting servitors.

There were drow priestesses and lesser tanar'ri led by hopping toad demons seven feet tall. A great, gaunt, vaguely humanish dog demon led the pack, its four misshapen arms opening to clack their pincers. The beast abased itself as Lolth approached, then stood to gabble out its report.

"Magnificence! Good news!" The creature opened its claws wide and beamed. "The spells are going well. Only a few small hitches. I regret to say the new body will not be available on time—"

The only reply from Lolth was an incoherent scream. She slammed her fist into the demon, clutching the creature's still beating heart. Screaming, Lolth hurled the useless thing away, the demon's blood spraying all over her naked flesh. Spiders as big as wolfhounds raced in to feed upon the bleeding demon.

"Now! *Get me that damned body!* Do it! *Do it!*" Lolth ripped her victim apart, the body still screaming. She tore out organs that smoked and steamed, her face an orgiastic mask of rage. "I want it now!" Demons scattered from her in fright. "No excuses! Now! *Now! Now!*"

A sudden wave of calm stole through the doors. Dripping wet, lean and magnificent, Lolth looked up as a demoness slithered into her hall.

Lolth's secretary was cool, slender, had a serpentine lower body and three pairs of arms. Halting before Lolth with a graceful bow, she spared a glance for the dead demon—fastidiously disdaining the filth all over the floor.

"The new body is ready, your Magnificence."

Lolth sprang to her feet, a stab of fire flickering across her skin. She raced along the rocking corridors of her mobile palace, her pet spiders following like a horde of excited puppies at her feet. The Queen of the Demonweb Pits strode through halls filled with giant arachnids, past metal walls where tiny imp-like quasits skittered through the dark. Tall and lean, with the body of a goddess and the soul of a black widow, Lolth strode into her workshops and stood in triumph in the door.

The lords of the tanar'ri were hard to kill. They would die only if slain while inside their own home realm. Outside of their own realms, death meant only a wait of a few hundred years until they could enter the plane once again. Lolth's body upon Oerth had been destroyed, and it had taken one hundred days to fashion a replacement. She had squandered resources and lavished her powers to make herself a new shell. Finally the new vessel was ready, magnificent, and awaiting its triumphant awakening. In her hall of mirrors, Lolth gazed upon it and gave a silken smile.

Finally. No more giant spider forms. Oerth would be taken by magic and steel and ruled by an empress of invincible glory. Lolth's new body was a copy of her current form—a long, lean dark elf female. She would tolerate no rivals for physical glory. Lolth's bodies were crafted to absolute perfection—powerful, agile, and stunningly sensual.

The new body lay in a shrine deep in the bowels of Oerth, in one of Lolth's few surviving temples. Her slaves had labored over it through Lolth's long frustration, polishing the flesh to perfection. Lolth gazed upon the new form critically through her magic gate, trying to conceal her eagerness.

*Perfect.*

Lolth gave the body one last, delicious glance, then strode past her minions and secretaries. She climbed the stairs into the chamber at the front of her palace and leaned out over the balcony.

The huge metal spider-palace stamped across a landscape bleak with ash. Ruined cities burned, and monsters cavorted amongst the carrion. Lolth's legions had been busy here, fighting a patient campaign of conquest. Her plans moved slowly and carefully, lest she evoke jealous anger from her peers. Slow and careful. Securing hidden bases, like spiders lurking in the woodpile—this was the formula Lolth had followed for hundreds of years.

But now it was high time to show the universe that the spider had a bite!

"Bring me the surviving high priestesses from Oerth."

Lolth paced like a leopardess, then flung herself into her throne. Two shabby, terrified female drow entered the room—creatures diminished by the magnificence of Lolth's dark beauty. Their white hair hung limp. Their black skins were unhealthy. Their robes had been pieced together from torn remnants scavenged from their ruined kingdom. The two high priestesses made obeisance to their goddess and waited, kneeling on the floor.

Slim, sleek and sensual, Lolth flowed up out of her throne. Her black skin gleamed in the light of the burning city as she leaned against a window frame.

"My children!"

"Magnificence." The priestesses were hoarse. Their city was in ruins, and their days were spent chanting spells to hold back the scavengers that closed in around the remaining drow. "Tell us how we may serve you."

"We shall serve *you*, children! We have a body in your temple again. We shall return to Oerth! We shall make your people safe, and then reward the faithful. Yes . . ." Lolth's voice bubbled like a chorus of elven girls. "You have done well. Now tell me: the vampire pool—have you found it?"

A priestess—scarred, burned, and downcast—failed to meet her goddess eye to eye.

"N-no, your magnificence."

Lolth glared, and the room seemed suddenly icy cold.

"Why not?"

One priestess licked her lips in fright. "W-we have no w-workers, Magnificence. No sorcerers! There are only a few hundred left. The collapse of the city—"

"No matter. No matter." Lolth did not care to hear excuses and depression. Oerth was coming into her grasp! "You will have sorcerers, and an earth elemental. Search! Uncover the pool!"

"Yes, your Magnificence."

The palace lurched as it crossed a ridge. At the palace's feet, Lolth spied capering flocks of harpies harrying her enemies. The demon queen gave an indulgent little smile.

"Yes. Dig. First—the pool. Then make tunnels. We will need accommodation for the assistants we shall be sending you."

"Assistants, Magnificence?" The priestesses looked at one another anxiously. The surviving drow were barely scraping an existence in the underdark by eating scraps scavenged from the ruins. "How—how many assistants?"

Lolth drew in a long, slow breath as she looked across her armies celebrating in the rubble below. There were spider beings and demons, undead legions and foul, slithering things taken from a dozen other worlds. On other planes, Lolth had army after army—hidden forces that lay in wait as their mistress matured her evil plans.

The two drow risked a glance at their goddess.

"Magnificence? H-how many assistants will you send?"

Lolth turned to face the miserable priests, and gave a seething smile.

*"Millions."*

The Demon Queen breathed raggedly, excited by the vision of revenge, of glory—of power! It was time to show the cosmos that Lolth was a force to be feared! She would unveil all her hidden pieces in a wild blaze of glory! She would strip a hundred worlds of their hidden troops and mass them all into a single tidal wave. Oerth would fall—obliterated and enslaved. A whole demon world would be made. The throne on which Lolth sat would be worshiped. The other tanar'ri lords would bow— sweet vengeance for the mockery Lolth had suffered since her defeat!

A whole world taken. A new era would dawn. Lolth would

become queen of the tanar'ri, mounted on a throne built from Oerth's rotting dead.

But before it began, there was a little time for fun. Lolth let it settle deliciously in her mind, and then spoke to her secretary with a voice that shimmered like a chorus of angels.

"Have the pilots take us back to the Demonweb. Take us home. Summon the commanders from each and every world to a conference in eight hours' time."

Lolth's long, serpentine secretary wrote notes upon three separate tablets at once, her six hands busy and her face in a frown. Orders were spoken. At the rods and wheels that controlled the spider palace, sleek succubi went to work. The palace poised, one huge spider foot hovering in mid air—then the juggernaut slowly began to turn. Its footfalls clashed like titanic cymbals as the metal monster trod slowly away, crushing the corpses of conquest underneath its feet.

Lolth savored the delicious smell of burning flesh caught in the breeze, and then turned, her violet eyes seething with delight.

"Now—let's get on with this, shall we?"

The demonic secretary gave an annoyed glare at her mistress, tucking a writing stylus behind one long ear. Of all Lolth's minions, only her secretary never showed fear—only an air of martyrdom and overwork that Lolth found extremely amusing.

"Magnificence, if we concentrate forces, we must find a way to feed them."

"Details, details!" The future was blooming like a flower, and Lolth danced with delight! "We're on our way at last! Think of it! Universal conquest! Cosmic domination! There are worlds to obliterate, slaves to conquer, enemies to destroy—orgiastic rites slithering in oceans of human blood!"

The secretary scowled. "Are you well, Magnificence?"

"Oh, I feel like a little girl!" Lolth paused mid-pirouette. "Have the cook send one up!"

Unamused, the secretary licked the end of her pencil and took notes on a pad.

"Magnificence? May I ask again about supplies for the troops?"

"We will live off the land! Oerth is rich. Find a pointless little city and invade it, then we'll use its populace as our supplies. We can let the monsters have their fun!" Lolth heaved a happy sigh as she contemplated the magnificence of her revenge. "We must enjoy ourselves, you sour little serpent."

The demonic queen turned, laid a hand upon her two high priestesses from Oerth, and smiled.

"Search. Find me the vampire pool again, and we shall reward you. Your kingdom will be returned to you a thousand fold!"

Lolth felt her palace walking the grounds of an alien world and sensed her legions and her armies like a fine-tuned instrument beneath her hands. She had the means to take her revenge at last. She had the power. She had the will.

The world of Oerth had mocked her, and it would die. . . .

# 2

In theory, they were still heading for Hommlet.

They marched through a range of dusty, tree-smothered hills on a day that seemed eerily hushed and still. In the lead walked the Justicar—huge, shaven headed, and grim in his armor of black dragon scales. Draped over his head and back was Cinders, a grinning sentient hell hound pelt that wagged his tail in eternal glee. Jutting through the Justicar's belt was a magical sword named Benelux. Despite its wolf skull pommel, the blade was talkative, prissy, and prim. Even when silent, the sword managed to radiate an impression that it approved of *none* of the current goings-on.

Behind Jus was Henry—eighteen years old, tall, skinny, and apparently made up mostly of elbows and knees. His blond hair framed a face smattered with freckles. A fine shirt of elven mail, threaded with green chords to keep it silent, betrayed an occasional sparkle beneath his cloak. He carried a sword, and a hefty magical crossbow sloped over his shoulders as he kept up with the Justicar stride-for-stride, bravely trying not to look tired.

Henry snuck sly glances at the happy female sphinx who walked beside him. Enid was larger than a lion—a shy, pretty creature with freckles on her nose, white feathers on her wings, her hair plaited in a thousand braids. Her big paws padded amiably in the dust, and her weaving tail cast its shadow onto the dappled light of the road. Riding on her back was a large badger who perpetually scribbled notes in a dog-eared journal. Polk the teamster, reincarnated as a lovable woodland beast, was, if anything, even more annoying than he had ever been.

Flitting madly from one end of the party to the other, dressed in a costume so sleek it was outlawed on six outer planes, Escalla the faerie was having a busy day. Full of energy, the little creature held a stick, flew level with Jus's head, and waved her hands in the air.

"All right pooch! Are you concentrating?" Escalla hovered above the roadway, paused, then threw a stick down the road. "Fetch the stick! Go on! Fetch!"

The stick hit the ground a dozen yards ahead. Escalla looked happily from the stick to Cinders where he rode draped across the Justicar's helm. She whooshed her hands forward, trying to will the hell hound into a run. "Go on! *Fetch!*"

Marching tirelessly along the road, the Justicar decided neither to ask nor comment. Henry looked from one of his friends to the other. Polk was busy trying to put his chronicles into heroic rhyme, and Enid was carrying sticks for Escalla.

Intrigued, Henry asked, "Hey, Escalla? Um, what are you doing?"

"Trying to teach the pooch to fetch!" Recording the moment on her slowglass gem, the little faerie happily tossed another stick for Cinders, full of boundless enthusiasm. "Come on Cinders! Fetch!"

"Oh." Henry struggled to set his crossbow properly in the crook of his arm. He leaned close to Escalla and whispered. "Um, isn't that difficult when he's . . . you know, an empty skin?"

Escalla shot a glance at Cinders, and then drifted Henry out of earshot of the hound.

"It's my plan to get him mobile."

"Mobile?"

"Look: the pooch can wag his tail, he can lift his ears. . . . I think getting him moving is just a case of mind over matter."

Escalla slapped a new throw-stick into her little palm. "That's why we're going to basics here! If we make instinct work for us, we can get over the mental barrier he has!"

"By fetching a stick?"

"Hey!" The faerie waved her hands. "Dogs fetch sticks! All the books say they do!"

"Really?" Henry peered thoughtfully over at Cinders's big teeth. "He's a hell hound. Maybe they fetch bones or skulls or something?"

With a heavy sigh, the Justicar looked at Escalla. "Escalla, I don't think Cinders is quite up to fetching any sticks."

"Ha! What you people need to learn is perseverance! You need some self discipline!" Escalla tossed a stick up the road. "Cinders! Fetch!"

There were at least two hundred sticks littered in the party's wake. Undefeated, Escalla eagerly made fetch motions at Cinders, who merely grinned. A tad annoyed, the girl speared him with a thoughtful glare.

"Are you really trying, or aren't you?"

*Fun!* The hell hound wagged his tail. *Good exercise for funny faerie!*

Escalla went into a sulk.

"Aw, come on, pooch! This is a serious experiment here!"

*Long day. Cinders tired.*

"Well, all right." Escalla tossed a final stick aside. "We'll give it a rest for a while. We don't want to strain your, um . . . whatever muscle things it is that let you move. But tonight, you practice for another hour! And you get a coal lump for each stick you snatch!"

The Justicar gave a patient arch of his brow.

"Escalla, the day he catches his first stick, I'll give him a whole wagon load."

"Hey, pooch! You hear that?" Escalla landed on Jus's shoulder and ruffled the ears of both man and beast. "See! He believes in you!"

*Cinders happy!*

"Good." The Justicar reached up to pat the hell hound's skull. "Good boy."

The path led through deserted forests, past the ruins of an ancient tower, and into lovely quiet hills. This empty country separated the civilized kingdoms of the south from the savage kingdoms of the north where the minions of Iuz lurked. Even this far south, the lands had been depopulated by the Greyhawk Wars. War bands had swept through years ago, done their damage, then disappeared. Now the hills were quiet, and old bones crumbled softly into dust.

There was no game. No deer started out of the forest. No hares or doves fled as the adventurers moved along the old deserted road. After a while, it became uncanny. The Justicar walked slightly off the trail and ran his hands over a disturbed patch of grass, looking down at a pile of deer droppings that had turned white with sun and rain. Henry immediately sank into cover, cocking the magic crossbow. Jus let the boy do his work and began sifting through the forest's sights and smells.

"Cinders?"

*No animal smell. No deer trail. No animals. Only bugs!* Cinders sampled the world with sharper senses than a man's, scenting magic on the wind. *Bad things were here. Now bad things gone.*

"Bad things?"

*Maybe troll. Maybe goblin. Maybe spider. Day-old smell.*

Escalla hovered overhead, invisible up in the trees, covering Jus and Cinders as they worked. The faerie faded slowly back into sight and drifted downward, her eyes on the forest eaves.

"Trouble?"

"Trouble." Jus swept his fingers through the grass. "There's no wild game. No animals bigger than a mouse. Cinders smells troll and goblin."

"Troll?" Escalla unslung her ice wand and readied for trouble. "Oh, that's fun."

"They can't be native. Not in this area."

Escalla fanned them both with her wings and asked, "So where did they come from?"

"Yes—" the Justicar looked out across the quiet hills— "where did they come from?"

From back on the trail, Polk's voice brayed into the silence. "What's up, boy? We're waiting! You're too slow. Unhardened to the trail. Sign of a sloppy life, boy! Slack! Undisciplined! You need to *crave* the open trail, son. Become a true rugged outdoorsman just like me!" Polk grandly puffed his chest. "You can use me as a role model, son. I don't mind. That's what I'm for! An example to the needy! A figure of inspiration!" The badger waved a paw. "Come on, son! We need speed! Need to find civilization, get some dungeoneering equipment, and then get you on a proper adventure!"

Jus and Escalla shot a dire glance at the badger. Jus rose up from the grass.

"Polk, we need food. We need beer. We need ingredients for Escalla's spells. If you buy any more damned rope—"

"Oh, yes!" Enid radiated good cheer. "And Escalla wants ingredients for lots more potions of giant size!"

Jus scratched his head. "What?"

"Shhh! Nothing!" Escalla jabbed Enid's ribs with her elbow and bit her lip. Flying backward, dressed in elbow gloves, leggings and skirt apparently sprayed directly onto her skin, she suddenly became aware of all eyes upon her. She blushed, tugged her skirt straight and glared at Polk, who was watching her expectantly. "What?"

"Are you deaf?" The badger was making a shopping list. "I asked if we need growth potions as adventure equipment?"

"Well, I sure hope it'll be an adventure!" The faerie whirred busily up into the air. "Polk! No adventure equipment! We are not buying holy water, wolfsbane, silver mirrors, or pack mules. And the only garlic buds I want are ones sizzling in olive oil with bay leaves and diced lamb!"

"We already have wolfsbane." Polk gave a sniff. "It's in with my scrolls. And garlic always gives me gas."

"We tried to warn you about that." Escalla hovered beside the badger and tapped her chin. "If the priests reincarnated you as a badger, shouldn't you be eating badgery things?"

"What? Bugs and bark and week-old rabbits?" Polk gave a superior little sniff. "I may be furry, but I ain't stupid! Now come on. Let's find a town. I want a steak, frog-apple pie, and a cold beer—and not necessarily in that order!"

"Hen?" Escalla waved Henry out of his hiding place. "Come on, hon! Time to get walking."

The road dipped into a valley, then swept up over a hill, finally looking down upon a shabby town on the plains below. A nearby river had broken its banks with the springtime floods, turning the lowlands into a morass. Floods lapped at the city walls. Refugees from drowned villages had flocked into the city, and the smell of the place was enough to draw flies from hundreds of miles around.

From the hills above, the adventurers looked down at the region's first, best claim to civilization. Enid wore a look of shock and waved her tail to clear the flies from her flanks. Escalla looked at the mess and gave an irritated sigh.

"So much for spending a night on the town!"

The only happy person was Polk. He unruffled a huge map and spread it out over Enid's bottom, his snout beaming full of smiles.

"Here we are at last! Greyhawk, son! Adventure capital of the whole of the Flanaess!"

"Polk, it isn't Greyhawk. Greyhawk is three hundred miles

that-a-way." The Justicar had long since stopped letting Polk plan their routes. "If those refugees we met two days ago were right, then that's the Att River, and Verbobonc is still at least a hundred miles south."

"Verbo-what?"

"I don't name them, Polk. I just find them."

"Well, then, what's this place?"

"I don't know." The Justicar shrugged. "Someplace in the west of Furyondy, I'm guessing." The Justicar felt Cinders avidly wagging his tail "Cinders?"

*Stinky!*

"I thought you were tired."

*Stick tired! Not sniff tired! Go city—have fun!*

The Justicar cocked a suspicious eye up at the hell hound and warned, "No burning. None! I mean it this time!"

*Cinders good dog! Never burns one little bit!*

"Remember Trigol City? Remember that tent city on the plains?"

*Was accident!*

"All right." The Justicar lay one hand upon the skull pommel of his sword. "Now—to get supplies."

The sword Benelux gave a lofty little sniff. *I believe we should file a complaint against our welcome in this country! We are superior quality travelers. At the very least, we deserve to be met at the border by a committee of nobles. Possibly even a king!*

"Good point, spiky." Escalla patted the sword's sheath. "All right, people! The sword here is going to file a complaint in writing right after she evolves herself a functional pair of hands. The rest of us—Jus, you and Henry go file the files and do the legal stuff. Enid and I will do the supplying. That gets us out of this cesspit in the fastest time."

Henry blinked. "Are you sure you'll be all right walking the streets without a man?"

"We'll take Polk. He's kind of a man." The faerie chucked Henry under the chin. "Hey, don't worry! This is our element!"

"Really?"

"Sure! Trust me. I'm a faerie!"

They decided to take a break before marching the last few miles down to the city. Polk trundled into his box of scrolls, looking for the deed to Hommlet and its surroundings—a purchase Escalla had made in the far distant past. Enid licked her paw and wiped travel stains from her freckled face. Seeing the Justicar move over to a log beside the road, Escalla drifted over, sat down beside him, and folded up her wings.

They sat together in silence for a while, the huge warrior in his black armor and the sleek little faerie with sly, laughing eyes. The two of them looked out across the hills, not entirely sure where to put their hands. Suddenly their friends seemed far away.

Long moments passed. Jus looked down at the reeking city—crammed with people and overflowing with trash, and he heaved a weary sigh.

"I'm sorry. I know you'd hoped this all might be more exciting."

"It *is* exciting! We have a wilderness to explore, there's evil ruins nearby . . ."

"So you really want to split up in the city?"

"Ooh, I think this smells like someplace we want to get out of in a real hurry." Escalla sat on her hands to keep them still and leaned forward, her long blonde hair cascading down across the log. "But Enid and I have . . . you know, stuff to buy."

"What stuff?"

"Um, girl stuff." Escalla blushed. "You know . . . stuff."

"Oh. I see." The Justicar ascribed it all to the female mysteries. "Well, we have a ton of gold left over from the drow caves."

"Yeah, I guess we can manage to spend it." Escalla gave a sudden smile. "I'm going to get some jewelry for Enid, though—

and a brush! I mean, how are we going to snare her a nice androsphinx if she stays stuck inside with her books all day every day? The girl needs a little romance to brighten up her life!"

The Justicar laughed at the thought. "Romance?"

Both Jus and Escalla froze their smiles and looked guiltily away from each other. The huge shaven-headed ranger turned pink, and Escalla felt her own cheeks blazing red. She covered herself by pretending enormous interest in the city far below.

"So . . . ready?"

"Yes." The Justicar heaved yet another sigh. "I'd hoped it would be more pleasant."

"Pleasant?"

"I wanted to stay somewhere halfway decent tonight." The big man was sitting on his own hands. "Maybe . . . maybe leave the other three and just go off somewhere with you for a little while." The Justicar coughed, blushing pink and staring at his hands. "Well, just talk to you about something."

Escalla swallowed. "Something?"

"Something really . . . important."

Behind Jus, the log gave off a hollow, rhythmic drumming sound. Both Jus and Escalla blinked, then looked up at Cinders where he hung in his usual place, cloaking Jus's helm and back. The hell hound's teeth gleamed, his eyes glowed, and he wagged his tail in glee. His tail thumped heavily on the hollow log.

*Funny!*

Escalla glared at the creature from one eye, and then turned her full attention back to Jus.

"You, ah . . . you wanted to be alone?" The girl faltered. "Together, I mean."

Jus had his hands out again, and was rubbing at his knuckles. He caught himself doing it and looked down at the ground, clearing his throat. "I . . . Yes. I mean . . . I just wanted to check something with you."

"Yes?"

"Something I've wanted to . . . to talk to you about."

Escalla's heart was in her throat, and she felt numb from head to toe. "T-talk?" She felt her voice quaver. "Um . . . fine!"

The Justicar tried to ease into the subject. "Well, it's just that I've been wanting . . ."

"Yes?"

"Look—I've been thinking."

"Uh-huh!"

Jus coughed and cleared his throat. "That is . . . I've wanted to ask . . ."

*Funny-funny!*

The hell hound thumped his tail even harder. Exasperated, Escalla leaped to her feet.

"Pooch!"

*Pretty faerie!*

"Look, Cinders. Do you mind if we just put you over here for a little while?" Escalla dragged Cinders over a stump. She crammed a large lump of coal into the creature's mouth. "Here. Eat!"

*Funny!*

Returning to Jus's side, Escalla sat, smoothed her leather leggings, and tried to get the conversation back on track.

"Talking? To me."

"In private, yes."

The Justicar had faced lich lords and tanar'ri in mortal combat. He had stormed breeches in fortress walls and had hunted demons in the dark, dead forests of Iuz, but at the moment, he found himself consumed with an idiotic terror. He slapped his hands on his thighs, heaved a breath, and determined to do what had to be done. He girded himself, took a deep breath, and decided to face the moment with a warrior's courage.

A prissy voice suddenly chimed in from his sword belt.

*Well, I do wish you'd ask her and just get on with it! Some of us have work to do!*

Benelux wriggled indignantly in her scabbard. Annoyed, Jus plucked out the weapon, sheath and all, and tossed it over to the grass beside Cinders. Cinders's big ears were pricked tall, and the hound sniggered. Jus signaled the hound to mind his own damned business, and then suddenly became acutely aware that Escalla's skin radiated a sense of warmth against his thigh.

She was pale white and beautiful, thin yet filled with her own glorious energy. Eyes as green as wild new leaves—cunning, inno-cent, and shy—looked up at him as she hung on his every word.

Jus reached out to caress a finger down the fine line of her cheek. Escalla held his hand quietly against her face, closed her eyes and nestled worshipfully into his caress.

"I found it! *Verbobonc!* Right here on the map!" Polk erupted from underneath the log, bulling his way between the two friends. "Verbobonc. Independent city-state."

Jus and Escalla moved apart, each blazing red with embarrass-ment. Polk ignored it all.

"Now what's all this about talk? If you've got something to say, then speak up, boy! Say what's on your mind! Information should be shared! That's called 'Exchange of ideas!' Backbone of progress!" The badger shoved Jus off the log. "Anyway, can't dawdle. Time to move on. Day's wasting! Life is precious. A stitch in time saves gathering moss! Here come the others!" Polk waved Henry and Enid over. "Now come on, boy! Let's get this paper-work done and get this adventure on the road!"

Cursing, Escalla kicked a toadstool to pieces. Enid, Henry, Polk, and Cinders all clustered merrily around, pushing Jus and Escalla onward down the road. Helpless before a wave of pure good will, Jus and Escalla were borne onward into the town, its stench, its crowds, and its flies.

Fuming, the Justicar tied Cinders into place over his helm. Savage with ill-humor he gripped his sword, swapped a look of mutual frustration with Escalla, and then took the lead down the road.

"When we reach the city, Henry, you come with me. We'll see if there is an officer of rangers, ask the best way south, then see if there's been any trouble we should know about. Escalla, you and Enid get the supplies, tools, whatever. . . . We'll meet just inside the gates when we're all done."

"Whatever." In a bad temper, Escalla sat on Enid's head. "Let's get this done and get back home."

Henry looked up at the faerie as she sat upon the sphinx. "Are you going to do anything about the way you look?"

Miffed, Escalla jerked her little black skirt. "Hey! This outfit was made from pure salamander skin! This is the shortest fireproof skirt in the Flanaess!"

"Um, I was just wondering if a faerie and a sphinx might not cause . . . a bit of attention."

"Kid, when you wear a skirt like this, you're not worried about attention." Escalla clicked her fingers. "It's all fine. I've got it covered."

"Really?" Henry hesitated, unsure. "Well, just as long as no one tries to make you show them a pot of gold or something."

"Hey! No one touches the faerie." Escalla gave an irritated sigh and then took off to scout the way ahead. "Come on! Let's get going so we can finally get a little peace!"

Escalla turned invisible. Jus hunched his head, gripped his sword, and walked. Polk sat upon Enid's rump reading a map upside down between his badger paws. With her eyes upon Jus's back, Enid leaned down to whisper quietly in Henry's ear.

"Psst! So did he ask her?"

"No." Henry pulled his elven mail shirt straight. "He never asks her. He keeps dithering! Why doesn't he just say it?"

"Ah, the poor thing. It must be difficult." The sphinx draped her wing companionably over Henry's shoulders. "I think all he needs is the encouragement of his friends."

3

The hills west of the Nyr Dyv, the Flanaess's inland sea, glowed a lazy velvet-purple in the sun. Spring had brought dew-speckled mornings and dusty afternoons. It seemed a land blessed with eternal slumber, a place where lizards could bask and rabbits scratch themselves in peaceful shadows.

In an ancient ruin covered with dead, black vines, a crypt door creaked open. Blinking in pain at the unaccustomed light, a drow high priestess winced her way out of the door, turned blinded eyes about the ruins, and then bowed abjectly toward the dark.

"Here, Magnificence. This is the sole remaining tunnel mouth near the inland sea."

Lolth came forth, making a face as light ripped like needles into her eyes. With a wave of her hand, she invoked darkness all about her as the tunnel from the underdark disgorged her priests, spiders, and demonic bodyguards. Lolth's secretary slithered forth—a six-armed tanar'ri with a woman's upper body and the lower boy of a snake, her hair black, short and efficient, and her serpentine lower body polished to perfection. She was laden with a drinking horn, a crystal ball, a shovel, and a collection of notebooks and pens.

Safe inside her pall of darkness, Lolth stretched her long, lithe body, and then wrinkled her nose.

"What *is* that ghastly stench?"

The high priestess kept her head bowed. "Open air, your

Magnificence. A miasma made from grass, pollens, cow flatulence, and the nests of animals."

"Well, it's horrid. We should burn something to keep the smell away." Lolth turned, paused, then threw a spell at one of her slaves. The creature burst into flame. "There! That's so much nicer!"

The Spider Queen's secretary gave a weary sigh, disgusted at the extra work required to find replacement slaves. She took notes with all six arms. Ignoring her secretary's silent reprimand, Lolth gave another delicious stretch, and warmed herself by the fire as she gazed across the hills and valleys of Oerth.

Something whimpered in the weeds. Flitting forward, light as a dancer, Lolth pulled back a curtain of old ivy and found a cringing human in the shadows. The man had a lamb clutched to his chest. Lolth clapped her hands, delighted.

"Oh, look! A shepherd! How deliciously rustic!" She held out a hand, beckoning the fearful man out of hiding. "Come here! Come on! We shan't bite you!"

The secretary winced and looked away, her coils lashing. The man's screams seemed to go on forever, and blood spattered over the old stones and quiet weeds. The secretary tuned back again when all seemed still.

Coated in blood, panting in delicious release, Lolth looked up and said, "Oh, yes. We are going to enjoy ourselves here."

The ruins formed an archway filled with cobwebs and old, dried flowers. At one end of the colonnade, a faint haze of magic flickered. Lolth danced over to the arch and caught a fly in her fingertips, thoughtfully feeding it to a little spider hanging from the stones.

The troops were already moving. In the next hour, the tunnel mouth would flood with abyssal horrors, ready to invade the settlement Lolth had chosen as her first "larder." The demon queen cast an eye on her secretary.

"There! We're all done? Our little food-capturing expedition is ready?"

"Yes, Magnificence. Everything is ready." The secretary irritably lashed her coils, then duly made notes. "One town—convert populace to foodstuffs. Details to be made up as we go along. . . ."

"But first, we have a few little, trivial tasks to do!" The Queen of the Demonweb Pits snapped a finger at her secretary. "Come! The rest of you, stay here and try not to do anything idiotic!"

The archway beckoned. Lolth pulled a pouch of black thorns from her belt and tossed a handful through the arch. Magic flashed, and a shimmering portal blazed into life. Shielding her eyes from the glare, Lolth stepped through the gate, beckoning her secretary in her wake.

"Come on! You're always such a dodderer!"

The magic gateway flashed, and Lolth and her secretary emerged from an archway made from pure black ivy deep inside a forest. Gigantic statues of long dead kings stood half-buried in old leaf mold, scowling at the demoness as she stood and spread her arms.

"One hundred and one days! A third of a year since the destruction of my underground kingdom." Black silk shimmered as Lolth's new demon body swirled like a girl. "Do you know what I have dwelt on every hour of all those hundred days?"

The secretary shot a droll glance at her mistress. "Affairs of state, Magnificence?"

"No, my dear dull darling. I have been contemplating *revenge*." Lolth sniffed and regarded her companion. "You're such a drab!"

"Yes, Magnificence."

Lolth walked amongst the trees. "There is a dreary proverb that revenge is a dish best savored cold." Lolth draped herself elegantly over a branch. "I believe revenge is a dish best savored alive and twitching."

The secretary answered with a patient sigh. Six hands held a total of three notebooks and three pens.

"These beings, Magnificence, destroyed an entire city. Do not take them lightly."

"Oh?" The demon queen contemplated the silver black widow brooches that were the mainstay of her clothing. "And how, dear dunce, would *you* deal with them?"

"I would dispatch twenty demons to kill them in their sleep." The secretary stabbed her pen into a notebook. "I would grind the pieces to a powder and scatter them grain by grain into the deepest ocean."

"And *that*, my dear, is why *I* am queen of evil, and not you." Lolth gave the serpent-woman a sidewise glance. "I don't want their death! I want their *despair!* Shock, horror, false hope, total panic! I want harassment for day after day, week after week. I want them in tears of fright and shame!"

The secretary looked at her mistress through lowered lashes. "And then kill them?"

"Obviously kill them! Eaten alive by giant spiders, their living skulls used as my chamber pot, their souls made my screaming playthings." Lolth brushed it all away. "But the *chase* is the thing! We're talking of revenge *quality*, not *quantity!* What we need here is applied irony, with just a teeny dab of sheer injustice!" Lolth used the head of a statue as her perch. "I have given two names to my itch: Escalla and the Justicar." Lolth crossed her legs and clicked her fingers, accepting the crystal ball from her secretary. "The process is simple. All we need to ask ourselves is what would enrage our little friends more than anything in the entire world?"

The time was drawing near when the first troops would come through the tunnel gate. The secretary tapped a pen against her notepad, bringing Lolth to order.

"Shall we get on with business, Magnificence? Surely the day is wasting."

Annoyed, Lolth dusted off the crystal ball. "You *try* me at times."

The secretary froze, flicked open her notepad, and met Lolth eye to eye, awaiting orders.

It was a delicate game that the secretary played. Lolth had trapped her into slavery—and in return, the secretary had made herself indispensable. They both knew it was a delicate relationship based on mutual scorn and exasperation.

"Escalla the faerie." With a snort, Lolth grabbed the crystal ball as Escalla's image glowed to life. "Vain, egotistical, and with a dress sense that could cause a riot at a succubus orgy—although I must admit, I *do* like the gloves." Lolth regarded her little victim with glee. "A prodigal child, much loved by her father—a fact that enraged Escalla's sister, Tielle. We were grooming Tielle to betray the Seelie Court into our hands. Too bad it failed."

Lolth tossed the crystal ball aside. Her secretary dived and saved the ball an instant before it smashed.

"In any case, here we are to set our first little wheels in motion!"

The rattle on the secretary's serpent tail gave a weary flick. "And where is *here*, Magnificence?"

"*Here* is the place where we get things moving!" Lolth looked annoyed. "Really, you're so dull. What was your name again?"

"Morag, Magnificence."

"*Morag?*" Lolth recoiled. "Erch! I should have guessed! How horribly appropriate. All right, I'll have one snake scale if you please."

Morag thought about arguing, then decided it was hardly worth the effort. She winced, plucked a single scale from her tail, then handed it to her queen. Lolth inspected the scale, sniffed at its scent of brimstone and perfume, and leaped from her perch. She wandered over to an arch made from two statues that had tilted over head-to-head.

The portal flashed as the demon's scale touched its surface. The gateway transported the pair to a deep, echoing underground chamber—a place lit by sickly blue stalactites and filled by a vile quicksilver pool.

Lolth twiddled her fingers. The scale had disappeared, consumed by the gate.

"A terribly convenient way to travel. The portals run all through this little chunk of the Flanaess. They're known only to the faeries! How convenient we had one on our team." The demon queen walked idly beside the great shallow pool. "Of course, the faeries don't know where most of them go. We found this little haven by accident. Isn't it delicious?"

The demon queen found herself a seat and relaxed. Left to her own devices, Morag the secretary bunched and flowed her body over to the silvery pool. It shimmered sluggishly, as though driven by a slow, living pulse. Setting her ball, her horn, and her notes aside, the secretary leaned over the pool and looked down at her own reflection. She frowned in puzzlement.

From behind her, Lolth's multi-tiered voice chorused, "It's called the vampire pool. I wouldn't touch it." Lolth inspected her nails. "It likes its blood very good or very evil, and it can't have yours. Not yet anyway."

Minutes later, a flash announced the opening of the magical gate. Lolth stood, her face radiant with smiles.

"Ah! At last we are all here!"

A male faerie hovered in the air—a sly, dark creature in the dress of the Seelie court. Black leathers and a mask hid the little creature's identity. Behind him, hovering in mid air, there was a large and heavy bucket full of weird pink goo. The faerie saw Lolth standing cool and glorious before him, her long silver hair falling in a cascade to the floor. He bowed softly and elegantly, averting his eyes.

"Magnificence. You do me too much honor."

"Yes." Lolth walked silkily between the eerie stalagmites, giving a coy glance toward the little faerie lord. "And have you brought me a gift?"

"Magnificence, I have brought you the present we discussed."

"Ah. Excellent." Lolth gave a droll wave of her fingers at the pulsing silver pool behind her "And here is your reward. Within this pool is the power to wreak your havoc. If you wish to carve an empire out of the bodies of your enemies, then here you are."

The faerie walked over to the pool and stared in fascination at the ebb and flow of patterns in the silver lake. Sleek and beautiful, Lolth tiptoed over beside him and smiled down into her own reflection.

"So much power! For evil blood, it gives the ability to sear your enemies to death!"

The faerie looked up at Lolth in raw greed and wonder. "Do I scoop it out? Bathe in it?"

"Why don't you try touching it?"

The faerie grinned, then plunged his hand into the water.

And died. One moment, he was standing there, one finger extended into the pool, and in the next, he was a desiccated husk, drained of all blood.

Lolth's secretary sniffed in disapproval. Standing by the edge of the pool, Lolth kicked the dried, empty husk into the pool. The corpse disappeared with a splash that left a new tide line of ripples. The liquid glowed red with energy, and Lolth looked over at Morag's irritated glare.

Lolth shrugged. "I'm a demon queen. Why would anyone take one of my suggestions?" She traipsed over to the bucket left beside the magic gate. "Now, to business."

The bucket was unceremoniously upended. Flowing sullenly out of the container came a pink puddle adorned with two eyes and occasional patches of hair. The eyes blinked up at Lolth, and turned wide with shock. Lolth twiddled her fingers, drifted a little shower of magic down onto the blob, and hummed a little tune as she worked, happy as a child.

"Up we come! Arise! Arise!"

Nothing happened. The blob blinked, Lolth frowned, and Morag sighed.

"You will need to expend actual power. The original spell was cast by the faerie Escalla."

"I am aware of that!" Lolth did it properly this time. Standing above the pink blob, she opened her hands, power arcing brilliantly between her palms. With a cry, Lolth brought her hands together in a clap. *"Arise!"*

Below her, the pink blob flexed and shifted.

It had been a savagely cunning combination of spells: flesh-to-stone, then stone-to-mud, and then the flesh-to-stone spell had been revoked. Tielle, Escalla's sister—murderess, schemer, and traitor to faerie—had been turned into a still-living puddle of flesh. The blob had been sealed in the dungeons of the Seelie court, awaiting the Erlking's pleasure. The goddess Lolth now sheared through Escalla's magic. There was a gasp, and Tielle lay in a ball on the ice-cold stone, her long blonde hair flowing all about her in a stream.

The faerie jerked upright—frightened, shocked, but alive. She threw out her arms in joy, staring at her reformed flesh, and then looked up at Lolth in abject wonder. She prostrated herself, only to be raised up and caressed.

Lolth stood with her head tilted impishly to one side. She gestured to Morag, who handed her a dainty drinking horn.

"Dear Tielle! The pool, I give to you. It's holy water—or reverse holy water, depending on the ingredients you add." Lolth dipped into it with the drinking horn, and the horn sucked in gallon after gallon of the water, tinging itself silver-red with the power of the pool. "Blood drives it. When you put in the life-blood of something evil, the water then burns the good! When you put in good blood, it burns the evil! The horn will allow you to carry a useful amount of the fluid—do you see? All you need to do to burn your enemies is sacrifice some worthless evil thing into the pool!"

Tielle stared at the pool, lost in shock, then looked wide-eyed at Lolth. The demon queen curled a finger sympathetically through Tielle's long, soft hair.

"Poor Tielle. Outsmarted by your sister. Chased, hounded, humiliated. Brought down before all your friends and family by Escalla. Total degradation!"

Lolth tossed Tielle the crystal ball. In it, there shone the tiny image of Escalla winging happily upon her daily chores.

"You have a pool, a horn, and a crystal ball." Lolth coiled silkily around the little faerie, resting her face to whisper in Tielle's attentive ear.

"Now, whatever will we find to talk about?"

**4**

The town of Keggle Bend was shockingly overcrowded. The population from dozens of outlying towns, farms, and villages had all come into the city—the only high ground in the entire region. They thronged the streets, made shantytowns in the alleyways, and huddled outside the city walls. Every government building had given up its lower floors to refugees, and every house and shop was filled with poor families.

Shouldering his way gently through the mob, the Justicar nodded. The city had made a superb effort to do justice to its citizens. The homeless were being sheltered, the poor fed. City officials led soldiers through the throng, trying to make order out of the chaos and clean away the filth that might lead to disease.

The Justicar approved. A good effort was being made. Feeling solid and calm, the man moved carefully through the crowds, opening the way for Henry who followed in his wake. The street ahead was hopelessly jammed. Jus stepped onto the stairs that led to the ramparts of the city wall. He grabbed Henry by the arm and effortlessly hauled the young man up onto the steps beside him. They stood a moment like castaways on an island watching the flotsam swirl about them, and then climbed steadily up the steps onto the battlements above.

Jus kept his hand on Henry's shoulder, steadying him. Henry had tied his untidy blond hair back from his face, and threaded cords through his mail to keep it silent. He was learning well. Jus nodded and led the boy up and away from the streets, looking out across the shale rooves of Keggle Bend.

"Crowds. Minimal danger from missiles. Maximum danger from daggers. But to do that, they have to get close. If the crowd is thick enough, they'll have trouble getting enough force to penetrate your armor." Jus's sharp, suspicious eyes flicked to check the streets and rooftops as he talked. "Deep in a packed mob, your sword blade is an impediment. The pommel is better than the blade. Draw from the scabbard and punch the hilt at an enemy's guts—hard! You can break his nose with your knee as he folds. A man with a broken nose is a man out of the fight for thirty seconds."

Henry hung on every word, his face serious. The Justicar remembered a younger self, and so he drilled information into the boy carefully and faithfully.

"Cities aren't frightening. The shapes here are angular; the shapes of enemies usually aren't. Check windows. Check roofs. Do it as you walk. Areas where light changes sharply are easy to hide in—both for you and an enemy. Always keep note of a place near you where you can defend. Always look for the nearest cover. Look for a place where you can drop out of sight, move fast, and attack from an unexpected angle."

These were the lessons that made the Justicar a lethal force. Attack with surprise; attack with absolute destructive force. Move swiftly; move decisively. Henry was a good pupil, but the boy still let violence shock him. He had not yet found the path that would let him ride it like a god.

They had reached the top ten feet of stairs. Cinders sniffed and slowly bristled up his fur. Instantly stopping to listen, the Justicar crouched with one hand on his sword.

"What is it?"

*Crash-a-boom.* It was getting dark, and it was hours still till sunset. Cinders jittered his tail, flattening his ears and sounding unhappy. *Bad crash-a-boom.*

Henry had his crossbow in his arms, watching his mentor's back. "Sir, what did he say? Crash-a-boom?"

"It's all right." Jus straightened, giving a shake of his head. "He hears a thunder storm."

"Oh." Henry looked at the agitated hell hound, which had begun leaking sulfurous steam. "Cinders is scared of storms?"

*Cinders brave! Big dog! Burn!*

The Justicar's scarred, stubbled face creased in a rare little smile. "When there's an S-T-O-R-M, he likes to H-I-D-E."

*Cinders* like *storm.* Cinders proudly lifted up his ears. *Storm be fun! Big boom! Tree catch fire—burn, burn!* The hell hound sniffed. *Rainstorm bad. Wet, wet. No fire. Makes man smell like old wet sock.*

Looking up past his helmet brim, Jus gave a thoughtful frown. "When did you learn to spell?"

*Funny faerie teach!* Cinders's grin gleamed. He was immensely pleased with himself. *Cinders know S-T-O-R-M storm, W-A-L-K walk, and B-A-T-H bath!*

"Remind me to thank her." Bath day for Cinders was always an experience to be endured. Escalla had just made the process a smidgen more difficult than necessary. "Why did she teach you spelling?"

*Let faerie sleep naked on fur! Warm!*

"Wonderful."

At the top of the city's curtain wall, guards armed with bows watched and waited. One man raised a hand in cautious welcome, wary of the Justicar's grim, forbidding presence. The big man looked as if he could easily clear the entire wall with his sword.

"Halt!" the guardsman shouted. "Garrison only. There's no housing up here."

"We're not staying." The Justicar nodded his chin toward the south. "We've come from the north. I'm looking for your captain of Rangers to ask about the road south."

Shrugging, the nearest soldier waved his bow at the city. The streets were packed like a cattle yard.

"He's somewhere down in *that*. You can wait here on the steps if you like. He'll be back soon."

"Fine."

They sat at the top of the steps, making themselves comfortable. The Justicar unshipped his camp flask, poured a beer for himself, one for Henry, then poured a drink for the nearest guard. The man hesitated, then took the drink. It was the last of the Faerie Court's best ale, imported from the outer planes and heavy as drop-forged steel. The guard took one hesitant sip, then another, then rested his backside on the battlements with his back to the big wide world.

He finished the drink, looking relaxed and relieved. Watching him, Jus sat with Cinders in his lap, brushing the hell hound's black fur to a shine. Jus took back the cup and snapped it into place on his canteen.

"Rough?"

The soldier looked at the city's ludicrous crowds and gave a dismal sigh.

"Noisy. Crowded. But the granary's full." The guard jerked his chin at the river. "Floods won't last. Happened like this ten years ago. Soon goes away."

*You should do something about it.* Benelux's voice echoed inside the Justicar's skull. *A true ruler should cure this at the source, not simply manage the symptoms. You should build retaining walls or drainage canals!*

"The wars might have disrupted public building projects." The Justicar glowered at the sword. "Always uncover facts before you make accusations."

He put the finishing touches on Cinders's coat with a wet cloth, making the hell hound gleam. The guard watched the hell hound's face assume a goofy look. The living pelt hammered his tail upon the ground.

"That thing real?"

"Yep." Jus cleaned the grooming brush and tossed the resulting ball of fur over the wall. "He's called Cinders."

The hell hound's huge teeth gleamed. *Hi!*

With a jerk of his thumb, Jus introduced himself. "Justicar. Henry. The sword's Benelux. We're heading to a village southward: Hommlet."

"Hommlet! And you came from the north?"

"Yep."

"Any trouble?"

"No. No trouble."

The Justicar was uncompromising and calm. His competence spoke for itself. The town guardsman stroked his chin and looked toward the northern hills—a barrier that seemed the end of the known world.

Jus drew Cinders back in place across his shoulders.

"Can we help?"

"Hommlet . . ." The guard tugged at wisps of his beard. "Would it have room for a few refugees?"

"I don't know. As much as you have here, I'd think. We could take a hundred people off your hands if you give us something to feed them with."

The guard shot upright and tugged his surcoat straight. "Wait here! I'll fetch the captain."

The man bustled off. Pouring Henry a second beer, the Justicar seemed perfectly at ease.

"Second lesson. An obstacle is a rock. If you can't break it, flow around it." The Justicar's black armor creaked softly as he relaxed. "Logic and instinct. They're your sharpest tools. In life, there are no mysteries that cannot be solved. No problems that cannot be fixed."

Henry frowned. "None at all?"

"None." Jus thought of Escalla and gave a heavy sigh. "Some just need a little more work than others."

Darkness built above the city. Far off in the distance, there was the rumbling of a sudden summer storm.

5

"Ah. Here we are. Oh, for once, it's actually quite pleasant!" Lolth stood in a wilderness of dead, twisted grass, a hillside where the bones of the slaughtered jutted through the soil. "That horrid fresh air smell is gone."

Black, polished, and magnificent, Lolth stood and let the fetid winds caress her hair. Behind her, carried along by Lolth's spells in the middle of her morning cup of tea, Morag glowered.

"Magnificence? What are we doing here?"

"We are eliminating trouble before it can begin." Lolth pulled two long thigh bones from the earth and enchanted them. "Do you have that bag I gave you?"

"Yes, Magnificence."

"Good. Drink your tea."

Holding the bones as divining rods, Lolth walked off along the hillside. Morag sighed, bunched up her coils, and followed, delicately picking a path past the bones of a dead wyvern. The place was wretchedly cold, abysmally dry, and Morag felt the day's carefully crafted schedules slipping away. She hurried after her mistress, planting herself so that Lolth's appointment diary could clearly be seen.

The spider goddess ignored her, happily scanning her divining rods over the dead grass.

"This is Iuz's territory, I believe. We shall take it over once we eliminate him." Lolth swung sideways as the two bones quivered and began to cross. She walked rapidly over the hill, led by her divining rods.

Morag impatiently folded all six of her arms. "Magnificence, the operation begins in sixty minutes."

"Yes, yes. I'm a goddess, Morag. I can teleport. I don't need a nag." Lolth shot a scathing glance at her secretary. "Your little shopping trip is safe and sound, never fear."

The divining rods crossed, and in the end, their target was obvious. On a hillside littered by the bones of monsters, one site had been conspicuously made into a grave. The earth had been heaped in a telltale fashion. Most interestingly of all, a froglike tanar'ri skull had been left to mark the grave—a skull impaled and pinned by a broken sword. Lolth reached out to draw the sword from the ground and instantly burned her hand.

"Damnation!"

"Magnificence?" Lolth was notoriously vulnerable to blessed artifacts. "Shall I fetch you a bandage?"

"Don't be impertinent!" Lolth blew on her fingers, hurt and angry. She kicked the sword and the skull out of the ground and shoved them away with one stiletto-heeled boot. "What sort of fool leaves an enchanted sword stuck in the soil?"

"Someone who has a better sword, Magnificence?"

"Brilliant." Lolth spared the grave a contemptuous kick. "Well what are you waiting for? You have six hands. Dig!"

Morag growled. Her hands were long and clever, and her scales had just been buffed and dried. She wearily unslung her collection of weapons, notebooks, pens, and diaries, and went to work, digging in the horrid, flinty soil. As she labored, Lolth opened her hands and cast a spell. An instant later, a savage vulture-demon appeared before her. Lolth accepted a delicate glass from the creature, allowed it to pour her some wine, and then lolled atop a varrangoin's skeleton to watch Morag at her work.

"Ah, wine. I always did like a glass in the afternoon. We must search this world and see if there are any novel vintages to be found!"

"Yes, Magnificence." Well down in her hole, Morag resentfully shoveled earth. "I'm sure the faeries will have a bottle or two to spare."

"Shut up. Dig."

The excavation took a good ten minutes of filthy work, by which time Morag was cursing. She had broken a nail, gotten grit in her eye, and was filthy from tip to tail. She finally uncovered a dried, withered skeleton—a figure clad in armor that had rusted to a flaky brown.

From above her came Lolth's imperious voice. "Don't hurt the bones, idiot! Now get out of there!"

No helping hand was offered. Morag angrily threw a spell and summoned some of her own vassals: hopping birdlike minions that stank like the pit. The beings reached down to help the secretary out. She jerked her hands free from their grasp and fastidiously cleaned herself while Lolth had the beings carefully lift the old bones out of their grave.

The corpse was well preserved—a withered husk dried like leather from the parched soil of the hills. The armor was elven mail, cut and ripped by claws. It had been torn open where the cadaver had once had its heart ripped out of its chest. The being bore a helmet fashioned like the open mouth of a screaming eagle. Lolth busied herself drawing an enchanted circle about the corpse, daubing her magic symbols with blood taken from an ivory chalice. Behind her, yet more tanar'ri appeared, dragging with them humanoid slaves, a troll, spider servitors, and treasure chests. The hillside had suddenly become crowded.

Lolth painted three final runes, then tore the heart out of a slave to activate her magic. Fastidiously cleaning herself, Morag looked away in disgust, reaching for her notebooks and weapons.

The enchanted circle flashed and flared into life about the corpse. Lolth opened bloody hands, chanted her spell, and a cold wind stirred her hair, lifting her silks about her magnificent body.

Slit-pupil eyes gleamed red as she opened her arms and trilled foul spells.

Lesser creatures fell dead from the magic. Insects, worms, and birds dropped lifeless about the hill. Lolth stood at the center of a storm of screaming energy. A ghostly image half-formed in the winds that swirled across the hill—an image that shrieked and wailed as it was dragged downward from the otherworld. Guardians tried to drag the spirit back, but Lolth flicked out with her hands and sent them spinning away into the storm.

The withered corpse arose slowly, lifted invisibly from the ground. Dead hair, long, golden, and littered with soil, whipped around in the storm's frenzy. The corpse arched, mold dropping from it as the winds raged and swirled. Lolth held her arms wide, her skin crackling pale with energy, then stepped through the circle of enchantment.

Reaching down, she wrenched open the corpse's rent mail armor and tore open its rotted ribs.

"Here is a heart for you, my dear. Fresh and new."

The sacrificial heart was jammed into the gaping chest. Lolth hissed in pleasure as she stabbed magic down into the dead, dried flesh.

"And now here is some blood for you to pump with it."

Demons dragged a black marsh troll forward, the huge creature raging with superhuman strength yet utterly impotent in the demons' claws. Lolth took a knife from a drow servant and stabbed the troll through its neck. Her eyes gleamed as she viciously twisted the knife in the wound, keeping it open even as the troll's flesh tried to regenerate and heal. She caught the blood in bowl after bowl, the troll growing weaker as it was drained. Finally she had the troll cast aside to heal, the monster whimpering as its blood was carried over to the floating corpse.

Lolth poured the blood into the cadaver's open chest, her spells wrenching at the air as the hissing fluid flowed. The blood soaked into the corpse's skin and bones. It drew into the withered, rotten veins. With a sizzle, the old body slowly began to fill and heal.

Finally, Lolth opened the corpse's mouth. With one hand she reached up and snatched the screaming spirit that flew about her ears. Wrestling it like a whirlwind she shoved the spirit down into the corpse and sealed it tight. With a wrench, the body heaved against invisible bonds. Arms reached, thrashing in horrific agony, and the throat roared in burning pain. Lolth stepped back, her head tilted like a little girl with one cheek resting on a bloodied finger. In the magic circle, the corpse writhed and spasmed in pure agony, until it fell hissing to the ground. The magic circle faded. The cadaver steamed with cold.

The corpse lay on its face. Slowly it opened one clawed hand and clutched at the soil of its grave. Light and happy as a lark, Lolth walked over to its side. She squatted down and dusted off the cadaver's eagle helm.

"Poor hero. Poor, poor hero . . ."

Lolth spoke in the tongue of the Grass Elves as he squatted, her face half lifted in a smile as the undead creature wrenched itself up from the ground.

The cadaver knelt in the dust, the ice-white pits of its eyes jerking in confusion from side to side. Its last clear memories were of battle. The creature's hand clutched at the rents in its mail—at the wound that had finally ripped away its life. Lolth watched it with a smile.

"Poor hero. Yes, struck down in the dust—betrayed and alone and surrounded."

The cadaver groped blindly in the dirt. It looked down in puzzlement, then anger as it saw nothing but dust.

"No. No sword. Stolen!" Lolth clucked in sympathy. "Your sword was taken away! You were betrayed, surrounded, abandoned, robbed. Poor hero. No sword to make you safe. No sword to take revenge."

Lolth reached out, and a demon threw her a sword. The goddess held the long, heavy weapon in her hands and drew it slowly from its sheath. The blade gleamed the foul red-purple color of clotted blood, smoking as she slowly bared the steel.

"Here is a sword. Yes! See?"

The corpse stared at the weapon. It hissed in lust and slowly reached out its hand. Lolth played a little, keeping the weapon just out of reach for a moment, then thrust it into the corpse's hand.

"There. I give you a new sword, a better sword. Strong, powerful! Now everything you lost can be regained."

The undead warrior jerked suddenly upright in shock, staring around. It hissed like a serpent, crouching into fighting stance as it searched from side to side, almost as if hunting for blood.

Lolth stood unconcernedly at its side. She pulled the hair back from the side of her face as she bent down to whisper in the warrior's ear.

"Yes . . . lost. Weren't you a leader? Weren't you alive? That's right! You were feared. You were a fighter! You had renown!" The queen of spiders crossed behind the undead corpse, her voice purring in its ear. "You were a great leader, but someone took your men away. He became leader in your place. He built on your fame, built on your legend. He stole your life away . . . and could you really have died here? Not you, not a warrior so great. Not the great swordmaster Recca."

Lolth covered her mouth in mock surprise.

"He betrayed you! Of course! It's the only way it could have been done!" The goddess looked quite shocked. "And after you taught him everything he knew! After you trusted him, raised him, treated him like a son!" Lolth leaned close to the monster and furrowed her brows into a frown. "He took everything you had. Whatever should you do?"

The cadaver roared. The skull-face bared its teeth as the

monstrous warrior raised its sword to the sky, screaming in mad hunger for revenge. Clustered about the edge of the magic circle, Lolth's demons, henchmen, and servants laughed in acclaim.

Smiling, Lolth arose and crooked a finger at the walking corpse.

"Well, now *I* must be your new friend. I gave you a sword, gave you blood and a heart. Such a good friend!" Lolth motioned to Morag, beckoning her close. "Come. Maybe I can help you a little more. I think perhaps I can take you to where you can find your revenge. After all, what are good friends for?"

Lolth walked happily toward her secretary, followed by the shambling monster. Twiddling her fingers at Morag, Lolth smiled.

"There we are! And just in time for our invasion to begin. Are there any other problems your tiny little mind can foresee?"

Morag regarded the walking corpse with a gaze rich with irony.

"Very few, Magnificence." Morag dotted a note in her diary with her pen. "Incidentally, Magnificence, the creature lacks a left foot and a sword hand."

Lolth whipped about and stared. Sure enough, the corpse had been buried by a dedicated soldier. Its sword hand and one foot had been cut off, then presumably burned and powdered to prevent the enemy from animating it as a walking skeleton. The missing pieces were not regenerating from the troll's blood inside the cadaver. Lolth felt Morag's smug smile and seethed, flexing her blood-sticky fingers in annoyance.

"It doesn't matter!" Lolth turned and walked away. "It will find new limbs on its own!"

"Yes, Magnificence. Superb foresight, Magnificence."

"He will adapt, Morag. That is the beauty of the spell."

"Yes, Magnificence. Of course."

6

Sitting by the town's front gate, Polk, for once, was doing just as he was told: staying put and staying out of trouble. He sat upon a table outside of a crowded tavern, waving irritably at serving boys. The tavern staff gave him a wide, wide berth, and patrons left Polk the whole table to himself. The badger squared his cap upon his head and grumbled about the falling standards of service these days.

Being a badger had mixed blessings. On one hand, he was dense, heavy, and had a bite like a crocodile. On the other hand, he was a furry quadruped most people viewed as a noxious pest or a danger to life and limb. It was this last attribute that finally brought a nine-year-old boy nervously edging up to the table bearing a large wooden bowl and a stone jug.

Polk waved a paw.

"Son! Over here, son! That's my order. It's for me—the badger. Quadruped, that is. Furry, black and white stripes. You can't miss me!"

The boy kept his distance, pushing his offering cautiously onto the tabletop. Polk scratched his ear with one hind leg.

"Son, you look frayed! A bundle of nerves, son. It ain't healthy! A boy like you needs courage! Needs discipline—some get up and go! Now what are you getting all timid for?"

"S-sorry, sir!" The child wiped his hands in fright. "We . . . we don't get many, um, bears here, sir."

"I'm a badger, son. Was human once, though. Reincarnation

accident. Magic spell cast after I heroically sacrificed my life for my friends. Part of the risks of the hero's profession, son. I'm not ashamed of it."

"A hero?" The boy blinked. "Were you in the war?"

"Hundreds of 'em, son! But no, I'm an explorer, saver of damsels, slayer of monsters." Polk trundled over to the wooden bowl. "That's my order you got there?"

"Uh, yes. That was one full bottle of fortified skull-crusher brandy poured in a bowl?"

"That's right, son. Keeps the coat glossy!" The badger wrinkled his nose. "Can I get a twist with that?"

"S-sorry, sir."

"Don't matter. But you have to uncork the bottle, son. You have to pour. I've got claws. Great for digging, poor for pulling the cork out of jugs! And get me about a hundred bottles of this to go!"

"A *hundred* bottles?" The child blinked. "How will you . . . you carry it?"

"I've got a portable hole, son. A trans-dimensional cubbyhole rolled up to convenient size. I never leave the burrow without it!"

The drink was poured, and Polk shook his head as the boy retreated. "Child's about as bright as a lamp with no wick in it."

The badger settled down to drink a restorative libation, managing to absorb almost his own body weight in alcohol. Surfacing with a sigh, Polk licked his chops, settled back on his furry rear, and cast his eyes out over the churning, tangled crowds.

Polk paused and frowned, then used his mouth to drop coins onto the table. He jumped heavily down onto the pavement and looked around.

The skies were pitch black with something that looked like storm clouds. Polk's badger nose suddenly sniffed the stench of magic in the air. The stink of evil.

A drifting cloud of silver strands settled on the nearby roofs. Thousands of spiders—tiny spiders tailing long web strands from their tails—landed, then sped over the roofs and gutters.

Moving under tables and chairs, Polk ran into an alleyway and watched a new team of spiders descend. A group landed close to Polk. They were black widows that shimmered with magic. Black widows that stank of drow.

Drow!

Polk almost fell over himself as he tumbled backward, found his feet, and sped off to save the city.

"Son! Jus, boy! We've got a problem here!"

\* \* \* \* \*

On the "Street of a Thousand Eateries," high prices had apparently chased away the crowds of refugees. A tall woman, her hair tied into a thousand pretty braids beneath a most extraordinary hat, teetered down the street. Walking unsteadily, staggering quickly forward to cling onto gutter pipes and walls, the woman let her hat coach her as she took one step at a time.

"Easy . . . easy . . . Left foot, right foot—left foot, right foot." Having shape-shifted into a stylish, pheasant-feathered hat, Escalla took the role of pilot, navigator, and deportment coach. "Come on—a bit of rhythm! One-two, one-two! There we go!"

Tripping over her own two feet, Enid yelped and grabbed a wall for support. Escalla had managed one of the finest shape change spells of her career, but Enid was finding life in the guise of a human a bit of a handful. Bipedal locomotion was not all that it was cracked up to be. Wobbling onward down the street, Enid held out her hands and tried to keep her balance.

"I'm not quite sure how you people manage to move around."

"You'll catch on in a bit. Now come on. There has to be a bakery somewhere in this damned town!"

Even here, in the most expensive streets of the city, the crowds were thick, though they seemed a bit more upscale than those they had encountered on their way into the city. A group of thirty monks stood in a silent ring, their heads bowed in prayer. There were families setting up tents in the alleyways and children running riot across the cobblestones. More monks stood on the street corners, collecting for the poor. The scene was total chaos, and Escalla rather liked it.

Most of the food shops were closed. The supplies had been requisitioned for the refugees. However, a few expensive luxury stores still seemed to stock an item or two. Escalla spied a pastry shop and clucked like a girl starting up a reluctant horse, jiggling herself to guide Enid in the right direction.

"There! That's what we're after. All right, now remember, keep one foot on the ground at all times!"

Desperately trying not to fall, Enid maneuvered her way along the street.

"Do I *have* to be human? I don't know where to put these silly arms!"

"Everyone has that problem! Just be glad you're not an octopus."

"You've been an octopus?"

"Hey, I'm a faerie!" Escalla's feather plumes gave a twirl. Her frost wand and lich staff were being used as hat pins. Two cherries on the hat served as her eyes. "Once a week back home, we used to take turns to scare the horses."

"You and your sister would take turns polymorphing?"

"My sister didn't have to polymorph. She had a face like a dog's bum with a hat on." Escalla-the-hat folded her feathers. "But anyway, this is a human town! You have to blend in. A faerie and a sphinx might draw attention, you know. This way, we're invisible. We're just a part of the crowd."

This particular piece of the crowd was well endowed, had

freckles, and was having a conversation with her hat. Still unhappy about her arms, missing her tail and wings, Enid tried her best to walk through the bustling street. She sniffed as she passed the ring of monks, then suddenly had to avoid a nasty fall.

"Arms are silly. Do they always just *hang* here like this?"

"Move 'em as you walk. Not like that! When your leg goes forward, your arm goes back. Anyway, you'll need the arms to carry all the cakes."

"What cakes?"

"The cakes we'll get at the bakery! It's on the list of provisions!"

Enid sheltered against a wall as carts of grain trundled past on their way to the town mill. She pulled out a pair of spectacles and perused the shopping list Escalla had provided for her.

"Let's see. Wine, honey, sugar, fruit, faerie cakes . . ." Enid read the list and screwed her pretty nose up in a frown "Is this what we're getting for rations? I thought we needed some other things too?"

"Hmm?" Escalla waved a feather. "No, just that. Oh, and maybe some meat, bread, vegetables, and cheese. I can't think of everything!"

"I see." Enid carefully put the shopping list away. Escalla had a metabolism like a hummingbird. "I believe you should leave the rest of the shopping to me."

"Sure! But can we get some cream? I really want faerie cakes with the tops cut into those little butterfly wings!"

They reached a shop that actually seemed to be open—a shop that proudly hung a wooden board painted with a cake from its eaves. The sign seemed new, clean, and neat. It was perfect. Escalla jiggled until Enid moved in the right direction, and Escalla was almost knocked off Enid's head as the tall girl entered the cramped, dim little store. Out in the street, the monks moved their circle closer to the store. The noise of the city dimmed as the door swung firmly shut.

A large, sticky cake sat on a bench. The cake was covered in honey, fruits, and sugar, and it had been freshly sliced into dainty little pieces. In a town given over to mass producing simple food for refugees, the cake was an utter treasure. Escalla saw the sweet and drooled.

Enid gave a sniff then narrowed her eyes and leaned over the cake, sniffing at it again. Escalla reached out with her feathers, but Enid stepped back out of the way.

"Oh, dear. I believe I've forgotten my purse."

Escalla shifted on Enid's head, looking carefully from left to right. The hat disappeared with a subtle *pop* as the faerie turned invisible.

The attack came from the rafters—a massive blast of lightning stabbing from the dark. Enid ducked, and the spell shattered against a shield made of swarming golden bees. The ceiling instantly caught fire from the ricocheting energy.

The globe of bees flickered and swirled around Enid. Escalla hovered in midair, naked, visible, and coldly furious as she readied her lich staff in her hand.

"Nice one, frot-head! I like your poisoned cake."

Enid hissed like an angry cat, hunched, and bared her teeth. Escalla looked idly at another blank patch of darkness.

The next spell hammered at them in a manic blast of ice. The rear wall of the shop smashed in, the serving counter torn apart under a raging storm of icicles and frost. Safe inside their sphere of bees, Enid and Escalla watched and waited.

The frost storm died, leaving the room ice-white and steaming with mists. Posing with her staff idly crooked across her shoulders, Escalla looked at the damage with a sneer.

"For the uninitiated, this is a lesser sphere of invulnerability. An anti-magic shield. Guess you'll just have to take me out hand-to-hand." Escalla's shield spell worked both ways—no magic could go in, and no magic could go out. With a sly smile, the faerie laid a hand on Enid and caressed her with a spell. "But hey! Lookie what I've got here."

Clothes ripped to rags. Enid warped up and outward into her sphinx form, her hindquarters knocking over the remnants of the rear wall. Clawed and bristling, a full-grown sphinx now crouched beneath the faerie girl. Standing on Enid's head, Escalla looked idly about the shop.

"Are you coming out to play?"

The answer came as a derisive female laugh, a laugh ringing with insanity. The roof fell, and Enid leaped forward, smashing through the wall and out into the street. Escalla sheltered from debris beneath Enid's wings. The shield spell danced and shimmered a golden light across the cobblestones.

Standing in silence, a ring of hooded monks made a cordon around Enid and Escalla. The monks stood in silence, crouched and intense. Their robes hid their hands and faces in impenetrable darkness. Escalla hovered with her staff in hand. The sphinx unsheathed her huge claws and spread her wings. There were easily thirty monks, but it was doubtful that any of them could fly.

The laugh came once again—a horribly familiar laugh tinged with a gay touch of madness. Escalla felt absolute loathing ooze through her soul.

"You."

Tielle, Escalla's sister, became visible at last.

She was better fleshed than Escalla, with rounder curves at chest and thigh. Dressed in a few tiny specks of adamantine and silver, the faerie hovered gaily in mid air.

"Sweet sister and her pretty kitty!" Tielle looked at Escalla in sick intensity, as though she had long adored and lingered over every inch of Escalla's hide. "It was very dark in prison. They left me as a blob, you know. A blob in a big, dark hole. Because it was your joke. Because dear beautiful Escalla thought it was funny." Tielle stared, her eyes wide and intense. "Oh, Escalla.

My wonderful Escalla." Tielle cradled a drinking horn and a crystal ball tight against herself, hugging them as though their love spoke to her soul. "I have so looked forward to feeling you die."

*     *     *     *     *

Running madly through the streets, Polk squinted at ankles, legs, and shoes. His badger nose smelled drow. *Drow!* People scattered, soldiers shouted. A woman screamed as he sped straight beneath her skirt. Polk wheezed as he ran, his fat fur rippling like an onrushing wave. Humans threw themselves out of his way, shouting in panic as they fought to escape the badger.

Polk ran, dodging as a soldier stabbed at him with a spear. The big badger finally found the city wall and raced growling along its base. He bowled over a pile of baskets, ripped clean through a row of tents, and scattered pots and pans in his wake. He bellowed, "Jus! Where are you son?" He got no answer, and so the badger lumbered on.

Three soldiers tried to wall him in with shields. Polk took them at a run, ploughing through a gap between their shields. He sped onward, scrabbling awkwardly up a set of stone stairs as he climbed to the city battlements. Overhead, the storm clouds shut away the sun.

"Son! Son, where are you? *Where are you, son?*"

"Polk! What in Cuthbert's name are you doing?" The Justicar sat at the head of the stairs with his sword across his knees, Cinders on his back, and Henry squatting beside him. Three town guards and a captain were with them, all gathered around a map. "Polk!"

The badger gave a savage roar. Polk leaped the last three steps, bowling Henry over as he landed on Henry's chest. Polk hurtled forward in a snarling charge beneath the magistrate and crashed into a vast spider that hauled itself over the battlements.

The giant spider was bigger than a horse. Polk shot under its jaws and attacked. Badger teeth ripped through chitin. Blood flew, and Polk wrenched the leg off the spider. Flailing its feet, the spider loomed over Polk, twin fangs bared and ready to stab down into the badger's heart. An instant later, the spider was smashed aside, Jus's blade smacking into the monster's face.

The blade hit hard, fast, and in savage silence. The monster staggered. The Justicar's sword hacked off one front leg, then another, then clove down in a massive blow that split the spider's head in two. He kicked the giant spider aside. The white blade of his sword shining, the Justicar looked across the city walls, and turned to roar back at the city guards.

"Get your men to the battlements! Move! *Move!*"

The captain stood, then lost his upper torso as a ballista bolt ripped above the battlements. Blood sprayed over the city walls. A second bolt whirred as it flew, and the Justicar raged forward, his big sword ringing as it caught the massive iron shaft and knocked it up into the air. Jus shouldered soldiers aside, then hacked his blade down into another spider's leg that came prancing over the wall.

Jus killed the spider with a vicious twisting thrust of his sword over the battlements. He cut away the web the creature had been laying as a ladder up the city walls. Soldiers stared, then grabbed crossbows, javelins, and bows, running faster and faster to their posts as the war cries and screams of an immense army sounded from the fields below. Signalers blew their battle horns as the whole world suddenly went mad.

The Justicar gave Polk a sharp nod, then helped him scrabble up onto the battlements. Polk and Henry looked out over the stone walls, off into the flooded countryside below, and both stared in ashen surprise.

"That wasn't there a moment ago!" Henry said.

Curtains of illusion faded and fell, revealing a vast army

rampaging toward Keggle Bend. The flooded, muddy fields were jet black, boiling with a vile carpet of screaming flesh. For miles around, the countryside was covered with a baying, ravening multitude. Monstrous black shapes raged toward the city walls. There were spiders as big as dinner plates, as big dogs, and some as big as mares. There were creatures with swords and monsters with spears. Here and there, titanic spiders stood above the boiling mass, their backs crowned with ballistae and howling warriors. Black widows the size of horses led the incoming waves, the creatures splashing through muddy fields to clamber up the walls. Other spiders had already reached the battlements, webs stringing to the ground behind them as they climbed. The first wave of warriors reached the webs, and began to climb upward in a mass of hate and steel.

# 7

Crowds scattered in panic. Facing each other across a stretch of cobblestones, Escalla and Tielle seethed with spells. Escalla laid arrow-wards and blade-wards over herself and Enid as she watched the circle of monks from the corner of her eye.

Tielle's costume consisted mostly of jewelry and spider silk. Looking at her sister, Escalla raised one eyebrow in disdain.

"Nice outfit, Thunder Thighs. I see prison food agreed with you."

"Insults." Tielle's eyes brightened. "Oh, I knew there would be insults!" Tielle looked at Escalla in yearning hunger. "And there you are, looking so beautiful. I *want* you to feel pretty! I want you to feel as beautiful and as glorious as you can." Tielle's breathing was deep and ragged as she wrung her hands about a large crystal horn. "And then I want to sear the skin off you. I want to burn you, Escalla, and I want it to last and last and last. . . ."

The bystanders had fled. Escalla looked at her sister and weighed the lich staff in her grasp.

"All right, so I'm guessing you have a few more issues than last time we met?" Escalla hovered behind her shield. "I don't know how you got out of prison, but this time you're going back in pieces! Now, are you going to keep wasting spells, or are you going to drag your butt in here and fight like a faerie?"

Shielded against magic, against missiles, and with sorcery able to deflect mortal blades, Escalla was ready for a fight. Beneath her, Enid gave a feline hiss. The sphinx was as big as a bull and a hundred time more deadly. Almost oblivious to the danger, Tielle flew brightly over to the edge of the magic shield.

"Oooh. A lesser sphere of invulnerability! What a lovely, powerful little spell." The girl looked coyly sidewise at her sister. "Escalla? Would you consider yourself to be a *good* little faerie?"

Escalla gave a disdainful shrug. "I fight the fight. I right the wrongs. Yeah, I'm good." The girl held her lich staff like a child about to play bat-and-ball. "What's it to you?"

"Oh, nothing." Tielle held her hands merrily behind her back. "But do you know what? I have a secret."

"Yeah? What?"

"This!"

Tielle moved. Escalla caught the motion and hurtled skyward. An instant later, a hissing blast of fluid shot out of Tielle's horn.

Escalla screamed.

Like red quicksilver, the fluid jetted outward in a solid beam. The spray clipped Enid on one shoulder, then swerved to catch Escalla as she twisted and flew. The blow hit Escalla on one thigh, the force of the blow knocking her spinning through the sky until she crashed against the cobblestones.

Escalla thrashed in mindless agony. She arched her back and hammered her head on the pavement as raw pain ripped into her leg. The fluid hissed and burned, bubbling away flesh and skin. The golden bees of her magic shield scattered madly aside as Escalla smashed herself against the road.

Tielle laughed and shook the horn next to her ear, smiling warmly as she heard yet more liquid sloshing away inside. She pointed the horn at Escalla and grinned.

"And now, your body. But not your face . . ."

Another beam of blood-silver shot straight at Escalla. She croaked and tried to move aside, but she was paralyzed with pain.

With a roar, Enid lunged, shielding Escalla with her back. Fluid blasted into Enid's hide, searing her to the bone. Tielle gave her insane, ringing laughter as the horn ran itself dry.

"Take them! Take them now!"

The monks threw back their hoods. Reeling in agony, Enid could only stare.

The opened hoods revealed hideous giggling faces, the eyes rolling mad and the flesh dripping wet with sweat. Their flesh was twisted and entwined with coil after coil of chains, mummifying them in steel. Thirty of the creatures gibbered and giggled as they whipped their arms forward, and chains lashed out to crack into Enid's hide. The sphinx staggered and thrashed. Chains wrapped around and around her legs, wings, and throat, dragging at her from a dozen different directions. Behind her servants, Tielle clapped her hands and made a little dance of glee.

"Aren't they lovely? They're from Pandemonium, where I serve the Queen of Wind and Woe!"

Tugging madly at the chains, the monks tried to drag Enid in a dozen different directions at once. Tielle watched it all in simple joy.

"You might have spells and powers, Escalla, but *I* have friends!"

One leg burned almost to the bone and her wings melted and useless, Escalla shook as she reached her hand up to Enid. The sphinx reared, trapped in agony, a dozen chains trying to wrench her from her feet. The sphinx fought back with huge strength and power, whirling and thrashing, sending Tielle's servants crashing to the ground. One chain monk flew and smashed into a wall, still giggling even as it died. More chains flew, links closed tight about Enid's throat, and Tielle leaned eagerly close as Enid started strangling to death.

Escalla managed to reach Enid's foot. A chain whipped out and crashed against the injured faerie, wrapping around and around. Escalla gripped Enid's fur. A chain monk screamed and leaped for her, chains flailing through the air, then suddenly fog exploded through the alleyway as Escalla coughed out a spell.

"No!"

Tielle hurled herself high above the whirling melee. Fog choked the alleyway, and the chain monks whooped and wailed as their empty chains thrashed at the air. Screaming, Tielle ploughed a spell into the fog's heart. The fireball blasted cobblestones into the air, tossing aside chain monks and shattering houses in the street. She fought her way down through the mist, waving her hands to clear her view. Molten stone and shattered shops collapsed into rubble and debris. No corpses lay splayed before her—only empty sheaths of chain.

"No!"

The faerie ripped at the cobblestones with her bare hands, trying to find her sister. Raving, Tielle tore the rubble apart with spells, smashing and gouging her way down to the dirt below. Panting, she reared up out of the filth, casting wildly from side to side with her face streaming tears.

"Where is she? Why did you release her? Why? Why?"

Chain monks fell back in terror. Tielle blew one of them apart with one savage gesture of a finger, her hair flying about her little body as she stamped and screamed in hate.

A chain monk crouched in the dirt nearby, hooting and moaning as it flapped a calming hand at Tielle. The monster pointed at an opening in one of the stone gutters of the street—an opening that led down into the flooded city sewers. A ferocious stench rose from the hole. Tielle flung herself over to the gutter and peered inside.

The hole was nothing but a slot a handspan tall, leading to a drop some twenty feet or more into the sewer tunnels down below. The faerie slammed her hand against the stone and roared in rage.

"Polymorph! Escalla and her mangy friend shape-changed and escaped!"

Tielle could shapeshift and chase her sister down into the sewers, but the chain monks would be left behind. Tielle needed the chain monks to catch and hold all of Escalla's little friends. She turned upon her servants and showered them with abuse.

"Tear up the streets! There must be a way into the sewers somewhere! Find it. Go-go-go!"

Tielle raged, and the chain monks raced to do her will. Left alone in the street, the faerie snatched up a torn ribbon of black skirt and hurled it to the ground.

Overhead, the sun suddenly dimmed. Darkness spread over the city, and the air trembled with a distant roar.

The legions of Lolth had come. The battlements would be stormed, the air would fill with abyssal bats, and Tielle's prey might be slain by any one of ten thousand monsters. Cursing, Tielle walked back down the streets as lightning cracked high up in the sky.

* * * * *

"Get down!"

On the battlements, the town guards flung themselves flat as a wave of spells shot upward from the onrushing hordes below. Lightning bolts smashed stone from the battlements and charred soldiers into ash. The Justicar pushed spearmen into cover, then whirled and cut an incoming lightning bolt clean out of the sky. Benelux shrieked, half in pain and half in exultation.

"Henry!" shouted the Justicar.

Henry had seen the enemy sorcerer. The boy slapped five bolts into his crossbow's magazine, took aim, and opened fire. The machine bucked in his hand, the magical bow blurring as it sent five shots hissing into the air. Down below, a drow sorcerer spun and screamed, pierced by three crossbow bolts and smashed to the ground. Henry reloaded, already picking new targets. Jus walked by, Cinders's tail swirling in his wake and the sword of light gleaming in his hand.

"Archers, pick your targets! Don't waste your fire! Kill the officers! Kill anyone who leads!"

The monsters down below had the same orders. An arrow sped up from below toward the Justicar, and he contemptuously swatted it from the air.

"Other soldiers, stay down! I want one man in three back at the stairs as a reserve!"

The Justicar strode the battlements, huge and powerful. His brilliant white sword steamed with blood, and the hell hound cresting his helmet leaked fire and brimstone from its fangs. Soldiers flung themselves into place along the battlements, and the Justicar shoved men to their stations. He caught a new soldier and spun the man around.

"You! Where are your officers for this section?"

"Dead!" Another man yelled over his shoulder, ducking a crossbow quarrel from below. "Spider bites! There's black widow spiders in the barracks! Millions of them!"

Polk moved backward, tugging a heavy box of crossbow quarrels over to Henry. Jus looked out over the battlements and saw a land turned black with hell.

No inch of ground showed beneath the onrushing horde. There were tens of thousands of creatures down below—spiders, some the size of wagons, others no bigger than coins. Troglodytes, reptilian and stinking like pus, shambled forward. There were trolls and gargoyles and demonic shapes made from molten bone and spikes. There were creatures half spider and half flayed corpse who fought each other to be first to the city walls, leaping and screaming as they fought through the fields of mud. Giant spiders the size of war elephants strode amongst the rabble, and from armored cabins on their backs, lordly drow directed the attack. Whipping the wave forward, roaring in insensate lust for blood, there were the hideous shapes of tanar'ri demons. Darkness spells turned the world around them into night, while abyssal bats flapped like flayed corpses through the skies.

Spiders and drow. Jus cursed and flattened himself against the wall of a tower as the arrow storm began.

*Lolth!* Benelux seemed stunned. *This is her doing!* Benelux was shocked when the Justicar seemed undismayed. *But we killed her! You defeated her. Good triumphed over evil!*

"Evil begs to differ." The Justicar made a practice cut with Benelux, the huge sword swirling like a toy in his hand. Jus had a sudden, clear vision of his responsibility for the invasion army down below.

Lolth. Coldly judging the enemy's rate of approach, the Justicar walked the battlements as a huge cloud of arrows flew up to smack and clatter from the city walls. Thousands of arrows fell down into the city streets, and the packed mobs living in the alleyways fought frantically to get into the shelter of the houses. Chaos broke out, and still the Justicar watched his enemy, unmoved. He cut another spider strand free, ducking back as a ballista bolt whipped harmlessly past his head.

"Polk?"

"Son? What is it, son? I'm busy here!" The badger had found a ballista crew, and was dragging spare ammunition over to them one bolt at a time. "There's a million of them down there, son. It's gonna be a last stand! Fight to the finish, backs to the wall, and the last defender dies atop a slaughtered heap of foes! I've gotta get ammo up here, then find somewhere to seal our chronicles. They can be a message of hope, son. A guiding light to the brave souls who will carry on the fight once we're dead and gone!"

"Polk, stop planning suicide notes and find Escalla! We need sorcery up here right now!" The big man felt the darkness growing over the city, the gloom deepening into pure pitch black. "Torches! I want torches on the wall!"

Henry wrenched a wounded man back out of the line of fire. He treated the soldier swiftly, tugging the arrow from him and

jamming the wound closed with spiderwebs. Pale white with
shock, the wounded man kept staring over the battlements.

"Th-there must be a hundred thousand of them."

"Most of them aren't real." The Justicar crouched, talking loud
enough to be heard by the defenders all around. "Cinders?"

The hell hound's red eyes watched the enemy and gave a feral
gleam.

*Front wave is illusion. Middle is real. Rear line is illusion.*

"Only the middle wave is real!" the Justicar bellowed to the
archers along the wall. "Concentrate fire on the middle ranks! Be
careful! There might be a few real ones mixed in with the phan-
tasms!" The Justicar cursed. "That still makes it forty thousand
troops down there. She wants this city taken fast." He yelled after
Polk as the badger blundered down the stairs. "Hurry, Polk! We
need magic up here now!"

Henry had his crossbow reloaded, this time with venom on the
bolts. He pulled his helmet strap tight and looked back at the Justicar.

"Here they come."

The shock of impact seemed to make the wall shudder to its
roots. Countless siege ladders thudded into place. On the walls,
soldiers began to rise, until the Justicar shoved them straight back
down.

"Get in cover and close your eyes! It isn't real!" The big man
strode like a god of war, the black hell hound gleaming on his
back, a sword made of white energy shimmering in his hand.
"Concentrate on dinner! What did you eat last night? How did it
feel between your teeth? Every bite! Concentrate!"

A soldier scrabbled back from the wall as ringing screams filled
the entire world. The Justicar stooped, grabbed the man by his
armor, and slammed him back into his post.

"Where in the abyss are you going?" Huge with anger, Jus
shoved his victim back in line. "If you desert your friends,

then you're one of the enemy! I'll kill you where you stand!"

Illusory monsters swarmed over the wall. The Justicar strode through the darkness, ripped by insubstantial claws. He passed through the monsters, laying a hand on the armored backs of the soldiers, forcing them to ignore the sorcery. As a real invader finally put a ladder on the wall, he reached over the battlements, snared the screaming goblin, and threw the creature straight down into the cobbled streets below.

"All right! Up! Now kill—kill them all!"

The soldiers surged to their feet as new scaling ladders thundered against the battlements. A screaming tide of monsters clawed against the city walls. Huge spiders climbed the stone, while demonic tanar'ri directed their slaves to scale the ladders in droves. Drow sorcerers wove a darkness black as pitch. Jus opened his arms and bellowed one of his own spells, and light spread out to rip into the darkness. In gloom lit with screams, lightning flash, and fire, the city guard met the first wave of attackers to crest their wall.

Swords crashed against goblin helms and lizard scales. Spiders clawed over the brink, rearing and stabbing fangs into warriors before being hacked to death by halberds. Henry fought in a surge of controlled panic, sheltering, reloading, then whipping over the wall to fire at the drow. Men lifted rocks, furniture, even water troughs ripped from the barracks and shoved them over the battlements to wipe entire ladders clean. Scaling ladders cracked and broke as boulders broke them from above. Falling monsters ploughed into their comrades and spattered in the mud.

The Justicar hung back with one third of the men, watching this one stretch of wall carefully. The soldiers fought in savage fury, swords and halberds butchering the monsters as they climbed the wall. Archers and crossbowmen fired in fast, professional rhythm. The soldiers had been hardened by decades of constant war, and the enemy was shocked by their sheer ferocity.

A chunk of wall shook as a spell thudded into it, and a choking cloud of gas made the defenders stagger clear. The Justicar took one look and waded forward, summoning his men.

"Reserves!" The big man fired off his best, most useful spell, dispelling the magic of the poison fog. "Archers stay here! Halberds with me!"

They came hissing and clattering over the wall—decaying corpses with black pits for eyes. Twenty men followed the Justicar as he crashed into the monsters. Cinders sheeted fire into the undead monsters, charring half a dozen into blazing, broken puppets. One cadaver fired a pistol crossbow, the dart ricocheting from Jus's dragon-scale cuirass, then the halberdiers fell onto the undead like a steel wall.

Heavy polearms shoved and cut. The Justicar roared like a bull, his white sword moving in a blur. The undead exploded the instant Benelux ploughed into them. Made of positive energy, the weapon caused the creatures to catch fire like paper dolls, burning from inside out. The undead screamed and fell, withering to ashes even as Jus kicked off their leader's skull. He hacked off a pair of arms that clung over the battlements, then heard Henry scream.

It was a varrangoin—an abyssal bat. Like an obscene, withered corpse the monster loomed over the men on the battlements, its bat wings open to show the spell runes burned into its skin. Its skull face screamed in fury as it landed among the men of the wall. The reserve archers fired, and their arrows rebounded from the monster's hide. The varrangoin reared in triumph and thundered a cloud of flames over the archers. The men screamed, charred instantly to skeletons. Twenty men gone, and the varrangoin blundered forward through the flames and screeched a cry of triumph.

The Justicar came at a dead run, Cinders streaming smoke in his wake. The varrangoin blasted out another cloud of flame, and Jus leaped, turning his back to the fire. Burned, in pain and still moving, he burst through the fire cloud with his white sword whipping around in a lethal swing. Benelux smacked into the varrangoin's skull, hacking into flesh as hard as teak and bone stronger than steel. The monster was wrenched sideways by the huge power of the blow.

Blinded, the varrangoin struck with its claws, lightning fast, only to have each stroke parried by the Justicar. Jus fell to the ground and spun, hacking for the monster's ankles. He felt his sword bite and was already rising, roaring like a maddened god, his swordpoint lancing upward as the monster fell. The varrangoin collapsed, impaled upon Benelux.

The Justicar twisted the weapon, wrenching it from side to side to open the wound. Wailing in agony, the varrangoin tried to stagger back. It fell, spewing blood across the battlements. With his hell hound's teeth gleaming above him, the Justicar poised his sword, gave a yell, and hacked off the monster's head. Splashed with blood, Benelux shrieked in victory.

Burned, his armor smoking and his white sword running with blood, the Justicar held up the head of the varrangoin and flung it into the enemy below. Troglodytes and goblins slithered back down their scaling ladders in terror, fleeing the walls. The assault stalled, then surged backward in panic. Huge tanar'ri tried to stem the flood, whipping and slaughtering their fleeing slaves. Henry and the surviving archers fired into the retreat, killing as fast as they could reload.

The next stretch of the wall hadn't been so lucky. There was a crash as battlements toppled, and a surge of bestial screams as monsters crested the wall. A tower door led through to the next wall. The Justicar wrenched soldiers from their post and led the charge.

"Even numbers! Follow me!"

Jus staggered, hurt and burned. He shoved open the tower door, led the way through the tower, and forced his way out onto the next strip of wall.

To see absolute and total defeat.

Here, the defenders had fought illusions while the real attackers planted their ladders and their grappling irons. The city guards lay dead, except for a few who screamed while being savaged for the pleasure of the tanar'ri lords. Troglodytes, giant spiders, and blood-crazed trolls were already spilling like a tidal wave into the streets, and panicked civilians surged away with terror stricken screams.

Hundreds of monsters were already across the wall. Thousands more flooded the breech in the city defenses. At the head of twenty men, the Justicar could only retreat with his men back to their own patch of wall.

"Retreat!" The ranger could hear another massed charge thundering toward the city. "Is there a keep? Do you have a rally point?"

"Yes!" A soldier wiped his face of blood. "The citadel is on the west side of the city!"

"Rally!" The wall could not be held. There were too many enemy and not enough soldiers. "Rally on the citadel!"

The enemy might only have attacked the west side of the city. There was a chance the population could flee to the east, if enough soldiers could be found to delay Lolth's forces. Roaring commands, the Justicar strode through the soldiers, pulling men back from the wall. Henry stayed with him, guarding his back. As a shower of grappling hooks came clattering over the wall, the boy loaded his last five crossbow bolts into his bow.

"Sir? Do we go?"

"We go!" Jus hauled the boy up by the scruff of his armor, pulling him back to the stairs. "Polk? *Polk!*" There was no answer. No sign of Enid or of Escalla. The sounds of demonic roars, screams, and slaughter came from the city streets. "All right! We go east! Run!"

Jus, Henry, and Cinders sped from the city walls. Behind them, the victors gibbered and screamed as they topped the wall, gleeful now that the real killing could begin.

# 8

Cutting through dark waters, a huge snake swam through the city sewers. Slits of light shone down to make pools of brilliance amidst the murk, but all the rest was stench and filth and gloom. The waters were stagnant and choked with garbage. Wounded and sobbing, the big snake swam, desperately retreating away from the sounds of death and battle up above.

Enid the snake finally found a ledge of rock lapped by flotsam. She slithered up onto the refuse, croaking with agony, and opened her mouth to drop a smaller snake upon the stone.

The little snake was burned over half its length. It held a wand and a little staff in a death grip in its tail, the hold so tight that the snake stayed rigid after it hit the floor. Escalla moaned, her snake eyes bright with pain, and then she tried to raise her head.

"E-Enid?"

"I'm here." Enid lay stiff with pain. "Just need to rest . . . a little while."

Blood trickled from a gutter slit twenty feet overhead. A hand clawed briefly at the slot, then disappeared. The world above rang with screams of the dead and dying, with bestial howls and demonic laughter. Slowly, Escalla lay her head on the stone and fought to breathe.

"E-Enid? What's going on up there?"

"Tanar'ri! There are tanar'ri in the streets. Drow and lizards. Hundreds of them!"

"Drow?"

"Drow. With spiders. They've overrun the city walls."

"Bitch!" Escalla scarcely had the strength to give a proper curse. "It must be Lolth. Tielle . . . must be working with Lolth."

The sound of distant splashing intermingled with hoots and cries. Something blundered through the sewer tunnels, laughing as it came. Escalla heard the sounds and tried to stir, but she was unable to move.

"C-can we go topside?"

"We'd be massacred."

"I can't move. S-sorry." Escalla swallowed. She lay rigid, upside down on the rock. "Can you carry me?"

"I can carry you."

"Swim—east if you can. The . . . river was east. There'll be a drain somewhere."

Enid looked at the filth lapping Escalla's injuries. Her own burned, scalded back was covered with sewer slime.

"Escalla? The wounds are infecting."

"Jus . . . will fix it. He . . . can fix anything."

Enid took Escalla, staff, and wand into her mouth, then slipped painfully back into the water. She turned, spared a glance for the gutter opening above, and then swam downstream.

A scream cut the air. Enid twisted sideways, and a chain smashed into the wall beside her. Clinging to the tunnel roof, a chain monk gibbered and lunged for Enid's throat. The snake dove. The monk hit the wall, landed in water a dozen feet deep, then managed to claw out of the filth and onto the little stone ledge.

The chain monk screeched, lashing fetters at its prey. Enid twisted aside, bashing the monster with her tail. The chain monk fell into the water, thrashing in panic as it disappeared, but the damage had been done. A dozen answering calls came echoing down the sewers as chain monks homed in on their prey.

Enid sobbed and swam, shoving through bobbing garbage and

trying to leave the monsters behind. The tunnels echoed with their screeching laughter until it seemed they came from every side. The shape-shifted sphinx swam onward, stiff with pain, Escalla jerking and shivering in her jaws.

It was pitch black. Suddenly, a faint glow of magic sparkled on Escalla's scales, and the injured faerie stirred.

"D-detection spell. We're being scryed." Escalla almost wept with the effort of lifting her head. "She must . . . have a . . . crystal ball."

Enid spoke though a mouthful of snake. "She can find us?"

"No." Escalla swallowed back a throat full of bile. "One . . . strip of dark tunnel looks like . . . looks . . . the same."

She coughed, and the effort tore her injuries. Escalla convulsed, then spasmed, going stiff as a board. Enid stared in fright.

"Escalla?"

Silence.

Enid swallowed, feeling her snake-blood run to ice. The faerie had fainted—or worse. The wand and staff were still gripped tight in her coils. Was that a good sign . . . or bad?

Jus would know.

Escalla was dying. Enid turned a frightened look up to the surface world, then painfully began to slither her way up a metal stepladder, rung by rung. Above her, flames sent red light shooting though the gutters, while the town rang with screams.

✳   ✳   ✳   ✳   ✳

Gargoyles landed in the streets, and the terrified refugees cowered away from them. The monsters ploughed forward, lashing with claws to rip the hearts out of shrieking townsfolk. One gargoyle carried its screaming victim to the heights of the city temple. Two others waded through a multitude, bathing themselves in blood and living flesh. The two monsters fought over one choice, screaming morsel, tearing it apart, laughing as they tasted fresh, hot meat.

And they died.

Jus's sword struck in near silence—sharp, horrific strokes chopping into stony flesh. The first gargoyle fell with its head split in two. The second turned then took a sword blow through its neck and into its chest. The monster bubbled—the white blade tugged free and instantly stabbed. Driven by the huge strength of the Justicar, Benelux punched through the gargoyle's back. The monster sank to its knees, dead before it fell. Jus ripped free his sword and held out a commanding hand to the refugees.

"Follow me, if you want to live!"

The mob of refugees split and ran, some fleeing east, some west, some hiding in the houses and the alleyways. Cursing, the Justicar ducked beneath the eaves of a house as three more varrangoin flapped overhead, showering flame and acid down onto the roofs.

Henry sighted on the monsters, but they flew onward. Jus swore, then pulled Henry away as the building behind him collapsed, flames billowing into the air. In the weird darkness of the city, the flames ran thick as treacle. Henry and the Justicar ducked and ran onward, while behind them terror spread out into the alleyways as the monsters ate their fill.

There were already monsters on the battlements of the citadel. Jus could see gargoyles, bats, and other creatures landing unopposed. The soldiers must never have made it to the keep. The streets had cleared, as every living thing in the city tried to claw its way out of the gates. Jus and Henry stopped inside a burning alleyway, hiding as a dark wave of flying monsters swerved a few feet overhead.

Cinders suddenly sniffed and growled. *Left!*

Jus turned. A badger shot out of a burning public building with a neat roll of black cloth stuck through its belt. Ducking a storm of sparks, Jus ran to catch the animal before it disappeared.

"Polk!"

The badger stopped and looked about, squinting. The Justicar ran over to him and picked the badger up.

"Polk! Polk, where's Escalla?"

"I'm a badger, son! Short sighted! If she's anywhere here, then I ain't seen her! She's gone! Disappeared!" Polk patted the portable hole on his little belt. "But look here, son! I've got a job to do. I better do it while there's still time!"

"Job?" Henry winced, using his cloak as a shield as a collapsing building shot coals across the street. "What job?"

"I've got the portable hole, son—the one we got from the underdark." The hole weighed nothing, no matter how much was put inside. It opened into a strange, otherworldly chamber ten feet deep and ten feet across. "I'm going to the library, son. The temple! We can save holy books and scrolls. We can preserve these people's great heritage for future generations to come!"

The Justicar pounded his fist against a wall.

"Polk, there aren't going to be any generations to come!" He handed the badger, portable hole and all to Henry. "Where did you look for Escalla? Did you look in the merchant's quarter?"

"Everywhere! All I saw was a war!"

Jus grabbed a piece of burning timber from the wreckage and passed it up to Cinders, who chomped on it in glee. Jus looked at the city streets, trying to think like a faerie, and drew a blank.

Cinders wagged his tail. *Down. Up dangerous. Faerie be down!*

"What?"

*Smart faerie. Clever, like dog!* Cinders grinned. *Abyss bat be up—faerie be down!*

Sewers! There were gutter openings in every street. Jus wrenched a corpse out of the way, uncovering a stone slab set into the street. He heaved it open, revealing a drain and stone-cut ladder that plunged down into the dark.

A scream came distantly from below—a feminine shriek tinged with pain and panic. The Justicar sheathed his sword and jumped feet first down the hole, plunging into total dark. Henry froze in shock, then heard a mighty splash from below. Moments later, a shout came from the dark.

"Henry! Jump!"

The boy did as he was told, keeping a tight grip upon the wailing Polk. He shot down through a dark well and crashed into warm, stinking water, sinking over his head before his feet could find the bottom.

With one hand, the Justicar heaved Henry half out of the water, crossbow, Polk, armor, and all.

"There's a ledge by the side."

Henry's feet found support, and the boy stopped believing he was drowning. Charging through the water like a galleon, the Justicar threw up a huge bow wave of foam. Throwing stealth aside, he forced his way downstream, his sword spilling a ghostly light into the air.

The scream came again. Jus ploughed out into an open space—another ladder to the surface—and stormed forward.

A huge snake hung limp from a rung halfway up the well. Below the giant snake hung a keening, babbling monster—a being like a cadaverous monk wrapped up in chains. The creature whipped its arms, shooting lengths of chain to trap and tangle around the snake. Burned and injured, the snake sobbed in a feminine voice of panic and tried to get away.

Jus smashed his sword onto the chain monk's back. Sparks showered from the creature's thick sheath of chains, blocking the blow. The monster gibbered in rage and tried to punch Jus with a chain-armored fist. The Justicar ducked two blows, caught another on his sword, then kicked the monster in its gut and sent it crashing through the water. He turned and hacked with his sword, severing with two huge blows the chains that bound the snake.

The chain monk surged back onto its feet, whipping out two lengths of chain that caught the Justicar. The monster wrenched, and Jus slipped and fell. Bulling forwards through the water, Henry erupted from the sewer tunnel, firing a quick burst of darts at the monster's chest.

Sparks flew as the crossbow bolts ricocheted from the dense mat of metal chains. The monk whirled and screamed fury at young Henry.

Bursting from the water like a behemoth, the Justicar surfaced behind the monk. His huge arms flew around the creature's throat, the forearm blocking the monster's windpipe and his other arm locking the hold tight. Jus's muscles bulged as he threw all his strength into his grip. The chain monk jerked and flailed backward with its chains, wrapping them around the Justicar's throat. Jus kept his grip, his neck muscles bulging as the chain monk tried to throttle him to death.

There was a cracking noise from the chain monk as it died, its neck crushed. Jus roared and shook his head, loosening the chains about his throat even as he held the monk to make sure the thing was dead.

A second chain monk burst from the dark. Jus whipped his head sideways, Cinders grinned, and then a white-hot column of flame thundered straight into the monster's face. It fell back, screaming yet still alive, the water around it hissing as it met burned flesh and molten steel. Throwing away the first monk's corpse, the Justicar lunged up the ladder. His damaged throat was hoarse as he laid a hand upon the giant snake.

"Enid?"

"Jus!" The serpent collapsed into his grip like coils of heavy cable. "Jus, Escalla's hurt!"

A little snake hung through the rungs above them. Holding thirty feet of exhausted Enid, Jus felt Enid shivering with shock. Henry slung his crossbow and clambered up the ladder, carefully retrieving the little serpent.

"I think it's Escalla!" Henry tried to feel for a pulse. "She's cold!"

"She's a snake!" Jus looked anxiously up the ladder. "She's burned?"

"Bad. Real bad." Henry tried to cradle the snake carefully as he fought his way down the ladder. "She won't wake up!"

The Justicar was hurt—burned, half strangled, and a rib felt broken. He had three healing spells to his name. He immediately cradled Escalla and punched two spells into her burned body, feeling the burns shimmer and heal. The snake was still horrifically injured—burned by acid until bones were exposed to the air—but it drew deeper breath, and she seemed alive. The third spell went into Enid. The huge snake heaved, croaking as the spell spread a tiny sensation of cool into her burns.

Polk came paddling madly down the sewers, angry at Henry for hurling him aside.

"Help! Son, help! I can't swim, son! I'm going to drown!"

"All badgers can swim, Polk." The Justicar snatched a handful of badger fur. "You're doing fine."

Henry held Enid's head in his lap, distraught and torn by her pain as he stroked her softly. The snake was still clearly in agony. The Justicar held Escalla and checked under her snake jaw for a pulse, then unclamped the wand and staff and shoved them under his cuirass. He draped the snake around his neck beneath Cinders's pelt as, somewhere off in the darkness, more chain monsters keened.

"Enid, how many?"

"Thirty." The snake coiled into Henry's arms. "At least. And Tielle! She . . . she has magic. Some sort of acid blast."

"Tielle!"

"There's a scrying spell." Enid sounded horribly weak. "She . . . she's tracing us with a scrying spell."

"Then let's move." Jus looked up the ladder. Monsters snarled, and the crash of falling, burning houses filled the air. "Polk, come here! Henry, you have to tow Enid. Keep her head up high." The man let Polk seize Cinders's tail and towed him through the water. "Downstream. Go!"

Sword in hand, the Justicar led the way. In the sewer tunnels, monsters screamed, while up above, an entire city burned.

*　*　*　*　*

The tunnels angled ever so slightly downhill. The sewers were apparently not draining, and water had risen from the river to flood the tunnel system. The result was that the water level rose higher the farther they went. Inch by inch the roof level grew lower. Struggling to tow an injured snake in his wake, Henry was scarcely able to keep his chin above the water.

One tunnel was alive with the chittering, screeching sound of stirges. It was clearly the best route, but Cinders had only one more flame blast left until he could find time to feed. Jus hoisted his sword and the badger higher and pushed onward, choosing tunnels from the maze of cross connections, twists, and turns.

Enid's snake eyes glazed with pain.

"Sh-should we go this fast? There might be . . . chain monsters in the dark."

The Justicar ploughed forward, dark, grim, and confident. "The last attack came from behind. If we move fast, we'll stay ahead." He checked a corner briefly, then looked left and right down a tunnel junction.

"Cinders?"

*Worstest smell to left. Stinky-bad-stinky!*

"Left it is."

Henry and Jus waded forward. At the tunnel junction, the water stirred, and a great rubbery eyestalk rose stealthily from the murk. Black-armored, with a hell hound as a cloak and a magical sword glowing in his hand, the Justicar turned and fixed the creature with a dire stare. "Don't even *think* it."

The eyestalk blinked once, then nervously withdrew.

The water became densely matted with floating garbage, until walking forward became a matter of shoving through a six-inch belt of flotsam. Henry foundered, holding Enid's head above him in one hand, and the Justicar held the boy up as he made his way through the gloom.

The tunnel fed into a hideous cavern. It was pitch black, the ceiling hanging mere inches from the water level. The pool here was stagnant, and the bottom was deep in slime and filled with sunken debris. With his chin only just above the water, Polk clinging fearfully to his back, and towing Henry and Enid behind him, the Justicar pushed forward until he reached the farthest end of the cavern.

The sewer simply stopped. There should have been some sort of tunnel leading out to the river—a tunnel that must have been entirely underwater with the river flooded. The drain was probably blocked by a metal grate. The Justicar peeled Polk away from his neck and rummaged in the badger's purse.

"Son! Son, you're hysterical! I'm not Escalla, son! She's the snake over there!"

"Quiet!" Jus retrieved the party's portable hole. Holding it up out of the water, he unfolded a corner of the weird black surface. "We'll have to make an underwater swim. Get in the hole—all of you."

"But son!"

Jus tossed Polk into the hole, then nodded to Henry. "Go. I'll lower you Enid, then Cinders and Escalla."

"Will you be all right, sir?"

"It's just a swim." The Justicar sheathed his sword and threw it in the hole, making the sword yell in anger and Polk screech in fright. He followed it with his helm. "Get in there—hurry!"

The boy climbed awkwardly over the lip of the hole, managing to splash water down into the space below.

"Sir? We could go back up there and try to save the city."

"Another lesson: Know when to withdraw so you can strike again."

The Justicar lowered Enid's head into Henry's hand, then Cinders. He peeled Escalla from his own neck, saw that the smaller snake still had a fluttering pulse, and made ready to go.

A wild peal of laughter came from the dark. Light sparkled, and an angler fish floated on the garbage, waggling the glowing bulb that dangled from its brow. In Tielle's voice, the fish celebrated its joy.

"Ah! Here we are at last! Where's your little dog?"

Behind Tielle, a dozen cackling shapes flailed through the water. The chain monks whipped their manacles to catch the jagged and broken ceiling stones, dragging themselves forward through the water. Cocking an eye at the Justicar, the angler fish smiled.

"I knew she'd still have her little friends with her, so I brought a bit of help along. They're precious, don't you think? It's so lovely to have friends." Tielle's voice was fragile and gay, and she watched the Justicar with sick eagerness. "Now that we're all together we can play a game!"

Escalla moved weakly in Jus's hand. With his eyes upon Tielle, he passed her down to Henry and folded up the flat entrance to the portable hole. He sealed the pouch in his purse, airtight and safe.

If Tielle expected a snappy comeback, she never got one. The Justicar simply ducked down beneath the water and shot away. The chain monks bellowed, then hurtled forward while Tielle fired ice darts into the dark.

"Get them! Get them now!" Tielle turned back into a faerie—filthy and naked without her spider jewels. "Block the sewer tunnels. Go!"

Chain monks wallowed forward, lashing at the water with their flails.

In the pitch-black murk beneath the surface, the Justicar felt the water boil and shudder. A chain streaked past him, but he brushed it as he swam across the bottom. Other chains crashed down. He hit buried debris with force enough to hurt—bunched his legs and used the obstacle to launch himself away. An instant later, chain monks plunged into the water behind him, their manacles lunging at the bottom like harpoons.

Jus hit a stone wall and groped for an exit. There had to be a drain to the river! He jabbed his hand against the floor, the water shuddering as more and more monks blundered into the cavern. Out of breath at last, Jus found a wall, surfaced, drew a breath then launched into a dive.

There were too many monks. Two of the monsters saw him and blundered in pursuit, and their wild cries dragged more chain monks to the scene. The Justicar twisted like a dolphin as a dozen chains speared point-first through the water. One crashed into his leg almost hard enough to shatter bone, glancing off the big man's boot.

The Justicar had long used water as a lurking place. Boots and dragon scale armor slowed him, but he was used to swimming with their bulk. As a chain monk plunged beneath the water and whirled on him, he shot forward and crashed into the monster's chest. They grappled underneath the water, the monk thrashing madly and trying to use its chains. Grabbing the monster's chain-covered flesh, the Justicar tried to dislocate a limb. The monk pulled away, its chain links slippery. Jus felt a chain wrap about his waist, then shot between the monster's legs. The chain yanked at him. He lunged up behind the chain monk, grabbed its head between his forearms, and surfaced, roaring as he broke the creature's neck with one massive twist of his arms.

Half floating in the water, Tielle screamed in alarm. "There! There, you fools! *There!*"

The chain monks surged and blundered in the dark. Jus dived underwater and shoved off from the corpse, heading straight for Tielle.

On the surface, Tielle raved in fury, then flung a lightning bolt at where she had last seen the Justicar. The lightning blast ploughed into the water, and the entire cavern lit with blue as the electric charge danced out into the water. Chain monks jerked and froze. Tielle screeched, the electric shock making her catapult herself half out of the water. Far from the blast, the Justicar twisted underwater, the shock hitting him like a hammer blow. He held his breath, spinning end over end and shaking his head to try and keep his wits.

The dazzle had shown a darker spot in the cavern floor. Jus blundered forward. The spot was almost directly beneath Tielle. He found a metal grill and grabbed it in both hands, bending all his strength against the bars of steel.

The iron bent. With Tielle right above him, Jus had no time to take a breath. He squeezed his bulk through the grill and found himself in a vertical tunnel. His ears popped as he plunged down into absolute pitch darkness. The pipe bent sideways. Jus crashed into the floor, then shot onward through horrible black water. Weed brushed at him. Once, something slithered and bit his armor, and Jus hammered the offending creature to a pulp against the wall. His lungs screamed for air, the pain almost tearing him in two.

The hole! Jus blundered for his purse, found the portable hole, and sucked a breath of air out of the hole. He breathed twice, then jammed the folded hole against his skin beneath his armor. His bald head scraped against the tunnel ceiling as he swam on.

He risked a light spell, making the area around him ghostly with a magic glow. Jus swam on, the water thick as soup and full of drifting muck. The tunnel continued slightly downward, making his ears ache with pain. He breathed from the portable hole four more times before he found the exit, covered by another iron grill.

The grill broke free to three savage kicks of his boot. Killing his light spell, the Justicar pushed out into the sluggish current of a river. He swam speedily downstream, crossing to what must be the opposite bank. Another breath from the portable hole, and he allowed himself to surge to the surface.

There were bull rushes drowned in the water from where the river had spilled over its banks. Pushing amongst the reeds, Jus surfaced. He dragged in a breath, keeping his head low amongst a forest of stems, and looked over the river to the fallen city.

Monsters lurked outside the eastern gate. As civilians from the city fled, Lolth's hidden troops rose from the muck. Bugbears led by massive trolls hammered into packed masses of refugees, forcing their captives up against the city walls. Drow officers stopped the slaughter, and the lesser monsters all obeyed. The city itself was in flames, and varrangoin, gargoyles, and other nightmarish shapes swooped through the smoke. The Justicar watched for a few moments as Keggle Bend was obliterated, then he withdrew into the reeds.

This far bank of the river was deserted. Jus slithered belly first out of the mud and lay gasping, wiping his face. His leg stung and throbbed where the chain had hit his boot, and his muscles were still stiff with electric shock from Tielle's lightning bolt. Rolling over, the Justicar pulled out the portable hole and opened it wide, dropping it onto a level patch of mud. Half-drowned and gasping, Henry and Polk struggled out of the hole. Polk coughed the sewer water from his snout.

"Son! Son, are we out?"

"We're out." The Justicar lay back and fought for breath, his huge chest heaving. "We're safe."

"Well don't just lie there, son. Our enemies can track us!

Crystal ball, son—that's magic!" Polk shook out his fur. "You have to get moving, boy. Get some distance. We'll stay in here and tend to the injured. You get running. And run fast!"

Rolling onto his side, the Justicar blinked. "Crystal ball?" He groped, and Henry handed him Benelux. "What . . . what stops a crystal ball?"

"You'll find a way, son. I have faith in you. I've taught you everything I know." Polk turned and muttered loudly into Henry's ear. "Wants me to molly-coddle him all the way. Boy's scared to stand on his own two feet!"

Cinders was handed up out of the portable hole, looking muddy and sadly bedraggled. He saw Jus and gave a wag of his droopy tail.

*Hi.*

"Hey."

*Bad day. Cinders want fetch stick game, then bed.*

"I'll see what I can do."

Managing to sit, Jus drew the bedraggled hell hound over his back and tied him into place over his helm. Staying flat, the Justicar folded up the portable hole and stuck it through his belt, then slithered backward through the mud, dragging his sword behind him.

Benelux seethed with indignation. *My scabbard is smothered in mud!*

"It isn't just mud."

Pushing carefully backward, Jus kept belts of reeds between himself and the city. He was watching for flying monsters, but Lolth's air armada was flocking to devour meaty fragments on the city walls. He made his way back through flooded weeds and grass until he reached an eroded mud brick wall. Hidden from immediate sight, he took a swift look for signs of pursuit from the river, then paused to scan the city.

Carnage was everywhere. People were being thrown from the walls or tossed like rags by the monstrous hordes at the gates, but the survivors were being systematically herded into mobs by the servants of Lolth. A scatter of slaughtered bodies were left behind as the terrorized citizens were driven like sheep. Savagely angry, embittered and helpless, the Justicar could do nothing but withdraw.

Outside the eastern gate, five hundred prisoners had been dragged into a huge circle two hundred yards across. While drow priests drew magic symbols in human blood, monsters killed the prisoners and strung their body parts into the titanic glyph. The circle flashed with power, turning brilliant white. . . .

And a vast bronze spider leg crept into view.

The magic circle now formed the base of a shimmering dome—a vast gateway into the Abyss. The gate looked into a place where the ground itself was formed from screaming souls, and where the air rang eternally with screams. From this nightmare heaved a spider shape so huge that it made trolls and ogres scatter like mice.

It was a machine—a palace made from a sickly bronze-green metal. It stood on eight vast legs, with countless windows sparkling like malevolent eyes. A hundred feet tall—the ground shuddered as it walked. Great fangs made of black steel arched above the armies of the damned.

With a hiss and roar, the spider palace trundled forward step by thunderous step, then halted beside the city walls. Its head hunted back and forth like a beast scenting prey. In the fields below, the drow, spiders, trolls, and troglodytes shook blood-spattered weapons and screamed in acclaim.

A door opened in the side of the palace. The vast metal spider sank down slowly, a staircase extending like an obscene tongue from between its jaws. As the palace settled into place with a deafening clang of brass, a small black figure emerged in the doorway.

She was perfect—lean, skin black as midnight and with silk-white hair so long that it trailed on the ground. Clad only in jewels, the apparition spread a pall of nightmare about herself. Lolth, Queen of Spiders, Mistress of the Drow, emerged from her palace to gaze upon her conquest.

Behind Lolth slithered a tanar'ri with a woman's torso, six arms, and a lower body shaped like a snake. Trim and sparse, the demon followed after Lolth and snapped commands to the troops, making them pull away from their prey.

The Justicar risked a moment more to watch the distant figure, and then he pulled carefully away.

"Lolth."

*Cinders think is time to go.*

"Absolutely."

The Justicar was alone and on the run again, with a nightmarish army all around him. It was as if the old, savage days were alive again. The Justicar remembered a figure in eagle armor holding a huge black sword, then shook the image off and kept himself in harsh reality.

Old times, old friends, old enemies were gone. . . .

It was a full invasion. Lolth had made a gate, and she would stage more troops into the Flanaess. The Justicar slid back through reeds, kept his sword naked in his hand, then ran west toward the hills. His leg hurt, and his body was in shock, but he pushed himself into a run that soon put the town of Keggle Bend far behind.

\*  \*  \*  \*  \*

Behind the departing ranger, climbing from the monstrous brazen palace, a figure stirred. Hissing cold with undeath, the figure killed the grass beneath its feet. Trolls and gibbering demons backed away from it in terror. Rusted eagle armor gleamed with patches of frost.

Dead eyes scanned the city and dismissed it. Dead eyes looked at roads and weeds and all the thousands of hidden places only a trained eye could see—and then settled on a slight swirl in the mud beside the riverbanks. A few bricks were hidden by the reeds.

The sign of man-made works feeding into the river.

The cadaver in its eagle armor stirred. It abandoned Lolth and her demons, leaving the burning city at its back. Walking down into the water, the cadaver disappeared with a sullen hiss of icy steam. . . .

# 9

The minions of the Demon Queen molded Lolth a throne from the flayed bodies of her victims. She shifted her weight. One or two of the furnishings were not quite dead, and Lolth idly threw a spell intended to keep it that way. She took the skull of the local high priest and poured herself a drink, regarding the fallen city with a sigh.

Bodies were being dragged from the still-burning city to the gates where frost imps froze them for storage. Hundreds of survivors had been herded into great lines beside the city walls. Relaxing with her drink, Lolth raised one brow as she saw Morag slithering along beside the prisoners and diligently counting heads.

Lolth gave a weary sigh and said, "Morag, you drabble-tail! What are you doing?"

"Accounting, Magnificence." The tanar'ri wrote upon pages made from human skin.

A human lunged out of the line of prisoners, armed with a jagged piece of iron. He threw himself straight at Morag's back. One idle flick of Morag's tail caught her attacker and slammed him against the nearby wall. Disgusted, Morag changed an entry in her files.

Annoyed by the display, Lolth leaned one elbow upon her squirming throne.

"Morag? Why, pray tell, are you counting cadavers?"

"I am tallying our stocks, Magnificence." The secretary stabbed at her parchments with her pen. "A little mathematics will tell us how long our stores will last."

Lolth sighed. "Morag, these wretches are to feed my teeming hordes. Now what is the one dominant characteristic of a teeming horde?"

Morag raised one elegant brow. "The smell, Magnificence?"

"No. They *teem*, Morag! They breed, they die, they subdivide like germs! They do not have fixed numbers and little record sheets!" The demon queen folded up her arms. "This is chaos, Morag! Chaos is expressive, adaptable, and incalculable! Sometimes you can be so . . . so *baatezu!*"

Morag folded up her notes. "Magnificence, we need to know how long the troops can be fed."

"We are attacking another city tomorrow, Morag. Then another and another. That's the way a conquest works. Eventually the entire population of the Flanaess will be our slaves and cattle through all eternity." Lolth slurped from her skull cup. "Improvise once in a while, Morag! I do. It's called genius."

Morag muttered something sour that the goddess failed to catch. Lolth sniffed and turned her eerie, flame-filled eyes upon her secretary. "Morag, are you wearing perfume?"

"I am wearing scent, Magnificence. Black lotus."

"How absurd. Whatever for?"

"I am meeting someone, Magnificence. An incubus."

Lolth looked at her secretary in mocking amazement. "An incubus! You?" The demon queen tried not to laugh. "Whatever do you do together?"

"We read." Stung, Morag sensed Lolth's laughter. "He happens to be highly intellectual!"

Wiping a mock tear from her eyes, Lolth tried to keep her face straight. "Oh, Morag, I always wondered why we never bothered having a court jester." The goddess's voice rang like a choir as she sighed in mirth. "Go slither off to your chores. Tell the commanders I will see them immediately. We need to start shuffling more troops onto this delightful little world."

The secretary thrashed her coils. Proud and angry, Morag jammed her notebooks beneath her arms. As she moved away, Lolth's mocking voice called after her. "Morag? Where did our cadaverous friend trot off to?"

"He left, Magnificence." Morag dropped her voice to a mutter. "About the time you plumped your mammalian arse on that chair."

Cocking a sharp eye at Morag, Lolth reached for another drink. "Excellent. Another little plan coming to glorious fruition!" The demon queen raised her skull-cup to her secretary. "Off you go! If you need me, my mammalian arse and I shall be right here."

Seething, Morag slid off through the bodies, blood, and rubble.

# 10

The Justicar had fought against supernatural enemies for his entire adult life. Blocking a scrying spell was far beyond him, but he could make Tielle's crystal ball almost useless to her. He kept himself in shrubs and trees, choosing nondescript terrain. He gave her no streams, no roads, no hillcrests as markers. Jus moved at a dogged run—loping relentlessly at a speed that would have soon left even cavalry behind him. These were the old skills learned in the wars against Iuz. Skills as natural to Jus as breathing air and walking earth.

He needed to find a stream, a place without rock outcrops and jagged bends—nothing a faerie might pick out from the air. The Justicar paused in the bushes above the banks, looking out over a clear rivulet with a bright stony bottom. Coming to a halt at last, the big man squatted like a troll and scanned the wilderness for dangers.

Nothing.

"Cinders?"

*Birds gone. No tasty animal.*

Jus nodded. Lolth's presence spread a pall of evil all over the wilderness. The sun seemed dim—colors were changing, like an old tapestry leeched and warped by time. He slithered down to the water, flipped open the portable hole, and kept his eyes on the skies as he heaved his friends out into the open air.

"Get in the stream and wash. There's soap in the equipment boxes. Use grit to scour your skins clean."

He propped Cinders over a bush, where the hell hound's senses could act as guard. Moving swiftly, Jus let Henry pass Polk up from the hole. Escalla the snake was passed gently into Jus's hands, then Enid came out, yard after yard, loop after loop. Henry scrabbled out, still armor clad and with his empty crossbow set aside in favor of his sword. The boy looked quickly about the stream, then squatted at the Justicar's side.

"Sir?"

"We wash here. Wash all your gear. Get rid of the filth before we catch a disease. We need to kill the scent in case Tielle has hounds. Wash out the portable hole and scour it clean."

Aware that magical eyes might be watching and magical ears listening, Henry asked no questions. He threw his crossbow aside and began struggling with his damp leather belts.

"I'll wash Enid," he said.

"I'll do Escalla, then Polk."

"Sir, the women are in shock." Henry winced. "We need a fire."

"No fire." Jus carefully laid Escalla's whimpering little length out along a warm, flat rock. "We'll deal with it when we're clean. Do your own gear first. The snakes go last."

The Justicar moved fast, stripping away his dragon-scale armor, his boots, his socks, even the bone ring that shielded him against charm spells. He took them all off and plunged naked into the stream. Jus sank, perfectly at home in the water, and brutally scoured himself with gravel, silt, then soap. He quickly did the same to his sword, scabbard, armor, boots, and clothes. Benelux squawked loudly as she plunged into the stream.

*Sir! Sir Justicar! The proper technique is to use an oiled silk—awwwk!*

The Justicar had been caring for swords for twenty years. He scrubbed blood away with grass, then silt, then grass again. Benelux's alien metal—hard matter from the plane of positive energy—never needed sharpening. Jus briskly wiped her with an oiled cloth, dried the wolf-skull pommel that now adorned the sword, and left her standing ready to hand on the shore. The sword cursed and sputtered all the more when her hilt was used to hold Jus's underwear out to dry.

Scraped bright red and raw, Jus tenderly lifted Escalla from her bed. He took her into the cold water and washed her as gently as his big hands could. The wound was bad—big, deep, and already inflamed. Jus's spells could deal with injuries, even disease, but his small reserve of magic had been exhausted for now. For the moment, they had to rely on simpler resources. The Justicar thought on the problem as he lifted Escalla from the stream.

"Cinders? The big rock there—the red one."

With his flames run down to a low ebb, Cinders could only manage the merest lick of fire. Jus laid the hell hound beside a large red rock, and Cinders heated it slowly. Escalla's snake body was laid out on a bed of dry grass beside the rock. Down in the stream, Henry carefully finished washing Enid. Jus helped him wrestle the huge snake out of the water and laid her gently down beside the stone.

Jus's bare ribs were livid black and purple—and two of them were clearly broken. He moved carefully, the pain clawing at him. He sat beside Escalla, glad of the slowly warming rock as he cradled her head in his hand.

"Escalla?"

She had no eyelids to open or close, and her snake eyes glittered. Was she awake or unconscious? Jus slowly stroked her satin scales, trying to be tender and insistent.

"Escalla, change back. We need you back to faerie form."

The little snake shuddered and groaned. An icy bath had

done nothing to cure her shock. Finally a forked tongue quivered. In a tiny voice, Escalla breathed a few painful words out into the air.

"Enid?"

"She's with us. She's still a snake."

"I have to . . . to ch-change." Escalla tried to lift her head but couldn't. She flopped back down, then stared at the injuries all over Jus's side. She lay there, panting and stiff with shock. The Justicar kissed her softly just behind the jaw.

Intelligence came back, quick and clear, into Escalla's eye. She looked at Jus's broken ribs.

"Jus?"

"I'm with you."

"Jus, where are we?"

She was hoarse. Jus's helmet served as a cup. He helped the snake to drink as he spoke.

"About twelve miles from the town."

"Is . . . is it the same day?"

"You've been unconscious for two hours."

With one hand, Jus threw his tunic onto the hot rock, where it sizzled and steamed. Cinders's flames had finally given out, and the hound lay exhausted, panting.

Escalla quietly regarded the Justicar. "You . . . you ran for two hours with . . . broken ribs?"

"You needed me to."

Escalla collapsed, weak with pain. She looked at Jus as she lay in his hands. "You have got to be the dumbest, most heroic bastard on the Flanaess."

The snake closed its mouth and went still—tensed—then shimmered in a magic field. An instant later its shape writhed, and Escalla turned back to her own form. The little woman lay gasping and absolutely shocked with pain. Her injuries took on a savage new life.

She had been burned by acid all over one leg, her hip, and back. Her wings hung limp and half melted. Giving her no hint of her desperate state, the Justicar carefully patted the burns dry. His healing spells had closed the deepest parts of the wounds, but the rest of the burns were livid and raw.

The burns were already badly infected. Escalla shivered, a fever starting to take her.

"Is it bad?"

Jus adoringly caressed her wet hair back from her face. "It'll do."

"Warriors for justice can't lie for crap."

Escalla reached out to Enid. Anxiously cradling the big snake, Henry moved Enid closer. Escalla shook with effort, framed a spell, and canceled the magic she had cast over Enid's body. The huge snake shimmered, then bunched and expanded to become a full grown gynosphinx.

Enid was burned across her back where she had shielded Escalla. The little faerie lay weak and shaking in Jus's arms, looking in horror at Enid's wounds.

"It was some . . . kind of . . . acid or something. It shot out of a drinking horn."

"Shhh. It's all right now." Jus carefully slid her off his lap. "Henry, keep them both warm. I need to give someone a W-A-S-H."

Cinders gave a a yelp and a wail, thrashing his tail and howling like a dog chased by a horde of scorpions. It was to no avail. With his flames run down, he had no chance to protest as he was dunked in the river, washed, scrubbed, wrung out—then sniffed, washed and dried again. Jus deposited him on the hot rock, where his fur steamed and seethed. Sulking, Cinders glared at the Justicar.

*Not funny!*

"Had to be done."

Cinders sneezed. His nose was stuffed with water, and his sense of smell would be muddled for hours.

*W-A-S-H means bath. Cinders remember.*

"Sorry, Cinders. We need you clean and dry."

*Cinders forgives you.* The hound ceased sulking. *Help pretty faerie and nice cat-lady to be warm.*

"That's the way."

Jus collected bull rush roots and pounded them in his helmet with Benelux's pommel. He crushed the juice out of the pulp with a massive squeeze of his hand, the tendons standing out as he wrung every last drop out of the mess.

"Henry, empty the portable hole and wash it out. Check the stuff we had stored in there. We should have a box of clean bandages."

Enid lay on her side, her face pale, and her eyes never leaving Henry as he worked. Jus salvaged a few sealed boxes—Escalla's wedding dress, a bag of coins, spare clothes—and found the bandages. He steeped the cloth in bull rush juice and lay bandages gently over Escalla's wounds. He tended to Enid carefully, dabbing the juice into the burns before softly covering them with cloth. Henry held Enid's paw, looking sick and worried as the big sphinx went pale with pain.

When he had finished, Jus measured out a little lotus syrup for both the girls against the pain. Escalla drank, made a face, and then relaxed slowly, looking sadly over at Henry and the sphinx. She watched them together and suddenly felt so very old and wise.

"I know something I didn't before."

Henry cradled Enid's face, looking at her with such love as he stroked her hair. Embarrassed, Jus cleared his throat and looked away.

"The lotus will make you sleep."

"Um-hmm."

"What can you tell me about crystal balls?"

Already drooping, Escalla sighed.

"Tielle has one." Escalla blinked her eyes rapidly, trying to think. "It . . . can see images, but can't hear. Blocked by . . . by shifting . . . to a different plane. Blocked by . . . thick metal. Heavy spells . . ."

She was falling asleep. Enid would be wilting too, and a quarter of a ton of sleeping sphinx would be impossible to move. Naked and holding his sword, Jus stood and walked over to the portable hole, levering himself down inside.

The hole was a tube ten feet deep and ten feet wide, the walls smooth, black, and slightly stretchy to the touch. Inside the hole there was a ladder, boxes waiting for equipment to fill them, and sealed tubes of scrolls for Enid's private library. Gravity always seemed stable, no matter what happened to the hole entrance outside. Wet and reeking like wet socks, Polk was busily mopping out the corners of the hole. Polk finished his work, carried his mops of dried grass out of the hole, then stuck his head back inside and frowned.

"Son, you're hurt! Did someone lay a glove on you?"

"Yes."

Jus tilted the hole back to its usual orientation, threw in grass and bracken to make beds for the ill. He jumped down, wincing as the impact jolted his broken ribs. He made a bed for Escalla, a larger one for Enid, then stowed their scanty boxes of possessions. They had no food and no water except the little that Jus and Henry could carry in their canteens. The woods were empty of animals—probably scoured clean by Lolth's own foraging parties over the last few weeks. Still, they would make do. Jus emerged from the hole, heaving himself over the rim, stonefaced with the pain from his ribs. He found Henry and Polk turning Cinders like a pancake on the hot rock, bringing great clouds of steam out of his fur. Jus squatted down beside them and retrieved his clothes.

"Let's get the girls back into the portable hole. We have to move away from the stream. It gives a landmark a crystal ball can fix on." He fetched clothes still damp and steaming hot. "We'll roll the hot rock into the hole to keep the girls warm."

Polk bustled over, long strips of bandage trailing from his mouth.

"First things first, son. We need to care for our assets. Protect the stock! Keep our ship in trim." Polk waved a paw. "Your ribs are broken, son. Henry here will tie them up."

The Justicar tried not to wince as he moved. "It's not the first priority, Polk."

*I agree. This is appalling!* Benelux's blade shimmered. *Get him a loin-cloth before the sphinx sees!*

Henry came to the rescue. He passed bandages around the Justicar's huge chest, bracketing the broken ribs, and pulled the straps tight. Tomorrow, there might be magic to heal the hurts, but for now, there was neither power nor time. The boy tied off the bandages, then fetched his own clothes.

"Sir, will you be all right?"

"I'll live." Jus put a hand on the injury, angry at the pain. "I can walk."

"I'll do it." Henry awkwardly pulled on his scuffed, worn boots. "You should rest inside the hole. I'll take a turn."

"I can't leave you out here alone."

"Then I'll accompany you." Henry looked stubborn. His expression was a cross between Escalla and the Justicar's. "Polk can stay in the hole."

Jus was too worn with worry to argue. He pulled out the last piece of snack coal from their baggage and stuck it inside Cinders's mouth, and the hell hound sucked avidly, trying to restore his flames. Jus allowed himself to be helped into his armor, scowling as Henry stopped to tie Jus's boots onto his feet.

"Henry, I'm fine!"

"Yes, sir."

"Just get the hot rock rolled into the portable hole and get Enid in there before she falls asleep. We have to leave!"

Henry rose to attend to it. As soon as his back was turned, Jus leaned heavily on his sword, eyes closed, feeling sick with pain.

Polk towed Cinders off the hot rock and cast a sharp glance at the Justicar. "Son, you all right?"

"I'm fine!" Jus fastened on his helmet. He turned and stared about the stream, blinking, and unsettled. "Come on, we'll get moving. "

"Son, if Escalla's in the portable hole, then she can't be tracked by a crystal ball!"

"The rest of us can, Polk. We have to move into terrain that can't be recognized. Something that gives no clue as to where we are."

"Hmph!" Polk sat up, liking the idea. "Sounds easy."

Jus pulled Cinders over his helm and let the hot hell hound pelt stream down his back.

"She's not an idiot, Polk. Once the sun starts to go down, she can look at the shadows and know which direction we're walking in."

The badger thought about it. "That's clever, son! Did you think of that?"

"I was taught it, Polk. I've done it before." Jus jerked his chin at the dense bushes and trees. "We've been sticking to thick scrub between hills. Overhead cover in case she has flying spies." Jus sheathed his sword and turned away. "We keep moving, we regroup, then we attack. That's the way we get the job done."

The sword flash came hard and fast—a red streak ripping dragon scales and flesh. The Justicar spun, blood flying from his flank as a huge scarlet blade twisted from the stream. Dense clouds of mist choked the air.

Henry stared, and then a mad, hissing shape shot from the water, the ground smoking at its feet as it trod toward the Justicar, who lay fallen by the streambed.

**II**

Henry screamed. The Justicar was down—his armor torn and a
red blade whipping through the fog to hack him down. Henry
moved, but Jus had hit the ground rolling, his white sword streaking
from its sheath to parry the incoming cut behind his back. Sparks
flew like a fountain as blade met blade, both weapons screaming.

Jus whipped about, hacking at his enemy's feet. The red blade
parried, cut, was parried and kicked aside. Jus thrust, rising from
the ground, his anger huge and terrifying. Like a massive black
bear he raged forward, his sword crashing down in a blow that
could have severed a tree. The enemy caught the blow in a lightning fast block, twisting and cutting at Jus's neck. Jus parried fast
and hard, hammered three sharp blows at his enemy in a rage.

The blades rang and howled, meeting each other time and time
again. Steam filled the air, emanating from the monster still standing in a cloud of icy fog. Only its screaming skull was visible, and
the blood-red gleam of its blade.

Jus parried a blow and dealt the creature a kick powerful enough to
shatter stone. He missed as the monster somersaulted backward, landing a dozen feet away and sinking into a crisp, deadly fighting pose.

The Justicar faced the creature with his huge sword ready. The
enemy stirred, swirling its blade in an identical pattern to Jus.

The mists cleared. Snarling at his opponent, Jus faltered, and
then suddenly wavered.

A golden eagle helm snarled at him: a helm made by Grass Runner artisans untold decades before. The armor was rusted and discolored, but he knew it inch by inch. In the dim past before he had a true name, the Justicar had slept, woken, fought, and bled with that armor beside him. The corpse inside the metal suit still bore traces of long, lank hair. The withered skin was scrawled with the traceries of Grass Runner tattoos.

Jus turned ashen, like a boy faced with the anger of a long lost father. "Master Recca?"

The corpse's head jerked up at the name, and eyes of blue flame searched the Justicar. The hand and foot that Jus had cut off with his own sword were back—bleeding, pale flesh stolen from fresh bodies. Jus's old master had risen from the grave. The cadaver opened its mouth in a wild hiss, then leaped with blinding speed to crash its sword toward Jus's skull.

But Jus was no longer there. He slid sideways, his sword catching the attack and ripping past the corpse. The eagle-armored monster jumped over the blow, barely touched by the blade. As the creature landed behind the Justicar, it struck. Jus parried sharp and hard, spun—only to find the corpse had already leaped away. A red blade clanged from his helm, cutting Cinders, then the hissing monster turned sideways as Jus beat its blade aside and lunged with his own sword.

The corpse stood ten feet away, snarling. It bore two wounds—long, shallow cuts that burned from contact with Benelux. The wounds stopped burning slowly and reluctantly, then began to heal as a fetid green blood oozed forth to cover them.

Jus staggered from a long narrow cut along his thigh, spreading a pall of ashen grey. It was as though the blood had been sucked out of the limb. Ten feet away, the undead monster swirled its sword, the blade glowing with an internal light of blood.

The monster spied Henry, the hole, Polk, and Enid. It sidled toward them, hissing slyly as Jus moved to block its way. Appalled, Henry lifted his sword and came forward to help.

The Justicar swiftly threw up a hand. "No!"

"Jus!" Henry came to an anxious halt. "Sir!"

"Back! Stay there!" The Justicar held a hand to keep Henry away. "Put Escalla and Enid in the hole and run! Keep running! Remember what I've taught you."

"Sir?"

"*Do it!*"

Recca had lost none of his old speed, none of his blinding skill. Undead and immune to pain, fatigue, and pity, the cadaver screeched as it stalked the Justicar.

"Henry, *go!*"

Henry turned and tipped Enid down into the portable hole. The undead swordmaster attacked, and Jus fought back, matching speed for speed, and pitting his vast strength against the corpse's shocking agility.

They fought, blades ringing, Benelux crying out in anger and agony as she struck. The swords moved fast—so fast that Henry could only stare in shock. The Justicar attacked with terrifying savagery, spinning and kicking at an opponent that blocked every blow. Punches rained but were slammed and parried aside by the undead warlord, who returned his own swift strikes.

Jus crashed his elbow into the dead face, broke its arm, and in return took a kick delivered by a shocking handspring that sent him reeling away. His broken ribs had been hit again, and his left arm hung drained of blood. He blocked a blow to his head, the two swords ringing, then staggered aside, dazed.

His left arm hung numb and useless. One leg could barely move. The Justicar snarled and staggered, managing to get his blade up to take another rain of blows. He had to fight long enough to let Henry get well clear.

Recca. Recca had taught the Justicar the sword—had always

mocked his student's rocklike style. As the cadaver shifted its weight, Jus knew exactly where the next lunge would come, and he caught the blow, already making a riposte, his huge sword clumsy when used in a single hand.

The Justicar had once been outmatched by his teacher, but ten years of hard fighting had taught the student vicious new tricks. Jus smashed his helmeted forehead into the corpse's skull, breaking teeth and knocking the creature back. He saw his opening and roared, lunging forward with his sword in a blow that would impale the monster through its spine.

He saw a red flash beneath his guard and twisted as he lunged. Benelux rammed into the monster's chest, and there was an intense blast of pain in Jus's side. The Justicar ran the monster through, his sword blasting out through its shoulder, but below Benelux, the corpse's red blade bit into his own flesh.

Jus screamed and hammered Recca back with his fist, sending the corpse flying. He staggered back, the red blade protruding from the bottom of his ribs. The evil sword sucked blood, drinking like a vampire. The undead swordsman lurched to its feet. Hissing in triumph, it lunged for the Justicar with its claws, suddenly fell spinning to the ground.

Polk spat out the monster's human foot just as Henry ripped the red blade out of the Justicar and crashed into the ranger with an impact that plunged both of them into the portable hole. Polk ran, snatched one edge of the portable hole in his jaws, and sped swiftly off into the grass.

Floundering on the dirt behind them, the undead monster snarled. Head down and running, Polk charged onward as fast as four clawed feet could run.

✳   ✳   ✳   ✳   ✳

They had run far into the dark—first Polk, then Henry—each

pounding onward in a dazed fatigue. Cinders clung about Henry's neck, trying to steer the boy past obstacles and trees. Luna, the greater moon, had not yet risen, her handmaiden Celene was only the barest blue crescent in the sky, and the night was black as pitch. Polk slammed into tree roots and bloodied his snout. Henry had tripped over rocks and crashed through brambles until he was running with blood. Somewhere behind them, the undead corpse was tracking them, and Tielle was staring into a crystal ball, watching each twist and turn. Mad with panic, Polk and Henry sped on and on until they finally collapsed into a gully filled with rocks.

Henry had done what he could. The inside of the portable hole was smothered in blood. The Justicar had been run through, the blade going through his right side beneath his ribs. In a panic, Henry had bandaged him—and he tried to remember all the healing lore Jus had taut him over patient evenings in camp. The blade must have missed Jus's lung. The man wasn't coughing blood but was breathing shallowly and in immense pain, and Jus was pale—shockingly pale. The blood seemed to have been sucked out of him by the terrible red sword, and he might still be bleeding internally. Henry made Jus drink, kept pressure on the wounds, and when he handed over to Polk, the boy ran in a daze.

He slammed down into the gully, with Cinders a hot, smothering cloak across his back. Henry heaved Cinders off himself, then tore open the neck fastenings of his elven mail, trying desperately to breathe. The portable hole landed on the ground, and after a moment, Polk managed to scrabble into view. Exhausted and bedraggled, the badger could only cling weakly to the rim of the hole.

"Son? Son, are you all right?"

"F-fine!" Henry's lungs hurt so much he was about to throw up. "Is . . . everyone . . . alive?"

"Bad. Real bad. Enid's getting fever from her wound, son. Nothing I can do."

Polk tried to climb over the lip of the hole, but he was too exhausted to make it. Henry heaved Polk out, then lay on his back crippled by cramps. The badger stirred, almost too weak to move. "It's fine, son. I can run now. Just need a bit of rest and . . . and a restorative libation."

"We used all the whiskey to clean the wounds."

Polk winced and slumped in gray disappointment.

"That hits hard, son." The badger worked his mouth. "Well, give me water, and I'll be fine to run."

They both lay there, exhausted, in a night so dark they couldn't even see the sky. Above them, Cinders's tail drooped in misery.

*Cinders worried. Cinders scared.*

"They'll be all right. We can fix them. The Justicar will know what to do." Henry groped for his canteen, but it was empty. "He'll be up soon, then he'll tell us what to do."

Cinders kept watch, his silhouette merely a darker patch of night atop a rock. Henry lay beside the panting badger, dazed and shocked, until finally he blinked and felt his mind grow clear.

"They're all going to die. If we can't save them, then they're all going to die."

Polk said nothing, choosing instead to gnaw his claws and try to think. Henry blinked blindly out into the dark.

"He *knew* him. The Justicar knew that monster."

"Workings of fate, son."

"No. They fought the same way. Didn't you see? The blade style—it was almost identical! I've never even heard of anyone who can use the sword like the Justicar."

Exhausted, Polk scarcely had the energy to argue. "Jus is a hero, son. He doesn't hold with monsters."

"But it went straight for *him*. Only for him." Sitting up straight, Henry suddenly saw it all clearly in his head. "Tielle was sent to kill Escalla. Do you think this other monster was sent for the Justicar?"

"By who, son? Who?"

"Lolth."

Rolling over, dazed and damp, Polk said, "Lolth's a demigod, son. Why would she worry her skull over us?"

Remembering back, Henry held his head and tried to reason it out. "Polk? We blew her body up, and . . . and I think that whole drow temple might have gone up in flames. Would that make Lolth mad?"

Polk blinked. "Son, that would make her bare-arsed, shoot-my-nanny, bat-crap, barking mad."

Polk stiffened, seeing the whole plot before him. He laid a paw upon Henry's arm and stared into the dark.

"Son! This is *great*, son! Do you know what this means?"

"Um, no."

"Son, this will be the making of us! If by a man's enemies ye shall know him, then we've made the big time at last!"

Henry resisted an urge to bash Polk across the skull. "Polk! Our friends are hurt real bad!"

"Oh, we'll fix that, son! We can just ask the Jus—"

Polk's sentence died mid-stride. The badger subsided and went back to gnawing nervously on his claws.

A stark wind knifed across the lip of the gully, making little stones shift and rattle. Henry kept stiff and still, reaching a hand out to Benelux, which now lay through Henry's belt.

"Cinders?"

*Wind. No corpse. No faerie. Cinders smell no animals at all.*

Benelux cleared her voice and said, *Henry, my dear. Do you think we should perhaps get moving?*

"Soon." Henry could scarcely sit, let alone walk or run. "Yeah, soon."

To buy a little time, the young man wiped his mouth and tried to clear his thoughts.

"Where should we run to? What do we do?" He looked at the sword. "Benelux? Any ideas?"

*Our comrades require immediate attention.*

"But Jus is hurt! How is he going to use his healing magic?" Polk coughed.

"You're thinking's flawed, son! You listen too much to the Justicar. You have to think on your feet. Improvise!" The badger tried to rise, but only managed to roll over. "Use yer logic. We have a job: Gotta heal the boy and the two girls. Now if *we* don't have the tools to do the job, then we have to borrow 'em from someone who has."

Benelux seemed suitably impressed. *Oh. Quite succinct. Nicely reasoned.*

"Thank you kindly. I'm a thinkin' man, Ma'am!" Polk scratched his belly with his claws. "Now, we can't have Henry learn the magic. We can't go to a town for a healer. So that means we need a *miracle*."

"A miracle?"

"Yep." Polk folded up his paws. "Happens all the time. Somewhere around here, there'll be a healing fountain, a wandering priest, a magic potion, or a sacred spirit just itching to heal our pals! All we have to do is find it!"

Henry gnawed his knuckles in despair and said, "Find it? That could take days!"

"Hell no, son! We need to be more efficient in our technique." Polk rose and took Henry underneath one furry arm.

"Son, what we need here is a crystal ball."

\* \* \* \* \*

"*Idiots!* Spread out and look for a trail!" Tielle hovered above her chain monks. She was scuffed, scratched, bedraggled, and tired. Half her spells had been wasted, and the search was proving more difficult than she thought. "Come on! Keep moving! Go!"

The night was pitch dark. Tielle's servants, still numbering about thirty, clanked and clattered up the hills, blundering through brush. Tielle snapped her fingers, and a chain monk brought her large crystal ball. The faerie stared into the bauble with a scowl. She stiffened, clearly liking what she saw. An extravagant hiss commanded her minions to silence.

The crystal ball glowed red, showing an image of Escalla sleeping by a campfire. Tielle jerked her head up and whirred high into the air, spying a faint glow of hidden fire over the next ridge. She descended and signaled her troops to encircle the area.

The chain monks clanked and rattled their way off into the night, heading for the distant glow of a small campfire.

* * * * *

Henry had hidden himself just as the Justicar had taught him: He lay buried beneath a thin layer of soil and scree. As Tielle and her monks drew away, he carefully lifted his head and said, "She took the bait!"

*Excellent.*

Benelux had accepted Henry as her bearer as a temporary measure. An apprentice warrior was far, far below her station, but needs must as the doppleganger drives. Henry rose carefully from the soil, trying to let it slide gracefully off Cinders's back, but the resultant rockfall sounded shockingly loud.

How did the Justicar do it? Silence spells? Magical rings? The big man could move in total silence when he needed to. Horribly conscious of every snapping twig, Henry slithered off in pursuit of the chain monks, his pulse hammering like a mad thing in his throat. Tielle could kill him with a single gesture. The chain monks could flail him to death. Henry crept carefully in pursuit of the enemy, painfully aware that this was a very stupid thing to do.

He managed to keep Tielle in view. Pure white and alarmingly under-clad, she showed up in the darkness as a pale little shape. The hellish clamor of the chain monks apparently deafened her to the sounds of Henry creeping quietly behind her. Chain monks paused at the edge of the hill, then charged down upon a little campfire hidden in a gully full of stones. Chains whipped through the air, smashing into rocks and stones, lighting the night with sparks. The chain monks shrieked and gibbered, turning the gully into absolute chaos.

Polk came running swiftly over the lip of the gully, leaving the monks stamping and wailing far behind. The badger held the folded portable hole in his mouth, having dragged Escalla back inside before he ran. Polk slid to a halt and went flat behind a fold of earth, blinking as he tried to see Tielle.

"Son? Where is she, son? Damned badger eyes can't see squat!"

"Shhh!" Henry almost couldn't be heard above the monks' manic screams. He held a hand over Polk's snout. "Keep still!"

The campfire had been beaten into flinders, and every rock in the gully had been overturned. Henry thanked the gods that Tielle had come to the fire before the eagle warrior, but the cadaver was possibly still minus one foot.

The young soldier lay flat and watched as Tielle brought order to the chaos. Well-built, blonde, and angry, the faerie flew above her minions and lit the night brilliantly with a spell.

"Stop that! They're not here! Fan out and look for signs!" The faerie adjusted the thong of her costume, casting an eye over her slaves. "You! Bring me the crystal ball. Now!"

Henry watched as a chain monk uncovered the crystal ball from its robes. The monk was surrounded by its comrades, and Tielle hovered overhead. There was no way to reach in and steal the prize. Henry squeezed himself flat against the ground as Tielle turned in his direction, the faerie activating the crystal ball with a quick pass of her hands.

"Show me Escalla!" Glaring into the ball, Tielle made a noise of frustration. "She's gone! I can't see." Tielle swore, then opened her hands above the crystal ball. "And the other one! Show me the Justicar!"

The crystal ball apparently didn't respond. Tielle swore. She tried shaking the crystal ball, then slapping it. She was aware Henry existed but apparently couldn't remember his name to ask the crystal ball. She finally cursed and glared out over the gully.

"They're in that damned portable hole again!"

Tielle hissed, chewing a knuckle as she thought. Finding a well-folded portable hole in the middle the night was impossible. The faerie gave a sudden smile, looking malicious and sly.

"This is all for the best! We'll return to the vampire pool. We need more water from the pool, and more spells to use on all our little friends tomorrow." Tielle whirred her wings in annoyance. "Come on! They're only walking. By tomorrow morning, they won't have gone far. We can play a nice new round of the game tomorrow, after they've lost a full night's sleep."

With that, Tielle dismissed the whole night's work. She had two of her chain monks whip their manacles about two small, scrubby trees, bending their branches together while she lashed them into place with cord. Tielle consulted a leatherbound book held by one of her servants, then quickly drew symbols on the ground, branches, and trees. She tossed a handful of something through the arch of the branches, the wind catching some of her offering and blowing it away. The space beneath the arch instantly blazed into life, forming a shimmering blue doorway of a very familiar kind, and Tielle chivvied her shambling chain monks through the magic gate. With a last sneering look over the hills, Tielle passed beneath the arch, and the gateway went dead as she disappeared.

The return of absolute darkness was a shock. Henry half

rose, blinking, with ghostly images of the glowing gateway dancing through his eyes. He kept a hand on Polk, keeping him still, while he tried to decide whether all of Tielle's monsters had gone.

The silence was absolute. Tielle's chain monks seemed incapable of stealth. Deciding to risk it, Henry rose and let Cinders take a sniff at the breeze. The hell hound made a careful check, then settled his fur.

*Monster gone. Bad faerie gone. Magic here. Maybe big bit. All on trees.*

"Thanks, Cinders."

Released at last, Polk sputtered in fury. "You let them go, boy! They got away!"

"Polk, there were a million of them!" Henry scuttled over to the tree arch, trying to think just like the Justicar. "No. The thing to do is follow them and steal the thing. Strike where they're off their guard."

"That ain't heroic, son! Man to man! Blade to blade! *That's* the way it's done!"

"Shh!" Henry felt Polk giving him a headache. He suddenly felt a lot sympathy for the Justicar. "All right. See if you can find what she used as a gate key. Some of it blew away in the wind."

Cinders did the hunting, sniffing as Henry thrust the hell hound's head at bushes and scanned him over the ground. All of a sudden, the big black hell hound thumped with his tail.

*Girlie smell!*

They finally found two long hairs caught against a bramble bush—fine golden hairs, almost a twin to Escalla's locks. Henry took them carefully in his hand and looked at the gate, then picked up Polk and made sure the badger had the portable hole held safe and sound.

"Right. We go in, we get the crystal ball, then use it to find a miracle!"

The badger gave a snort. "It's not too late to opt for a direct duel to the death, son! Go blade to blade with the minions of evil! Think of your career!"

Henry let the comment go. He advanced, waving one golden hair before him. As the hair flashed and disappeared, the gateway bloomed an eerie blue, and Henry stepped through into an echoing, empty cave.

**12**

Henry slowly straightened, blinking as his eyes adjusted to the light. He let Polk slip from his grasp and looked owlishly about himself, hoping to escape notice simply by keeping still.

They stood in a limestone cavern. The walls gave off a strange silvery light, making the dead black spaces of the cavern soften at the walls. Henry saw shapes silhouetted down a tunnel far ahead and heard the rhythmic noise of chains as the monks marched away. This particular cave was lined with entrances and tunnel mouths—some high, some low. The magic gate had opened from one amongst a dozen identical holes.

Henry needed a way to mark this escape gate in the darkness. He ran his fingers underneath Cinders to scratch his own skull, then hit on an idea.

"Polk! Pee!"

"What was that, son?"

"We need a way for Cinders to sniff his way back here. Badger pee!" Henry kept his voice in a whisper. "Come on. You always wanted to make your mark."

"Son, toilet humor is beneath you."

Polk wandered off to have some privacy, and Henry kept watch on the distant, swaying shapes of the monks. He grew more nervous as the monsters slowly disappeared into the gloom.

"Polk! Haven't you finished?"

"I got stage fright, son! Now just hold your horses." Polk finally sighed. "All right, there! Are you happy? Now let's get moving!"

They moved. Henry scuttled forward, half bent over as though this might offer some sort of concealment. Polk walked his badger walk, his belly fur brushing at the dirt. They walked along a floor unnaturally clean and cared for, descending slightly downward as they followed the chain monks' trail.

The tunnel opened out into a cavern filled with hideous shapes. Skeletons hung chained to the walls, and an old wooden torture rack lay broken and rotting on the floor. A skeleton shrouded in sackcloth sat in an iron cage. The cage dangled from the ceiling at eye level, its door half-open to let the skeleton's hand trail the floor. Giving the skeletons a careful berth, Henry padded over to check the three exits from the room.

Each one gave off a distant, ringing sound of chains. Each one echoed to faint hoots and giggles. Henry could see no movement, nor find marks on the floor that might have been brand new footprints.

With a polite cough, Benelux shimmered inside her scabbard. *I can sense evil up ahead, child. A very great intensity of it. Try the doorway to the right.*

"Oh." Henry never quite knew what to say to Benelux. She always made him want to tug his forelock and bow. "Uh, thank you. Thank you, Ma'am."

Over at the left tunnel, Polk suddenly scrambled backward in fright, hissing, "Son! They're coming, son! Thousands of them! I can hear them marching up the tunnel!"

More rattling chains sounded from the way behind. Chain monks had followed down the same route Polk and Henry had just come. Polk dashed beneath the old rotten rack. Henry looked wildly about, then leaped up and caught the iron cage, wrenching open the door and bundling himself inside. He threw the old bones out of the sackcloth and wrapped himself and Cinders inside the reeking shroud. He sat there, the cage swaying and swinging, as the first chain monks marched through the room.

Two columns of the creatures shambled past, giggling and shrieking like maniacs as they walked. The creatures dragged their chains along the floor, making an atrocious din. One line of a dozen monks came from the left. A full score more came from behind. Henry's face was hidden, his body covered, and the monks never gave the terrified boy a glance. They shambled off down the right-hand tunnel, hooting and screaming at each other in the dark.

The instant they were gone, Henry slid out of the cage. His hands shook as he pressed them against his head, trying to reassure himself that he was still alive. He kept an eye on the right-hand tunnel and sidled over to another set of cages. He wrenched the feet from two dangling skeletons and removed the chains that had once bound their legs together.

"Polk, stay there! Open up the hole and check the others. I'm going to follow the monks and steal the crystal ball."

"Right you are, son!" Polk was buried under the old rack and showed no inclination to emerge "I'll just keep an eye on your back. Watch the rear! Guard your blind spot!"

"Right." Henry pulled the sackcloth over Cinders's head, hoping he now looked like a chain monk. "I'll be back."

He walked in a silly stagger, dragging two lengths of chain out of his sleeves and trying to titter like a maniac. Somewhere up ahead, cacophony reigned. Henry tried to stop his knees knocking together as he followed the great shaft downward, finally seeing the backs of chain monks as the creatures shuffled slowly out of a congested tunnel mouth.

The silvery radiance shone brightly ahead. It came from farther on within the broad, vaulted cavern that opened outward from the tunnel. There was a lapping sound, as though a huge, slow lake washed itself against an unseen shore. Henry shuffled behind the monks, his eyes darting as he tried to keep his head down and make sense out of the caves.

Fifty of the mewling, screeching chain monks had entered the cave. At the cavern's heart lay a great pool of silver liquid—like a quicksilver lake that shone and glowed. The lake gave off a more intense version of the radiance that spilled from the walls. Far more disturbing was the way the quicksilver fluid moved and quivered, as though it were a living entity that *breathed*.

Tielle stood on a rock outcrop beside the eerie pool. Her monsters had gathered in a mob that fell quiet as Tielle scathed them with her glance. Henry attached himself to the back of the mob, now so deep in trouble that he felt light-headed. Tielle glared up the side tunnels, making sure that all her minions had gathered, and then planted her fists on her hips and gazed at them all in disdain.

"You let them get away."

The monks cringed a little, and Henry followed suit. Furious, Tielle flicked open her wings.

"Which of you idiots was holding Escalla and the sphinx in the city? *Which one?*"

Half a dozen monks shuffled slightly then lifted their chains, hooting like children trying to mollify their nurse. With a snarl, Tielle flung her hand at the nearest one and spat out a magic spell. Ice darts blasted through the monk. It staggered, blood spraying from its skin. Tielle snapped her fingers, and hooting, joyous chain monks pushed their injured comrade straight out into the pool. The bleeding monk screamed and thrashed as its blood was sucked from it. The wizened corpse sank out of view, while the entire lake suddenly took on a sinister red glow.

Watching, laughing, and screeching in glee, chain monks leaned over the pool's edges. Annoyed, Tielle put her hand out and received a drinking horn from one of her minions. The horn sucked up red liquid from the pool, gallon after gallon flowing inside.

"Evil blood to burn the good. Good blood to burn the evil!"

Tielle shook the rod clean. "Right, so now it's evil water. Which out of you idiots is injured? Hurry!"

Some of the monks were damaged—cut by the Justicar or with broken limbs or damaged throats. Tielle used a common kitchen ladle to scoop red water from the pool and pour it over the creatures' wounds. The injuries flashed and disappeared. Knocking out the last drops from the ladle, the faerie rose fluttering into the air, followed by a chain monk bearing her crystal ball. The other monks dispersed, some following after Tielle, and others going off into alcoves at the far side of the cave. The hoots and hollers drifted in the cavern like sounds from a nightmare.

The lakeshore was quiet. Henry blinked and edged closer, trying to pierce the gloom and see whether he truly was alone. The boy licked his lips and fumbled with his helmet buckles. He pulled off his helm and cradled it carefully in his hands, then walked swiftly over to the ladle Tielle had left lying by the shore. He gave a quick look over the caves, then knelt and scooped the heavy, silky liquid from the pool. He filled his helmet with as much as it would take and then carefully set the ladle aside.

A scream came from behind him. Henry left his helmet and hurled himself aside. An instant later, a chain smashed down where he had once knelt, shattering limestone. A chain monk stood screeching and yammering, looming over Henry as it whipped its chains at his head.

Henry dived and rolled, drawing Benelux with the smooth, lightning-fast motion he had learned at the Justicar's side. He hit the monk beneath one arm and felt Benelux's edge shear through three whole thicknesses of chain. Chain links and manacles went flying, and one of the creature's massive arms dealt Henry a blow. He flew backward, falling and skidding on his back. Henry's hair touched the hideous red liquid of the pool. There was a sucking sensation at his neck, and Henry jerked his head up and away in fright.

The chain monk threw itself at him, two manacles streaming as it prepared to crash them down onto Henry's skull. Henry saw his own rusty chains lying an arm's length away. He dropped Benelux and snatched a chain, whipping it at the monk's legs as he rolled wildly aside. Flails crashed into the stone beside him; Henry felt his own chain go tight, and he gave a ferocious tug. With a huge crash, the heavy chain monk tumbled down, its legs entangled and its arms flailing wide. Henry planted his boots against the monster in panic, gave a mighty shove, and the monk spilled so that its arm fell in the pool.

The monk screamed as blood was sucked from its body and into the lake. Lashing its chains, it tried to smash Henry's skull. The boy shoved it with his boots again, and the monk fell into the silver-red fluid, its mouth open in a silent scream. It fought wildly, draining white before Henry's horrified eyes.

Henry panted, numb with shock. An instant later, a chain came flailing from the lake to wrap about his leg. Still alive, the monk dragged Henry to the edge of the pool, dragging the human with an irresistible strength. Clawing at the smooth stone floor, Henry fought to hold on. He saw Benelux lying on the stone. In one lightning move Henry released the floor, snatched Benelux and smashed the magic sword's blade against the chain. Links parted in a flash of molten steel. The monk catapulted back into the lake, jerking madly as it was sucked dry of blood and died. Scrabbling away from the lake, Henry stared at his enemy and felt his whole skin running with a cold sweat of fear.

Benelux caroled happily inside his head. *Oh well struck! Your technique is coming on quite well.*

"Th-thank you." Henry's voice was ragged with shock. He scuttled over to his helmet, saw it still sitting there, hale, hearty, and full of red liquid. The cavern seemed still and quiet. No monks came to investigate the noise. Shaking, Henry took his helmet and ran quickly into the same tunnel he had first come from. He crushed himself flat against a wall and looked behind with dread.

No one had noticed. No one came. Tielle was off doing whatever it was that maniacs did in their spare time. Carefully cradling his prize, Henry ran up the long tunnel, passing a dozen twists and turns, then came into the old moldering torture chamber once more.

"Polk! Hssst! Polk, quickly!"

The badger emerged from beneath a pile of rusted thumbscrews, holding the folded portable hole in his mouth. He dropped the hole and stared at Henry in concern.

"Son! What's wrong, son? You look pale!" The badger squinted. "Is that a crystal ball?"

"Quick—I think I've got something. Open the hole!"

The badger flipped open the hole like a sheet of canvas and laid it on the ground. Henry slithered over the edge and down into the gloomy space within, smelling sickness and fever in the air. He lit a lantern from the sealed box of supplies, then ran across the grass bedding to kneel between Enid and the Justicar.

Jus was awake, his shaven head sheened with sweat. Henry laid Cinders down beside him and used the hell hound's fur to steady the helmet full of liquid. The Justicar groped a pale hand over to Henry and held the boy by the arm.

"H-Henry? What's . . . h-happening?"

"All be fixed soon, sir. All soon." Henry had scrounged a bandage, then unsheathed Benelux. "Lie still. I think I can fix it all."

Henry held Benelux, winced, and bared his arm. Alarmed, the magic sword gave a rapid pulse of light. *I say! Steady on! No need to suicide!*

"It's not suicide!" Henry cut himself on the arm—didn't do it right and swore as he had to cut himself again. This time the cut ran fast with blood. He held his arm over the helmet full of liquid and let his blood drip and mingle, watching anxiously as the liquid swirled.

There was a flash, and the fluid in Henry's helmet turned a faint, pale blue—a healthy color, cool and soothing. Henry stared at it, then took a breath and jammed his little finger into the brew. He kept his eyes shut tight, expecting to have his finger burned to the bone.

The only sensation was a cool tingle, and a sense of peace and calm.

Henry worked fast. He tore away Jus's bandages, oblivious to the pain it caused, then slopped a measure of the blue liquid over the wound. Blood hissed, and the big man spasmed. The wound closed right before Henry's eyes, the skin looking healthier by the second. Henry struggled to his feet and ran over to Escalla. He poured blue fluid over her injured leg and side, then over her poor burned wings. The last of the liquid went over Enid's back, covering her burns and regenerating them. Henry tossed his helmet away and wrapped a bandage about his injured arm.

None of his patients were awake. They slept, but at least they were sleeping in peace. Wounds knitted with magical speed— infected flesh turning peaceful and healthy once again. Henry leaned against the wall of the portable hole and closed his eyes as relief flooded through his soul.

"Polk, I think I did it! We can go!"

The entrance to the hole suddenly closed, sealing out the faint light from above. Henry blinked, then sat down and held on tight as he felt Polk grab the hole and begin to move.

✦  ✦  ✦  ✦  ✦

In the torture chamber above, Polk dived into his hiding place and stared. Emerging slowly and relentlessly from the gateway tunnel, there came a savage figure. A tarnished golden eagle helm over a cadaverous skull emerged first, and it was soon followed by the rest of the armored body, lurching on the stump of one foot. The monster paused as it looked carefully over the room. Polk froze, not daring even to breathe as the undead creature sniffed for a scent.

Distant echoes of laughter came from the caverns, and Recca turned. His blood-red sword glowed in the gloom, and the apparition was gone. Polk unfolded the hole and let Henry emerge. The two of them crept to the tunnel mouth and stared after the undead monster.

Polk and Henry fled back through the magic gate. Their last strand of gold hair flashed, and an instant later they were running out among the trees. A cold dawn was creeping over the Flanaess, bringing with it the distant smells of blazing homes.

13

"Fetch! Fetch the stick!" Escalla's voice bubbled, bright and gay. Morning sun streamed across Jus's eyes as he lay on something soft. "Come on! Just try!"

*Cinders can't run.*

"So fly!"

*Cinders can't fly.*

"Sure you can! Just jump and forget to come down." Escalla threw another stick. "So-o-o-o . . . *fetch!*"

The stick thudded onto bare soil somewhere to Jus's left. He became aware of a little bottom—a rather pert and silky one—perched on his stomach. He opened one eye and cautiously felt his sword wound, but he found nothing but his own smooth skin.

Then he felt other smooth skin. Jus lifted his head and saw Escalla—unblemished and perfect—sitting on him in her leggings, long gloves, and little skirt. She rested one hand on his hairy chest and looked down at him with a smile.

"Hey, J-man!"

"Hello." The Justicar levered himself up into a sitting position, moving cautiously, but finding no pain. "You look healed."

"All better." Escalla stood and turned a pirouette. "See? No one touches the faerie!" She bowed, her eyes directing Jus's gaze off to one side. "The kid does good work."

They both looked over at Henry. The party sat in a dense thicket of brush—a place as deliberately nondescript as the Justicar could ever have wanted. A little way away, Henry sat beside Enid, helping the freckled sphinx to plait and bead her hair. Henry saw that Jus was awake, and he blushed as he gave the man a wave, turning back to his job while Enid flexed her claws and purred.

Cinders lay beside Jus on the dirt, his fur brushed and a few new rents in his hide. As he saw Jus, Cinders drummed his tail against the ground.

*Hello!*

"Cinders, you helped Henry?"

*Cinders help! Fun! Went to where bad faerie lives and wore big disguise!*

"Henry did good." Escalla settled herself in the crook of Jus's arm, sitting easily and lovingly against his chest. "Seems he and Polk had an adventure."

"We'll let Henry tell it." The Justicar rubbed his eyes. "It'll make him feel ten feet tall."

Escalla turned a little smile. "We'll let him tell it with Enid there to hang on every word."

In the end, Henry told the story three times, end to end— once with Polk beside him supplying embellishments and once in private with Jus and Escalla, filling in the concise details. Finally, he told it again in private to a wide-eyed, admiring Enid, who did indeed hang on every word.

The party kept on the move but stopped for frequent rests. Jus felt hale and hearty, perfectly unscratched. He marched in silent meditation, fixing spells in his mind. Perched on his shoulders, Escalla flipped through pages of her spellbooks doing exactly the same. She wore reading glasses that made her look deliciously prim—an image at odds with her leather skirt and cleavage line. As the party descended a ridge, she lowered her glasses down her little nose.

"Give me another five minutes, and I'll have a spell up to block the crystal ball. That lets us go on the offensive."

His unloaded crossbow slung, Henry looked back at the faerie.

"We're going on the offensive?"

*Oh, indeed.* Having insisted on returning to Jus's sword belt, Benelux glowed with self-satisfaction. *Offensive action is the only heroic course. Sir Polk would clearly agree.*

"What? Oh, sure!" Polk waddled along. "That's the heroic thing to do! The tactical thing. We turn on the hand that bit us!"

Escalla glared at Polk and snapped her spellbook shut. "To Baator with that! I'm getting Tielle, tattooing her arse red, and chucking her in a cage of crazed baboons! Then I'm gonna sink her neck-deep in a pond full of those little tropical fish that have a thing for the urethral tract!" Escalla tugged her long black gloves. "No one touches the faerie!"

Everyone was staring at her. Escalla gave a big wave of her hands.

"Oh, come on! What? Just because I'm a little blonde faerie, I have to be *nice?*"

She jumped down, took a quick look at the horizon, and unshipped her frost wand from her back. Using it as a stick, she began drawing glowing symbols in mid air.

"Right. Scrying shield coming up! Any sign of Tielle or our skeletal friend?"

Cinders waggled his ears and replied, *No sniff! No hear!*

"Well, when Tielle sees this spell, she'll come running!"

Jus stood with his sword drawn, the blade turning between his fingers as he stared intently at the scrub. He was not watching for chain monks and a faerie but for something far more deadly. Escalla, circling slowly, worked quickly and professionally behind him. She opened her hands, the spell molding between her palms, and the glyphs she had drawn into the empty air flashed with power. Magic rippled away from her like a breeze, and Escalla opened her eyes and clapped her hands.

"Right! *Go!*"

Jus, Polk, and Henry dived into the portable hole. Escalla

folded up the hole and stuffed the parcel under one arm as she swung up behind Enid's neck. She held on tight to Enid as the big sphinx flipped open her wings, gathered, and sprang powerfully up into the sky. Enid flew with big heavy beats of her wings, shoving through the air with astounding speed. Escalla clung on tight and whooped for joy. Enid was always wonderful fun to take for a fly.

Enid stayed low, weaving below the treetops as she flew for miles and miles. Any pursuers would have lost sight of her in a second. Escalla fought back Enid's billowing nest of hair braids. She managed to gain a forward view just as Enid folded sideways and dived like a falcon straight down into a river chasm. The faerie cried, half cheer and half screech of fright as Enid plummeted three hundred feet, caught herself mere inches above a river torrent, and then shot like an arrow above river rapids that jetted, foamed, and raged.

Choosing her landing place carefully, Enid landed on a rocky island in the middle of violent rapids, with twenty yards of savage white water to every side. There was timber for a fire, brush and boulders to hide in, and a clear view for miles both upstream and down. Ten miles from where she had first taken to the air, the sphinx settled down on all four big furry feet, then folded up her wings. Escalla flew up and shook out the portable hole, then threw it down onto the ground.

Peeking from the hole came Jus, who flowed out of the depths like a vast black panther with Cinders grinning from his helm. Polk was boosted up by Henry. The group nested amongst the boulders and heaved a collective sigh. Surrounded by wild rapids and by yards of thick, hard stone, there was a small sense of security.

They had no rations—no food other than a bag of flour that had been sealed up inside the equipment box in the portable hole. Cinders set a fire going, and thin pancakes were made. While they cooked, Jus found a pine tree that was leaking sap, and he brought branches of it for Cinders to suck. The hell hound lay on a rock, stuffing pinecones in his mouth and complaining bitterly about the taste, while Henry fried pancakes carefully one by one.

They ate, with the lion's share going to Enid. Still with most of his attention on keeping guard, the Justicar finally broke the silence.

"We got our arses kicked."

It was an uncomfortable thought. Tielle had put them on the run with a single blow. The Justicar would have been killed without the fast rescue work performed by Henry, Polk, and Cinders.

The group sat, tearing at the unpalatable pancakes, while the river rapids threw up a numbing shield of noise.

Jus levered up the soil beneath their little fire and placed sticks where they could bake into charcoal: Cinders needed feeding, and his fire-breath was vital. Henry passed Jus a bundle of firewood then squatted at his side.

"Sir? Who was that . . . that thing?" Henry nervously fiddled with his hands. "You *knew* it. You'd fought against it before. . . ."

"I fought *for* it before."

Jus knocked out Cinders's brush and curry-comb. Escalla sat on his knee, resting her face against his shoulder as the big man began brushing Cinders. The Justicar stared at Cinders's jet-black pelt as he worked.

"His name was Recca."

Pinecones in the fire popped and crackled. Escalla took a tighter grip upon Jus's shoulder and listened in silence. The fur brush hissed as the Justicar brushed Cinders to a shine. He watched the hell hound's pelt and stared at the gleaming surface as he spoke.

"They were a good people, the Grass Runners. Elves. They lived on the plains, gathered and hunted. Good fighters—fast, clever. I was raised in a village on the borders near the Bandit Kingdoms. I used to sneak off with the Grass Runners to learn.

Their chief was old, clever, careful. He taught me how to hide and trail, track and hunt. He had a son—three hundred years old, but still his son: Recca the Swordmaster. High elves came to him—even a prince. He taught only a few of them, only the ones he saw something in, but he taught me. Took me right from the very start. I don't know why."

The big man had let his brush glide to a halt.

"There was a brotherhood, back then, a network of rangers who patrolled the borderlands, kept the bandits in check, gathered to defend villages from raids. A noble band." Jus's voice held a ghost of cynicism as he remembered ideals long gone. "I wanted to be one. He put me on the path and showed me how. Even gave me the letters and the gold I needed so I could do the journey and learn."

Jus finished his grooming. He took the loose hairs from the hell hound and put them in a little bag. It was pointless tossing them on the fire. Escalla claimed she was going to use the fur to knit flameproof underwear.

"I went south to the forest elves, learned my spells from the hermits there. Studied hand fighting when I met the monks, learned my fieldcraft from the Oleads. Went to the dwarves to learn more swordcraft, to Greyhawk to read my letters. Came back to be a ranger, but I'd been away too long. I only had—what?—a month? Only a month before the invasion came.

"First I knew of it was a fight—a pack of some kind of giant skeletal birds. I trailed them back to their base and found a whole army of Iuz rolling over the villages, then the towns. They killed everything—horses, cows, dogs, sheep in the fields, every deer in the woods, every squirrel in the trees . . . Cut the villagers' throats so they could animate the corpses. I started trailing the army, killing them in ones as twos best as I could. Kept at it for three months. Got in trouble, and then there was Recca, flying into them with his sword."

The Justicar carefully tore his pancake in two and passed the largest piece to Escalla.

"He gathered about a dozen folk—rangers, Grass Runners . . . The Grass Runner tribes were gone, the villages dead, so we took the war to Iuz. Killed his couriers. Killed his foragers and his reinforcements. Went deep and far, right into the guts of Iuz lands. There were about a hundred of us all told, different groups, all working together.

"Iuz started to hurt. They pulled troops back from the front lines to deal with us. Set ambushes and began wearing us down. We killed a lot of them, though. Hundreds. We'd break into a camp at night and just butcher them in their sleep—slit a hundred throats and fade away . . .

"They got frightened of us. They'd only move in huge, marching columns—big squares with varrangoin flying overhead, or tanar'ri or a wyvern. Nothing we could do but watch and follow. Then Recca got wind of an Iuz general who was traveling with only a few zombies as guards. He wanted a general. In all the war so far, no one had ever managed to kill one of Iuz's warlords."

Shifting his sword, Jus shrugged his huge shoulders.

"Didn't work. It was a trap. They had wights shape-shifted to look like infantry. We got cut up. Recca and I covered the retreat, but a tanar'ri got him, killed him while I was caught in a fight. I killed the tanar'ri, buried Recca, and met the survivors. There were only five of us left. They went to join another group. I stayed back and decided to fight on alone."

Sitting crosslegged, Escalla looked carefully at Jus's face and asked, "So what is it? So why is this Recca guy after you?"

"It's not him!" Jus's anger snapped across the island. "It's an animated puppet! A nothing! Just a corpse that moves. It has his brain, uses his skills, but it isn't Recca!" The man flexed his hands and cracked a branch in two to feed the fire. "They did it to the villagers I grew up with—and I cut *them* down too! I took them out! They aren't the people you knew. It isn't a betrayal!"

Escalla flicked a look at Henry and Enid, who both had the

sense to be looking busy. The faerie kept a hand on Jus's shoulder as the ranger finished kicking at the fire and spoke on.

"I was his second-in-command. We were both good—swordmaster and apprentice. I did the scout work. He led the raids."

"Yes . . ." Escalla toyed with her own hair. "And you didn't want to do that last attack, did you? The one that got him killed. It was you that told him not to go."

"It was pointless! All just show of strength. We should have gone north into Iuz where they weren't expecting us. Always attack with surprise. Always hit where they don't expect you." The Justicar was angry. "He dropped his own rules out of pride. They were frightened of him, and he reveled in it! It gave him power, gave him a thrill." Jus rammed a branch into the fire. "He wasn't fighting for anything but vanity."

Enid looked to Escalla, then quietly cleared her throat. "So he just . . . got beaten in a fight?"

Jus pulled out a few inches of his sword. Benelux now sported a black wolf-skull hilt—a hilt taken from Recca's old blade.

"We——he——challenged a demon. He went for their general but never planned the fight. The demon did to him what he always did to others: got behind him, cut, then moved again. I killed my own enemy, but Recca was down. I took out the tanar'ri. It was too late for Recca. He died."

Escalla sat very, very still. There were black depths here that Jus had left unsaid. "Died how?"

"Died the way he had to! He went down fighting. We attacked to let our surviving people escape." The Justicar slammed his sword back into its sheath. "I cut off his hand and foot to stop anyone from re-animating him, then buried him. I swapped swords with him, so Recca's sword could keep up the work he should have been there to do."

Escalla winced. Enid looked away. Squeezing Jus's shoulder, Escalla softly touched his cheek with the back of her hand.

"Are you all right?"

"Of course I'm all right." Jus's face was stern but pale, and he refused to meet her eye. "I'm fine."

"He's after you."

"Lolth put him after me. She outfitted Tielle to take you, Recca to take me." Carefully easing Escalla down, the Justicar stood and turned away. "We just have to take them out one at a time."

"Can you beat him? I mean . . ." Henry faltered in embarrassment. "He seems to just . . . fix himself! And I . . . I never saw anyone match you with the sword."

"It isn't him. It isn't Recca! He was father and brother and teacher to me!" Jus hurled a stick into the fire. "It's just a cadaver, a tool. It's just a puppet made of rotting meat."

Escalla looked sadly at Jus. "And if it's really Recca?"

There was no answer. Leaving Cinders and the others by the campfire, the Justicar strode away to the dark, private places of the island. Escalla kept her eyes on him, then reached aside to fumble in the box of provisions. She came up with a little bottle on a string, hesitated, then walked after the Justicar.

"Guys? Keep an eye on everything."

Henry looked up from carefully smoothing down the fire. "Where are you going? What's that bottle for?"

"It's just a bottle." Escalla hovered, looking anxiously after Jus. "It's in case I get thirsty. I'll just be a while."

She flew off, and Henry rose to his feet in concern. "It could be dangerous! Should we come with you?"

Enid cleared her throat then helped arrange Cinders upon a rock where he could watch the river for a while.

"Henry? Perhaps we can see if there are any fish in the river. And we can find some willow branches to make you crossbow bolts of a kind."

Henry looked back anxiously as he was led away. "But will they be all right?"

"They'll be fine."

He was taken down to the riverbanks where Enid could stand in the water, flicking big fish onto the banks with her paws. Henry worked, Enid's freckles gleamed, and Cinders watched over everything with his big teeth bright and bare.

*Everything fine.*

Sun gleamed on the waters, and Cinders wagged his tail.

\*  \*  \*  \*  \*

The ceaseless rush and surge of the river lay like a blanket across bare skin, kissing little droplets across Escalla's side. She lay naked in the plush velvet moss, soaring in an infinite sense of peace. Half comatose, five foot nine, and tired over every inch of it, Escalla kept her head pillowed in her man's arms and listened to him breathe. Long hair, finer than softest silk, sheeted over her skin and spread like spun gold over the Justicar. She kissed him and felt him smile—felt big hands caress her pointed ears, her antennae—smooth down her slim back to her wings.

They should have done this long ago. The thought was shared in perfect communion as they kissed again, then lay with Escalla held in Jus's arms, watching the river gleaming in the sun.

Adoringly, Jus brushed Escalla's hair away from her face. "I've tried to work up to asking you to marry me for so long."

"I've been trying to be asked for so long." Escalla snuggled, contemplating her follies. "Idiots?"

"Idiots."

Stained green with moss, they rose and sat together. The Justicar fished something out of his purse and held it in his hand.

"But I saved this from the drow treasure. This is what I wanted to give to you."

It was a ring—an elven ring, delicate and beautiful—silver

inlaid with jet, and with a diamond as clear as a summer sky. The Justicar put it in Escalla's palm. Suddenly pale, he looked at the ring.

"So I . . . wanted to ask you. To marry me, I mean. Because I love you. I really do."

Escalla had thought of a thousand ways of answering. They all failed her. She made a squeaking noise and felt herself cry. Her hand shook like a leaf as he slid the ring onto her finger. She threw herself on him in an adoring embrace, rolling on the moss with him beside the foaming river.

There was a bright flash, and Escalla felt herself suddenly shrinking. An instant later, she was two feet tall again, feeling more properly in scale, and crying like a fool. She sat in Jus's lap, looked up at him, and laughed through tears, brushing her long hair back from her face. She gave a watery smile, then went back to hugging him and looking at the empty potion bottle that lay amongst the moss and stones.

"Small again." She sighed. "Ah, well."

Jus smiled, admiring her delicate, wild beauty as he helped straighten out Escalla's flowing hair.

"How many potions do you have?"

"Seven now, but I've got the recipe—though I don't really know how to milk a purple worm. I think I'll use cow." Escalla lounged back against Jus. "Oh, Enid is *so* going to know what we've just done!"

She rolled into him and kissed him, then lay listening to his breathing. Serious at last, she contemplated the oversized ring that lay in her palm.

"Married."

"Soon. Whenever you want."

"And I'm going to have your kids. One day, when its time. A little scowling Justicar."

"Or a girl." Jus smiled. "Bright as a hummingbird."

Escalla heaved a sigh, troubles edging in around her. She looked sadly out at the riverbanks.

"Marriage. But only when we fix it." Escalla stared at the water rushing by. "We're responsible. We stirred up Lolth, and look what happened to Keggle Bend."

The Justicar held Escalla protectively in his arms.

"No. Lolth was always going to kill, but we did determine what world she would strike." Even here, Jus's sword was only a handspan away. "Her victims need justice."

"Here's to Justice."

They shared a cup of river water. Retrieving clothes, Escalla sat on the moss with her heels tucked into her rump and turned the problem over in her mind.

"Lolth didn't hit Keggle Bend just because we were there."

"She's invading." The Justicar ran his hands across the velvet stubble of his skull. "If we don't stop her, there'll be more towns going the same way as Keggle Bend."

Escalla thoughtfully combed moss out of her hair.

"All right, so we go for Lolth. Stop Lolth, and you also should stop Tielle and Recca. Without Lolth, her armies are toast. All those monsters would be at each other's throats in a minute!"

"That's the way. That's the weakness." Jus scowled at the water. "But she's a tanar'ri, a powerful one. The tanar'ri lords only truly die if they die on their own home plane. We have to kill her when she's in the Abyss." He skimmed a rock into the stream. "When she returns to the Abyss, we have to be there."

Escalla stared at splashes in the stream. "Can we take out a god?"

"Like any other god, Lolth is a deity only because she says she is. Gods are just creatures with enough power to bully and destroy." The Justicar looked at the old holy symbol that hung about his neck—a solar symbol cut through by a blow of his own sword long, long ago. "If it lives, then it can die. It's time we brought the gods a taste of Justice."

Escalla winced. "Some honeymoon!"

"There's another problem. Recca and Tielle will be trying to find our trail. We'll have to move fast, before they reason out what we're going to do."

"Ambush the ambushers?" Escalla shrugged. "Bring 'em on." The girl ran fingers through her hair and thought a moment. "Right. The Abyss. Fine! So what gear do we need? We need crossbow bolts for Henry."

"We'll take them from the enemy."

"We need gems for Enid so she can make ink for her stun symbol."

Jus gave a snort. "Polk kept five emeralds. He was going to use them to buy booze."

"Fine." Escalla ticked off the last point on her list. "Most of all, we need to protect you. I can do a stoneskin spell that'll block the first half dozen hits you take, but for that, I need to powder up a diamond."

"Diamond." The Justicar hissed and scowled. "There's no diamond."

Escalla gave a wan little grimace and waved her engagement ring. She threw it into the party fund.

"No point having a rock with no husband. Get me a bigger one from Lolth."

They rose, dressed, and held each other quietly by the river. Finally Escalla ruffled Jus's stubble and gave him a smile.

"Someone finally touched the faerie."

Jus smiled. They paused at the edge of the boulders. Jus held up his fingers, and Escalla clasped them in her hand.

"Forever and always?"

"Forever and always."

They drew apart in a thin attempt to pretend they were as pure as driven snow. Escalla flew gaily on ahead, suddenly in the grip of a food frenzy. Left behind, Jus felt suddenly weak at the knees.

He sagged and held onto a tree for support.

Jutting through his belt, the sword Benelux was scandalized. *Sir. I am agog! I realized a warrior's weapon must always be at hand. But sir, there are limits to what I can try not to overhear!*

Mortified, Jus blushed. "So you, ah, heard?"

*I did indeed! Most undecorous!* Benelux gave a sniff. *What question did you keep asking her, and why did she keep agreeing so vigorously?*

The Justicar ducked his head and walked doggedly through the trees.

"Never mind!"

\* \* \* \* \*

About twenty large fish were smoking over the fire when Escalla came out of the bushes. She looked neither right nor left, blushed bright pink, and held herself stiff as a brush. She busied herself ineffectually arranging the fish, while Enid crept over to her side.

They worked side by side where Henry could not hear. Enid kept her voice a little whisper. "Psst! Did he . . . ?"

"Uh-huh!"

"Did you . . . ?"

"Uh-huh."

"Was it . . . ?"

*"Unbelievable!"* Escalla snatched food and headed for the nearest place where they could gossip.

**14**

In all the legions of all the armies of all the forces of Lolth, not one officer had the foresight to bring along a map of the Flanaess. It was left to Morag to churn through the burned remnants of Keggled Bend's library. Filthy with soot and cursing bitterly, she tried to make sense out of the scraps of ash and rubbish left by a thousand rampaging demons.

She summoned her own vassal tanar'ri—hopping demons shaped like frogs, vultures, or rotting canines with crab claws. None of them were any earthly use. They merely upset the piles of scorched shelves and rubbish to make yet more mess. Apparently the only creature in the Abyss with any hint of intelligence, Morag did the filthy job herself, digging through ruins that still reeked of blood and fire.

Fastidious as a cat, Morag swore at each smudge and smear. Rotted bodies, putrefied entrails, blood, and sludge revolted her. All she wanted was a little home—a neat tower made of bone she would set beside a waterfall. Somewhere quiet. Somewhere clean. Somewhere a book could be left open without a quasit ripping out the pages to line its nest! There should be more to life than this! Cleanliness! Friends! Someone to talk to—even someone to curl up against. No more pain, no more blood, no more fear. But she was trapped. Lolth had discovered her secret, true name, and now Morag was bound to centuries of servitude. There was nothing Morag could do—no escape, no freedom, nothing while Lolth still held Morag's true name in her claws!

Morag heaved over a fresh pile of intermingled bodies, burned books, and fallen roofing tiles, swearing openly as she set about her work.

"I could have taken service with Demogorgon. I could have been with Jubilex, but no-o-o-o-o!" She worked in a flurry, all six arms hurling ruined parchments to the winds. "The queen of the drow will have manners! The queen of the drow will have dry quarters! Intrigue, cunning, plot, adventure! We'll get it *all* from the queen of the drow!"

"Mora-a-a-ag? *Morag!*"

An imperious summons came from the streets. Cursing as she pulled her sleek black clothing straight, Morag slithered over to a broken window and looked out.

There she was—near naked, wild, and magnificent. Lolth, looking rested, relaxed, and competent, walked upon a carpet of terrified slaves as she conferred with her generals.

"*Morag?* Where have you slithered off to now, you slimy little spinster?"

With a weary sigh, Morag perched herself in the window and called, "Yes, your Magnificence?"

"Morag!" Lolth looked over at the ruins in disdain. "What are you doing? You look like a charcoal burner."

"I am searching for maps, Magnificence."

"Whatever for?" Lolth waved toward some drow noble who followed adoringly behind her. "The drow have maps!"

"Maps twenty years old, Magnificence. There has been a major war since then."

Lolth gave Morag a pitying little sigh. "Oh, Morag, we have scouts out on the winds! The generals have all that sort of thing in hand. Surely you trust my generals?"

Morag turned away from the window with a mutter. "I wouldn't trust them to sit the right way around on a toilet."

Eventually, she uncovered a map—or part of a map, at least. Though smudged and leaked upon, it clearly showed a city a hundred miles to the northeast. Morag shook the parchment out and slithered her coils down to the street. She would summon some dark elves and have them make clean copies—in triplicate, one set of copies to each army commander.

Morag slid past a half-eaten corpse left moldering in the street. She found a ruined house that still had curtains, and she used the cloth to wipe herself clean. As she finished, she saw a figure leaning carefully over footprints in the mud, sniffing at them like a hellish dog.

It was a figure in eagle armor. One of its feet was brand new, contrasting against its withered, mummified skin. Morag watched it go, then slithered over to join Lolth's bustling entourage. Varrangoin—huge cadaverous shapes with bat wings—crouched before the goddess as they gave their reports. The creatures scattered and beat heavily into the air as Lolth dismissed them with a wave.

Morag handed over her maps and installed herself at Lolth's side. A vast ring of tanar'ri had formed—jagged creatures that hopped and flapped, monsters with claws so hard they scored the cobblestones. These were the elite of Lolth's legions—her officers and her warlords, creatures who had slaughtered innocents in their tens of thousands.

Morag leaned close to Lolth, frowning, and whispered quietly into her mistress's ear. "Magnificence, I have seen the Eagle warrior—the undead ranger. He's back inside the city walls."

Not particularly interested, Lolth stood with her demonic generals—vast, towering beings wreathed in flames. She issued imperious orders, her body gleaming from the heat of her advisors, then turned to face her secretary with a scowl.

"What? You saw it?"

"Not a hundred yards away, Magnificence."

"Absurd! What was it doing?"

Morag gave an elegant shrug of all six shoulders. "Searching for a trail, magnificence. Unsuccessfully."

Lolth fumed, reflecting that her plans for vengeance had failed. But there was an army to muster and enemies to tame. Revenge could wait until another time. Lolth allowed slaves to clasp a cloak about her neck, then she signaled for her spider palace to be brought to the city walls.

"We'll deal with it later." Lolth's eyes were silver flame, her naked skin pure liquid ebony. "Once this little world is ours, we shall pull it apart stone by stone until we have found that faerie and her Justicar."

In a sudden explosion of rage, Lolth whipped her fist back to pulp the head of a human slave. Blood geysered, and Lolth stood, flexing her fist, eyes wild as she clenched the gore.

The fit passed. Lolth moved on, turning to make sure Morag fell in behind her.

"Well? Did you find those maps or didn't you?"

"I have maps, Magnificence."

"Then bring them to the palace!" Lolth walked through howling, shrieking ranks of servitors. "Come! We're returning to the Demonweb."

Lolth marched away. Morag signed for her clerks and followers and hastened along in Lolth's wake. Behind them, chaos broke out as the towering generals drove their troops into ranks and columns, ready to crush all of the Flanaess under her heel.

## 15

A drider—part drow and part spider—lurched along the road from Keggle Bend. The centaur creature clicked along the ground on eight long legs, cradling a crossbow pistol in its hand. Behind it on the plains, thousands of giant spiders wrapped paralyzed humans into bundles of silk. The spiders chittered and screeched as they worked—vinegaroons and scorpions dragging the prey away to stack it like cordwood beside the demon hordes.

With the armies of Lolth at its back, the spider-centaur was now far beyond fear. It wanted prey. The monster sensed something in the air—something elusive, something invisible. The creature cocked its crossbow and stalked sideways off the road. Sly and sinister, it slid to a stand of bushes to lie in wait.

The invisible *something* hovered, hesitated, and then suddenly backed away. The drider blundered out of the bushes in pursuit, taking aim with its crossbow.

An instant later, a section of the grass burst upward and a shining white blade smacked into the monster from behind. Headless, the creature staggered forward. Streaming soil and grass, the Justicar rose up out of the mold and hacked off the creature's arm. The crossbow fell to the ground and fired uselessly into the dirt. Jus let the headless body stagger through the bushes and die. No other monsters were close enough to care. He stripped the corpse of its case of crossbow bolts and threw them to Henry, who rose from hiding in the grass. In the air between, there was a *pop* as Escalla became visible again.

"That eight-legged bastard could see me!" The faerie was indignant. Invisibility was a faerie's pride and joy. "How'd the creep manage that?"

"Spiders sense vibration." Jus inspected a pot of viscous green liquid he'd found on the drider's belt and threw it to Henry. "Arrow poison. Here!"

Still in a huff, Escalla fluttered with her arms folded tight. "Oh, great. How am I supposed to infiltrate and spy?"

Emerging from the portable hole, Polk and Enid crept out to stare at the ruined town in the far distance. Giant spiders crawled all over the landscape, like a scene ripped out of a nightmare. Over the town, the grotesque shapes of flying tanar'ri spread an aura of dread. Enid blinked, her face beneath her freckles turning pale.

"Oh, dear. All those poor people."

The Justicar rose, Cinders's teeth streaming sulfurous smoke and flames. "The best we can offer them is to obliterate Lolth."

The hellish legions on the mudflats below were gathering into mobs and columns. Lolth's generals were about to march, spreading the massacre and terror out into all the Flanaess. The adventurers fell flat amongst the bushes as abyssal bats swept overhead, their hunting cries chilling the very air.

There were tanar'ri in their hundreds—some thirty feet tall and wreathed in flames, others human sized and hopping like mad insects, the grass beneath them dying where they walked. The fields boiled and surged with giant spiders and scorpions. Titanic black widows and tarantulas the size of elephants thudded along beside the animated corpses of giants and writhing carpets of carnivorous worms. Somewhere in the middle of all these beings was Lolth, the mistress of the drow.

Polk wrinkled his snout in thought. "Son? Have you ever considered the advantages of issuing a heroic challenge? A duel in the sun! Man to goddess! Your blade, flesh, and bone against her mighty spells?"

Escalla kept her eyes on the shrieking, wheeling, battling mobs of monsters on the plains as she replied, "Polk, we were thinking more along the lines of stabbing her in the bladder in her sleep."

"Oh."

The spider goddess's armies were being reinforced. The magic circle made from butchered corpses acted as a planar gate, and a multitude of screeching, filthy beings were shambling out of the circle and forming into ranks. The Justicar watched from cover, lying with Escalla at his side.

"A gate to the Abyss?"

"Yeah. Those critters there are called manes." Escalla was the resident expert. Her people had lived amongst the outer planes. "Must have come straight from the Abyss. Slow and stupid. So that's our way in."

In the heart of the crushed, smoking ruins of Keggle Bend, Lolth's spider palace loomed like a behemoth. The metal of its structure looked like brass, yet it shimmered with fleeting images as though it were somehow alive. The palace crouched above shattered temples and roofs, towering a hundred feet high. The jaws formed a ramp guarded by demons—a gateway into Lolth's private home.

Escalla leaned on her frost wand and stared at the mobile palace. "Wow! Look at that place! Hoopy! Why leave the comforts of home when you can take them on campaign?"

Henry stared at the spider palace in awe. "That's where she lives?"

"Looks like it. Part palace, and part war machine."

"Yes." Lying beneath Cinders's black pelt, the Justicar stared in calculation at his prey. "That's where we have to be. We have to get into that palace, then find a way to ambush Lolth when she returns to the Abyss."

Henry gnawed a thumb nail as he spoke. "Will she return there? Why?"

"She has to. It's the source of her power," Escalla replied. "If she wants to recharge her magic, she has to go back home and suck up the ambiance."

The Justicar kept his eyes upon the city ruins, thinking and planning. Escalla used him as a chair.

"All right, that metal spider is as big as a castle. If we get in, we should be able to hide out."

Lolth's armies swarmed all over the roads and paths. The ruins moved subtly with hints of lurking shapes. Enid looked over the view and bit the end of one huge claw.

"So . . . how do we get in?"

"No problem!" Escalla gave a confident little pose. "I change myself into a quasit or a little tanar'ri-thing. Everyone else gets in the portable hole, and I just fly straight through Lolth's front door! She'll be dead by lunchtime; we'll be home in time for tea!"

Enid gave a frown that wrinkled up her nose. "Can we do that? Don't these creatures have the ability to detect good?"

"Why's that a problem?" asked Polk. "It's Escalla."

"I'm good, thank you very much!" She shot a glance at the Justicar. *"Damned* good!"

Enid blinked. "So that means we can't just sneak in?"

*Goodness no.* Benelux sounded stuffy and impatient. *They will sense me. My energy signature is unique. And you certainly cannot kill a goddess with any weapon other than me!*

Ignoring the conversation, the Justicar had Henry beside him. The two men were carefully studying the lay of the land—the flooded fields and the fallen walls. Henry pointed out a feature to the Justicar, and the big man nodded as he agreed. Enid, Polk, and Escalla eventually became interested, and all came over to watch the fun and inquire.

Escalla lounged silkily against the Justicar and raised one brow. "Having fun?"

"There's a way in." The Justicar traced a path with his finger that wended beneath fallen roofs and fields drowned neck deep in slime. "We go through the fields by swimming—then cross the river where it laps the city wall. Through the breach and into the city. Then we can try to find a way aboard the palace."

Enid lashed her tail in thought. "What if there are monsters in the river?"

"Lolth's creatures are mostly spiders and fire creatures. Watch them. They try to avoid the water—all except the trolls."

"Ah. Trolls."

"We can take trolls." The Justicar had no fear of mere claws, scales, and bone. "Easiest if only one person makes the swim. I'll carry you in the portable hole until we get into the city. After that, we'll need the whole team."

Sitting beside the furry bulk of Enid, Henry looked a little pale. "Then after that—the Abyss?"

"The Abyss."

The party froze, letting the fear of that dark place settle in their minds. Unperturbed, Escalla whirred up into the air and clapped her hands.

"Abyss? What's in a name? Any of you guys ever been to the Inn of No Return in Greyhawk?" The faerie whipped up enthusiasm. "Ever had a bottomless cup of brew? Did the cup have a bottom? I hope to kiss a duck it did!" Escalla dismissed all their worries with a little wave of her hand. "It's just hype! The kind of stuff Polk writes!"

The badger gave an indignant squawk. "Hey!"

"Sorry, man. Motivational speech." Strutting like a coach with a reluctant team, Escalla pounded Enid on one wing. "Now the Abyss is just a place! Things live there—thousands of things. All right, most of those things are tanar'ri, and they like to eat people, *but* they live, they goof off, and snooze between meals. The Abyss is a world like any other—big ecology, wide open spaces, with cities and towns! We keep away from the towns, stick to the empty bits . . . it'll be a doddle!" The girl saw doubtful looks on Henry and Enid's faces. "Hey, trust me! I'm a faerie! Cinders! Back me up here. You're a hell hound. What have you heard about the Abyss?"

*Fun!* The hell hound's big fangs gleamed. *Nice hot lava, sulfur jets, hot fires! Dead things everywhere!*

"And . . . and then there were all those *other* bits that were not life-threatening to the non-fireproof in any way at all!" Escalla hit Henry on the shoulder. "So come on! We're the team! We're adventurers with heroism written in our eyes! The world is our oyster, and we like it raw!" Turning to face the ruins, Escalla posed in magnificent defiance. She stood with fists on her little hips, and murmured to the Justicar. "Did they buy it?"

"No."

"Sod it! Let's go."

Escalla chased Polk, Henry, and Enid down into the portable hole. "We should put a couch in here—maybe a real bed or two." Polk she helped down with a boot in his tail. "Come on! Time's wasting!"

Alone at last, Escalla put her arms about Jus's neck and buried her face against his cheek. He held her, eyes closed, loving the deceitful little creature heart and soul.

"It'll be all right. We can do it."

"Sure we can." Escalla held him tight. "I love you."

"I love you."

*Cinders love you, too!* The dog grinned away, his tail wagging. *Fun! Hush, Cinders.* Benelux sniffed importantly. *This is a private moment. Be a good dog and be still.*

With a dire glare for the interlopers, Escalla tugged her little chain-mail skirt straight.

"True love might be easier without the chorus of eavesdroppers!"

*Eavesdropping? I never!* Benelux bridled in indignation. *That is an uncouth suggestion. Young lady, the only words I overheard were your continuous agreement.* The sword sniffed. *Very vigorous agreement!*

"You know, one day you are going to get a crush on a big handsome broadsword, and then I am gonna go to *town* on you!" Escalla flicked the sword hilt with the tip of her finger. "Now look after my betrothed, or I'll store something rancid at the bottom of your sheath."

Jus kissed Escalla tenderly, and the little faerie did a swan dive down into the portable hole. The ranger folded up the hole and made it safe.

"Cinders?"

*Faerie agrees! Funny!*

"Very funny." The Justicar lay flat, waited for a swarm of bat-winged severed heads to fly over the river, then slithered belly first into the mud of a flooded field. "Eyes open. Let's go."

From inside the portable hole, voices drifted up—Escalla scolding Polk for the twentieth time that day.

"Polk! What are you doing?"

"Updating the chronicles." The badger sounded positively overjoyed. "We're going to the Abyss! The pit of evil itself! Best place a hero could ever hope to carry the blade of the just and true! It's time to put in some illustrations!"

"You're a very sick person, Polk. You know that, don't you?"

Cinders wagged his tail. Jus shook his head and began the careful business of penetrating the defenses of hell.

*    *    *    *    *

"Out! Quiet and quick. Hide over to the left."

Wet and lying flat in the wreck of a house, Jus carefully helped his friends out of the portable hole. They were inside the ruins of Keggle Bend where giant spiders had strung webs hung with corpses. A gargoyle lay dead on the ground—characteristically sliced from head to groin with a single blow of Jus's sword. Enid flowed out of the portable hole like a gigantic panther and hid herself, brown fur and freckles invisible in the gloom. Henry took one brief look from the edge of the hole, then slid into position with his crossbow covering the ruins. Polk and Escalla emerged, and Jus folded up the hole and put it in his pouch——shutting out the stench of dried fish from within.

Polk trundled over to the lip of the ruined house, his cap set at a jaunty angle above his eye. "Son! Where are we? Where's the demons?"

"They're leaving. There's no garrison." The Justicar motioned toward the bloodstained towers of the citadel. The back of Lolth's spider palace loomed above the battlements. "They're using the populace for food and moving on. The front door to the spider palace is guarded, but there are portholes in some of the sides. If we can get on top, we can find a way in."

Henry kept careful watch over the ruins. "Won't they see us from the air?"

"Might. But their fliers have all gone. They're abandoning this site and marching north."

With a shrug, Escalla pulled off her gloves. "Well, let's take a peek. Me first. You guys keep hidden."

Skirt, leggings and halter followed, Escalla kicking her clothes into Jus's hands. Henry blushed as he stared rigidly off at the ruins, and Escalla kissed him on the ear.

"Wish me luck, Hen." Escalla cracked her knuckles and prepared to change shape. "Were the tanar'ri imps or quasits? I forget. Wait! Wait! It's quasits! Right! Got it!"

There was a brief *pop*, and Escalla disappeared. In her place stood a hideous little demon——horned, clawed, with a sting on its tail and a cookie-cutter mouth filled with teeth. Escalla's distorted voice came from the beast as it skittered off into the rubble.

"Back in ten!"

Enid watched her best friend go, and arched her brow. "Eerie."

Escalla the quasit kept a hard grip on her frost wand. It was too late now to ask her to leave it behind. The hideous little demon shape hopped up onto the rocks, then disappeared.

Long, anxious minutes passed. Beyond the lingering sound of screams, a strange rustling sound could be heard. It was the sound of a vast multitude of creatures on the march—an army moving slowly away. The wind blew through the ruined city, making the rubble shift and hiss. Jus kept Benelux in his hand, and Cinders's red eyes scanned the ruins. Henry kept watch. All seemed quiet.

A giant spider came out of the ruins, dragging a corpse wrapped in silk behind it. It moved awkwardly, finding the burden heavy. As it worked, a quasit came bounding out of a window. The little demon ran fearlessly beneath the spider's legs. Annoyed, the huge black widow hissed but left the quasit alone. The spider disappeared around a corner as the quasit slipped into the shadows and sat happily beside the Justicar.

There was a *pop*, and the quasit now wore Escalla's face.

"Right! They're loading that spider palace up with loot. Gold and stuff. They're getting ready to move out." Escalla lashed her little demon tail. "I think the west tower of the citadel might give us a way up onto the spider palace roof. From there we can slip across without being seen." The girl stood, took a peek out of cover, then waved the others on. "Coast is clear! Let's go!"

She changed her head back into quasit shape. The Justicar moved like a vast, silent bear as he followed her. Next came Enid, with Polk running at her heel. Henry spied a coal lump in the ruins, pocketed it for Cinders, then scuttled awkwardly backward, covering the rear with his crossbow.

The entire town lay empty. The gates were smashed in, and the few small towers crumbled from blows made with demonic force. Bloodstains splashed the walls in dry brown crusts, and the court-yards reeked of death. But there were no bodies—no slaughtered guards, no dead ladies-in-waiting. Lolth's minions had scoured the city clean, taking every corpse for the value of its meat. Escalla the quasit waited in the shattered gateway as her comrades caught up. She peeked about a corner, scampered across a dangerous patch of open ground, and waved her friends to follow. Jus crossed at a dead run, disappearing into darkness as he dived behind a door. With a nervous glance at the walls, the others followed swiftly and slipped into the empty castle halls.

They descended into a kitchen that had been thrown all awry. Pots and pans were crushed and buckled. A charred, twisted human skeleton lay over the cooking range where it had burned. Enid leaped over the party and landed at the opposite door, where she stood peering and thrashing her tail.

"I hear singing!"

A strange music drifted through the air—joyous, carefree, the sound of a girl without a care in the world. The music was unearthly, and strangely unsettling. Her fur standing on end, Enid nosed open a door and peered into a long, dark corridor.

The singing was louder. Enid edged forward, her nose sniffing. Hurrying across the kitchen, the Justicar caught up with the sphinx. "Enid, careful!" he whispered.

There was a hissing squeal as a giant black widow spider launched itself out of the corridor straight at Enid's face. Jus lunged, but Enid merely stamped her foot. Her big paw smashed the spider to the pavement, swiftly followed by another spider clinging to the wall. She trod the monsters as she walked into the corridor.

"It's only spiders. Come on!"

Jus looked down at the squashed spiders, met Escalla's gaze, and shrugged. He followed behind Enid as the big sphinx padded down the hall toward a glimmer of light.

The singing grew louder, more gay, and beautiful. Enid settled down on her haunches beside a shattered wall, peering curiously out into the light.

"Oh! Look here!"

Escalla avoided squished spider, scampered over to Enid's side, and joined in the view.

A courtyard spread itself under the sky. The walls were lined with flayed human corpses that had been nailed to the stones so that the impaled bodies formed a grisly collonnade. Once-graceful flowering trees now had skulls hanging from their branches like fruit. A portable stove seemed to be cooking toasted cheese, and the broad fountain, beautiful with mosaics, now brimmed with milk and almond oil. Sitting happily in the bath was a drow woman of stunning beauty. In the pool her silver hair floated all about her sheer black skin. Her eyes were quicksilver fire, and an aura of darkness shimmered from her skin. The drow beauty sang as she lolled in perfect happiness. She sang like a choir of angels. Behind her, shambling, imbecilic slaves milked a cage of butter-flies to help top up the woman's bath.

Standing at the edge of the bath and looking extremely annoyed was a strange tanar'ri female. A thin, sharp featured woman with bobbed black hair with a tart expression on her face, she was consulting a notebook and shooting meaningful glances at a big hourglass propped beside the bath.

Watching the scene below, Escalla cocked her frost wand.

"Check it out! Hoo-hoo! Bathing in butterfly milk! Gal after my own heart!" Escalla changed back into normal form, buck naked, armed, and dangerous. " 'Course, I'm still gonna have to kill her nasty."

In the courtyard below, the black-skinned beauty stood to rinse her hair. Henry stared at her naked figure in shock. "You mean that's Lolth?"

Escalla stretched and posed. "Sure! Check out her arse! You only get perfection like that in goddesses and faeries!"

"You can tell just by her bottom?"

"Yeah. Well, that and the pall of total evil that surrounds her."

Escalla kept her back flat against the stone wall, looking for a way to creep closer to Lolth. "Come on. Maybe we can get closer." Escalla risked another peek at Lolth. "Hoo-hoo! Natural blonde!"

She moved onward.

Henry followed, whispering in fright. "I thought Lolth was a sort of spider!"

"So she smartened up her grooming habits a little! Now come on!"

Down in the courtyard, the six-armed demoness finally convinced Lolth to leave her bath. The six-limbed woman was forced to set her notebooks aside, find the goddess a towel, then pour Lolth a drink. The Justicar watched the creature at work, feeling almost sorry for her. The woman's six arms were always busy.

"I wonder who she is?"

"Easy." Escalla leaned close and gave everyone a nudge. "See? She's a *hand*maiden! Get it?"

A dire glance came from Jus. "You've been working up to that one for a while?"

"I'm a comedy natural!"

Lolth was leaving. The adventurers moved swiftly into the castle, following with all due stealth. Lolth's voice could be heard in conversation with her six-armed assistant. They spoke in the language of the tanar'ri—sibilant, hissing, and in Lolth's case, almost beautiful.

Jus levered open a door. Lolth's voice sounded louder, closer. The goddess was capable of all manner of magical spells. Their one chance of eliminating her was a surprise attack. Jus crept across a bloodstained room to another door, let Cinders listen, and then signaled Henry to take position to open fire.

"Wait!"

Escalla dived into the portable hole and returned with a little folded packet. She sprinkled diamond dust over Jus, her wings fluttering and her eyes crossing as she wove her spell.

"There! Stoneskin! It'll block the first half dozen hits you take." The faerie looked regretfully at the packet, mourning the passing of her engagement stone. "If she lays a glove on any of us, we're finished!"

Escalla readied a spell. Enid unsheathed her claws. Polk settled his hat, and Henry knelt with his magic bow pointed and ready to fire. The Justicar took one brief look over his comrades, gave a nod, and flung open the door.

They had reached a balcony overhung with a crushed and broken ceiling. The view looked out over another open courtyard, and the tail end of Lolth's procession could just be seen exiting through a distant gate. Shambling slaves carried milk buckets and clothing. The six-armed demon brought up the rear, three curved swords jutting through her belt.

Lolth's party drew out of sight. With a glance to make sure they weren't seen, the Justicar led a stealthy advance along the balcony.

*Down!*

Cinders's warning came a split second before a red streak flashed. Jus dropped to one knee, his sword catching a blow that should have smashed his head in two. Sword blades rang—brilliant red against blinding white. A figure tumbled from beneath the ceiling, spinning as it fell, and then the blades crashed against each other in a blur. A red blade hit Jus across the back, spitting sparks as the sword uselessly struck Escalla's stoneskin spell.

The eagle-helmed warrior had clung upside down between the roof beams. Hissing, it fought in a mad stammer of speed, the red sword like a streak of light as it strove to slaughter the Justicar. Jus blocked the attacks, then Cinders blasted out a massive gout of flame that engulfed the far end of the balcony.

The cadaver leaped clear an instant before Cinders's flames struck, and it clung to the rafters like a bat. Annoyed, the hell hound fired again, and this time the corpse shot away like an arrow, leaping over Jus's head. The Justicar spun, blocking a sword stroke that sheared at his head. Cinders's flames boiled and thundered along the balcony, sending the others diving madly away. Hovering in midair, Escalla worked the arming slide on her frost wand.

"Hey, bony! Suck on this!"

The Justicar swore and dived aside. Enid crashed into Henry and covered him as she threw herself into cover. Cackling with glee, Escalla fired her wand, a blast of ice smashing into the balcony. The undead monster turned agile handstands, bounding away. Escalla followed, playing a storm of lethal cold and razor sharp ice shards all over the creature as it fled.

"And that, my friend, is *that!* You took on the wrong gal's squeeze! No one touches the faerie!"

Deadly clouds of frost cleared. The cadaver emerged, its teeth set into a snarl, silent and deadly. The red sword in its hand sheathed the creature in a glow that had kept it safe from magic.

The grin fell instantly from Escalla's face. "Holy mother puss-bucket."

The Justicar struck from behind, blindingly fast, but Recca caught the blow. Sparks showered from their blades, and Benelux screamed in pain.

*That hurt!*

Jus tumbled free, and in his hand, Benelux's gleaming metal showed a scar.

*The red sword!* Benelux fluttered in panic. *It's full of blood from last time! I think it gets sharper the more blood it has!*

Enid roared and leaped, and Jus swung at the cadaver. They tried to bring it down from both sides. The monster parried Jus, twisted away from a punch that could have snapped its neck like a twig, then turned a somersault over Enid's two hefty claw blows. The cadaver landed at Enid's side and slashed with its sword, ripping a gash along the girl's flank. Blood was instantly sucked into the sword. Enid reared and roared, cracking a wing out to try and bowl Recca over. The corpse jumped easily over the huge wing, then staggered as Henry leveled his crossbow and opened fire.

The magic crossbow blurred, hammering out five bolts that tore into the screaming cadaver. The monster staggered back, then surged forward again, shot through the neck, chest, and skull. It tore the crossbow bolt out of its own eye, and the wound flared and healed. The withered body glowed with light as the hellish creature rebuilt itself. It started toward Henry, then whirled and parried as the Justicar's blade stabbed a lightning-fast blow at its spine.

Henry drew his sword and tried to fight, only to have the weapon struck out of his hands. Escalla whirred in with her lich staff, but the corpse leaped and dodged, spinning over her. Only the Justicar held his ground. He locked blades with the monster, then shot his arm over Recca's forearm, trapping him tight. Perfectly partnered, Cinders opened fire. The hell hound's flames blasted into Recca's face, blinding the monster and melting the helmet's surface. The undead cadaver hurled away, then staggered and fell as the Justicar severed its leg at the knee. Enid attacked again, but her blows were blocked, then the one legged monster leaped clear, hurtling back at the Justicar.

A miss from the red blade hit the wall, and solid granite shattered like porcelain. The Justicar roared and swung his sword down in a blow so massive it drove the undead monster to its knees. Sparks showered as blade met blade. Jus's huge strength kept his enemy crushed to the ground, and he kicked Recca's face with one heavy boot, breaking the corpse's neck, skull, and jaw. The monster ploughed over the balcony and smashed to the ground two dozen feet below.

"We did it!" Escalla was exultant. "The dead dude's toast! Teamwork rules!"

Everyone rushed to the balcony rails. Below them, Recca sat, reached hands to his head and reset his own broken neck with a *crack*. Green blood pumped from his injuries, and where the blood touched his dead flesh, his wounds disappeared. His eyes were still regrowing, but already footsteps thundered as Lolth's guards came to investigate the noise. Jus grabbed Polk under one arm and threw himself back through a door into the citadel. The others followed suit, Enid staggering and weak. The Justicar slammed a hand against Enid's wound and sent a pulse of healing magic into her. The wound closed after the second spell, and Jus instantly led the way up a shattered flight of stairs.

Outside in the courtyard, there were yells and screams. Something had apparently interfered with Recca's healing. The Justicar raced up a flight of circular stairs, pounding hard and fast. Escalla shot through the air and took the point. Enid squeezed the whole stairwell shut behind. They ran and ran until the stairs ended in a door. Jus smashed heavy oak and steel open with one crash of his shoulder.

The door opened upon a rooftop. Wind whistled, and from this great height, all the world seemed exposed. The flattened, ruined city lay all about. Flooded plains stretched for miles around. To the north, a vast army scuttled, slid, and marched beneath a cloud of abyssal bats. Beside the citadel stood Lolth's titanic mobile palace. The huge machine squatted like a tarantula. Lolth and her entourage were mounting steps into the monster's maw. A gap of fifty feet led from the citadel roof to the spider palace's gleaming back.

Jus flicked out the portable hole and leaped inside. Henry and a protesting Polk were pushed in after him. Holding the hole in her mouth, Enid gathered and sprang out into the open air. Her wings lofted her effortlessly across the gap, while Escalla flew beside her, covering the jump with her wand.

Enid landed on the spider's broad metal back—and everything went wrong. Her feet skated out from under her. The metal was as slick as butter. She thrashed her wings impotently, unable to fly, and began to slide toward the ground a hundred feet below.

Hovering nearby, Escalla landed—had her own feet shoot out from under her, and began to slide. Her wings wouldn't lift her. As Enid slithered past, the faerie turned into a snake, her clothes hanging loose on her coils, and whipped herself out as a lifeline to hold Enid by the paw. Eyes bulging—tail wrapped around Enid and her neck wrapped about a jutting piece of metal, Escalla gagged as Enid hauled herself up to safety and tried to cling flat against the slippery, greasy metal.

Flailing at the end of Enid's paw, Escalla the snake tried to get a grip on the metal hull. "Jus. Help! We can't fly! Something's wrong! We can't fly!"

Escalla was being torn in half. The Justicar shot out of the portable hole and slipped. Groping for the magic rope on his belt—a rope taken from an erinyes a few short months before—he grabbed Enid by the scruff of her neck and lashed the rope like a whip. It wrapped itself about a porthole cover. The Justicar roared and tried to hold on, but Enid's weight was too heavy.

With a ponderous lurch, the spider palace began to move.

It rose from its crouch, its legs straightening. Hanging desperately on the magic rope, Jus felt the whole world give a sickening sway. Rocking like a ship in a mad sea, the spider palace trundled over the ruins of Keggle Bend. With Enid slipping in his grasp, Jus gripped the sphinx and Escalla, the magic rope cutting into his hand.

Ringing like monstrous bells, the spider palace's feet crashed over stones and splashed into muddy fields. Jus felt his grip giving way as the palace moved ponderously toward its gate to the Abyss. The magic circle gave off a sickly light. A stench of death, decay, and filth leaped into the air.

Jus's grip slipped. He roared and caught himself, blood leaking from his palm where the rope burned through his hide.

"Hold on!"

Henry appeared in the mouth of the portable hole and tried to stab a handhold into the palace's hull. Escalla turned into an octopus, her flailing suckers failing to take hold of the alien metal. Jus slipped again. The air around them turned thick with sulfurous smoke, ash, and death, and suddenly the whole team fell.

The bronze hull slipped past in a blur, and then the group was falling free. Escalla turned into a bat. Tumbling free, Enid thrashed her wings, felt resistance, and thrashed madly at the air. She broke the fall and saved them all from death. With a lurch, she crashed into the ground. The universe shook as titanic metal feet thudded to the ground beside them, and the spider palace marched on its way.

They lay on a field of ashes. The sky above them was purple as venous blood. Distant shapes wheeled and screamed in heavens that stank of death. Lolth's spider palace clanged and crashed, disappearing into the murk with frightening speed—and suddenly the adventurers were alone.

Escalla fluttered down and returned to form. Henry and Polk had fallen from the portable hole. They lay beside Enid, who blinked in shock, staring at the sudden change of scene.

Jus sat slowly and looked into the dull, thick air. They sat on a terrace hundreds of miles wide, a flat ridge at the edge of a vast chasm. The Abyss yawned before them—an infinite drop into eternity, ringed by six hundred and sixty-six descending rings of hell. The view was numbing—awesome and horrible.

The air shivered all about them like a dying scream. Locusts made of wormwood and brass skittered and chittered in the dust. The group could only stare at the vast gulf of the Abyss and shiver. Unperturbed, Escalla beat the ashes out of her little skirt and looked around.

"Hey, guys! It's the Abyss!" Happy to be making real progress, Escalla clapped her hands. "Well, we're here!"

❉  ❉  ❉  ❉  ❉

Sadly diminished, Lolth—Queen of the Demonweb Pits, Lady of the Drow, and Mistress of Spiders—walked into the control room of her palace. Two succubi worked the controls. Each one seethed in annoyance at having to work. Lolth was greeted by her pack of pet spiders, scorpions, and miscellaneous arachnids, the creatures stretching up to their mistress for a pat. Mistress of all that she surveyed, Lolth allowed slaves to bring her a throne, and she lazily sat down.

"Morag?"

The secretary trailed behind the rest of Lolth's entourage. Seeing the drab, skinny creature enter, Lolth held a cup out and demanded tea.

"Morag, what was all that commotion behind us just now?"

Somewhere in her treasures, Lolth had written down Morag's true name. An order prefaced with that name would have to be obeyed—even an order to suicide. Morag poured the tea oh-so-nicely, then found an adamantite sugar spoon.

"Nothing, Magnificence. A brawl in the town ruins."

"Something attacked my guards?"

"No, Magnificence. It was lower creatures having a difference of opinion."

Lolth detected no untruths. She pinned Morag with a careful eye then lounged back in her throne, planted her feet on the back of a squatting slave, and drank her tea. She snapped her fingers at the succubi guiding her palace along the paths of the Abyss.

"Full speed for the Demonweb Pits." Lolth sipped her tea, found it insipid, and handed it back. "Morag, you bore me."

The secretary folded up her hands. "Yes, Magnificence. I will try to be more entertaining in the future."

16

The foul air shuddered with an immense, unending roar. Bruised and dazed, the party crept carefully to their feet. The dirt beneath felt like volcanic cinders—clinking, hollow stuff that leeched the skin of heat. The air brought no sense of life, wafting thick and dull as a mist of powdered lead.

The shuddering roar came from a titanic waterfall. A river too wide to see across flowed to the lip of the abyss and plunged straight down. Whole oceans of water thundered into the void, crashing into all six hundred and sixty-six layers of the Abyss on its way to the bottom of the pit. The mist of the waterfall was full of wheeling, shrieking shapes—skull-headed ghosts lost in time and mind. The waters stirred as dark shapes looped and slithered in the deeps. Numbed by the sight, Henry let his crossbow slip in his hands.

"What is that?"

Enid, Polk, and the Justicar joined him in staring at the river. Behind them, Escalla did up her clothing, sparing a glance to see what everyone else found so fascinating.

"Oh, that? River Lethe. That's the little river here in the Abyss. If you wanna see something *really* impressive, you ought to see the Styx!" Escalla checked the set of her thong—perfect, as usual. "The Lethe flows through about half the outer planes. Crosses whole worlds! This is the muckiest end of it." The faerie finished tying up her leggings. "There's another river, about half a dozen realities away: Mnemos. Or maybe it's actually the underside of the Lethe. It holds lost memories. Sort of the counterbalance to this one. Hoopy scene, though! Look at the size of this thing!" Escalla held up the slow glass gem to scan it slowly across the scene. "There! At least we can watch it all again and laugh in about two weeks."

Enid blinked, her gaze still on the river. "Counterbalance? Why does a river need a counterbalance?"

"Yeah! I told you, this is the Lethe! If a mortal falls in that water, they lose all their memories." Escalla held one end of a tie between her teeth as she affixed her mail gloves. The roar of the river made it hard to hear. "These are the outer planes! A lot of these places are what you guys think of as 'the afterlife.' If you die, you get reborn into one of these other worlds here!"

"Really?"

"Hey, trust me on this one. I'm a faerie!" Escalla waved a hand. "They're all out there in the planes: Elysian fields, Hades, Valhalla . . . and the Abyss! This here is where you go if you've been a real arsehole!" The girl waved her slowglass gem at the river. "The river's like a tool. A lot of gods have their worshipers emerge from the river once they die. You know, a baptismal sort of thing. But what it really does is wipe minds! It makes lost souls into blank slates. Perfect servitors."

"Servitors?" Enid seemed bemused. "Whatever do you mean?"

Escalla exchanged a shared glance with the Justicar then hovered up into the air. "All right, these 'god' guys? Hasn't it struck you that they're just beings a bit higher up the power scale than you and I? They're a scam! They're living egos scrabbling for power. But anyway, if you believe in one, then when you die, you become the god's little puppy dog! Born into his afterworld. Maybe you get to live in ease, maybe you get to plow the holy fields and sweep the palace floors, or, if you were a bad boy, maybe you end up here as food for demons."

"The gods can't be like that!" The sphinx bridled. "The

afterlife is a place of beautiful reward. Dead sphinxes go to the court of Thoth in the deserts of endless dreams!"

Escalla raised a brow. "And what happens in the palace of Thoth?"

The sphinx puffed in importance. "Well, there we have access to the riddles of the universe! The library of Thoth. The knowledge of the ages! There we are allowed to file the scrolls, dust the shelves, and issue tomes to visiting . . ." Enid's face fell as realization struck her. "Oh, bugger!"

Escalla tipped her finger to her friend. "Yep! Got it in one."

The sphinx hunched, then suddenly shot a concerned look at Escalla. "You don't have any gods?"

"None I'd cross the street to say hello to."

"What happens to you if you die?"

Escalla hugged her hands against her face and batted eyelids. "Oh, *good* little faeries are supposed to turn into forest lights somewhere in the Seelie woods." The faerie sneered. "Which is why I'm a *bad* little faerie. I intend to take up a role as a ghost with fashion sense. Not that it matters. None of *us* are going anywhere!"

"Eh?"

Escalla spread her arms to encompass her friends. "Hey! I'm a faerie princess. I don't let death screw up a perfectly good partnership!" The girl turned a barrel roll in midair, flying with her back to the vast river. "Now come on! Let's get this spider bitch squashed flat so we can go home and have some fun!"

They walked to the riverbank, the roar of the waterfall so huge that they all had to shout to be heard. Instinctively they moved upstream, away from the river mists with their looping, screaming ghosts. Escalla kept up a monologue for the uninitiated mortals.

"This is the Abyss! Six hundred and sixty-six levels straight down! Each level has the surface area of several worlds, and each one is the domain of a lord of the Abyss. They call themselves gods, but they're just demons with a few ego issues!" Escalla waved her lich staff like a guide, shepherding her friends between the massive footprints left by Lolth's palace. "We read up on tanar'ri at school. Magic resistant; fire, frost, and lightning resistant. Pains in the arse!"

Henry hunched forward against the noise, trying to be heard. "How do we take out Lolth?"

"Steel!" The Justicar took the lead, spying a ragged path to the river. "Ambush and close combat."

"Close combat." Henry listened anxiously. "How do we get close? Do we have anything we can use?"

"Yes."

The Justicar marched grimly on and said no more. Escalla whirred up and took Henry underneath her arm.

"Anything we can use? Sure! Jus has a stoneskin spell on him, and I've got combat spells up the wazoo! We have a stun symbol from Enid, a portable hole, a tangling rope, a frost wand, a lich staff, Benelux, your bow, your sword, Enid's claws, and my brain! And a little dog, too!" The faerie slapped Henry between the shoulders, dangling the slowglass gem on its string. "Hey! We've even got slowglass so we can watch the action and laugh when it's all done!"

Henry reached for the slowglass, dropped it, then almost trod on it. With a screech, Escalla whipped down and snatched the prize to safety!

"Hey! Watch it! Don't break the damned slowglass!"

"Sorry!" Henry looked anxious. "Um, would that be bad?"

"Bad? Hell yes, breaking it would be bad!" The faerie waved her hands excitedly—almost shattering the slowglass against a pinnacle of rock. "This thing screws up time! You break it, and it'd trap us all in a field of slowtime. Lasts maybe two seconds for *us*—and half an hour everywhere else! By the time we snapped out of it, there'd be six hundred monsters all around us ready to party-hearty with our spleens!" The girl carefully stuffed the gem down her cleavage. *"Definitely* non-hoopy!"

"Oh. Ah, yes." Henry blinked, looking at the gem nervously. "Definitely."

Enid came swiftly to Henry's rescue. "Henry understands. Now, where is Lolth?"

"Hmm? Oh, over the river, I guess." Escalla lofted higher, squinting into the thick, foul air of the Abyss. "All we have to do is cross."

As Escalla rose from the path, something streaked from behind a jagged spray of glass and sped straight for her. The Justicar caught the motion from the corner of his eye, drew his blade, and whirled, just managing to clip the creature.

It was one of the brass locusts, its poisoned stinger held beneath it like a lance. Escalla dived aside and only just managed to swipe the insect with her staff. The locust struck the magic staff and exploded, the blast bowling Escalla through the air. Enid leaped and caught the girl, ducking as a fresh storm of locusts spat like slingstones from the dust. Forewarned, the Justicar shielded Enid, his blade whipping up to send one locust ringing off into the dust. Others hit a wall of flame from Cinders, their wings melting in the heat. The survivors looped back to make another pass, then Henry cut the leader in two with a single shot from his crossbow. The other locusts turned tail and fled, screeching like beaten children.

The comparative silence was shocking. The attack vanished as fast as it had come. Poison from a dead locust's stinger leaked into the ash, hissing and melting the dirt into glass.

The Justicar angrily grabbed Escalla by the feet and shoved her onto his shoulder where she belonged. "Quiet! And keep your eyes open!"

The locusts had come out of nowhere. The ash, dust, and smoke of the Abyss was thick as fog.

"All of you! Cover your quadrants, stay together, and keep down!"

Everything here was deadly—the soil, even the air. The Justicar kept his senses tuned to the hunt.

"Recca will be through the gate soon. The air here feels like slow poison. We can't afford to lie in wait to ambush him." The Justicar looked over the river, a place dotted with islands that Lolth's vast palace had simply used as stepping stones. "We need to get to Lolth's palace before he can catch up with us."

The sphinx creased her freckled nose. "Will he be fast?"

"He's only got one foot again. The spare parts he takes from other creatures don't seem to re-attach or regenerate."

"Oh." Ever genteel, Enid looked a little ill at the thought. "The ones you cut off when he died?"

"That's them."

*Bad skelly-man walk funny!* Cinders grinned, the river light chasing blue patterns through his fur. *Cinders burn him good next time. Burn off kneecaps! Burn top of head! Make him go crunchy! Burn! Burn! Burn!*

"Good boy." Jus seemed wary and disturbed. "But still . . . his technique is nothing to be trifled with."

"Ha!" Escalla had salvaged a piece of smoked fish from the portable hole. "We did better against him this time!"

"Not well enough." The Justicar walked onward to the river. "He's still kicking."

*       *       *       *       *

The poisoned air of the Abyss was hot and thick, and yet the place felt chill. Worst of all was the oppressive sense of evil. The ground seemed hazed with a maze of skeletal shadows—maddening shapes of bones, claws, and screaming skulls that jerked out of view the instant a head turned. The breeze echoed memories of torture and infinite, screaming pain.

By the river grew great putrid yellow trees with writhing vipers for branches. The trees hissed in hunger, forming a dense thicket that blocked the way to the riverbanks. The ground was covered in a jagged, saw-edged grass through which hissing maggots crawled. The party came to a halt and looked at the air above the river. A flock of wheeling shapes—possibly gigantic abyssal bats, possibly something even worse—kept station high above the isles.

Across the river—just barely seen—lay a white gleam of spider-web. The monstrous net rose into the sky, disappearing in a silver haze of magic. Climbing steadily up the web, gleamed a fat brass dot—the spider palace clambering for home.

Escalla looked over the river and pulled thoughtfully at her chin. "What do you think those flying things are?"

"Dangerous." The Justicar looked at the river carefully. "Watch carefully. They keep away from the river."

"Hoopy! They avoid the river. Problem solved!" The faerie was overjoyed. "There's trees here! All we do is make a raft and float across!"

"Escalla, the trees are made out of snakes."

"Well, I can't think of everything!"

Wearily, the Justicar pointed at the dark shapes seething beneath the water. "Escalla, the flying things keep away from the water because something in there has *teeth*."

"Hmmm." The faerie hovered. "Look, if we make a raft out of living trees, then the snakes and vipers will scare away the things in the river!"

The Justicar gave the girl a scowl. "No rafts."

"All right already!" Escalla thought a moment, then clicked all ten fingers on her hands. "I got it! I got it! All right, here's the plan. We get everyone inside the portable hole, then I change into something that looks amazingly evil, and I fly across the river."

Jus definitely didn't like the plan. "And the flying things?"

"I just avoid 'em! Easy." The girl put an arm about Jus's

shoulder, infinitely confident. "Hey, trust me! I'm a faerie!"

Polk and Enid were already laying out the portable hole, as happy as clams. Henry secured his water bottles, crossbow bolts, and sword and then followed his friends inside. Unwilling to leave Escalla unguarded in the Abyss, the Justicar glowered at the brink of the hole. Escalla gave him a kiss, then tried to push him in.

"Come on. We have to get moving!"

Jus watched the girl carefully. "You won't do anything silly?"

"Me? *Me!* Hey! Get real!"

"If anything wants to fight, you drop onto an island and yell for help."

"What? No fights! No one touches the faerie!"

Sighing, the Justicar looked over the dreadful scenery. Only the fact that there was nothing in the Abyss to touch, borrow, or steal convinced him to go.

"You go fast and stay away from the water. You fly as fast as you can, and don't touch anything!"

"Jus, get in the hole before I pinch you!"

Escalla tipped him in, turned into a horrific, scaly little skull-faced horror, and flapped up into the air. She grabbed the folded hole in one taloned foot, her lich staff in the other, and flew happily away.

Inside the hole, Benelux simply glowed with pride. *I do so love a woman with true heroism in her heart!*

Jus looked up at the closed entrance to the hole, his big hands working with worry. "She has no idea how dangerous this is."

"Relax, son! Just watch her and learn!" Polk was busily eating a badly smoked fish, which was stinking up the entire portable hole. "See that girl? Now *that's* true heroism! Bravery in the face of danger. Courage in adversity. Total overconfidence no matter what the odds!"

"Polk, shut up."

"Son, that gal's one of a kind!"

"Yes." The Justicar sat hard against a wall and glared. "Thank the great sky-goat for that!"

\* \* \* \* \*

Disguised as a flying imp, Escalla whistled tunelessly to herself as she whirred high above the river Lethe. Far below, skeletal serpents coiled and slithered in the water. The air seemed to be made from a pattern of old nightmares—broken, jarred, and clattering like glass. Escalla had never before seen a place so absolutely ugly. Annoyed rather than frightened, she flew gaily between geysers of Lethe-water, the cursed drops missing her by inches. Two large bat-shaped creatures chased her, then veered off in panic as she skimmed a wing's breadth above the churning waters. A bat dived toward her, Escalla kept a sly eye on the water before looping high, and a split second later a hideous rotting sea serpent blasted out of the water. It missed Escalla and clashed its jaws shut upon the bat. Escalla looked back pityingly at the opposition, then gave an expressive little shrug.

"Gods but it's good being me!"

At the far bank, forests of viper trees lunged and uselessly spat venom. Brass locusts launched, screeching for Escalla's blood. Annoyed, the faerie hovered and smashed the locusts apart with a swarm of her golden bees.

"Scram! Go on!"

There was no point dragging the others out of the portable hole. Escalla was clearly right on top of the dangers of the Abyss. Nothing here she couldn't handle. She followed the clear track of Lolth's spider palace straight to a vast cleft in the Abyssal wall. The web arose a thousand feet, then simply disappeared into a silvery mist, clearly interfacing with another plane. Lolth's home plane.

Escalla tucked her frost wand under one arm, held her lich

staff and the portable hole in taloned feet, and soared up along a titanic strand of spider web. She slowed near the silver mist and edged into it slowly, blinking her eyes against the sudden change in atmosphere.

The place smelled even worse than the Abyss. Escalla had found a dead tarantula in a box once, and this new reek had something of that eye-watering stench about it. Coughing and wiping her eyes, the faerie fluttered over to a strand of web and looked around.

The webs formed giant roads that led to a solid silver wall. One strand headed to vast doors six stories high—apparently the entrance for the spider palace. Escalla headed over to another strand, looking for somewhere decent to set down, then spied a small door of arsenic green.

The door was attended by two figures—one female, blindfolded with a shawl over her hair, and the other a tiny demon sitting at a desk and surrounded by quills. Alcoves to either side showed the presence of at least twenty armed and armored drow.

No problem. Escalla flew straight for the imp, bypassing the drow entirely. From the mouth of the portable hole, Jus's voice came hissing out.

"Escalla, are we across the river yet?"

"Almost! Now shh! There's a big fish or something here!"

Escalla flapped up to the little demon, wrestling madly with the portable hole, and screeched to a halt. Her command of tanar'ri language came from one term of classes she had slept through at school. Bawling in a panic, Escalla skidded onto the desk outside the door.

"Hey-lo! Hey-lo! Deliverings is! Special things deliverings—yes! Moment is impregnated with urgency. Hoopla!"

The little demon scowled and tapped an absurdly long quill on the desk. The blindfolded woman leaned forward, and something hissed and writhed beneath her shawl. Escalla pretended to fight with the struggling portable hole, wailing in panic and trying to hold it back.

"Yours now! For you! Not mine! I go!"

In theory, the demon would fear the bag and wave her through. Unfortunately, the creature hopped up onto the desk and pointed at the portable hole, sensing something alarming inside and apparently demanding an explanation. Escalla screamed and ran out of patience a split second before the demon.

"Tedious conversation anyway." Escalla hit the creature with her lich staff, slinging it across the desk to crash into a pile of papers, and turned into her beautiful faerie self. "Hey, uglies! See this faerie butt? Silken pure!" She whirred backward, dashing off into the mists. "Lolth sucks rocks! Lolth sucks rocks!"

There was a roar of rage. A female voice screamed, and there was a hissing of snakes. Drow yelled at one another, armored feet tramping as they poured from their guardrooms. Escalla fled on foot, theatrically dragging one leg and wing behind her. The snakes hissed a foot or two behind her, and then Escalla laughed and broke into a run.

Another alcove opened up in the wall. Escalla dodged into it, finding a short corridor that took a sharp turn to the right. The maddened hiss of vipers followed, and shadows on the walls showed a woman with hair made from a writhing mass of snakes pelting behind Escalla, followed by a dozen angry drow.

Escalla fired her frost wand at the wall ahead then dived, hitting the wall and running madly around the bend. She screeched to a halt as a sound of crashing stone and breaking glass filled the corridor.

The wall at the corner shed a last few jagged shards of ice, the sheets crashing down onto a pile of broken stone at the foot of the wall. The medusa had been confronted with a wall of reflective ice, and her gaze had totalled the entire guard contingent. They had turned to stone, hit the wall, and broken like a pile of garden gnomes. Escalla flew over the wreckage, spotted one drow still alive and unparalyzed, and bopped it unconscious with a single blow of her staff.

From inside the portable hole, Jus's voice whispered in panic, "Escalla, what happened?"

"Ha! The inevitable happened!" Escalla blew a wisp of frost from the tip of her wand. "The faerie is dealing with inferior mentalities! Now come out of that hole! We're at Lolth's back door."

The faerie threw the portable hole down on the ground. Escalla posed happily over the broken statues as her friends dazedly emerged.

"Hey, look! Wreck of the Medusa!" Escalla spied some gems gleaming about the rubble pile. "Hoopy! All this fun and cash, too!"

Annoyed, the Justicar looked over the scene. "Escalla!"

"Hey! She has some nice stuff here, and we're out of treasure!" The girl found a necklace of amber. "Ooo! Hey, Enid! Catch! This ought to pick up the color of your eyes!" The faerie coiled close into Enid's hair as she fastened the necklace about her friend. "You know a girl has to look her best."

"Best?" Enid flicked a glance at Henry and blushed pink. "Why?"

"No special reason." Fluttering upward, Escalla led the way to Lolth's back door. "All right! Tour leading to the Demonweb Pits, now departing!"

The Justicar seethed with ill humor. He kicked shards of petrified drow out of his way and pursued Escalla up the corridor.

"You promised you were just going to cross the river."

"We're across the river! Hey! Riverbanks can be kind of vague! I mean, what's a riverbank, anyway? Is it where the river stops? Is it where the river once dried? Wetlands, water meadows . . ."

"Escalla!"

"Hey! We're here! Trust your favorite faerie." Escalla inspected the petrified demon and stored it in the portable hole for later use as a garden ornament. "We can sneak in here. I did good!"

The Justicar looked at Henry as Polk bustled happily past them for the door.

"This is the way it's done, son! Direct, forthright, to the point!"

"Polk, shut up. Don't touch the door. It probably has an alarm spell or a trap on it." The Justicar carefully inspected the little demon's desk. "Everyone look around carefully. Watch for traps. There might be a key or a password somewhere."

"What about this?" Enid laid her face sideways on the ground, where she could take a closer look at a silver sphere the size of a lemon that had fallen off the desk. "Is this a key?"

"Oh! Is it valuable?" Escalla shot over to Enid like a lightning bolt. "Is it a pearl? A giant pearl?"

"No. I think it looks more like a spider egg." Enid batted the object with one paw, and it broke. "Oh, dear."

The sphere had been hollow, and it contained a collection of little objects: a tiny iron pyramid, a silver ball, a little bronze star, and a pale blue crystal. The Justicar took possession of them before Escalla could take one and break it.

"Keys or identity passes." The green door itself was horrible to look upon. The metal seemed to have been pressed out of tortured, screaming faces. "No one touch the door. Polk, do *not* touch the door! Polk!"

Polk touched the door. The badger simply butted his head against it to push it open. The door instantly glowed a blazing, hellish green, and three bolts of energy shot silently along the corridor. Jus and Enid ducked. Escalla looked up with interest. Having managed to miss the entire group, the energy bolts faded, and the door was open.

Polk looked back at Jus in irritation and gave a superior little waddle of his feet.

"Son, what are you doing lookin' for clues down there? The adventure's this way, son! This way! You're addled, son." The badger walked through the door. "Got to sharpen up your game. Fate keeps pitchin', and you keeps missin'!"

Through the door came a deep silver mist. Stinking and sour, it was as impenetrable as quicksilver. The Justicar unsheathed his sword and moved carefully for the door as Cinders searched the mist. With Escalla at his side, Enid behind, and Henry covering the rear, the Justicar edged into the Demonweb.

*　*　*　*　*

At the edge of the River Lethe, amidst the surge and roar of the titanic waterfall, a shape stood over a butchered body. Golden armor and an eagle helm flaked shards of rust, torn across the chest to show the ragged wound where a living heart once had been. A human hand ended one arm, and the undead monster stooped to sever the foot from a dead, bleeding denizen of the Abyss. The living cadaver held the foot against the stump of its ankle. Tendrils of flesh bound the new foot in place. Able to walk once more, the snarling corpse looked through the soot of the Abyss toward the titanic spider webs beyond.

Behind Recca lay a hissing raft of vipers. Recca stared across the howling Abyss, turned his back upon the river Lethe, and walked onward, hunting for his prey. . . .

17

They stood upon a pathway of slick, polished stone suspended in the middle of a yawning, empty gulf. The path was wide, flat, without walls or ceiling, like a bridge through an abyss of fog.

Faces distorted in pain and terror formed and vanished in the mists before being torn apart by violent winds that never seemed to stir the air. Inside the stone surface of the path, flattened figures scratched and pleaded. Escalla looked about, a little crestfallen, and pulled on her chain mail.

"Oh, this is *so* un-hoopy." The girl winced and shifted her feet. "Jus, I think I'm treading on someone's soul."

*Only the soul of a sinner.* Benelux gave a prim little shimmer of disdain. *Go ahead, dear. Scuff your feet. The blighter deserved it.*

"Spiky, go stick your head up a rust monster's bum." Escalla decided to solve the problem with flight, and her wings whirred into action.

Staring about the mists, Henry jerked his crossbow left to right, covering shapes that screamed and swirled.

"What is this place?" asked the young soldier.

"The Demonweb." Of them all, only the Justicar seemed undisturbed. He scanned the pathway, looking for tracks. "This is the antechamber to Lolth's home plane."

Henry looked around and slowly stood straight. "So where's the spider palace?"

"Looked like it went above us." The Justicar rested a hand upon Henry's shoulder and pointed overhead. "Somewhere up there."

"Can we fly up and see?"

Still whirring her wings but still very much on the ground, Escalla's face had gone red. She flapped with all her might, the rising whine of her wings drawing the party's attention one by one. The faerie jumped madly up into the air, and still she failed to get aloft.

Enid carefully scratched her ear with one hind paw. "Oh, dear. There may be a few technical difficulties with that plan."

Escalla leaped and jumped, rapidly losing her temper. "Fly! Come on, damn it! Fly!"

"Escalla?" Jus finally solved the problem by grabbing the angry faerie by the scruff of her clothes. "Escalla! Stop. This is Lolth's plane. Laws are different here."

"Laws!" Escalla kicked and struggled. "I hate laws! Law represses freedom, and loss of freedom is tyranny!"

"*Physical* laws, Escalla. Like gravity."

"You mean we have to *walk* while we're in here?" Escalla allowed herself to be put on Jus's shoulder. "That is so un-hoopy! People will think I'm a brownie or something."

"Not with a backside like that. Perfect lift and pinch." The Justicar studied the mists that surrounded the path. "On top of the spider palace, none of you could fly. The same laws must have applied."

Enid blinked. "Oh, meaning we're supposed to walk along these paths?"

"Meaning the paths are a guardian maze." Shrugging, the Justicar looked around. "This is the way Lolth guards her door."

The Justicar and Cinders took point, with Escalla sitting on Jus's shoulder, her frost wand cradled on her knees. Enid, Polk, and Henry came behind. They moved silently, while all around them, lost souls screamed inside a universe of fog.

Footfalls had an unnatural silence. There were no walls to throw back echoes, no stones to shift and rattle. Enid's big soft paws, the Justicar's careful tread, Henry's boots, and Escalla's feet—none made more than the slightest sound upon the horrible pavement. The floor with its images of screaming faces and clawing hands throbbed as warm as flesh.

The path turned at sharp ninety-degree angles—turning, then turning again. Escalla edged as close as she dared to the brink of the path and looked down. Below her through the mist, she could dimly see another path identical to the one she trod.

"Hey! Look!"

They all looked down and traced the shape of another path that ran at right angles to them forty feet below. It was almost invisible in the horrible, haunted mist. Escalla looked carefully about, her sharp eyes spying other shapes in the mist up above. There was a maze of paths above and below, locked together like pieces of a puzzle.

"The palace was headed for the top of the web. Should we try and climb up?"

"Don't put temptation in front of the boy." Polk sat on his haunches like a mouse, unable to see more than a few feet into the mist. "We have to do the maze. Defeat the guardians! We can't complete the adventure without killin' all the guardians."

"Polk, shut up." The Justicar looked up through the mists, judging their jerk and flow. "How do we get up there?"

Escalla rubbed her hands together in glee. "We have the tangle rope! The one Jus got from the erinyes!"

"Too short." Cinders had burned through that rope in a fight long, long ago. It was now only twelve feet long and hung from the Justicar's sword belt. "And there are ghosts in the mist."

They turned and surveyed the horrible shapes in the mist. By unanimous consent they all moved on, looking for the stairs and ladders they all felt sure must be there.

The long, quiet walk went on—turn after turn, yard after yard. Walking softly at their head, the Justicar suddenly sank to his knees in silence, and the entire group froze in response.

"Henry."

Around the next corner, dimly seen through the mist, four horrible shapes pattered along the path. They were whip scorpions the size of wolfhounds. Henry looked, knelt, and fired in one smooth action. His crossbow shuddered and threw out a stream of bolts from its magazine. Two scorpions staggered sideways, already curling as the poisoned darts struck home. The remaining two lifted their claws high like dogs locking the scent, and they raced straight at the party. Enid and Jus surged forward, but a swarm of golden darts shaped like bees streaked through the air, smashing chitin and blowing holes through the scorpions. The creatures staggered and died as a second strike blasted them off their feet.

Escalla stood, her spell finger trailing a wisp of magic. The girl blew it away and gave a little shrug.

"Henry and I will clean up the little stuff on the way." The faerie used Cinders's tail as a handhold as she scaled the Justicar. "Jus's stoneskin will only block a few hits. We want to save it for when he fights Lolth."

The scorpions all wore silver bands about their tails. They had moved in unison, like a purposeful patrol. The party gave their bodies a wide berth, mistrusting the way the monsters twitched and oozed.

The pathway led on. There were more turns, more twists, until finally the way fed into a junction. A door gleamed in the mist— a door that seemed to lead to nowhere. Jus pointed, and the party fanned out. Enid and Henry watched the other pathways while Jus, Cinders, and Escalla moved carefully to the door.

The door simply hung in space, its bottom joined to the pathway, and its rear opening onto empty fog. Escalla peered behind it, shrugged, then cracked her knuckles. A careful search for traps, the approval of Cinders, and Escalla listened at the door with one pointy ear. She crept back to the others, her voice a sly little whisper.

"There's a room behind the door. I hear big things moving and arguing."

The Justicar nodded. "Cinders?"

The hell hound's nose wrinkled as Cinders was allowed to sniff at the crack beneath the door. Big fangs gleamed, and the dog wagged his tail.

*Stinky trolls!*

Escalla happily wagged her wings. "Oh! Hoopy!

"Guards!" Polk was overjoyed. He opened a tiny notebook stuck through his belt and began jotting notes into his endless chronicles. "We're in luck, son! Killing guards is heroic! Blade to blade! Man to man! Pure heroism against the cunning of evil!"

The rest of the party ignored him. Escalla leaned against the doorjamb, molded magic between her hands, and nodded. Jus kicked open the door, and Escalla gleefully launched a fireball into the space beyond. Everyone dived aside, leaving Polk blinking until Jus grabbed him by the fur and yanked him to safety.

The fireball exploded, billowing flame across the path. Chunks of debris hurtled out the door, across the path, and were snatched by the fog. The Justicar jumped up. Henry stood in front of the door and drew his sword. As a burned, raging troll came lunging through the portal, the Justicar's white sword sheared its head from its trunk. Benelux whipped blindingly fast into the stomach of a second troll. The big man kicked his victims back into the room and followed, his blade severing an arm from another troll, all in a single blur.

Damaged trolls and severed troll parts began to grow and regenerate. The Justicar swept his gaze across the room, then parried a troll claw with his forearm before burying his sword in a monster's skull.

"Cinders!"

The flame crashed like a wave across the trolls. The monsters screamed, reared, and writhed as they died. The hell hound gave a feral growl of pleasure as the trolls burned to a crisp. Jus flicked Benelux clean and sheathed her all in one silky, fluid move, rising from fighting stance to turn his back upon the room.

Escalla was holding the slowglass gem up to her eye, recording the moment.

"Got it!" The girl popped the gem back into her cleavage and then looked at the burning, ruined room with a sigh. "Gods I love it when you go all homicidal!"

Escalla looked back along the path outside while Jus tore the burned hide from the corpses of trolls. Enid carefully smudged her feet in soot and walked out into the passage with Henry at her side.

Escalla went suddenly stiff, and her antennae lifted high, quivering with alarm. She froze, as if listening, then said, "Jus, he's back there. Recca. Coming fast."

"He heard the fight with the scorpions." Jus shook out scorched pieces of troll hide. "Stun scroll?"

"Oh, I don't think it works on undead." Enid frowned. "Sorry."

"No matter. Get moving. Polk, go with them." Moving through the smoke, the Justicar trailed scraps of troll hide in his hand. The room was filled with vile smoke. "Get to your places. Move!"

\* \* \* \* \*

The door hung open, burn marks fanning out across the path. A charred troll's head lay upside down and forlorn. The Demonweb seemed alone with its fog, ghosts, and eerie winds.

Until a movement flickered on the path.

He came fast, running with a tireless stride—feral and horrible. A rusted eagle helm kept its beak open in an eternal scream. Dead eyes searched ceaselessly for hints of prey.

The scent of burned flesh made the creature slow. Recca's sword swept out. The black blood inside his blade gleamed and seethed. Sidestepping the dead scorpions, Recca crept to the junction, his skull turning to look carefully up and down the way.

A shattered door into nothingness hung open before him. Burn marks, charred troll bodies, smoke, and stink leaked onto the path. Sphinx footprints and a single set of boot marks led off along the path. Recca sniffed the air and looked at the room behind the door.

He dived through the door in a somersault, arcing high into the air, blade blurring as he spun. He landed with his blade on guard but shifted rapidly. He ran his blade through three troll corpses, viciously twisting the blade. No blood spurted. The Justicar was not hiding beneath a cunning shroud of charred dead flesh. The monster turned, dead eyes gleaming. Moving with supreme caution, Recca walked back through the open door.

The blow, when it came, almost cut him in two. Recca twisted with serpentine speed, blocking with his sword, and the white blade only managed to hack halfway through his waist. Recca tore free, spilling onto the path, his flesh burning and smoking where Benelux had cut.

The Justicar stood beside the door. He had hung beneath the pavement, suspended above the howling fog, his hands hidden by a scrap of troll hide as Recca passed overhead. Now he strode toward the staggering monster, his blade snapping back, ready to thrust. Recca's wound smoldered, and this time the Justicar saw what happened. Green blood pumped into the open wound, flashed, and sealed the dead flesh shut. An instant later, the wound was gone.

The Justicar assessed Recca's tools. He shifted fighting stance,

saw the move countered, shifted his weight, and saw the respond-
ing twitch of stance. Recca was active, responsive. Alive. The Justicar watched him over the point of his own blade.

"You're in there, Recca. . . ."

Escalla and the others were still waiting for Recca to reach the
perfect position. The Justicar changed fighting stance, choosing
movements learned in a hundred fights, skills picked up far, far
away from Recca and his schooling. He watched the animated
corpse respond. The Justicar remembered being awed, shamed,
and in worship of this man, remembered the scorn the elf had
poured over his human student.

If he were jealous, why had Recca taught him if he knew the
student would someday equal the master? Perhaps because the student was never expected to match Recca in skill? Had Recca seen
him as a threat rather than a triumph?

The Justicar moved slowly and carefully, circling the undead
master. Recca moved away slowly, always keeping just out of
range. He danced with the same old skill and speed, using the
moves he had been so unspeakably proud of.

They were too close for Escalla to risk a spell, and Henry and
Enid knew better than to try to fight Recca hand-to-hand. Coax-
ing Recca into position, the Justicar adjusted his blade.

"The tanar'ri tore your heart out, but I killed it." The big
ranger was dark with anger. "Jealousy, Recca?"

The corpse hissed like a cobra, fangs wide. The Justicar could
feel the hate. It was a weakness. Recca fought for pride. Pride was
a weakness. Justice was balanced and controlled. The Justicar
could beat this thing, this swordmaster. He felt the certainty of it
as if it were cast in bronze.

The Justicar let his point drift a mere tenth of an inch and
growled at his enemy. "You lost, Recca. You lost because you never
had a *code*."

He had given Recca an opening. Recca screamed and cut. The

corpse's attack came exactly as Jus knew it would—timed and planned. This time Jus took the blow on the flat of his blade, doubling Benelux like a quarterstaff. The blades met, and the Justicar punched with his hilt, the blow shattering Recca's jaw and sending the cadaver sprawling back along the path.

The broken jaw clicked and healed as Recca flipped onto his feet and came at the Justicar behind a whirling web of steel.

They fought hard and fast, the swords smashing sparks from one another in a maddened dance. An instant after the swords met and crashed, Recca tumbled and leaped over the Justicar to attack from behind. He landed, sword poised, the Justicar only half way through a turn, and then a blast of frost crashed into him from the side. The magic dissipated, blocked by the aura of his magic sword.

"Hey, boney!" The troll's head stood on two shapely little legs, and a frost wand waved from one ear. "Hey! Remember me?"

Recca wiped frost from his face. From around the corner, Henry appeared, taking aim with his crossbow. Recca flicked up his sword, caught the first two crossbow bolts on his blade, and had three more smash into his chest. The impact knocked Recca over the edge of the path, and he fell into the howling mist. Rushing to the brink, Escalla and Jus looked out to see Recca carried up into the fog storm before smashing into a pathway overhead and disappearing from view.

Escalla shed her hollowed-out troll's head and cursed. "Damn it! You were doing it! You were getting on top of him! That was our best shot at snuffing him!"

"He'll find us again." The Justicar flicked his blade clean. He felt heavy, tired, and burdened. "Next time."

"Hey, Jus?" Escalla clung to his knee and looked up in concern. "Hey, come on! It's just a monster with a sword. We can outdo him!"

The Justicar sheathed Benelux. Recca was alive and revealing the hatred Jus had always pretended wasn't there. Escalla held Jus's hand and looked into his face.

"We did better this time."

"He's brilliant." The Justicar felt Recca's hate still lingering in the air. "He's as good as he always was."

"Yeah, but you're better."

Suddenly Jus could see it. He could feel the change between himself and Recca.

"Recca is too proud to change." The big ranger turned to look up into the mist. "Yes. For three hundred years, he was sword-master and a chief of the Grass Runners. He wants his victory to prove his perfection."

Jus glanced at the pathway overhead, then turned away, his hand gripping the hilt of his sword. His other hand took Escalla's, and they walked back to their friends.

Henry spared a hard glance for the overhead fog, then peered briefly into the troll-littered room as he passed. He gave a sudden frown and held up one hand.

"Justicar, sir? Look at this!"

A neat white folder lay in the middle of the ash. The group stared at it in puzzlement. Cinders gave a sniff, paused, sniffed again, then his grin brightened.

*Girlie girl smell!*

"Girl?" Escalla sniffed, almost choking on smoke and carbonized troll. "What? Like a little girl?"

*Big girl. Nice skin!*

"There speaks the connoisseur." Escalla crept toward the folder then stroked her lich staff. It grew to the size of a broomstick. "All right, people! Let a professional handle this! Heads down!"

Enid hid outside the door. "Escalla? Do you really think you should touch it?"

"Sure we should! Hey! This is my professional opinion!" The faerie displayed her tiny skirt. "So just duck and let me do my job!"

Everyone dived for cover as Escalla flipped the folder open with her staff. No spells discharged. No poisoned needles shot out. No trap doors opened or monsters appeared. Emerging cautiously from cover, the party gathered to find Escalla holding the folder and shaking it in disappointment, as though hoping some gold and jewels might fall out.

"Hey! I think it's a map!" She tossed the folder at Jus. "All right! I solved the dungeon. Here! Find me Lolth, or I'll let Cinders lick you!"

*Yuck.*

Escalla leaned on the hell hound and whispered, "Don't knock it till you've tried it." She leaped onto Jus's back. "Well, am I hot or am I hot?"

"You're hot." The Justicar looked at the open folder. It showed a maze of interlocking lines that seemed to be the pathways in the fog. Someone had even thoughtfully penciled in neat marks to show their initial point of entry, a dot to mark the trolls' room, and a big red X at a far point of the maze. Other places were marked with discrete red numbers—two "ones," two "twos," and two "threes." Each one was marked with a "travel" rune. Traps? Ladders? Stairs?

The map was a godsend. Too much of a godsend. It had appeared as if by magic. It all smacked of an elaborate trap. The Justicar weighed the implications in his mind then cast a careful search over the room.

The ash had been disturbed. Marks lay in long strokes—diagonally parallel. The Justicar rubbed ash between his finger and thumb.

Henry squatted at his side. "Drag marks, sir?"

"Snake. A big snake." Jus showed his student how to tell the marks by shape and distance. The ash had been compacted quite hard, which meant the snake weighed at least as much as a man. "Lolth's handmaiden."

Demons could teleport. That would explain how she entered the room even while the party fought outside its door. A layer of airborne ash had not yet settled on the folder's cover. She must have left the folder only seconds before Henry peered into the room.

Henry scratched the thin stubble of his newly sprouting beard and asked, "Why would Lolth's handmaiden give us a map?"

"If Lolth knew we were here, I would expect crueler traps than these." The Justicar breathed slow and hard. He took a piece of charred troll and passed it up to Cinders, who ate it with noisy glee. "We'll use the map, but we'll be careful." The big man put a finger on Henry's shoulder. "Very, very careful."

✳    ✳    ✳    ✳    ✳

"Morag! We have rats! Nasty, furry little rats!"

Recharging her magic, Lolth lolled with her feet in a bath filled with the blood of a few hapless sacrifices. She had been idly planning her conquests, making slaves plant pins on her maps of the Flanaess when Morag arrived in the throne room.

Her long lashes tilting in elegant surprise, Morag poised in the door. "Magnificence?"

"Intruders, Morag. In the Demonweb. I sense something *different* in my home."

Morag bowed gravely. "Escapees from the prison levels, Magnificence?"

"Perhaps." Lolth carefully watched her secretary. "Morag. I do hope we have had no little break-ins from outside."

Morag spoke carefully, knowing that she played for very, very high stakes. One slip, and Lolth would command her to pull her own intestines out—slowly—yard by yard.

"Magnificence, the guards at the gates have reported no trouble."

"Have they not?"

Lolth's voice, sly and acidic, dripped with irony. She shot a sidewise glance at Morag.

"Morag, how long have you been with me?"

"One hundred and one years, three months, three days, six hours, and twenty-seven minutes, Magnificence."

"Ah. Leaving eight hundred and ninety-eight years, nine months, twenty-seven-odd days, seventeen hours and thirty-three minutes until our little arrangement comes into review." Lolth paddled her feet, lounging back in her throne. "I do so hope it is a *good* review, Morag."

Morag rippled her long tail. "I'm sure everything will be properly dealt with, Magnificence." Her swords clattered as she shifted her weight. "Our reentry to the pits has been normal. All guard posts were changed immediately after we docked. I have unleashed a hundred extra spiders into the Demonweb." Morag flourished an order for Lolth to sign. "Here are the hatchery reports from the spider pits. Here is the oath of allegiance from the Ixitxachitl of the Flanaess's inland sea. And here is an execution order for that priestess you thought had bigger breasts than you."

"Oh, just polymorph her into something nasty for an afternoon." Lolth signed, already bored with the procedures.

"Yes, Magnificence."

"I shall be refreshed in about ten hours, Morag, so have the stokers raise a head of steam, and get my dinner. Oh, and nothing *living*, this time! Not if it can speak. I don't want my appetite spoiled by another idiot trying to give me three wishes if I let him go free."

Morag bowed, her six arms spreading in obeisance, then she slithered back out of the room. Lolth sniffed a vague scent of soot upon the air, scowled, and then went back to her plans for conquest and slaughter.

18

The adventurers squatted at a bend in the path as Jus, Polk, and Henry puzzled over the new map. Letting the boys pretend to navigate, Escalla amused herself with a spider leg, tossing it off the path.

"Hey, Cinders! Fetch!"

The leg bounced. Cinders lay beside her, thump-thump-thumping his tail. Escalla gave an unhappy sigh and collected the spider leg for later.

"Are you really trying, or what?"

*Cinders trying. Stick moves too fast.*

"Oh, all right! I'll try to roll it slower or something. Maybe we should make it smell of coal?" Escalla looked over at her friends. "Have you guys figured out what that map means yet?"

"I think these paths are all different levels. The levels never seem to link. No one level is entirely below or above any other—all except for this top level here, where the red X is marked." The Justicar looked down a pathway and scowled. "So there's no way to communicate between levels, unless that's what's been marked here in pencil. The paired numbers on the map might be link points."

Henry scratched underneath his helmet. "Can we be sure?"

"They're the only things marked on the map at all." The Justicar looked down at the tortured tangle of lines marked on the map. "The first number marked is over that way. Past another door and to the left."

Enid came and settled on her haunches beside Escalla. The big sphinx folded up her paws and lowered her voice so that only the faerie could hear her. "That undead ranger is unpleasant. I hope the Justicar can find him soon."

"Yeah. Well, we'll get him. Jus just has a little problem with him."

"You mean he's holding back?"

"No. But he's pretty miffed."

"Oh." Enid thoughtfully kneaded the path with her big claws. "I wonder where your sister is? She's been remarkably quiet."

"Oh, she's a *lady*. She won't work unless she *has* to." Escalla snorted and threw Cinders's spider leg once more. "If I know her, she'll sit there glued to her crystal ball, waiting for my scrying shield to fade."

"She won't come hunting for us here?"

"You don't get as plush as *that* girl by walking the wilderness and camping under trees. Nah. She'll use magic to look for us. She's probably still back in her cave."

Cinders was wagging his tail more happily. Jus returned and picked the hell hound up, smiling fondly as he dusted the dog's pelt clean of ash and troll. He swept Cinders back into place across his back, then lifted Escalla onto Enid's back, where the faerie could ride comfortably upon her friend.

A distant glimpse of a path far below showed a horrible pack of giant spiders skittering along the roadway. The adventurers kept back from the edges and speeded their pace, passing by doors and side paths as they followed the map for turn after turn, path after path. Finally the Justicar held up his hand as the road led up to another floating door.

Escalla slithered down from Enid's back and peeled off her long gloves. She kept her voice a whisper as she handed her wand and staff to her friends. "Stay here. Henry, turn around! Mama's going natural again!"

Henry blushed and turned around. The faerie shucked her fine black mail, tossed it to the Justicar, and changed herself into a flat-worm. She slithered her front portion carefully under the bottom of the door, remained half in and half out of the room for a long, silent minute, then stealthily withdrew. She converted back into her usual form and motioned her friends to gather a few yards away from the door. When she spoke, she spoke in a careful whisper.

"All right. There's four demons in there. Big vulture guys!" The girl scanned carefully, staying quiet and unhurried. "The floor's covered in broken skeletons—all busted up, legs broken and stuff. The demons are in the corners on pillars about a hundred feet high, all facing the center of the room and just sitting there. They must be guarding something!"

"Four demons?" The Justicar kept careful watch on the paths and mist. "Real demons are important. Lolth and Iuz use them to control whole regiments. If there's four demons there, then it's an important room."

"Should we try to take them?"

"Yes."

It seemed easier said than done. Escalla picked her teeth and tried to come up with an idea. Henry looked nervously about his circle of friends.

"Vulture shaped?" Henry was all at sea. "Are they dangerous?"

The Justicar said nothing. Escalla took it on herself to answer.

"You bet your pearly white buns!" She kept her voice in a care-ful whisper. "Tanar'ri are about as bad as it can get. Pretty much immune to magic, tough as iron, dirty as a roach, and just plain nasty. All sorts of powers. You know—teleporting, making dark-ness, telekinesis . . . If we take them out, it has to be *fast!* Real fast. We can't let them teleport out and raise the alarm."

Enid brightened. "I could try to coax them out with a riddle!"

"They're demons, hon." Escalla shrugged. "They get their jol-lies from other things."

"Oh." The sphinx folded up her paws and frowned.

The Justicar took a piece of charcoal saved for Cinders's dinner and made a sketch of the room upon the floor.

"Escalla? Are there enough skeletons to interfere with footing?"

"Not too thick. I dunno—maybe a dozen dead guys."

"The bones on the floor are all broken?" The Justicar took on a meaningful look. "Like they've been dropped from a height?"

Escalla sat back, looking displeased. "Telekinesis! These guys can lift weights with their minds. Crap!" The girl explained Jus's point to Henry. "That's the trap! *Telekinesis.* They use mind power to lift you up a hundred feet, then drop you to the floor. Simple."

Henry looked at the rough sketch of the room and blanched. "So how do we kill them, and do it fast? They're a hundred feet above us!"

Still naked but supremely confident, Escalla spread her arms and said, "Oh, tanar'ri? You want to see how I handle tanar'ri? Insanely bloodthirsty, outnumber me four to one, outweigh me by three hundred pounds. Watch this! A great mind is at work beneath the pretty face."

The Justicar sensed a stupid stunt about to happen. He leaped forward to stop her, but it was too late. Everyone scattered madly aside as the faerie danced over to the door and raucously knocked on the demons' door.

"Hey, you! Hello in there! Anyone here order a two-foot-tall goddess in a thong? Yoo-hoo! I'm too short to reach the handle! Open up!"

The door gave a click and swung open as if by magic—or as if by telekinesis. Escalla shoved it wide open and gave a happy cry. She fired a lightning bolt high into the ceiling of the chamber, blowing apart a ledge that a vulture demon was standing upon. The creature fell, and Escalla whooped as the tanar'ri spread its wings. She dashed into the room and fired a spell up into the ceiling, which immediately became clogged with a pretty pink fog that smelled of strawberry flowers. Outraged, all four tanar'ri howled in anger.

Escalla turned herself into a huge limpet and stuck herself fast to the floor. A mouth tube stuck out from one side and showered abuse on the demons above.

"Hey, vulture boys! Do you guys fight as bad as you smell? You call that telekinesis? Come on! Put your frontal lobes into it! Pull! Pull!"

Escalla the limpet was having the time of her life.

The tanar'ri abandoned all pretense at rational planning. Berserk with rage they fell on the limpet with their claws, pounding at its thick shell and trying to wrench it from the floor. Huge, stinking, with vulture heads and verminous bodies, the demons screamed in rage.

"Is that all you've got? Hey, you! The one with the beak! Yeah, I'm talking to you!"

The savage ring of Benelux smashing through tanar'ri flesh was pure music to Escalla's ears. She grew an eyestalk and watched as one vulture monster staggered, the white blade protruding from its shoulder and into its chest. A kick of Jus's boot freed his blade. A second blow, then a third smacked into the tanar'ri and killed it.

Henry's crossbow hammered five darts into a demon's side. The monster spun, leaped to attack, and tripped as Enid pounced on it from behind.

The melee spread, Jus furiously defending himself from a vulture's talons with his sword. Henry whip-cracked the Justicar's magic rope and sent a tanar'ri spinning to the ground, choking to death.

Escalla whistled, turned back to her usual form, and dashed outside for her clothes. She fetched her lich staff, pelted up behind a tanar'ri, and took its leg off with a single well-placed blow. Demon claws ripped empty air as Escalla made a fantastic handspring onto a tanar'ri's back and smote the monster upon its skull while Polk bit it in the rear. The last of the creatures staggered as Enid ripped it apart like a cat shredding a chair. Feathers flew, then Henry drove his sword into the last monster's chest.

The party had a mass of wounds and scratches, but nothing too severe. The Justicar issued his healing spells, while Escalla dusted off her hands.

"A-a-and that's how we do it in the bad side of the faerie forest!"

Panting, wounded, and a little dazed, Henry leaned upon his sword and said, "Wow! You . . . fought tanar'ri . . . before?"

"Who, me? Nah! I'm daddy's little angel." Escalla shrugged. "But you should have seen me in pillow fights!" The girl picked up her slowglass gem and scanned it about the room. "All right! Here we are in tanar'ri central, our heroes standing triumphant above piles of four vulture things!"

The Justicar scowled. "Will you stop doing that?"

"Hey! These are precious memories! In two weeks' time we can watch all this and laugh!"

The Justicar cleared his throat and murmured in Escalla's ear. "Most of what we see will be a view down your cleavage."

"Oh, yeah." The girl looked down at her bosom. "Well, we can put a bag over Henry's head at those points. All right! Let's look for treasure!"

The promised cache never came. The tiny iron pyramid they'd found outside Lolth's gates rose up out of Jus's purse. It twirled, flared with light for a moment, and disappeared.

With a blink, the dead tanar'ri, skeletons, and blood were gone, leaving the adventurers standing in a blank stretch of open path. Mists swirled. Ghosts moaned.

Fastidiously washing her paws, Enid sat on her haunches and looked around. "Oh, I say! That was jolly well done. I do so dislike stairs."

Wide-eyed, Escalla looked around. "Hey! My treasure!"

"Do vultures keep treasure?" Enid blew vulture fluff from her nose. "I thought they mostly liked decaying bits of bone?"

"Maybe they had gold fillings or something! This is an adventure, damn it! I demand financial rewards for acts of homicide!"

The Justicar sheathed his sword and knelt to examine their map. He pointed at two bends in the corridor and tapped the markings penciled down in red.

"We're here on the map. This corridor junction is a match. We just climbed up one level of the maze." The big man flipped the map into a strip and put it through his belt. "We were given an accurate tool."

He moved away to stare down the paths. Behind him, Polk looked up from his notebooks with a quill pen quivering in his paw.

"Wait, son! How do you spell 'lissome'?"

"E-S-C-A-L-L-A." Dressing, the faerie leaned helpfully over Polk's notebook. "And those things in my bottom are called dimples, not divets."

"Oh!" Polk crossed out a few words. "That's all right. That's fine! As long as the gist of it's there! I can get the prose really purple when I edit it after the adventure!"

The badger kept writing. Enid picked him up with her teeth and carried him down the corridor. They were deep into the Demonweb, and Polk still had half an empty notebook to go.

**19**

They walked onward through half an hour of silent footfalls and sobbing ghosts. The only food they had was a few preserved fish, which they washed down with canteens of lukewarm river water. Time was of the essence. Lolth had to be caught before she could return to the Flanaess.

And so the party ambled on, eating as they went.

The food was not to Escalla's liking. Dressed in her skin tight, silky smooth, and strangely see-through clothes of black elven chain mail, she glittered like a fish as she lolled on Enid's furry back. The occasional sparkle of pixie dust drifted from her as she flicked her wings.

Escalla had decided to bolster the party's morale with a riddle game—a game at which Enid always did well. The sphinx had an endless memory for facts and figures, rhyme and poem, as well as a huge library of scrolls sealed in a watertight box inside the portable hole. Wagging her foot in thought, her slim arms behind her back, Escalla chewed her bottom lip and tried to concoct a rhyme.

"All right, um . . . here!" The faerie composed on the fly.

"Restless snake, ever stirring
  Never hissing—too much purring
  Proud e'en though it always bows.
  Sweeping paths where e'er it goes."

With an arch look over her shoulder, Enid smiled. "Simple. It's my tail."

"Drat! One guess gets you three questions." Escalla lounged happily upon her friend's warm fur. "Fire away!"

Velvet soft, golden brown, and girlishly sly, Enid cast a blushing glance at the Justicar and Henry up ahead. She motioned to Escalla, who came over and hung down so that Enid could whisper in her ear. Escalla stayed hanging over her friend's shoulder, then scratched her chin when the sphinx had finished.

"Hmm. That would be 'ten,' 'I doubt it' . . . and bipeds don't bite necks, dear. Not unless you ask them nicely."

"Oh!" Enid again shot a furtive glance at Henry. "Not even a little?"

"Well, there have been cases."

"Oh, good." Enid nestled closer. "And does he really have dimples in his bottom?"

The faerie shot up in glee. "Yeah! And it's all furry right down where——"

"Escalla!" Enid turned red.

"Well it is!" The faerie sprawled over Enid's back "Is Henry's?"

"No! It's really perfectly . . ." The sphinx blushed a most remarkable pink and caught herself mid-sentence. "Um, no, not that I'm aware."

"Uh-huh."

Escalla was enjoying herself. Henry cast wan looks in Enid's direction as they marched, and Enid remained protectively close to Henry.

Escalla lounged back on the sphinx's furry back and continued the riddle game. "Two little birdies in a birdie tree . . ."

*K-I-S-S-I-N-G!*

"Thank you, Cinders!" Lying on her back, Escalla raised one finger to the sky. "You're getting better at this spelling stuff!"

*Cinders clever!*

"So fetch a stick!"

*Cinders not that clever.*

"Wuss!" Escalla levered herself up on one elbow and saw that they were passing by another door. The Justicar glanced at the map and moved on.

Escalla jumped from Enid's back and pointed eagerly at the door. "Hey! What about in here? We didn't look in here!"

"It's not part of the mission." His hand always ready with his sword, his eyes always searching for danger, the Justicar kept the door in one corner of his eye. "We're only interested in doors marked with teleport symbols on the map."

The faerie's face fell, and she instantly turned petulant. "But *Ju-us!* What if there's monsters in here? Ambushers? Evil? What if there's something that's going to follow after us once we've gone?"

"You mean—what if there's something valuable in there you can get your hands on?"

"Sure! That, too!" The faerie lived a life free from guilt. "Hey! Taking from a demon queen isn't stealing! If Lolth's evil, then all her riches will be used for evil! And gold corrupts! This stuff is her tool. So by removing her gold, we're diminishing evil." Escalla rubbed her fist, keen to get cracking. "See? We have an honor-bound duty to rob this bitch blind! It's the only socially responsible course of action!"

The Justicar glowered at her. "Cute."

Persuaded by Escalla's moral argument, Enid regarded the door. "We *do* have a wedding to pay for."

Polk immediately put his pen down. He had been doodling a picture for his chronicles, showing himself beheading a tanar'ri with one bite.

"Come on, son! Where's your sense of right? A hero shows superiority over evil by sappin' it on the head and emptying evil's pockets!"

"Polk, shut up! Leave the door alone." The Justicar waved to his companions, signaling them to move on. "We're running out of time."

Escalla had already bustled over to the door. Polk stretched high, and Escalla used him as a ladder as she peered in through a perfectly ordinary key hole.

"It's empty. Just a big black room."

"So leave it alone." The Justicar sighed in annoyance, turning back to deal with the delay. "Come on!"

"Cool room, though!" Escalla turned the handle, opening the door. She jumped down from Polk and stood in the doorway. "See. There's nothing in here. Just a big flat shiny wall made out of iron."

A loud hum came from the room. Escalla took on a funny look for one brief second, and then she shot into the room and slammed spread-eagled onto the middle of the iron wall. Suspended three feet off the ground, Escalla's eyes bugged out. She tried to move, but her chainmail clothing was stuck fast to the wall.

"Ow! Jus! Jus, get me offa this!"

A roar erupted from the chamber as hidden doors slammed open all around the walls. Dozens of huge bugbears—stinking goblins, eight feet tall—raged into the room. All bore branches and wooden clubs.

Jus and Henry ran into the room. Henry wailed and flew through the air, plastering himself to the iron wall inches from Escalla—his own elven mail stuck tight. Jus's helmet broke its straps and flew through the air. Benelux screeched as she tumbled end over end to crash into the iron wall right beside Escalla's head. The bugbears looked at their trapped victims and gave a scream of joy as they scrambled toward Escalla and Henry with clubs ready to smash and pound.

Jerking like a fly on flypaper, Escalla squealed, "Jus! A little help here!"

The ranger was already on the move. "Enid!"

With Enid beside him, the Justicar flung himself into the room, and ten bugbears rampaged toward them. Jus caught a club bare-handed and spun into the blow, slamming the bugbear to the ground. A savage strike from his elbow broke the teeth of another bugbear behind. Jus caught another blow, then kicked a bugbear with enough force to break the monster's knee. A club crashed against Jus's shoulder, and Escalla's stoneskin spell fended off the blow in a shower of little bees.

Enid pounced into a knot of bugbears. Clubs lashed at her, and she took the head off a bugbear with one huge swipe of her paw.

At the iron wall, Escalla found herself the focus of a dozen charging monsters. She shrieked, turned into a small pink blob, and flowed out of her clothes, which stayed stuck to the wall. Clubs crashed onto the wall, and the blob-faerie rose up, boiling with fury.

"Bastards!"

Bugbears slammed a blow onto Henry's helmet, making the metal ring. An instant later, Escalla trilled a twisted scream, and the ground before Henry boiled with huge black tentacles. The black tentacles lashed out to crush and strangle half a dozen bugbears, shielding Henry from harm. Escalla-the-blob wiped her nonexistent nose and turned back to the fight, just in time to be hit by a club and go ricocheting from the walls like a rubber ball. She landed like a splat of pudding, shook herself in anger, and mottled herself polka-dot in rage.

"That does it!"

Power flashed, and a flaming point of searing heat appeared. Twisting a bugbear's arm and breaking it, the Justicar took one appalled glance and dropped flat beneath Cinders's fireproof hide.

"Enid! Duck!"

The sphinx wailed and leaped over a dozen bugbears, landing

behind Escalla as the blob fired. A fireball flashed into the far side of the room and exploded with apocalyptic force. At the center of the blast, bugbears vaporized. Others flew in smoking chunks through the air. Ecalla-the-blob laughed in maniacal glee, then stared in shock as a wave of heat raced straight toward her.

The force of the explosion bowled her and Enid back into one of the bugbears' alcoves. Still stuck on the wall Henry screamed as the hedge of black tentacles in front of him vaporized. Scorched but alive, the boy opened his eyes and stared in dazed amazement at a room that smoked in total ruin. The only uncharred thing in view was Cinders's gleaming teeth. The dog sniffed the breeze and happily thumped his tail.

*Big bada-boom! Funny!*

"Real funny." The Justicar, scorched around the edges and extremely annoyed, rose from beneath Cinders. He kicked a flaming bugbear out of his way then stuck his head into the alcove where Enid and Escalla staggered.

Enid was totally devoid of fur and feathers, and the tuft of her tail was on fire. Escalla-the-blob was now charred black, her two eyes showing white, dazed shock. The Justicar staggered over to Enid and used his last healing spell to repair her burns and restore her dignity. The big man held Escalla by the scruff of her protoplasm and shook the blob free of soot.

"I am now out of healing spells, and we have no healing potions. You *personally* have done more damage to us than the entire Abyss."

"Just me?" The faerie-blob coughed smoke rings. "H-hoopy! D-did we find any treasure?"

A gem lay on the floor amidst a nest of rags. The Justicar swept it up and shoved it in Escalla's mouth, planting her on the floor. He then returned to Henry and wrenched him free of the magnetized wall. Walking against the vast pull of the magnet, he wrestled Henry outside, then returned to retrieve Escalla's clothing, his helmet, and Benelux.

The magic sword cursed and babbled in absolute outrage. *It won't do, sir! It shall not do! I have never been so humiliated—not since the day that I was forged!*

Struggling to tow the sword out of the room, the Justicar merely growled.

Warming to her tirade, Benelux's voice rose like a matron-martyr. *No, sir, it shall not do! I have been wielded by kings, sir! By demigods! Demigods! By heroes bold!* The sword lacked lungs, and so had no need to pause for breath. *That it should come to this—a victim of mere clumsiness. To be dropped in combat by a chosen warrior . . .*

The Justicar opened his hand, and the sword flew through the air to clang against the magnetized wall. Benelux squawked in shock and pain and then went into a magnificent sulk.

*Very well. We shall acknowledge that there may have been extenuating circumstances just this once.*

Not bothering to answer, the Justicar wrenched the sword off the wall and began towing her back outside.

The sword squawked at her rough handling. *Hmph! I had thought that romance might mellow your attitude toward the social graces.*

"Nope."

*I can see that.*

The party gathered out on the open path, dusting blackened armor, snuffing out flames, and trying to repair their gear. The Justicar—flameproof in his hell hound skin and dragon scales—looked at Escalla with an expectant air.

The faerie had just changed back into her normal form and was contemplating the charred ruins of her underwear. She caught the Justicar's look and instantly went on the defensive.

"Like it was my fault!" The faerie tossed the blue bugbear gem into the portable hole. "Who killed all the bugbears anyway? Me!"

The Justicar simply looked at her, and Escalla squirmed.

"*Fine*. It was my suggestion to go into the room in the first place, but that does not make me actually responsible!"

No answer came, and Escalla wriggled on the hook.

"Oh, man! I thought love meant never having to say you're sorry!" Jerking her clothing on, Escalla fussed with her straps and skirt. "All right. Sorry! But I'm saying it in a sense of regret for mutual misadventure—not in responsibility! What do you want me to say?"

The Justicar retied his helmet's chin strap. " 'Sorry everyone for blowing you up.' "

"Nnnng!" Escalla took it all with extreme ill grace. "Sorry everyone for blowing you up!"

" 'I promise not to blow up my friends for at least another week.' "

"All right already! Don't rub it in!" The girl kicked at a smoking chunk of bugbear. "Damn it! I promise not to blow you all up for another week. Two weeks! There! Are you happy?"

Enid was looking between her hind legs in shock. "What happened to my tail?"

"Nothing!" Escalla busily dusted the sphinx's new-grown fur. "Get your spare clothes out of the portable hole, honey. You're suffering from fallout here. Hey, guys? Great new plan! We open only the doors Jus tells us to—and leave the other ones alone!"

Henry rubbed the lump on his skull and said, "Good plan."

Escalla's underwear and accessories gave up the ghost, falling to earth in a dust of ashes. "Damn it! That was my best silk!"

Cinders grinned in glee. *Funny!*

"Yeah, hilarious." Escalla fed charred underwear to the hell hound. "There! Live it up!" Angry, scorched, and with her clothes smelling of soot, Escalla stamped off along the path. "Lolth had better have some decent treasure! This adventure is playing havoc with my wardrobe." The girl left sooty clouds behind her as she walked "Come on! Let's get into the palace while we still have a sense of style!"

✳    ✳    ✳    ✳    ✳

The paths twisted back on themselves for another half mile. With one eye peering down the long, empty pathway around the next corner, the Justicar checked for marks and signs. The pathway seemed clean and untouched. The only sign of life was a blundering pack of giant spiders that moved steadily away along another road. The Justicar let the spiders go, then waved his friends to follow as he moved out into the path.

Henry stood quietly beside the Justicar, examining the door that hung in space up ahead. It was the next point marked upon the mysterious map.

"No sign of Recca, sir?"

"None." The Justicar nodded to the door ahead. "But these doors are probably guarded. There's no way past the guards without leaving signs of a fight."

"He can't have keys, sir. Not the way we do."

"He knows we're heading for the spider palace. He might find a different route."

Leading the way, the Justicar crept up to the door and inspected it carefully for traps. Escalla cracked her knuckles noisily, approached the door, then changed into a sea slug with eyes upon long stalks. She inserted her eyes through the crack of the door and carefully looked about. Her voice spoke through a breathing tube behind the slug's red mantle.

"All righty! We've got water. Big room, about a hundred feet square. Flooded. Looks like a raised path leads from the door over to some kind of island. And"—the slug snorted—"there are some really bad illusions of two tanar'ri standing on the island. Eww! Those are awful! Is that someone's idea of a decoy? Get real!" Coming from a home where illusion was often preferred over the real, Escalla had high standards for fake reality. "There's nothing on the ceiling. Might be something hiding in the water. No way to tell. Uch, it stinks! Something in here reeks like a lycanthrope's laundry!"

The slug withdrew, slid backward, and changed back into faerie form.

"Sorry. That's all I can see. I don't know what sort of guards it has."

"No. No, that's good." The Justicar squatted on his haunches, drawing a map of the sealed room with a piece of charred bugbear. "The last teleport room was guarded by tanar'ri. If the rooms marked on the map all get you closer to the palace, then they probably all have tanar'ri guards. Tougher and tougher guards as we get closer to Lolth."

Cloaked by her long blonde hair, Escalla sighed in frustration. "Frot! The last ones almost killed us, and I'm out of decent spells! I need to restock on heavy stuff!"

Trying to reason out the problem, Henry scratched his brow. "What spells have you got?"

"Lessee. Well, I loaded up with combat stuff. Missiles, webs, fireballs . . . got me a vampire touch spell that's a doozy!" The faerie counted off the spells on her fingers. "I had my black tentacles, plus I've got a lesser sphere of invulnerability. Oh! And I've got my grease spell ready!"

"Grease?" Henry blinked. Why grease?"

"It's a comedy natural. Trust me, I'm a faerie!"

"O-o-oh!" Enid crowded close, suitably impressed. "What's 'vampire touch'?"

"It's totally hoopy! Sucks your enemy's life energy and gives it to you! I found it in an old book."

"That big black one that warned us not to open it?"

"Yeah! That's the one!"

Ignoring the girls, Polk worked at copying the Justicar's map into his notebooks, showing the route they traveled by the means of badly drawn stick figures boldly led by badger. "Son, why water? What sort of guard wants to stand knee deep in water all day?"

Scowling, the Justicar regarded the door. "Aquatic ones, Polk. Tanar'ri."

The Justicar looked meaningfully at Henry, who frowned, trying to see a deeper point, then suddenly got the idea. The boy turned to Polk and tried to explain.

"Yes! You see? It's another telekinesis trap! You charge the island along the path, then hidden tanar'ri use their power to drag you off the path and drown you in the water."

Standing, the Justicar stood facing the door and said, "Simple. Well done."

And hard to counter. He breathed slowly, thinking, when suddenly Henry gave a sound of joy and opened up the portable hole.

"Oh, yes! Escalla has something to fix it!"

He dived into the hole.

Instantly curious, Escalla raced over to the rim. "What? The frost wand? We freeze the water to ice?"

"No!"

"Spare underwear? We leave a trail of it to tempt them out here into the open!"

"No-no! Wait! I've got it!" Henry erupted over the lip of the hole, dragging a bag of clinking bottles. "Look! Potions of giant growth!"

Escalla gave a possessive yelp and clutched the bag. *"No!* Not the giant growth potions! No! No! No-no-no-no-no! *No!"*

"Why not?" Henry shrugged. "Don't we have tons of them?"

Using fingers and toes to clutch the bag shut, Escalla flapped her wings in panic. "No! We only have one left! And that's . . . for emergencies!"

"But I counted them! Only one's gone! We still have seven potions." Henry pointed at the the the bag. "Right. We all grow to giant size—me, the Justicar, and Enid. Then no tanar'ri can telekinesify us! We'll be too heavy! And at giant size—swords, armor, everything—we can kill the tanar'ri just like that!"

Wringing her hands, Escalla whined, "But that's three whole potions gone!"

"That leaves four! We can do the same trick again at the other rooms marked on the map!"

Turning pale, Escalla gripped her precious potions in her arms and screamed, "No-no-no-no! That's all the potions gone!"

Henry was confused. "So why do we need so many growth potions?"

"Be-be-because it's . . . it's . . . medicine! Yeah! Medicine!" The faerie hid a potion behind her back. "My medicine! Yes! I need it for a, uh, female complaint. You know! A girl thing!"

"Do you get it often?"

"Well, I'm sure planning to!" Escalla shoved the potion bag behind her back. "Go on! Scram! You can have three! Three, and that's all!"

The party portioned out bottles, ignoring Escalla entirely. She danced about trying to get attention.

"Hey! Giant size doesn't solve the problem! We still need tactics and stuff. Hello? Is anyone listening to me?"

"We're listening." The Justicar held up a potion bottle, peering through the glass thoughtfully. "We need to stop them from teleporting out. That means killing them by surprise or enraging them so they want to fight."

Irritated, Escalla said, "All right! The faerie has it under control! I'll get Jus and me in there first, then you two guys come in a minute later. We'll do a tanar'ri sandwich."

Henry looked surprised. "How?"

"Mist spell. Jus and I slip into the water and make like sharks, then you two guys charge. J-man and I hit them from behind after you two guys engage." The faerie shrugged. "Best I can do."

"Oh?" Henry looked suspicious. "No fireballs?"

"Oh, for the love of . . . ! You blow a bunch of people up just *once*, and do they let you forget it?" The faerie lost her temper and headed for the door. "Just keep hold of the potions and let *me* worry about the magic!"

The faerie waited by the door, clicked her fingers imperiously, and the handle was turned by the Justicar. As the door opened just a teeny crack, Escalla leaked her mist spell into the room. She waved to Jus, crept silently forward, and the whole plan went straight to hell.

# 20

Thick fog spread over the water. The Justicar edged into the room behind Escalla. In one blinding moment, he whirled and hammered his brilliant white blade into the water. In the murk, the sword struck something that screamed and roared. Jus dived, his sword cleaving the water before him and crashing into a huge toadlike tanar'ri. The monster screamed and slashed at the Justicar with its claws.

On the surface, mist covered the front half of the room. Escalla coughed and waved the mist aside with her hands as splashes and roars filled the air.

"Jus? Jus!"

Enid and Henry chugged down their potions and charged into the room. They thundered along the bridge, shimmering as the magic took hold and enlarged them to four times their normal size. Twenty-three feet high and waving a twenty-foot-long sword, Henry plunged into the water and grappled with a toad demon. He took a grip on the monster's head and wrenched, using the huge strength of a giant to tear the tanar'ri to bits. Behind him a titanic sphinx smashed her paws into the water, bucking and plunging until she ran another tanar'ri down.

Above them, Escalla waved her hands and tried to shout order into the chaos. "Guys? *Guys!*" The faerie fired a stream of her magic bees at a tanar'ri and watched the magic ricochet away. "Guys! A little discipline here!"

A demon sped through the water like a hungry crocodile—a bloated, fang-slathered demon angling straight for Henry's back. With a curse, Escalla unshipped her lich staff and sped into a maddened run along the bridge. She leaped into the air, landing on the tanar'ri's back and smacking it across the skull. Power flashed and detonated, blowing chunks of toad-monster across the water. The demon screamed, reared, then plunged deep into the water while Escalla clung like grim death. The faerie turned into a lamprey, attached her sucker jaws, and began burrowing madly into the demon's stinking flesh.

Henry's victim blinked out of existence, reappearing behind him and raking him with its claws. Henry staggered, then whipped about with a swordblow learned hour after painful hour from the Justicar. Driven by gigantic strength, the blow cut the tanar'ri in two, scattering the demon into the pond.

Jus reared from the water, twenty-five feet high, one hand holding a tanar'ri's head. He pulped the creature against the wall, crushing it like an ant. Enid worried her own monster to death, shaking her head to fling bits of it about the room.

The sounds of combat died out—all except for the screams of a single tanar'ri. The toad monster bucked and heaved, smashing its back against the walls—each blow being accompanied by a muffled squawk. A vile spray of fluids jetted from the tanar'ri's back, where a lamprey's tail could be seen slowly disappearing into the tanar'ri's guts. The monster was blind with rage and agony, trying to reach behind itself and blinking out of existence to reappear a few feet to one side. The lamprey was always with it, burrowing into its flesh in a frenzy and cursing all the while.

Henry slipped, surfaced, then ploughed to Escalla's aid.

"It's going to teleport!" Henry blundered forward, a behemoth in the water. "Justicar! Your silence spell."

Magic silence might stop the demon from speaking the syllables to cast its spell.

Instead, the scarred titan that was the Justicar rose, poised, and threw Benelux like a javelin. Twenty feet long, the huge blade whooped with glee as she flew and pierced the tanar'ri's shoulders. Heart and spine were severed, and Benelux thudded point first into the wall. The toad demon hung stone dead, its body twitching like a broken puppet. The gigantic Justicar waded through the chest-deep water, wrenched the bottom of the demon from its top, and retrieved his sword.

A lamprey head emerged from the guts of the demon, grew Escalla's face, and retched in agony.

"You almost killed me! That only missed me by an inch!"

"It missed you." The Justicar's bass rumble sounded larger than mountains, deeper than the Abyss. "You're fine."

"Oh, *eeeew!* That was the most disgusting, stupid thing I've ever done!" Escalla was violently sick, disgorging the bits of tanar'ri she'd packed into her lamprey gut.

"Are you all right?"

"Oh, ick! That thing did *not* taste like chicken! Well, except for some spiced chicken I once left lying in the sun all afternoon and ate for dinner. But this is not funny!" Escalla emerged from stinking demon guts and turned to her normal form. Jus obligingly held her in his palm and shook her rapidly back and forth in the water to clean her. Rattled like a dice in a cup, Escalla lost her temper.

"Enough! You guys are even worse gigantic than when you're all just huge!" The faerie fought her way out of Jus's palm and retrieved her staff and wand. "Cinders? Cinders, where are you?"

*Here!*

Left lying on the bridge when the Justicar dived into the water, the hell hound watched with his big grin. Polk was using the hell hound as a seat, intently writing down a blow-by-blow account of the fight, clucking his tongue and shaking his head.

A high-pitched whine came from the portable hole on Jus's belt. A little silver sphere—another one of Lolth's keys—rose up out of the hole and began to glow in the air over their heads. Escalla, still naked, looked at it and instantly leaped to her feet.

"No! My clothes! That mail was specially crafted!" Her black chain mail now lay somewhere on the bottom of the pool. "Those are my last clean clothes! Wait! *Wait!*"

Escalla shot into the water and turned into an angler fish, a light dangling from a rod atop her head. She had no sooner disappeared than a hum came from the little sphere. There was a blinding flash, and suddenly the giant sphinx, two titanic humans, a badger, a sentient hell hound pelt, and an enraged angler fish were all in a new, dry section of corridor. Escalla cursed and raved, while huge streams of water cascaded from her gigantic friends.

"How the hell is a girl supposed to adventure if she doesn't even own clean leather?" The faerie was drenched and furious. "Jus! Open the damned portable hole!"

Snarling and cursing, she disappeared within the hole. There was the sound of tearing cloth. Escalla reappeared wearing a strip of white fabric printed with big red dots.

"My clothes are wet and my wardrobe is full of demon guts and water!" She realized she was the center of a ring of derisive glances, and she straightened her new dress. "Oh, you can laugh! This was ripped out of a pair of Jus's shorts!"

*Funny funny!*

"Laugh it up, pooch. Next bath you have, I'm gonna tizz you up like a duchess's pet!"

There was nothing to wash out the taste of tanar'ri from her mouth—only a flask of river water. As she fussed and bothered, Henry rose, so high that his head stuck into the howling mists. His voice boomed into the air like a god.

"Um, how long do these potions keep us this way?"

Escalla was sorely put out. "Not long enough to do it twice."

"Huh?"

"Nothing." The girl kicked at a puddle of water on the ground.

"All right, big guys, which way down the path—left or right?"

"Left." The gigantic Justicar opened the wet map—now sadly smudged. "It's only a little way away."

"Great. Well, if we run, maybe we can save on potions." There was a flash, and everyone suddenly returned to normal size. "O-o-of course not!" With a sigh, the faerie led the way. "Come on, you bold spirits. Get moving!"

Back in place over Jus's back, Cinders sniggered at Escalla from behind. *Hee hee. Love funny faerie!*

Escalla looked sideways at the hell hound, managing to look lofty despite her attire, and said, "Keep laughing, pooch. Just keep laughing."

❋    ❋    ❋    ❋    ❋

Converted once again into a slug, Escalla moved her tail slowly back and forth. Her eyestalks were peeking under a door—the next teleport room marked upon the map. Her mouth whispered back to her friends as she carefully surveyed the room beyond the door.

"Eh. Looks like more of the same—long path, big fires beside the path, then the rest of the room seems normal. Guess they want to do the same ol' plan. Hide, then use their power to try and tug us into the flames." The worm thrashed in contempt. "Real smart boys. They get one good idea in their entire lives and just have to keep using it again and again."

The Justicar squatted beside her, ready to intervene at the first hint of trouble.

"Where are they hiding?"

"Don't know. In the fires? If they're flame proof, I guess that's their best bet." Escalla's slug body stiffened in sudden suspicion. "Ah, now *there's* something. Anyone here know about tanar'ri?"

The Justicar raised one brow. "I thought *you* knew all about tanar'ri?"

"Hey, so some days I paid less than total attention!" Escalla pulled her head out from under the door.

Stiff and hurt by a demon's claws, Henry rubbed his eyes and looked at the closed door. "Um, Escalla? Why did you ask about tanar'ri?"

"Just wondering if they can change shape." The faerie sniffed at the edge of the portable hole, smelling the stink of fish. "Has anyone noticed any vermin around here? I mean, in this whole place—apart from giant spiders—has there been a fly, a rat, a cockroach . . . anything?"

There was a general moment of thinking and murmuring. No, no one had seen anything. The paths and rooms were so clean as to be sterile. The Justicar pondered it and shook his head.

"Empty. Why do you ask?"

"Because there's a bunch of mice sitting over in the far corner of that room."

Everyone gathered around. Cinders was eating the last of their supply of charcoaled troll, making noises of total rapture as he did so. The Justicar tried to borrow a piece of it to draw a map, and Cinders petulantly closed his snout over the treat.

*Yummy troll!* Cinders *keep!*

"We'll get you something better in a minute."

Escalla leaned close to whisper in Jus's ear. "Don't worry. You hold his M-O-U-T-H, and I'll make the G-R-A-B."

Cinders thrashed his tail. *G-R-A-B spells grab!* The hell hound chewed and swallowed as fast as he could. *No flakes! Troll all gone, see?*

"You and your damned spelling lessons." The Justicar settled on a piece of scorched fish from their rations to serve him as a pencil. "Right. So the room has a path, like this—fire trenches. No other doors?"

"Nah. None I could see." Back in faerie form again, Escalla hitched her horrible makeshift dress about herself. "Mice are over in this corner. They're probably some kind of tanar'ri, shapeshifted to try to fool us."

"Not the smartest disguise." Looking at the map, Jus rubbed his tired face. "Right So we need to eliminate the tanar'ri. That seems to activate the teleport."

The company leaned over the crude map in thought. Her nose wrinkling prettily, Enid tapped at the map with one long claw and said, "We could have Escalla attack them with a spell. Even if they're resistant, one or two of them might drop dead."

"I'm *out*, hon. You wanna know what spells I've got left?" The faerie always became didactic when tired and bothered. "I can do you a grease, vampire touch, a fire shield, a cloud kill, my invulnerability globe, and a web spell. Real tanar'ri-shattering stuff."

"I was only asking!"

Holding up a hand, the Justicar imposed peace. He looked up at the mists overhead and stared at the half-seen shapes of a pathway overhead. Lolth's maze was doing its job, paring away their spells and magic, weakening them steadily before they could confront the Spider Queen herself.

Always take the unexpected path. Always attack with surprise. The Justicar looked up at the pathways overhead then rose up to his feet.

"We avoid this room."

The others all looked inquiringly at him, but the Justicar never spoke until his facts were all in place. He turned from the map to the mists then folded the chart away.

"If we skip one guard room, Lolth and Recca will have no way of knowing which level of the maze we are on. We will jump up one level, then find a place to rest. We need Escalla with her spells. We need Henry healed."

Enid switched her scorched tail from side to side.

"The other paths are forty feet above us. How do we reach that high?"

"Giant growth potions. Enid, Henry, and I take the potions, Enid and I make a ladder up to the next level. Henry carries Escalla and Polk up, then gives Enid and I a hand up after him."

The mere mention of drinking giant growth potions instantly threw Escalla into a fit of panic. She fluttered about like a mad moth in a bottle.

"No! No! Look—we can get past the mice! You know—talk our way out of it or something!" Everyone was looking at the map, trying to find the best overpass to climb. "Hey! Is anyone looking at me? Hello? Hey! I can get us past mice! Mice are my speciality, I swear! I could turn into a cat or something!"

Trying to be patient, the Justicar inclined his head toward her and said, "Escalla, tanar'ri are not going to be scared of a cat."

"Jus! Those potions are for our honeymoon!" Escalla tried to whisper, painfully aware that Cinders, Enid, and Benelux were all listening. "I've got about a hundred years of theory I wanna put into practice!"

"Escalla, we need the potions."

The faerie waved her hands. "Can't we just throw a rope or something? Why hasn't Polk got rope and grappling hooks and ten-foot poles anymore?"

"Because we used to give him so much grief about it."

"Well, when did he start listening to us?" Escalla gave in with poor grace. "All right! All right! Drink the damned potions!" She kicked the potion bag over to her friends. "You know, if I didn't have Lolth to blame for all of this, you people would get me in such a huff!"

It was a brief walk to the needed overpass. Paths crossed over and under each other like a puzzle knot, but the map showed every twist and turn with total accuracy. Potions were drunk, and the giant adventurers formed an awkward human ladder through the mists.

The fog tugged and shoved at them like a living force as they climbed. Faces screamed in the mists—horrific skeletal figures were blown apart in the currents, only to reform into horrible weeping shapes. The Justicar grimly ignored it all, getting on with the job at hand.

Enid proved to be the major obstacle. They managed to boost her up onto the overhead path with some very indelicate shoving and tugging that left Henry blushing and speechless. The giants collapsed in a heap, panting and exhausted. Clambering out of the portable hole, Escalla and Polk walked over Jus's heaving chest. Polk looked about the empty pathways and gave an irritated scowl.

"Son! Are we there yet?"

"Not yet." Big as a titan, the Justicar raised his head to look at Polk. "Soon."

"Well, come on, son! We have to move. Keep the opposition off balance! Haven't you absorbed any of my tactical training?" Polk leaped to the ground. "The boy procrastinates. Hard thing to say, but the boy just lacks any get-up-and-go."

Surveying the panting wreck of her friends, Escalla frowned as she dragged Cinders from the portable hole and unrolled him on the floor.

"What's wrong with you guys?"

The Justicar sat up, towering vast and grim above the path, and replied, "Enid is bigger than we thought."

"Enid, lay off the stirges for a while, hon." Escalla hopped over to the blushing sphinx. "We have to keep you sleek."

There was a warning flash, the giants all looked up as the potions wore off, and suddenly everyone was back to their own natural sizes.

They unfolded the map, looking carefully up and down the new paths. According to the diagrams, this was the final, topmost level of the maze. Unfortunately, the area seemed identical to a dozen others. The Justicar carefully checked the floors for the slightest sign of use, then waved the others forward as he led the way.

As they walked down the screaming pathway, they drew nearer and nearer to an incongruous marble doorway. This time the door was ornately inscribed, jet black, and gleaming new. A wide, clear window at shoulder height gave a view of the room beyond.

The party ducked down out of sight of the window. In a drill honed carefully over their adventures, Jus and Cinders crept close and examined the area for traps. Cinders sniffed the door, and Escalla listened carefully against the wood with one pointed ear. Hearing nothing, Escalla threw off her clothes, lay on her belly and began to shimmer, changing into a slug so that she could peek beneath the door.

The shimmer of magic went jarringly off-color. Escalla changed shape into a bizarre multicolored slug with something shaped like a flower planted on her behind. Her eyestalks wrenched around to stare at herself in shock.

"I'm a nudibrach!"

Benelux cleared her throat. *A what?*

"A type of sea slug with exposed gills and a brightly colored venomous integument." Escalla waggled her floral backside, making her anemone-like gills wave. "I didn't plan this! Why am I a nudibrach?"

Henry slithered closer, trying to keep his voice to a whisper. "It isn't what you were trying to be?"

"No!" Escalla tried to move. "Damn it! I look ridiculous. Hang on and I'll change back."

There was a glow of light, a jangling note of discord, and Escalla changed shape. Where once there had been a slug, there was now a short, gnomish creature with a huge pickle-shaped nose. The creature reached for its clothes, then cast a patient glance at the rest of the party.

"What? What are you all gaping at? If you don't like the view, then quit steaming up the window!" The creature muttered as it wrapped itself in Escalla's little dress. "Faerie butt. Does it every time."

The Justicar reached into his pouch and came out with the small mirror on a stick he used for peering about corners. Escalla took the mirror, gazed levelly into it and immediately had a fit.

"All right! Who's trying to be funny?" The girl frantically tugged at her nose. "Ouch! I'm a brownie! This is not funny!" Escalla suddenly jerked her hand away from her new nose. "Ick! I touched a brownie! I *am* a brownie! Ewww!"

She began to change shape again, but the Justicar leaped in to stop her. "Wait! Something's wrong."

"Jus, I'm a brownie! A lovable icon of childhood fun!" The bulbous-nosed creature did a jig of wild anger. "I have to change back before I puke!"

"Just wait." The Justicar let Cinders sniff at the air. "There might be something strange about this room or this level. Let us check it out first."

The Justicar carefully edged up to peek through the window in the door. Seething, Escalla sat down, one hand propped up her chin and the other propped up her huge nose.

"This is so unfashionable!"

Sitting beside her, Enid frowned. "Are brownies unfashionable?"

"Ha!" Escalla clicked her fingers. "Have you got any idea how many parties brownies get invited to?"

"Millions?"

"None!"

"Oh." The sphinx shrugged. "Well, I knew you would only have asked if it were really big or really small."

The Justicar stood peering through the window in the door. He examined the view very carefully, then signaled Henry to join him. They both looked through the window, staring into a slice of an alien world.

The window looked out onto a gloomy twilight. Ruined walls surrounded a castle courtyard littered with drifts of old, dry leaves. An empty fountain filled with sculpted hippocampi stood at the center of the open square. The sky held an eerie blood-red moon that stained the stones with a horrible venous purple light. Henry took a searching look at the scene, then ducked down to consult in whispers with the Justicar.

"Sir, do you know where that is?"

"No." The Justicar glowered, scratching the stubble of his chin. "But it's a gate into another world. That much is obvious."

Benelux made self-important throat clearing noises at Jus's side. *If I might be permitted a glance? As you know, I am a multi-planar artifact. My erudition is clearly one of the party's strongest assets.*

Jus drew the sword and lifted the edge of the blade over the window. He moved the sword slowly so that Benelux might see the view. The blade mused, brim full of wisdom and experience.

*Yes . . . yes, yes . . . clearly not Oerth.* Benelux mulled her thoughts. *A double moon, characteristic blood-red sky. Did you note the architecture? Extremely distinct.*

The Justicar kept the sword held high. "Do you recognize the place?"

*Hmm. No.*

Deeply annoyed at the waste of time, the Justicar shoved at the door. It swung open upon an alcove that ended in a clear, slightly reflective wall. The Justicar carefully touched the surface—pushed—and saw his hand penetrate as though piercing clear water. He withdrew his hand, sniffed his fingers, and then waved the other party members through.

"Come on. Escalla, sweep the path behind us. Henry, close the door."

Guarded by the ever-watchful Justicar, one by one the party stepped through into another world. They breathed alien air, trod alien stones, and crossed swiftly into cover. Polk waddled through a drift of leaves, his footfalls the only sound in the breathless gloom.

The scent of the Demonweb had gone, and with it, a strange, bleak sense of depression lifted from their souls. Each of them stood a little straighter. Escalla looked at her hand, then shimmered and changed—this time flickering back into her usual faerie shape. She heaved a huge sigh of relief. Vain as a cat, she inspected her naked self, front and behind, with Jus's mirror, suspiciously searching for the slightest hint of brownie lingering on her skin. She tried her wings, found she could fly, and then joyously turned invisible and whirred away into the sky.

The Justicar looked up at the row of grim, blank windows that faced the courtyard. Nothing stirred, and yet the castle was filled with a sense of dread *presence.* He carefully examined the fallen leaves, the dust and dirt, kneeling in the shadows of a crumbled hall.

"Cinders?"

*Cinders smells undead.*

Jus held up a hand to keep his friends still and motionless in the gloom. He went flat and slithered through the long weeds that grew throughout the courtyard, moving under brambles with scarcely a whisper of sound. The Justicar found old, gnawed bones—human bones. A long-dead body lay nearby, the skin waxen and drained of blood. Eviscerated and gnawed, the body still held a vile pallor. The Justicar rolled the corpse over. No blood had pooled at its back. The body had been drained of blood before it died.

Jus crept back to his friends, and Escalla popped into place beside him.

"Hey, Jus?" she whispered. "What do you think lives here?"

"Vampire."

"Oh. Whacko."

They both took it so matter-of fact that Henry and Enid

could only stare. Polk scribbled in his chronicles. Benelux muttered to herself. The Justicar gathered the party in the shadows of a tower—well out of sight of the castle windows.

"We can stay here and rest. We just have to be careful. A vampire is not a problem if it never knows we're here." The Justicar said it as if he'd just told them to fetch water or cut wood—all part of the job. "Escalla will go see if the vampire is near. We'll find a secure room. We need to rest and replenish our magic. Then we go straight for Lolth's palace and hit it hard."

"Vampire scout away! See you in ten!" The faerie saluted Jus and flew away, turning invisible as she went. While they awaited her return, Henry knelt beside the Justicar and looked at the dark spaces around the castle yard.

"Sir? Is it dawn or twilight?"

"It probably stays like this. Perfect for undead." The Justicar moved stealthily over to a set of stairs. "Watch the others. Don't let Polk wander off."

He knelt above a tiny smear on a flagstone, then followed the trace to the base of a tower. There were slight marks in the dust that filmed the stair—long, broad smears. The Justicar touched the marks, lifted his fingers to his nose and sniffed, then lifted the scent up to Cinders.

*Snake smell.*

21

Escalla reappeared with a soft *pop*, turning visible, combing out her hair with her fingers. Clearly, she was thrilled to be flying once again. She settled down with Jus and Henry, keeping her voice low.

"Found something?" she asked.

"Snake tracks. Tanar'ri." Jus traced the tracks for her so that she could see. "Might be our six-armed friend again."

"Oh, if you liked that, you're gonna *love* this!" Keeping low, the faerie beckoned the group upstairs. "Come check it out!"

She led the way into the tower, staying visible and peeking cautiously about each corner as she went. The door swung open to reveal a room with a drab wooden table. On the table stood a bottle of wine, a jug of water, a cob of bread, and lengths of hard sausage. A bag of dried fruit lay beside a bleeding haunch of mutton—raggedly torn from a carcass and inexpertly skinned. No flies had come to the meat, and the blood was still fresh.

Escalla signaled everyone to ignore the food, and then she opened another door.

In a huge hall hung with moldering old banners, a vampire lay sprawled on the floor. The creature had been utterly demolished—sliced, decapitated, and a stake driven through its heart. The stake, made from the leg of a chair, had been driven through the vampire's torso with enough force to penetrate the floorboards beneath. Escalla ushered her friends over, waving her hands toward the corpse.

"This is seriously icky! Have you guys met Count Bisecto, Master of Homicide Hall?"

Moving swiftly to the vampire, Jus knelt to examine the damage. Polk trundled over to a fallen jug, sniffing eagerly as he caught the scent of crab-apple brandy. Mincing over the floor and avoiding extravagant pools of black sticky stuff, Escalla made her way to Jus's side. The Justicar was carefully examining the wounds on the vampire's body, while Cinders grinned away, his big teeth gleaming.

"So what did him in?" Escalla asked.

"Curved blades." Using the tip of his hunting knife, the Justicar opened up a wound. "A cut from a very sharp blade. Body weight behind the blow, pushing forward. Good technique."

"Hoopy!" Escalla drew the man away. "You think it was the snake lady?"

"Almost certainly. Swords, tracks . . . she killed him in a single pass—three hits, all at once."

"Creepy." Escalla pondered memories of the tanar'ri. "She had nice hair. And a nice butt—for a snake, I mean." The faerie turned. "Polk! Careful, man! You don't know what's been in there!"

Polk had taken possession of the fallen jug, smacking his lips. Every cell of his body craved an alcoholic interlude, and crab-apple brandy would surely hit the spot. He held the jug in his back feet and inverted it, eagerly opening his mouth. Thick vapors swirled from the jug and pooled out over the floor to gather in a mist behind him.

Behind Polk, Escalla hovered in front of the Justicar.

"So Jus, are you sure about this? How does someone manage to kill a vampire with a single blow?"

The mist behind Polk suddenly flashed. In its place, appeared a female vampire, black clad and arrowing toward Escalla and the Justicar. Escalla squeaked and sped skyward. Screaming, claws reaching, the vampire streaked below her. There was a sharp whisper and a blur of light, and the vampire stopped and stared in shock.

The Justicar held his pose for an instant—sword out. He reversed the blade and sheathed it, sliding Benelux slowly back into her scabbard.

The vampire's severed head tilted back, burning slowly as it fell. The decapitated torso stood swaying, the undead flesh beginning to wither from contact with the metal of Benelux. The torso finally fell. Staring at it, Henry blinked then snapped a crossbow bolt in two and hammered it straight into the vampire's heart.

"Um . . . all right!" Escalla looked at the corpse. "Yeah, like that! That was good."

Completely unconcerned, Polk had already begun helping himself to the dregs of brandy in the jug. "That's just the way I would have done it, son! But you need just a little bit more style."

A horrific scream came from the courtyard below, followed by the sound of claws scrabbling beneath the windows. The Justicar directed his friends back from the windows and doors, guiding them to the center of the room.

"Henry, back to the middle of the room! Enid and Escalla, up in the rafters. Polk, play dead!" The Justicar drew his sword. "Here they come!"

Through the doors and windows, a howling mob of ghouls—jackal-thin, stinking, skeletal, and crazed—rushed into the room and ran madly at Henry and the Justicar. Henry coolly opened fire, his magic crossbow stuttering. A stream of five crossbow bolts tore through one ghoul, sent it crashing to the ground, then Henry drew his sword and followed the Justicar as the big man ploughed into the foe.

Cinders snarled and sent a blast of flames writhing through the ghouls. The creatures twisted and screamed, burning as they fell. The Justicar wielded Benelux in a savage blur, the ghouls burning like paper as they fell. The ranger's stoneskin flared and died.

Henry blocked a ghoul's claws and ran the creature through. Another ghoul sprang at him in a fury, only to be torn apart by a stream of golden bees shot from the rafters. Enid fell atop the last three ghouls—swatted one so that it simply fell in half—and discovered another flat beneath her paws.

The last ghoul turned to flee. Jus whip-cracked his magic rope about the creature's torso, jerked it from its feet and rammed Benelux through the monster's head. The body flared into flames, and Jus yanked on the rope, spinning the burning corpse across the floor.

Still sitting in the rafters and nursing her unused wand, Escalla looked suitably impressed. "Hoopy! What was that—nine in, nine down?"

"Nine! Are you blind, girl? It was a dozen!" Polk happily jotted notes into his chronicles. "For every piece of evil seen, there's three waiting in the wings, so that makes four-dozen defeated! Forty-eight ghouls! Not bad for a minute or two."

"Polk, shut up." The Justicar kicked a ghoul's corpse over and examined the body. He stabbed it once more to make it burn. "Scavengers that serve the vampires. They eat bodies drained of blood."

Still panting and pale, Henry wiped his mouth. "Why did they attack like that, sir?"

"If they can stop us from killing the vampires, then they still have their meal ticket." The Justicar burned away the last remnants of both vampires' skulls. "Everyone check this room, then retreat back into the tower."

Escalla had already begun a search. Rummaging behind a painted throne, the faerie gave a whoop and dragged out a sack that clinked and clanked.

"Treasure! Finally we find a treasure!" She upended the sack. Out spilled gold coins, silver coins, bent copper pennies, wooden slugs, little gems, big gems, potion bottles, and a scroll. "Look, guys! Treasure! Whoever offed the vampire just left the stash lying around!"

Beside herself with excitement, the faerie flung herself atop the gold and wallowed atop the pile. "Enid, come over here and try this! Oh, I'm so excited I can see through time!" Escalla plucked a bottle from the treasure pile. "What's this? Magic potions? O-o-oh, a regeneration potion!" The girl unshipped the slowglass gem from down her front. "All right! Everyone pose with the money and wave! Smile!"

The Justicar found the discarded bag that the treasure had once been in. He lifted it to Cinders's nose, and the hell hound sniffed at it carefully.

"Tanar'ri?"

*Tanar'ri snake!*

"Yes." Rising, the Justicar signaled Henry to his side. "Get back into the room with the food. Barricade the door to the courtyard. I'll bring Escalla and the treasure."

"Yes, sir."

They retrieved the treasure through the simple expedient of opening the portable hole, then pushing the entire loot pile inside—faerie, potion bottles, and all. Escalla gave a squawk and looked out over the edge of the hole as Jus dragged it over the floor to the other room.

"Hey, Jus! Hey look! Treasure!"

"Yep."

"Real treasure! There's gold and potions . . . and jewels! One of them's a diamond!"

"Uh-huh." The Justicar nodded. "Exactly the right size to use for a stoneskin spell?"

"Oh—oh, yeah. Did yours run out yet?"

"Just then."

"Ah." The girl suddenly took on a thoughtful look, ducked into the hole and came up with one of the potion bottles. She gave it a sniff. "Healing potion, Flanaess style."

"The sausage in the room is lying on a bag. The bag is stenciled with the seal of a Keggle Bend merchant." The Justicar reached the far room, where Henry was busily dropping a bar into place against the outer door. "Our snake woman is a busy girl."

"A busy girl with an agenda." Escalla climbed out of the hole. Her eye took in the food, doors leading off to two other small, quiet rooms filled with bedding. "She wants us to rest."

"She took care of the only thing here that was dangerous. The chief vampire would have been a lot tougher than his bride." Jus spied a fireplace and checked it—a metal grate sealed off the chimney flue. "We each need at least four hours to rest and get spells back. Polk and Cinders can keep guard. We can put that mutton on to cook."

Enid looked up guiltily. The stripped mutton bone lay on the floor before her, and she covered it up with her paws.

"Um, aren't you all going to fry up that nice sausage?"

"I guess we are." Escalla looked about the table and sighed. "Any faerie cakes? Honey? Jam? Sugar?"

"No. Sorry."

"Sod it. If I don't keep my sugar intake up, I get into such a mood!" Escalla tugged at the Justicar, dragging him over to one of the little side rooms. "All right. You meditate, I'll grab my spell book, and we can grind that diamond. Let's get rested up."

The next room was small, dark, and had windows bolted, sealed, and shuttered tight. Spreading Cinders out over a chair to keep guard in the kitchen, Jus closed the door on the sounds and smells of dinner. He dropped down into the portable hole, retrieved blankets and a pillow made out of an old sack, then clambered wearily out again. He found Escalla sitting surrounded by her loot and tools—lich staff, frost wand, spellbook, and potion bottles.

Peace at last. Still dressed in her awful makeshift dress, she gave Jus a wan little smile.

"Hello."

He kissed her softly, and she curled into him. It was a simple, powerful love with so few complications. Escalla wound her arms about Jus's neck, leaned her forehead against his skin and sighed.

They held each other for a long, long time. Escalla rested a hand on Jus's skull as they drew apart, and she scratched his stubble with a smile.

"Stubble." She loved the feel of it beneath her hands. "Let's get you shaved. Can't have you facing ultimate evil with afternoon shadow on your head."

He was tired, but he laughed. She sat on his thigh and raked through the loot, shaking the potion bottle beside her ear. Jus looked at the writing on the label and scowled.

"Elven?"

"Drow." The girl nodded. "Yep. All drow. Looks like about five healing potions and five spider venom antidotes: one each. Convenient, eh? Plus we've got a potion of regeneration. All are labeled."

"I thought so."

"So what's going on?" Escalla rattled the bottles with her foot. "You think Lolth's playing with us? Wants us to make it to the palace so she can flatten us?"

"No. The problems we're facing aren't cruel enough." The Justicar sighed, feeling tired. "There's nothing specifically intended to make us suffer. It's been just guards."

"Heh. And Recca and Tielle."

"Them, too." The Justicar looked over their weapons and tools. "Is your frost wand holding out?"

"Yeah. Running low on charges, though. Lich staff too." The girl ran frustrated fingers through her hair. "I have to relax! Clear my mind! I can't memorize spells while I'm all keyed up."

There were empty bottles amongst the full. Jus picked up a familiar little vial and shook it.

"Giant growth potion?"

"Yeah. Last one left." Escalla picked it up and looked at the liquid gleaming through the clear glass bottle. "Ah, well. I guess we'll make more some day. I'll find the ingredients somehow. . . ."

Jus rubbed his eyes.

"We should meditate. We only have four hours. Do faeries do anything special to relax?"

Escalla laughed. All of a sudden, she looked at Jus, and Jus looked at her. They looked at each other, then Escalla pounced, tearing at the potion bottle's cork.

Hanging from the door handle nearby, Benelux wailed. *No! Not again! No! I demand to be put in another room!* The sword buried herself inside her sheath and sang to try to block away the noise. *La la la la la!*

\* \* \* \* \*

Outside the door, Enid blinked. She pushed more wood into the fire, hoping the crackling flames and sizzling sausage would mask other sounds. Diligently slicing sausage at the table with Polk, Henry looked at the door in puzzlement.

"What's that noise?

"Mantra!" Enid managed to go pale and blush bright red at the same time. "Escalla's meditating."

Polk pricked his ears. "Mantra? Sounds like she's just yelling 'yes!' over and over again."

"It's a very happy mantra." Enid cleared her throat. "Mmm! Sausages smell nice, don't they?"

She stirred the sausages in the pan and burned her paw. Henry leaped to her aid and knelt with her, cradling her big paw in his hands. They looked at each other, turned pink as crabs, and both hastily looked away—yet stayed sitting as close beside each other as they possibly could.

Draped over the back of a chair, Cinders saw all, heard all, and knew all. He sucked on a lump of prime new coal and slowly wagged his tail.

*Funny!*

## 22

"What do you mean there's no sign of them? Have you looked?"

Wild, furious, worn, and thoroughly annoyed, Tielle hovered above a hillside with her wings beating like a mad dragonfly. She had been so certain that today would be the day of her revenge that she had dressed herself in her most outrageous outfit. It consisted of a few threads and thongs—all pulled as tight as comfort would allow. The effect was like a pale white pudding bound up with string. With thirty chain monks spread about the hillsides, with spells and imps and bloodhounds sniffing the ground, she had still failed to find Escalla's trail! The crystal ball was useless, drawing a blank hour after hour. It was as though Escalla had disappeared without a trace!

"Damn her! She can't possibly have a scrying shield! Not every hour of every day!" Tielle sat on a tree stump, the bark agony to her bared bottom, and snatched her crystal ball out of the hands of a monk. "Where is she? If she's on this plane, then why can't we find her?"

A monk dragged its chains and gibbered at her, waving its arms in a mad attempt to be understood. Blonde, plump, and underclad, Tielle tossed the useless crystal ball into its arms.

"Don't be an idiot! I know exactly what to do. All we need is a little patience. I'll flay her alive and use the skin to make a puppet show!" The faerie stood, dusted herself irritably, and rose into the air. "Come on. Gather those other idiots here. We'll head back to the gate and go home!"

The chain monk made a pathetic, hungry noise. From above, Tielle gave it a look of angry contempt.

"I know my sister. Escalla is nothing but a strutting, puffed up little peahen. We've bested her, so she'll want her revenge! All we have to do is wait for her to come into our lair."

Tielle watched her minions gathering. The search had been long and annoying. To escape her, Escalla must have hidden in the darkest bowels of the earth or the foulest swamps of some other plane. The girl hovered, looking nastily out across the wilderness, consoling herself with the thought of her sister in humiliation and agony.

"Well, wherever she is, at least she's suffering!"

\* \* \* \* \*

A few hours of rest had worked miracles. The castle remained quiet, the fried sausage had a hint of garlic, and the wine was a Verbobonc vintage that must have cost a hundred crowns. Escalla had to be ladled out of bed like limp, boiled noodles. She was slipped into rough new clothes made out of a soft cloth, and draped over Jus's shoulders like a collar. As the group edged into the castle courtyard under a blood-red sky, Henry coughed politely to attract her attention.

"My Lady? You seem less tense." The boy leaned closer. "Did you study your spells?"

"Hmm? Spells? Yeah. Hoopier than hoopy!" The faerie girl gave a dazed thumbs up. "Recharged and rarin' to go. You have a problem, and I'm right on the job."

With that, she curled back down to snooze again. One part of her brain registered something new, and she sleepily eyed off her brand new clothes.

"Where did these come from?"

"I made them out of a polishing cloth," Henry replied. "Enid and I thought it was, ah, more dignified than the others you were wearing."

"Henry! You are just the sweetest thing!" Raising her head, Escalla made long streams of her golden hair cascade down Jus's back. "Hey, you two guys just earned yourself a faerie boon. Straight from the faerie princess to you!" The girl rolled luxuriously, spreading her hair into watery drifts of light. "I'll do the 'true heart's desire' thing right after we get back home."

The doorway to the Demonweb Pits stood as it always had, but lying beside the door was a tiny, glittering snake scale. The Justicar knelt over his find and carefully pocketed the evidence before clearing the scene. He jumped through the barrier between worlds, emerging into the stench, the prickling light, and formless dread of the Demonweb. The others followed him one by one as he carefully examined the path in each direction, opened his map, then signaled the way forward.

They had shared out healing potions, water bottles, and tools. Escalla sat up, her spells firm in her head and her frost wand in her hands. They all moved to the end of the path to a great bronze door that marked the entrance to another world.

Again, there was a clear window. This time, the view revealed a bleak plain of windswept obsidian boulders and cracked rivers of volcanic glass. Electrical storms sheeted across the sky, revealing the sinister shape of Lolth's palace squatting on a hilltop a mere hundred yards away.

The palace seemed deserted, and yet light leaked from the huge windows that served as its eyes. The Justicar dug in his pouch for the remaining key and fitted it into a depression on the door. He swung the door open, and the party stood before a transparent barrier that led into Lolth's private, most secret home.

The Justicar checked the fit of his equipment, using the same quiet, careful moves that had seen him through a hundred battlefields.

"This is Lolth's inner sanctum. Touch nothing you don't have to. Look on everything as a deadly trap. Watch for magic. Watch for enemies. Your enemy can shape change, teleport, cast magic and illusion . . . so kill first and strike hard."

He looked from Enid to Henry, Escalla to Polk, and then reached up to tie Cinders into place.

"I'm yours, and you are mine. You never abandon your people. If any of you get in trouble, remember: I *will* come for you." The big man turned and waved the others in his wake. "Forward."

Escalla turned invisible to scout ahead. Polk and Enid moved forward stealthily into the black glass boulders. Henry followed, his magic crossbow hunting at shadows.

They had scarcely crossed the threshold when the folded map on Jus's belt caught fire. He scowled at it as it burned against his dragon scales, then dragged the map free before it could damage his sword belt. He stamped on the ashes then took a swift look across the plains to see if the fire had been noticed. Lightning flashed and obsidian sparkled. Hopefully, one tiny little fire had not been seen. Escalla cocked an eye at the last few wisps of crumbling map and gave a wry little smile.

"Smart girl, isn't she?"

"Smart girl." The Justicar abandoned the map and moved on. "Everyone move carefully."

*     *     *     *     *

Vast and foreboding, Lolth's palace was watchful. The brass metal of its hull swam with images of screaming faces and clawing hands, as if it were pressed out of the souls of the dead. Vents high upon the hull leaked smoke into the sky, and steam hissed from its joints. The body rested just above the ground, stairs spilling out from the spider palace's monstrous head like a tongue feeding into its cavernous jaws. Little quasits scampered through the boulders like monstrous rats, their demonic shapes casting immense, terrifying shadows in the unclean light.

Two gargoyles sat on guard at the bottom of the stairs. Bat winged, stone skinned, and hideous, the two monsters tore the carcass of a halfling between them, squabbling over the spoils. They were still fighting as a little figure popped into view beside them and cleared its throat.

Small, blonde, and dainty, Escalla posed on the path, gave a little wave, and interrupted the guardians.

"Hey, guys? I just wanted to say that you got me! I'm caught! Damn! There's just no way past real professional guards like you, so I'm giving up! I'll come quietly. I mean, if anyone gets to reap the *huge* rewards for bringing me in to the boss, then I want it to go to two professionals!"

The two gargoyles stared for an instant, gore dripping from their open mouths, then pounced on Escalla. One caught her in its stony fist, while the other tried to grab her feet. The two creatures snarled and squabbled with one another, cuffing each other across the scales. Finally Escalla managed to bring peace to the fight, waving her arms to keep the gargoyles apart.

"Whoa! Whoa! Whoa! Enough! All right! The guy who is holding me can keep holding me. That's fair, right? The other guy, he can go upstairs and report that you've got a prisoner. Right? Happy?" The faerie chased one of the gargoyles away. "So go! Go on! Report upstairs! Open the front gate and go!"

A gargoyle shambled up the steps to the locked front door of the fortress. The creature disabled a guard spell and gave a password to someone on the far side of the door, snarling and gabbling in rage. Relaxing in her captor's claws, Escalla watched the whole process with approval.

"Wow! Now that's partnership. Two guys workin' as one." The girl leaned her elbow on her captor's fist. "It's great to have a partner, eh? Someone you can trust. I mean, you two guys, you obviously work as a team. And why? *Trust*, that's why! I mean, he can trust you to sit here on your arse looking after the prisoner, while he goes and makes the report. And you! You trust him to tell them all about you *both* catching me. Equal shares plus equal rewards equals equal promotion!" The girl gave an admiring sigh. "Partnership. I tell you, it's beautiful to watch."

Escalla's captor blinked, turned to watch his partner disappearing into the spider palace, and then screeched in rage. He pelted up the stairs, wrenched the other gargoyle about, and another furious argument began. Escalla was shaken about as she was used as a prop for the argument. The two gargoyles finally came to a decision. Escalla swapped from one gargoyle to the other, and her original captor now proceeded into the palace. Eating a piece of garlic sausage, Escalla watched the other gargoyle go.

"Yeah. He's right. I mean, *he* should go. He's the one that caught me, so he should make the report. It's only fair. I mean, the boss knows your pal is the brains of the outfit. If you go in there, it's only going to look suspicious, right? I mean, give your partner credit where credit's due. If *he* carries the load, then *he* ought to get the reward!"

With a howl, the gargoyle ran after its partner. The two creatures screamed, leaped, flapped, and squabbled. Finally, they came to another decision. Both gargoyles totally abandoned their guard post and went to make their report together, with Escalla held between them in their claws.

Locks and bolts opened from the inside. One of the gargoyles grabbed Escalla and pushed his partner towards the doors, yelling at him to open the way. Escalla joined in the general shower of abuse.

"Yeah! You open those doors! And don't even suspect that your friend might sneak in a bite now your back is turned. Because he's a great guy! Your friend through and through!"

In homicidal fury the gargoyle at the doors whirled and flung itself at its partner. Escalla was hurled aside as both monsters fought. The faerie sat on a balustrade, pulled out more sausage, and ate while strips of gargoyle flesh flew all over the stairs. She looked at the carnage and sighed.

"Tragically, the faerie is forever condemned to face inferior intellects."

The Justicar stamped irritably out from behind a boulder, crossed the open ground, and mounted the stairs. Both gargoyles now lay in a single bleeding heap. Jus was not amused.

"I thought I told you just to sneak up and find a way past the guards."

Escalla had her mouth full of sausage.

"Sho I got ush pasht the guardsh! No prob'em!" Escalla wiped her lips and jumped down onto the stairs. "See! I even got the door open! Come on! Let's go."

She scampered on ahead. Growling, Jus turned and signaled the others to make a run for the stairs. He turned back just in time to see Escalla disappearing through Lolth's front door. From inside the spider palace, the faerie gave a happy little cry.

"Oh! Hey, guys! Yep! You got me! So which one of you wants to go and report that you just got a prisoner?"

Enid looked at Jus, and the two of them charged headlong up the stairs and through the door.

# 23

The inside of Lolth's palace was shocking and surprising. Beyond the entrance alcove, with its dead gargoyles and guards, there was an area of clean white walls—a wide room with a rug upon the floor and paintings on the wall, all tasteful and incredibly beautiful.

Behind a desk sat a slim, cool woman with bobbed black hair. Her six arms were busy all over the desk, writing, sorting, doodling and filing all at once. Long snake coils draped elegantly over a perch that was half office chair and half shoe tree. As Jus cautiously edged into the room, she turned her back to him and deliberately concentrated on her files.

"Greetings, Justicar. Come in." The demon spoke in a very, very ordinary voice—officious and beautifully spoken. "You've done well. She still doesn't know you're here."

Escalla became visible. She ambled into the room, looking eagerly at the furnishings. Enid flowed through the door, her eyes on the tanar'ri woman and her claws unsheathed. Polk and Henry stood in the doorway and simply stared.

The six-armed tanar'ri never once looked at her visitors. Instead, she concentrated on her files.

"You may call me Morag. That is my common name, not my true name. Lolth has my true name. She has it written down. While she holds it, I must obey her to the letter. I must always answer her with the truth. If she wants to, she can use it to destroy me."

Looming huge and dark, the Justicar thoughtfully regarded the tanar'ri girl, then said, "If Lolth dies, the name is lost, and you are free."

"Yes."

"Why should we help you?"

Morag kept her back to him, sitting straight and stiff.

"You are not helping me. I have never discussed plans with you. Therefore, when asked by Lolth, I will say I have never conspired against her." One slim hand motioned to a large book upon the table. "Your names are penciled into the appointment list for the day. Therefore, there are no intruders in the palace. My duties will shortly call me away from this room." The woman made a careful entry into a ledger. "I can even say that I have not *seen* any intruders. I have never laid eyes upon you."

Escalla had been poking about the room. Perched on the desk was a painted portrait of a tanar'ri male—a handsome creature with a longing, slightly wistful expression. Escalla took one look at the picture and whistled in glee.

"Hubba-hubba! Oh, wow! Is he yours?"

"Give me that!" Morag snatched the picture away and hugged it against her breast. "And no, he is not mine. He . . . he . . ." A blush actually crept up the tanar'ri's cheeks. "He's an acquaintance."

"Oh . . ." Walking along the desk, Escalla cast a sly little eye backward at the tanar'ri. "But, ah, an acquaintance who's pretty nice to you. I mean, I can tell! He has great eyes." Escalla looked at the rugs, the paintings, and tapped her index fingers together "You really caught something special in that painting. You did all these, too?"

Morag straightened, tugging at her neat little black skirt.

"Yes. Yes, I painted them."

"And I bet you write, too!" Escalla was now sitting on the edge of the desk companionably next to the tanar'ri. "You do history, right? But there's a novel you've been working on, too?"

"It's a trilogy!" The tanar'ri sat up, and then subsided into misery. "We . . . I'm Lolth's secretary. Her vassal. Her . . . her slave." Morag swallowed. "I'm not supposed to . . . to waste time, to form attachments."

"Wow! You poor thing!"

Escalla was quite distraught. She looked up to see Jus looking patiently irritable at her. The girl waved her hand, shooing him away. "What? Hey, just because she's a tanar'ri, we can't both talk like girls?" The faerie snapped her fingers at her man. "We have a problem here! Helping ladies in distress is in the line of Justice! This is right up your alley!"

Morag was still hugging her portrait of her paramour. Escalla cleared her throat and came a little closer, staying out of view.

"Um, right. So this fella of yours . . . I mean, you'd like the chance to know him better, huh? You made a dumb mistake with Lolth, and now you're stuck! Regrets lead to frustration. Frustration leads to anger. I mean, we have to catch this problem now before it ruins your life forever!"

Morag hung her head. All six hands clenched tight. "Yes."

"Hoopy. Well, girl to girl, I'm glad to help." Escalla waggled her little bare feet. "So tell me: How do we get Lolth? What's the secret?"

"I can't tell you. Not . . . not directly."

"Hints are fine." Escalla lounged on the tabletop. "Shoot!"

Morag slithered from her chair. She gathered files and folders, checked the set of her curved swords, and tugged her skirt down straight. She headed for a door, then paused to speak into thin air.

"When thinking of Lolth, remember this: Power breeds superiority. Superiority breeds contempt. Contempt breeds a need to control." The tanar'ri exited through a door, her beautiful coils shimmering as she moved. "I believe it was Saint Cuthbert who said, 'Evil is a stain. The darker the evil, the more pure the waters must be to wash it clean.' "

Morag swept majestically out of the room. "The ship is powering up. We leave for the Flanaess within the hour."

The door closed with a bang, and Escalla sat up, scowling.

"Actually, I was hoping more for something on the lines of 'Two doors on the left, her bedroom's just great! You can ambush her there. Lolth goes shut-eye at eight.' " The girl shrugged. "Ah, well . . ."

"It could have been worse." The Justicar came over to Escalla's side to examine the desk. "It could have been a poem."

Polk shambled forward, his belt fur dragging. "It *should* have been a poem, damn it! Don't that snake know anything about adventuring? It should have been a rede!"

Escalla recoiled. "A reed? What? Like a bull rush?"

"No, a rede, girl! A rede! A saying! A phrase put into rhyme so it won't be forgotten!"

"The Flanaess has been literate for a couple of thousand years now, Polk. Some might think rote-learning is a tad old fashioned." Escalla was happily poking about in the desk. "Huh! What do you know? Some old decorator's plans for the palace. They even wrote in the titles of the rooms so workmen knew what furniture went where." The girl flipped out the map. "Morag is so careless. This should have been filed!"

The spider palace was laid out in a series of decks—engine rooms in the belly, a control room in the head. The rest of the place seemed to be palatial audience chambers, throne rooms, and guards quarters. Perfectly able to read any language ever written or devised, Enid took charge of the charts, smoothing them flat upon the floor. One big lion claw traced scribbles in the tanar'ri script written over some of the rooms.

"Let me see. The private chambers are right at the very top. Handmaiden chambers, guard chambers . . ." The sphinx gave a pretty scowl. "What exactly are we looking for?"

"Lolth." The Justicar's hand scratched as it ran over the stubble of his chin. He pondered Morag's words carefully and thoroughly. "Superiority breeds contempt. Contempt breeds a need to control . . ."

"Easy!" Escalla was changing entries in Lolth's appointment book, booking up her lunchtimes for the next seventeen years. "Contempt! She's a goddess. She won't see us as a threat, so if we challenge her, we can draw her into a trap! You know—slap Enid's stun symbol over a door, then I moon Lolth and we beat her when she runs through the door and gets hit by the spell!"

With a sigh, the Justicar regarded the faerie. "Lolth's magic resistant."

"Well . . . then we attack from behind the door!" Escalla shadowboxed back and forth between the legs and tails of her friends. "We bind her in the magic rope, use a silence spell to stop her casting magic, and give her the fist-beating of a lifetime!" The faerie was overjoyed. "This is gonna be simpler than I thought! Hey, Cinders! Fetch!"

She threw a pencil. All eyes followed it as it clinked onto the floor and rolled. Cinders wag-wag-wagged his tail, his teeth gleaming in the overhead lights.

*What?*

Everyone looked wearily at the faerie. Escalla shrugged.

"I'm lookin' for an instinctive reaction. I'm gonna sneak it up on him!" The faerie slapped Jus on the shoulder. "All right, big J! Got a route? Let's go!"

The Justicar was not yet ready to move. He stood over the map, one hand resting on Enid's warm shoulder as he looked down at the diagrams.

"Wash away evil. Wash it clean . . . ?" The Justicar tapped Benelux's wolf-skull pommel. "It's a clue. Enid, you're our riddle consultant. Any ideas?"

"Um, not really. Unless the washing-thing is a clue to a room we should use?"

Jus scratched the stubble of his chin. "Is there a bath house on the map?"

"There's this!" The sphinx carefully read Morag's beautiful round handwriting. "It says, 'Black Dragon Lair. Please grout tiles properly.'"

"That's not it." The ranger heaved a frustrated sigh. "Escalla? Henry? Any ideas?"

Henry could only shrug helplessly. Escalla merely cocked her frost wand and stuck her lich staff through her belt like a dagger.

"We'll keep an eye out as we go. What's to worry? You're all stoneskinned up, we have a map, and the faerie's taking point! What could possibly go wrong?"

They moved onward into the palace, and Enid leaned closer to Henry as they walked. "Henry, I get such a shiver down my spine whenever she says that."

"Absolutely."

Inside the palace were Lolth's private quarters——her treasury, audience chambers, and carefully prepared lines of defense. She would have long ago planned her retreat and her tactics in case of invasion. The Justicar looked at his map then chose a door. Above him, Cinders looked slyly left and right and made a happy growl.

*We go find spider lady?*

"No. No, we make the spider lady come to us."

*Burn spiders! Wheee!*

Cinders's grin turned to the palace above, and the party walked into the spider's lair.

*     *     *     *     *

Lolth stood in the center of her audience chamber, arranging one of her nasty little triumphs of ingenuity. The floor was a dead, leaden gray, made from quicksand gathered from the swamps of the Abyss. Lolth had a secret bridge running across the floor, hidden an inch or two beneath the sand. Anyone crossing the floor without knowledge of the secret path would end up dead and drowned! The goddess watched her giants bring in the last buckets of quicksand, and she flicked out her long hair in glee.

"Excellent."

A door opened, and Morag cruised serenely into the chamber. She saw the arrangements and flipped open a notebook, jotting down an estimate of the costs. Lolth saw her at work and raised a droll little smile.

"Morag! How good of you to join us at last. All your little files and folders stowed away?"

"Yes, Magnificence."

"Ah." The spider goddess walked the length of her hidden bridge. The aura about her made the air crackle with power. "Have you seen any intruders, Morag?"

Morag tucked her pen behind one ear. "I have seen no intruders, Magnificence."

"Yes." The goddess stood, held her arms outstretched, and horrible amorphous handmaidens oozed from under a door and removed their mistress's lounging clothes. Lolth allowed herself to be accoutered for war. Her handmaidens stripped her naked—all except for the delicately engraved gems she always wore about her neck. "Yes, Morag. Still, I have a little inkling that something might be wrong. Have you any thoughts upon that matter?"

"Your intuition is divine, Magnificence." The secretary flipped open her notebook. "I will rouse the palace guards and have them begin an immediate search. The webs, the palace, the boulder fields. It will delay our departure for at least two hours."

"No delays!" The goddess whirled, scornful and magnificent. "We will return to the Flanaess! I have to renew the spells that bind my armies. Have you any idea what those fools will be doing without my genius to guide them?" Lolth shoved her handmaidens aside and strode along the rim of her quicksand pool. "I can't trust any of you idiots to do anything right. How long until we leave?"

The secretary coolly pulled out a little timepiece—handcrafted modron work that she greatly admired. "Thirty minutes, Magnificence. Web fluid is still being loaded into the palace tanks. We still have only three boilers on line."

"Tell them to hurry!"

"I will tell them, Magnificence." Morag closed her book. "But we may find that water will only heat so fast. There are laws of physics in operation, even here."

Lolth stabbed a look of pure calculation at Morag. The goddess tapped at the gems hanging from her neck.

"There is something very un-tanar'ri about you, Morag."

"Yes, Magnificence." The secretary proudly settled her swords and pens. "That is why you enslaved me."

Lolth whirled. She looked at her quicksand floor in satisfaction and folded her hands.

"Yes. And you toil so very well. Dear, dull, drab, beige little creature that you are. But if you can shapechange, I do wish you'd at least make a pretense of a proper bosom. You really do tend to bring the team down." Lolth allowed the last of her own new clothes to be fixed into place—covering her own plush bosom in a thin net of spider web. "Stuck here for half an hour! I am annoyed, Morag. I wanted to be on my way ages ago. Today I hear nothing but delay delay delay!" The goddess immodestly hitched the thong of her garments. "Well, we shall be here for an hour, then. We shall make the best of it. Morag, are there enough demon vassals still here for me to be depraved?"

"I am sure you'll find a way, Magnificence." Morag acidly took notes. "Will that be all?"

"Oh, yes, Morag. Quite all." Lolth waggled her hand. "Off off

off! Go on! Slither back to your little hutch and start totting up things. You can at least be useful if you can't manage to be ornamental. Off!"

Morag slid silkily away and closed the door behind her. Lolth signed imperiously to a handmaiden, who opened up a door. Lolth turned and looked into the space beyond and gave a sly, evil little smile.

"Yes. We all have our little secrets." The goddess walked past the figure standing silently in her hall—a nightmarish shape of rotted flesh, dry skin, and bone, wearing an eagle fashioned helm and tarnished armor. "I have a plan for dealing with intruders, so be careful of the traps, my dear. But do please make yourself at home."

24

Pressed flat against a wall, the Justicar looked cautiously
around a corner. Beside him, Escalla frantically tugged at his tunic
to get the man's attention.

"Jus! This route leads downstairs! What are we going downstairs for? All the really hoopy treasure will be up in Lolth's
rooms!"

Jus glanced at Morag's map, then drew the faerie after him as
he went around the corner.

"Lolth will have her best traps and guards around her own
apartments. What we need is to strip those guards away from her.
We need her unprepared, rushed, and unfocused." The Justicar
looked around a corner, then signaled Henry to watch the rear.
"We need to get Lolth extremely annoyed. . . ."

"O-o-oh! Pissed off spider goddess? Hoopy! Yeah, I can see
that!"

Silently drawing his sword Jus approached a door. Somewhere
up ahead, there was a hum that transmitted through the metal hull.

"*Control.* That's what our 'associate' meant. Lolth holds all other
beings in contempt. She trusts no one else to do anything right."
Jus nodded at the door ahead. "According to the map, downstairs
is the machinery that makes this palace walk. If we can destroy the
machines, she'll come down herself to see what's wrong."

Polk rose up onto his haunches, clearly dismayed.

"But son! This way we don't go into the actual lair of evil! We don't fight her step by step through the palace, facing every single trap, guard, and power she possesses!"

Escalla dropped down and patted the badger on his head.

"Ah, that's great, man. Let's call that one Plan B. We'll get onto it right after we have our brains torn out and replaced by cauliflower." The girl pointed at a door. "So the machine room stairs are this way?"

The Justicar listened at the door, then signed for Henry to prepare his crossbow. Jus stove the doorway in with a single massive kick, sending wood splintering into a big space beyond. There was a roar from inside, and two huge shapes surged up from a heap of garbage on the floor. Startled, the giants snatched for clubs even as Henry's crossbow hammered crossbow bolts through the air. One giant snarled as the little darts ripped into him, then went wide eyed as the sleeping poison smeared on the tips went to work. The Justicar was about to charge into the fray, when Escalla shot between his legs with her frost wand in her hand.

"Whoa! Mine!" Escalla fired her frost wand into the room. "Jus, back! Don't screw up that stoneskin spell!"

A blast of icy cold smashed into the remaining giant. The creature bellowed and recoiled. Invisible, Escalla sped into the room. A club hammered down at her as the giant blindly tried to smash her to a paste—then Escalla's frost wand opened fire from an indelicate position below. The giant arched and froze solid, dead as a stone. Reappearing, Escalla blew a wisp of frost from the tip of her wand, twirled it like a baton and tucked it into place beneath her arm.

"And that's how they do it on faerie turf!" The girl seemed pleased. "Hey! Who wants to search for treasure?"

Jus was in action. He swiftly passed the rest of the party through the room, propelling Polk with his boot. He opened the door that led to the rear of the ship, moving fast, always watchful and ready to kill.

"Move! Move fast. Go!" He picked up Escalla in passing. "No treasure hunting!"

"No treasure hunting?"

"Get moving before the guards come!" Jus paused at a door, kicked it open, and led the way through a storeroom. He paused outside another door—a door leading to a stairwell—and gripped Benelux tight. "Go!"

The door burst open. Four ogres rose from their nests beside a spiral stair. A hail of crossbow fire and a blast of frost met them, and the creatures were dead before they hit the ground. Jus ran to the top of the stairwell, looked down, then immediately led the way downstairs. He moved fast, and Escalla had to sprint wildly to catch him up.

"Jus! Jus, we should be careful!"

"The guards will be after us. There's no time!"

He had to shout. The stair was filled with an awful noise coming from below—a metallic clash and shudder that rose to a deafening roar. The air was thick with heat and steam. Soot caked the walls, hiding the faces of the damned inside the metal skin. Enid squeezed down the stairs behind Jus and Escalla. Polk and Henry brought up the rear. Stifled, the group descended echoing metal steps into a deafening universe of noise.

They stood in a vast metal hall choked with smoke. Huge furnaces ran the length of the chamber, each one a doorway into a raging hell of flame. Blank-eyed monsters, fanged, listless, and maggot-ridden, slowly shoveled coal into the fires. Some of the creatures even walked about among the coals, arranging white-hot embers with their bare hands. Pipes arched across the ceiling, some dripping water, and others jetted lethal blasts of steam. Tubes shuddered with force as steam drove through them. Others hung still and caked with soot as little quasit-imps ran skittering in the gloom. Furious heat struck the party like a physical blow.

Shuddering machinery made a hellish racket. The Justicar leaned in to Henry, Enid, and Escalla, and bellowed at the top of his lungs, "Does anyone know how this thing works?"

Everyone looked at Escalla. The girl shrugged.

"I'm the world's most deadly fashion statement! What do I know about machines?" The girl waved at the furnaces. "Look! There's a process going on here! Stop the process, and you stop the machines!"

"All right." Jus waved the others into the hellish room. "Keep away from the pipes! They look dangerous. Look for something we can break. Something important!"

The floor was covered in fallen scraps of coal. The Justicar salvaged a piece to feed to Cinders, then signaled the party to fan out. Enid and Henry flanked him. Escalla turned invisible and flitted about just ahead. Staggering and stumbling across a coal-littered floor, Polk hurried his short little legs to keep up. He pointed out the creatures servicing the furnaces and tried to swerve Jus's attention.

"Look, son! Tanar'ri! Demons just itching to be slain!"

"They're called manes, Polk. They're like zombies, only dumber!" Jus pressed Cinders down atop his helmet as a steam blast hissed by. "They won't even bother to look at us. They only do what they're told." The big ranger looked at the solid furnaces, the deadly pipes, looking for something that might cause Lolth to come and rage at her subordinates. "Benelux! Have you seen anything like this before? How does it work?"

*I, sir, am a sword. Not a mechanic.* Ever petulant, the sword shimmered in the Justicar's hands. *If it is information you want, I suggest you ask one of the bright red gentlemen over there.*

Dimly seen in the smoke and flames, the far end of the hall rose to a platform atop a pair of steps. Here were forests of rods, wheels, and control levers, all overwatched by a trio of hideous serpentine monsters. The creatures were shaped like anacondas with human arms, but they seemed to be wreathed in living flame. Jus dived into cover. Enid and Henry flattened themselves behind a pile of coal. The group froze, but apparently they had not been seen. The serpent creatures snarled at one another and attended to their mechanisms, twisting wheels to bring a scream of steam from pipes up above.

Escalla found a fresh lump of coal for the ever-greedy Cinders. "Jus, what are those snake-things?"

"No idea." The Justicar squinted through the steam. "Salamanders?"

*Salamander!* Cinders spoke with his mouth full, coal crunching between big teeth. *Dumb selfish bad! Steals coal. Chase hell hound. Kill human. Bad!* The hell hound gave a little growl. *No burn. Is made from fire. Cold kills him dead!*

"Woo-hoo! Little Miss Frost Wand is having a good day!" Escalla patted her favorite weapon, then noisily worked its arming slide. "Hoopy! I'll creep up, shoot them all with frost, and they'll be dead before you can say 'premeditated homicide'!"

She turned invisible again before there was any chance for discussion. Jus half rose out of cover, trying to bring the girl back to heel.

"Escalla! Escalla, be careful!"

"Hey! Trust me! I'm a faerie!"

* * * * *

She looked so hot it was a shame to be invisible all the time. Still . . . it had a delicious sneaky feeling to it! Invisible Escalla flitted gaily across the room, leaving footprints in the coal dust. Struggling to hoist herself up the control platform stairs, she stood in the middle of a scalding hot floor and grinned at her prey.

The salamanders towered four feet over her, with tails four times as long as she was tall—but none of it would help them. They were faerie fodder now! Escalla struck her sexiest, most aggressive pose and gave a raucous little cry.

"Eat frost, you disgusting serpentine weirdo!"

She triggered the wand. There was an asthmatic wheeze, followed by a flatulent sound. A tiny trickle of frost and ice gurgled out into the air and instantly disappeared. All three salamanders jerked their heads about, staring at Escalla with uncanny accuracy as she suddenly ran with sweat.

"Oh *frot*."

A salamander lashed at her with its coils. Escalla tried to fly over the blow—forgot that she was grounded, and was caught by a blow of the red-hot scales. The tail-strike hurtled her between a mass of rods and levers, throwing switches and spinning dials as the faerie squawked and tried to battle free. From the coal heaps, crossbow bolts fired as Jus and Enid charged. A salamander took one look at the intruders, whirled and hauled on a lever, making a piercing whistle blast thunder through the air. An instant later, a crossbow bolt ricocheted from the creature's skull, shattering a dial and making steam hiss into the air.

Escalla wormed madly through the levers, dodging from side to side as an enraged salamander stabbed at her with a spear. She sheltered behind a control bank. Mad with rage, the salamander jammed its weapon clean through the control panel, severing tubes and pulleys. Squeaking in fright, Escalla jerked back from the weapon, leveled her finger and blasted a lightning bolt right through her enemy. The salamander roared, shook itself, then caught Escalla in the grip of its red-hot coils. The faerie flashed up a heat shield spell, then struggled furiously in the salamander's grip, unable to get free. The monster squeezed. Escalla cursed, worked her lich staff free, and hit the salamander on the tail. The staff detonated flesh and scales, blasting its way through the monster to leave the salamander thrashing mutilated on the floor. Escalla threw the coils off her, then dived aside as two more salamanders came at her in a rage.

"Jus! Jus, little help here!"

\*    \*    \*    \*    \*

Charging the salamanders, the Justicar saw a flicker of motion as Enid galloped past a furnace door. A spear flashed for her flank. The Justicar bellowed a warning, and Enid dropped, the spear flying over her back instead of piercing her heart. A second spear came for the fallen sphinx, but Jus was already in its path. He hacked the weapon from the air then charged straight toward a salamander that stood inside the heart of a furnace. The creature snarled in triumph, falling back to make its enemy fight it inside the white heat of the coals. Instead, Jus slammed against the furnace and kicked the door shut, dropping the locking bar in place. A mane shambled over with a shovel full of coal, dumbly reaching for the door. Jus killed it with his sword, hacking it in two, then whirled to smack the head from another mane behind him. Inside the furnace, the salamander pounded on the door in rage, its fury wasted on half an inch of solid steel.

Jus whirled. At the control platform, Henry was locked blade to blade with a salamander. The creature lunged and Henry parried, then jammed his blade home in a thrust with all the power he could command. He twisted the sword in the wound, just as he had been taught by the Justicar. The salamander screamed and caught him tight in its coils. Henry abandoned his sword, ripped a crossbow quarrel from his belt, and stabbed the salamander in the throat. The creature fell back. Henry tore his sword out of the creature's chest and felled it with a huge blow that clove it through the skull.

Escalla and Henry fell on the last salamander. The creature, backed into a corner, held them off with its spear. The Justicar ran forward, leaped over Escalla and smashed Benelux down on the monster. The salamander parried, but Benelux blasted down through its spear and into the salamander's shoulder. Jus wrenched and twisted the blade, the salamander's bones cracking as he viciously opened up the wound.

Coughing and screaming, the salamander fell, and Jus decapitated it with a single blow. He stooped and grabbed Escalla by the wings, jerking her back from harm just as a valve exploded in a lethal jet of steam.

"Escalla! Here!" Jus tossed healing potions to Escalla. "Pass them to whoever needs them, then break something. Anything that will stop the palace from moving!"

The whistle was still screaming. Jus marched past it and smashed it with his fist, buckling solid brass as if it were paper. The noise gurgled to a stop. He pointed Polk to a line of pipes and levers.

"Polk, destroy!"

"I'm on it, son! Anticipating ya! Thinking one step ahead already!" The badger charged past, almost losing his hat. "Son, I think that whistle was some kind of alarm!"

"No! You *think?*" Escalla raced past, throwing levers and twisting safety valves shut all over the control panels. "Polk, sabotage something! Hurry!"

A huge pipe ran overhead between the furnaces. As boilers overloaded, one by one their valves popped and steam thundered into the pipe. Escalla saw the writing on the huge brass tube and yelled out to the Justicar.

"Jus! That's the safety vent! If we can close it, we might blow open some of this machinery!"

Instead of hunting for a control lever, the Justicar took a simpler route. At a dead run, Jus thundered through the engine room. Benelux shone a blinding white. Shambling manes tried to block

Jus's path as he ran, and he killed two of them without slowing stride. He gave a huge roar and smashed the flat of Benelux into the titanic pipe, and the whole room rang to the blacksmith crash of blade on steel. The pipe buckled, bent almost shut, and immediately the engine noise rose to a manic scream.

Steam exploded from the pipe, but the Justicar was already gone, diving and rolling away. A boiler wheezed, then suddenly swelled, rivets cracking like sling bullets as they popped and ricochet into the hall. Far behind Jus, Escalla took one look at the boiler and dived behind a pile of coal.

"She's gonna blow! Get your arses down!"

The boiler exploded like a volcano, blasting steam and fragments of metal into the room. The blistering hot shrapnel severed surrounding pipes and splintered the engines. The mechanisms seized, screaming and breaking—more steam pipes burst, and others collapsed and fell from the ceiling in a crash. Jus, still gripping his magical white blade, hunched beneath Cinders as steam jetted through the room.

The entire hall was choked in an impenetrable cloud of fog. From beneath a chaotic mass of shattered pipes, the Justicar rose up, then ducked beneath a scalding blast. The engine room was a madhouse of destruction—engines screaming, metal shattering.

A figure suddenly formed in the steam—a shape slim, jet black, and magnificent. A tall, disdainful, and beautiful dark elf stepped through the clouds—a figure with eyes filled with dancing silver flames. When she spoke, it was with a dozen voices torn from the throats of her prey.

"Just as I thought. Two little rats—Escalla and the Justicar."

Behind Lolth slithered Morag—pale and annoyed. Lolth unclipped her cloak of spider web and threw it back to her secretary.

"An infestation in the engine room. I so hate having to deal with little creatures." Lolth clicked her fingers to her secretary and smiled. "Morag, kill the faerie. Make sure he sees her die."

Jus leaped through fires, his hell hound wrapped around him and his sword a brilliant, blinding white. The sword should have smashed the goddess in two, but it met another force and blasted sparks through the steam. A blood red blade locked with Benelux, and Recca, emerging from a cloud of steam, screeched in rage and attacked in a mad, hate-filled blur. The Justicar fought hard and fast, parrying blows from the vampire blade as Recca drove him back and away.

Lolth watched them fight then gave a peal of droll, derisive laughter. She walked away into the steam without a worry in the world, heading for the Justicar's friends.

"Enjoy yourself, little elf corpse! Sweet revenge! Sweet, sweet revenge!"

Blade to blade with Recca, the Justicar retreated back into the steam. Recca shifted, anticipating an attempt by Jus to aid his friends. Seeing the move, Jus swatted at his old master's sword, then circled slowly through the steam.

The Justicar paced like a vast, angry bear, side to side, his sword now just out of engagement range. Recca matched him step for step. The Justicar spun Benelux, watching the cadaver of his old master, his old friend—his old enemy.

"You're no zombie. You're in there! Aren't you, Recca?" The big man watched Recca carefully. "So this is all for revenge. You abandoned them to their deaths, and now you think they owe you for all that lost glory." Benelux snapped up into attack position. "You never, *ever* abandon your people. Without love, there is no Justice."

He attacked in a blinding arc. Recca spun and caught the blow—leaped, dived, twirled, and cut. The Justicar ploughed forward, blade smashing, lunging, crashing into bright red steel. He fought to win and win fast. Roaring, he smashed and hammered at his enemy, ripping fountains of green blood out of the monster's withered hide.

✳   ✳   ✳   ✳   ✳

Hiding beneath blinding clouds of steam, Escalla hugged the
floor. She found Enid and Henry side by side, lying flat to look
for the feet and shins of incoming enemies. Polk had disappeared,
as had Jus. The din of steam, the clamor of machinery, and the
screaming of enraged manes made speech almost impossible.
Escalla scuttled over to Enid and Henry, bellowing into their ears.

"Find a spot to ambush Lolth. Over near the broken pipe!"
The faerie slapped Enid on one haunch. "I'll find Jus and bring
him back!"

Enid yelled something that might have been an answer.

A mane lunged at her, and Henry killed it with one blow of
his sword. He rose to a crouch and waved Enid into the din.
Escalla paid them no more attention. She sped through the
choking clouds, invisible and moving fast, looking for a pair of
conspicuously booted feet. She finally saw a spatter of sparks in
the steam—sparks flashing fast in a pattern she knew all too
well.

Swords crashed together—one white, one red. Escalla pulled
out her lich staff and pounded it in her fist like a cudgel. She
charged straight toward the fight, happily determined to blow
both of Recca's kneecaps off.

A blade flicked at her, almost too fast to see. Escalla made a
tumbling leap—a second and third blade missing her by the width
of a gnat's arse. An instant later, the blades were back, and the
faerie hopped aside, saving herself through the brilliant luck that
always attends pure genius. She flung herself backward in a handspring, leaped a random course through the steam, and heard
blades clashing on the floor behind her.

Escalla landed on an intact pipe and climbed it in panic, looking frantically through the steam.

Morag coiled, wielding three curved swords in her hands, her tail lashing behind her. She cut at Escalla again, and the faerie dodged by, leaping onto Morag's head. She clung to the tanar'ri's hair in panic, unwilling to club the woman to death with her magic staff.

"Morag! What the frot are you doing?"

"Lolth must be obeyed!" The tanar'ri hovered between panic and fury. "She has my secret name! She must be obeyed!"

Morag's tail grabbed Escalla.

The faerie turned into a slimy worm, wriggled away, and sprang like a javelin into the pipes above. She flashed back to her true form and shot her best web spell at the tanar'ri, plastering her to the floor. Morag instantly teleported away, leaving a blank spot sagging in the middle of the web.

Escalla ran like a weasel, fearing a reappearance of Morag from behind. She ran hard through the fog, running straight into Recca and smashing her lich staff into his shin. The leg exploded and the monster collapsed. The Justicar took off his foe's arm as it fell. Recca planted his remaining foot against a piece of wreckage and shoved hard, shooting himself back into the steam. Escalla made to fire a spell, but Jus grabbed her and sped into the fog.

"Lolth's here! She's after the others!"

They ran.

Steam billowed all about them. Manes lurched and blundered with outstretched claws, but Jus never stopped. He charged toward faint sounds of combat. Exploding through the steam, his sword was already swinging as he reached Lolth. She ducked by bowing forward and pivoting on one leg. The other foot caught Jus in a savage kick that clanged against his stone-skin spell with enough force to shatter steel. Jus spun away from the impact, Benelux rebounding from a silver buckler on Lolth's forearm. Lolth let the kick spin her around in a turn, then blocked a blow from Enid and hammered a vicious punch into the sphinx's hide.

Enid was thrown back by the goddess's titanic strength. Lolth gleefully blew on her fist and looked about the fog.

"Next!"

Escalla launched a spell at the floor beneath Lolth's feet, turning solid metal to quicksand. Lolth turned a backflip and flew away from the danger zone, smiling quietly in amusement.

A rain of crossbow darts from Henry was blocked by one quick gesture of her hand. The darts clattered away in a splash and shower of sparks—and then the Justicar came at her from a cloud of steam. He bellowed his silence spell, snapping open a sphere of total quiet. Lolth was inside the sphere, unable to cast spells. She clapped her hands together in silence. Teleporting away and landing behind the Justicar, she raked him with a poisoned sword. The blow flashed against the stoneskin spell—and there was a blast of light as Escalla leaped onto Lolth and cracked the lich staff against the demon's neck.

Jewelry flew in all directions—spiderweb cloth shattered, flesh tore. Lolth staggered aside, her scream of pain silent in the spell field. One furious sweep of her hand knocked Escalla aside, but the faerie broke her fall like a warrior monk and came up snarling, her lich staff already pulsing with power.

Wounded, Lolth sped free of her shattered necklace and teleported away. Enid rolled to her feet. Henry drew his sword and looked wildly through the murk—then the flash of a healing spell in the boiling clouds betrayed the goddess's position.

Jus charged, Enid springing to her feet to follow. Henry and Escalla made to follow, and Escalla dived into the fallen mass of Lolth's jewelry and began picking up the biggest, shiniest bits. Henry hesitated beside her and gave a panicked little cry.

"*Escalla!* Come on!"

"Wait!" The girl found what she wanted. "Ha! Here!"

Escalla grabbed jewels in one of her hands, then went dashing off to the fight.

\* \* \* \* \*

Jus's charge ended in a crash. The huge man ran at Lolth, and the spider queen threw back her long hair and laughed. She braced herself and punched empty air. Five yards away, Jus felt Benelux twist out of his hands.

*Telekinesis!*

The Justicar never faltered. He aimed a punch at Lolth, missed, then spun into a vicious kick. Her flesh was like teak, but still she fell sprawling. Snarling in rage, she punched empty air. Yards away, the Justicar staggered as savage blows hammered into his arms. He kept his guard up, wading forward like a boxer as the demon used her telekinesis to pound him to the ground. The stoneskin spell flashed, flared, and finally died. Lolth punched with vicious fury, and still the Justicar fended the blows. She gave a savage flurry of punches, then one huge upward shove. Jus deflected it with a boxer's dip and roll. He spun, kicked, twirled, and punched, smashing a steam pipe in two. The steam shot at Lolth's eyes.

The spider queen leaped away, landed beside Benelux, and ducked as Henry and Enid both attacked. Henry cut with his sword, the blow slicing empty air as Lolth swayed, turned, and kicked. Henry flew backward, and Enid struck with her claws. Lolth snarled—still in the field of Jus's silence spell—whirled, and broke Enid's forepaw with one blow of her hand. The sphinx reared in pain. Lolth drew a short sword, aimed a blow—and then an enraged badger suddenly had her backside in its jaws. The spider queen screamed in outrage, trying to dislodge Polk from her rear.

Enid limped back, shook her head clear, then lumbered back into the fray. Polk was thrown clear and smashed to the ground— dazed, injured, and coughing blood.

Arriving at the melee, Escalla hesitated, looked for her chance to attack, then saw Morag emerging from the steam. The tanar'ri was about to slaughter Henry from behind. Escalla gave a piercing whistle and waved Lolth's gems over her head.

"Morag! It was written on her jewels! Your name was on her jewels!" The faerie threw a stone to the six-armed tanar'ri. "Here, you're free! Now come and help!"

Morag caught the jewel, took on a look of dawning joy—and simply teleported away. Escalla stared at the empty space in absolute outrage.

*"Bitch!"*

Henry spared a despairing glance over his shoulder. "She's evil! What did you expect?"

Escalla waved another pair of gems in the air and bellowed at the roof. "Yeah—but Lolth kept all her records in triplicate!"

Jus went for his fallen sword.

Lolth saw the man dive, threw up her hand, and Benelux sped off into the steam with a telekinetic shove. As the demon queen watched the sword, Enid leaped. The sphinx was caught mid-jump by a telekinetic punch on her wounded leg. She landed in a tumbling heap, crashing to the ground in an agonized daze.

Escalla fired a spell at Lolth, but the magic simply died away. The distraction let Henry swipe at Lolth with his sword. The demon queen caught his blade with her buckler, smashed it from his grip, and felled the boy with a punch from her silver shield.

Lolth laughed. Wiping her eye in malicious joy, she spread her arms wide. Her form flashed and changed, swelling as she changed shape. Legs erupted from her sides, her black body bulged obscenely, her remaining gems changing shape to cling to her new form. Lolth turned into a vast, vile spider ten feet high. Huge poisoned fangs arched above the floor. Escalla ran at her with her staff and slammed it against Lolth's foot, only to discover that the staff had run out of magic. Swatting Escalla aside, the spider reared and turned its attentions to the Justicar.

Still radiating a spell of silence, Jus stood without a weapon in his hands, already measuring his next attack. Escalla sprinted behind Lolth, heading for her blind side. Polk coughed weakly, Henry lay unconscious, and Enid dazedly tried to stand.

The Justicar moved to drag Lolth's attention away from the fallen. He ran at the giant spider. With a cunning squint behind her, Lolth surged backward and squirted a cloud of web out of her spinnerets just as Escalla charged into the attack. Escalla was hit dead center by the webbing and flung ten yards away, slamming hard against a steam pipe that scalded and burned. The faerie girl wrenched at the webs helplessly.

The Justicar grabbed Lolth's monstrous fangs and heaved, his huge strength enough to start tearing the spider apart. The goddess threw herself from side to side in a rage, and Cinders flew free to slither over the floor. An instant later, Jus staggered as Lolth teleported away, leaving him holding empty air.

The titanic spider appeared on the ceiling ten feet overhead. Jus's silence spell was shattered as Lolth dispelled it from afar, her voice finally free to cast magic of her own. Shrieking with laughter, Lolth cast another spell, and instantly a dozen spiders the size of wolves blinked into existence all about the room.

Steam slowly cleared as the pipes ran dry of water and the furnaces burned down. Lolth clung to the ceiling, rocking with mirth. Her spiders closed in from all sides.

As Escalla changed shape and escaped the webs, Recca limped forward, his severed limbs oozing green blood and regrowing right before their eyes. Only his borrowed hand and foot did not regrow. They stayed as always—pale flesh torn from another creature. Escalla returned to faerie form, her eyes flicking from Lolth to Jus to Recca as a dozen huge spiders tightened their cordon.

Lolth was clearly having the time of her life.

"Little playmates! I so love having little playmates!" The spider rubbed her forelegs together, looking at the adventurers through all eight gleeful eyes. "What's next?"

Recca stood beside Benelux, looking down at the blade. Enid crawled away from him, dazed and shaking her head. The Justicar rose beneath Lolth and cast a proud, grim look toward his old master.

"Recca! You crave the honor that you lost? You want glory? Then fight! If you want to be remembered as a hero, kill the demon queen!" The big ranger held out one hand to the undead monster. "Stand with me! The way it should have been."

Recca looked down at Benelux, then at the Justicar. He took a pace forward, thoughtfully tapped his chin . . . then Recca ran Enid through.

He did it slowly, with precision, jamming his blood red blade through her hide behind her foreleg and straight into her heart. Enid wailed. Escalla gave a despairing cry and fired a spell that smashed Recca from his feet, but his blade stayed buried in the sphinx, glowing horribly as it filled with Enid's lifeblood.

Roaring, the Justicar flung himself at Enid, launching into a desperate attempt to rip out the deadly sword. It was the move Lolth was waiting for. She dropped from the ceiling, turning like a cat. She slammed to the ground behind the Justicar, and both her fangs blasted through his back, the points jutting through the front of his chest. Poison squirted out onto the floor, and Jus coughed, holding the fang points in his hands.

Escalla shrieked, her whole body chill. Lolth reared over the Justicar. Henry and Polk lay bleeding as a pack of spiders sprang at them in a wave of death. Enid coughed a shower of blood, and Escalla saw the life leave her eyes. Lolth pulled her fangs free of the Justicar and laughed as he fell to the ground. She whirled to face the little faerie, who stood alone, naked but for the slowglass gem hanging at her neck.

Escalla ripped the gem free. She hurled it at the goddess and fired off a spell. It was a tiny spell—one of the first she ever learned. A stream of magic missiles shaped like little golden bees. Lolth laughed to be attacked by such pathetic magic—but the bees struck, smashed, splintered—

And atomized the slowglass gem into a thousand shards.

There was a pulse of magic. A sphere of force shot outward from the gem. The sphere caught Lolth and the Justicar, flashing out fast, then expanding with a dream-like slowness. Inside the globe, all time stopped. Gem shards hung in midair—poison hovered where it dripped from spider fangs.

The sphere continued to expand. Escalla raced forward, grabbed Polk, and tore the portable hole from his belt. She worked feverishly fast. The globe enfolded Recca, Henry—Polk's head, then his body. The spiders pouncing at Henry and Polk all simply hung frozen in midair.

Escalla wept as she ran, shaking, numb, and blank.

She backed away as the sphere slowed its rate of expansion. It ground to a halt and shimmered—freezing the death and destruction of everything the faerie loved. She cried lost, hopeless tears. The girl bit one hand, trying to make the pain focus her. She had thirty minutes—no more. The time sphere would fade, Lolth would be free, and everyone would die. Escalla backed away, her mind racing in mad panic as she tried to form a plan.

*Ouch.*

The hell hound's voice rang in Escalla's head. She whirled, and there lay Cinders, upside down and crumpled. Escalla sped over to him, her hands shaking as she untangled her friend.

"Cinders!"

*Cinders fall down. Spider lady tough.* Cinders seemed a little dazed. *Cinders want faerie make plan now——kick spider butt! No cry.*

"Yeah. Yeah, that's right." Escalla wiped her face. She ran a thousand thoughts through her mind at once. "I'm the faerie. The faerie always has a plan!"

Morag had led them right so far. But there was something else . . . something at the edge of Escalla's memory. Words spoken in a rhyme . . .

"Wash away sin . . . wash away sin!"

Moving fast, Escalla grabbed one of Lolth's gems and waved it above her head, bellowing into empty air.

"Morag! I'll use it! I swear! Come here . . . *now!*"

There was a flash. Morag appeared—resentful, fearful, and with a panicked eye at Lolth frozen in time nearby.

"What? What do you want?"

"Help." Escalla pushed Cinders into the portable hole. "Teleport me! Now!"

The tanar'ri blinked in astonishment.

"Where?"

"You *know* where! Now go!"

Escalla grabbed the portable hole, leaped astride Morag's back, and the demon teleported them both away.

## 25

The Flanaess. After the dead stench of the Abyss, the smell of grass and dirt struck the senses like a fist. Escalla knew the shadows, the light, and the grass. She hadn't grown up here, but this was home now.

Morag had gone to Lolth's gate in the Abyss. From the Abyss to Keggle Bend, and then to a cave deep in the earth.

Even the dank caves smelled clean and pure compared to where they'd been. Enveloped in gloom, Escalla whirred from Morag's back. She hovered above a floor of hard limestone in a place that had the soft, slow echoes of an underground lake. Escalla levered open the portable hole. Cinders lay with his nose just peeking out into the dark. Escalla took a quick look about the cave and saw a dozen tunnels leading off into the dark.

"Morag, which way?"

"The lower tunnel." The tanar'ri thrashed her tail, undecided. "I can't go with you. Lolth will know I helped you."

"Fine! I don't frazzin' need you!" Escalla was already on her way. "Just stay here! You move one scale, and I use that secret name of yours to blow you open like popcorn!"

The faerie moved fast. Time was racing. With Cinders to guide her, she stormed down a corridor into a darkness that clinked with hidden chains.

"Sis!" Escalla bellowed into the darkness as she flew. "Hey, sis! Expecting a call?"

The sound of her shout echoed though the tunnels. Somewhere in these caves Tielle lurked, and nearby would be the horrible pool Henry had described. Speeding through the air, Escalla swerved madly though tunnels and caves. In the Abyss, time was passing fast and hard.

"Tielle! It's family reunion time!"

They entered a long, low cavern, and Cinders's voice hissed inside Escalla's mind.

*Left!*

Two chain monks had been hidden by a strip of illusory wall. Escalla detonated a fireball amongst them, blasting the monsters apart. The chain monks flailed forward in a mass of chains, dying as Escalla shot past.

Six more chain monks erupted from the nearest tunnel. They threw chains ahead of them, screeching in eagerness to drink Escalla's blood. She blasted a lightning bolt through the dense-packed tunnel, knocking chain monks into a shattered mass of bone and steel.

Escalla caught the glint of light from behind them, and she flew over the molten wreckage in a red haze of panic, grief, and pain.

"Tielle!"

She burst out into a huge cavern filled with silvery light. A narrow shore of limestone ran about a lake that shimmered an unwholesome quicksilver hue. Sluggish waves moved toward the faerie, as if the lake were a gigantic amoeba yearning after the scent of living flesh. Escalla sped above the lake to the distant shore and an archway of stone that stood conspicuously alone in the cave. It was a teleportation gateway, like a thousand others Escalla had used all her days.

"Keep an eye open!"

Escalla dropped the portable hole, propped Cinders's head on the floor where he could keep watch, and dived past him into the hole. She rummaged in the boxes stored deep in the hole, found

Enid's stun parchment, and felt sick as she crushed it against her breast. The parchment still smelled of Enid's spicy, feline scent. She saw the regeneration potion—the tiniest of vials—and weighed it in her hand.

"There's a plan! The faerie always has a plan." Escalla shot up out of the hole and planted the stun parchment beneath the arch. "Trust me, I'm a faerie!"

Cinders suddenly scowled, his eyes burning bright red.

*Duck!*

The hell hound blasted a huge gout of flames into a rock crevice. Chain monks leaped out of the hollows where they had been hiding, recoiling away from the flames. Escalla flew back to the lake, leaving Cinders and the portable hole where they lay.

"I'm bored, Tielle! One more minute, and I'm gone!"

Motion stirred at the far end of the lake. Emerging from her own luxurious apartments, Tielle posed in midair, attired in leather, gauze, and jewels. She held her magical drinking horn in her hands.

"Escalla! Come to taunt?"

The lightning spell almost caught Tielle square in the stomach, but she hurtled aside with only a hair's breadth to spare, slamming hard against a wall. The girl's magic horn flew off into the gloom. Still thoroughly alive, Tielle wiped blood from her mouth. Over the center of the vampire lake, Escalla hovered inside her anti-magic shield. Naked and coldly savage, the little blonde faerie waited for her sister. She had no lich staff, no sword or dagger, just bare hands, skin, and eyes that glinted murderous green.

"Come on, you fat git! Come over here and drop dead! Make my day!"

Chain monks capered on the banks of the lake, hurling chains into the air to fall well short of Escalla. Tielle looked left to right—saw none of Escalla's friends lurking in the darkness, and came flying low over the lake. Quicksilver fluid surged up at her, hungry for blood, and the whole lake trembled in need.

Tielle closed carefully with her sister then paused. She hovered just short of Escalla, tilting her head carefully, looking for hidden dangers and traps.

"No staves, no poisoned rings, no daggers . . ." Tielle flexed her fingers, suddenly intent—her skin tingling with building pleasure as she thought of her sister's life being choked out between her hands. "And just how were you planning on hurting me, Escalla? Have you been off training with the monks?"

Escalla bunched a fist. "Nope. But I'm shacked up with someone who has!"

She flew at Tielle and punched her with a savage left hook. Tielle tumbled in midair, then caught herself and attacked in a wild fury of fists and nails. Tielle screeched, howling in bloodlust as she attacked, and Escalla whirred about, punching fast and drawing blood with her hands.

Tielle grappled Escalla and choked her. The two faeries smashed into the roof, then Escalla had her teeth locked in Tielle's arm. Tielle screeched and changed shape into a flying serpent, crushing Escalla in her coils. Escalla flashed, changed into a spiny urchin, and pierced Tielle in a hundred places with her spines. The snake dropped the urchin, which turned into a flying squid and grappled the snake in a mass of tentacles. Turning into acid slime, the snake wrenched itself free.

The two faeries battled in a raging fury, shifting shapes almost faster than the eye could see. They hacked and battered at each other with tentacles, stingers, arms and tails, gored with horns, and ripped with claws. Escalla turned into a flying puffer fish and fired a stream of poisoned spines. Tielle switched into an armored ribbon-snake and whip-cracked Escalla, spinning the puffer fish away. Both faeries tangled again in a welter of blood and screams, shifting shape into lizards, wasps, and crayfish high up in the air. They surged and fought even after Escalla's anti-magical shield finally faded away. The smacked into stalactites, crashed into walls, then crashed into the shoreline in a tumbling mad fury of hate.

The monks gathered in shock around the battle. A stonefish lurched out of the fight, and changed into Tielle. She pointed at her opponent in a foaming rage as she screamed orders to the monks.

"Kill her! Do it! Kill her!"

Chain monks lashed at the other faerie, who wailed and turned back into Tielle. Shaking herself, Escalla dropped her last, most repellent form, no longer pretending to be her own sister. She watched the chain monks flailing madly at Tielle. They were tightly packed, like jackals ripping at a kill. Torn and hurting, Escalla rose into the air.

"Hey!"

The chain monks whirled, saw Escalla hovering in midair— and then disintegrated as she detonated her last fireball spell. The chain monks flew apart. Tielle jerked up out of the wreckage, having formed into a stone tortoise to save herself from her own monsters' chains. Bleeding and exhausted, she took one look at Escalla and fled toward the faerie gate at the back of the cave. Tielle hit the portal—Enid's stun scroll flashed—and the faerie crashed down, beaten unconscious by the magical blow.

Escalla scarcely bothered to give the fallen girl a glance. She sped into the dark, searching the cavern floor, and found Tielle's magic horn. She dragged horn, portable hole, and Cinders over to the lake. She dived into the hole and found their paltry few grooming goods—Cinders's fur brush, her own hairbrush, soap, and the straight razor Jus used to shave. The razor was absurdly sharp. Escalla tried not to think about it. She laid bandages, razor, regeneration potion and Tielle's magic horn out by the edge of the lake. Cinders lay watching her, beating at the cave floor with his tail.

*Faerie have plan?*

"Yeah. Faerie has plan."

*Safe plan?*

"Maybe. A bit." Escalla stopped, retrieved Lolth's gems from the portable hole, and popped them into Cinders's mouth. "Cinders, if this doesn't work, then call for Morag. Tell her that her true name is on the gem. Make her take you and Tielle to my father. He'll look after you, all right? Good dog." Escalla shook, mortally afraid. She put her arms around Cinders's head and hugged his beloved furry skull. "Love you."

*Faerie? Faerie what do? Faerie?* Cinders panicked as he saw Escalla flip open the razor. *Faerie, no!*

Escalla slit her wrist with one long slash of the razor. She tried to keep quiet, but one awful sob escaped her as she sliced open her artery. Faerie blood squirted out over the shore, and Escalla held her arm over the silver lake and let herself bleed into the horrible liquid.

Her blood ran fast, driven by a pounding little heart. There was so very little faerie to go around. Already drained white, with her blood spattering fast out of her arm, Escalla flipped open the potion of regeneration. She hoped Morag had played straight. She quaffed it down.

It tasted like spring water.

Escalla swayed, then felt herself fall. She caught herself at the last moment before pitching into the lake. Slumped sideways, she lay on the shore, her arm stretched toward the lake and her blood running in a shocking stream down into the fluid. Yawning, she felt her legs go numb and knew she was bleeding to death.

Beside her, Cinders mewed and thrashed in place, tail pushing at the ground and his chin smashing at the stone.

*Faerie! Faerie!* The dog sobbed, helplessly trying to reach her. *Faerie no die! No die!*

". . . 's all right, Cinders." Escalla wanted to blink but couldn't move her eyes. She felt like a rag, all washed out and worn. "Don' cry. Don' cry. . . ."

*Faerie, no!*

The room faded, and Escalla wasn't frightened anymore.

＊　＊　＊　＊　＊

Escalla felt something nuzzling her face—Cinders's nose, cold and firm. Blinking, she stared at her arm. Blood flowed out of the gash she had cut from wrist to elbow—far more blood that any faerie body could hold. Her heart beat slowly, weakly—but steadily. The girl watched herself bleed for a while, then felt an image of Recca's regenerating flesh settle in her mind.

"Blood. He does it with green blood. That's how he heals."

Cinders nuzzled more insistently, and Escalla sat up. Giddy, she reached for a length of cloth and carefully bound her arm. The bandages were stained red, but she kept winding the cloth tight until the bleeding stopped. The severed muscles hurt. Her arm was useless. She tied a knot awkwardly with one hand and her teeth. She found herself sitting, staring at the lake, and patting Cinders's warm, furry head.

"It's all right, Cinders. It's all right now. See? No one touches the faerie."

The lake glowed a pleasing, restful blue—like liquid sapphire or a perfect morning sky. Escalla looked down at her arm as it tingled. She could feel her feet again, and her heartbeat grew stronger. Beside her, the empty potion bottle rolled twinkling in the light.

Morag had given them a real potion of regeneration. Escalla prodded the empty bottle with her foot and felt her little body beginning to heal.

"Hey, Cinders."

*Hello, faerie.*

Morag had told Escalla the secret. The lake was blue. Blue for healing, blue for good—a blue that would burn evil just as the red water burned good. Escalla picked up the magic horn and filled it, then dipped the edge of the portable hole into the lake and topped it to the brim. She folded the hole, took Cinders and planted him over her head, then marched back to where Morag waited in the caves.

The tanar'ri stood, trying to appear serene. Her thin, beautiful face betrayed her nervousness. She looked anxiously at Escalla as the faerie appeared.

"What happened?"

"I got it. The vampire pool's water, charged with the lifeblood of a good creature." Escalla nodded. "Lolth's vulnerable to holy water."

"Shockingly vulnerable!" Morag shrugged her tail. "In the Abyss, it is hardly a disadvantage. Nothing stays holy there for more than a few minutes."

"I have the tools to win. I can go."

Escalla thought for a moment, heaved a sigh, then handed Morag Lolth's jewel.

"Morag, take me back there, and then go do what you please. If you take my sister to my father's court, he'll give you refuge and help you make a home. There are places quieter than the Abyss for you and your friend."

"You're giving me back my name?" Morag stared at the jewel. "You're trusting me?"

"There was no name on the jewels. I lied." Escalla shrugged. "Sorry. Hey! I'm a faerie."

Morag looked extremely annoyed. She grabbed Escalla, planted her on her shoulders, and growled.

"Meaning Lolth still has my secret name. So now I *have* to help you."

"Yep."

"I am annoyed."

"Hey!" Escalla looked acidly at the tanar'ri girl. "Remember when you nicked off and left us in the middle of that fight?"

"All right, all right!" Morag seethed. She had been outmaneuvered. "Let's go."

"Hoopy."

Morag summoned one of her followers to collect Tielle.

"So this place your father knows . . . it's much quieter than the Abyss?"

Still numb with shock and grief, the faerie gave a nod. "Much."

Morag teleported out of the caves, first to Keggle Bend, then the Abyss, the Demonweb—and finally through the brass door to Lolth's home plane. They returned to the spider palace.

The battle against Lolth was about to be rejoined.

*    *    *    *    *

Morag teleported them into the engine room. The boilers lay dead and hissing. All powers of flight lost as the physical laws of Lolth's home plane took hold, Escalla leaped down. She ran to the edge of the time-stop field and stared at the weird changes that had taken place.

Manes had come blundering to the rescue. There were perhaps six of them now, all frozen where they had walked into the time field. Escalla ran frantically around the rim of the field, staring in at the scene and trying to plan what she should do.

Enid was dead. Henry and Polk were unconscious and about to be deluged in giant spiders—all of whom hung in mid-leap. Recca had risen halfway from the ground and was reaching for his sword. Jus was on his knees, hanging forward, one hand crammed against the wound in his chest and a look of apocalyptic fury on his face as he turned toward the spider queen.

Working fast, Escalla flung Cinders down on the floor.

"Time!"

Morag had a time-keeping device. She retrieved it from her pocket and opened the cover.

"Time's up."

"Right! Quickly!" Escalla ran fingers through hair made limp with grief and worry. "Put a rag over your hand, grab Benelux, and shove it hilt first at the Justicar. *Move!*"

The tanar'ri went one way, Escalla went another. She gave a roar of rage and began firing her last few spells into the time field. Magic golden bees froze as she aimed at the giant spiders. Her black tentacles spell hung half formed, frozen in time, ready to choke Recca to death. She swung Tielle's magic horn into her hands, braced herself, and opened fire. Bolts of blue liquid shot into the field and stopped. She aimed to hit Jus right in the chest, then Henry, Polk—and finally Lolth. The girl refilled the horn, fired at Lolth again from another angle, and then she saw the figures in the time field twitch.

"Morag! *Show time!*"

Cinders lay beside the open portable hole. Escalla turned to refill the magic horn, and Morag threw Benelux in a glittering arc at the Justicar.

The engine room erupted into noise.

Spellfire flashed. A swarm of Escalla's magic bees blasted into leaping spiders, hammering them apart mid flight. Tentacles blasted up from the floor and seized hold of Recca. Water splashed and spellfire came from a dozen directions all at once.

Caught mid-run, Escalla looked wildly at Lolth as great bolts of blue liquid gouted through the air toward her. Escalla screamed in victory, her cry turned to a howl of despair as Lolth teleported away an instant before the blue waters crashed home. Escalla slid to the portable hole, plunged her horn into the blue liquid and felt it sucking in a titanic draft.

She whirled, ready to fight, and saw a vast shape looming over her. Lolth lashed out with one leg and smashed into Escalla. The faerie went cartwheeling away, the magic horn flying from her gasp.

Lolth pursued Escalla as the little faerie crashed against a wall.

"You pathetic little gnat! I'll make you scream for all eternity!"

Morag tried to attack but was smashed aside. Escalla looked wildly about for the magic horn. It lay ten yards away. She sprinted for it, but a wall of flames shot up in her path. Escalla skidded away in panic, backpedaling across the floor as the vast spider, fangs bared, towered over her.

"Morag! *Die!*" The spider queen hissed in hate. She began to speak the snake-girl's secret name but had only managed the first syllable when she staggered sideways, blood flying from her side. The spider screamed, her titanic body rocking as something smashed with the force of a meteor.

A huge bellow shook the hall. The Justicar, his wounds healed by the magical blue waters, stood sheathed in blood, massive and wild with anger, as he ripped Benelux from the demon queen's shell. The titanic spider turned, and Jus chopped into one of her legs, hacking through the carapace to tear the limb free. Lolth screamed out a charm spell, but it spattered harmlessly from the counter spell of Jus's magic ring. Lolth recoiled backward and opened fire with a magic missile storm.

Red fire darts blasted at the Justicar. The big man roared and moved his sword in a blur. Glowing darts hit, spun, and ricocheted. Others stabbed home, ripping his armor of dragon hide and spraying blood across the floor, but the ranger stood his ground. Morag attacked from behind Lolth, cutting in a frenzy with her swords. She drew blood, and Lolth stabbed out another spell. A huge shockwave hit Morag and flung her against the ceiling. The snake-woman crashed to the deck, stunned and immobile.

Escalla flung herself at one of Lolth's feet and tried to climb up the demon. She planned to turn into a lamprey and gnaw through the demon's guts. Lolth stamped, kicking out her leg and throwing the faerie off. The Justicar ran at her. She turned, fired web from her spinnerets, and almost drowned the human in an avalanche of strands. Escalla flew free, rolling as she fell, the breath driven out of her as she tumbled like a ball across the floor. Bleeding, she managed to lift her head as Lolth reared over her prey.

With a flash, Lolth shapeshifted back to her dark-elven form. Mad wild with the ecstasy of victory, the demon queen paced past Morag, Henry, and Polk—past dead Enid and the trapped Justicar. She advanced on the faerie, panting with a lust for blood.

"No fast talk, Escalla? No clever little plans?" Magic crackled about Lolth's hands as she prepared to inflict an eternity of agony. "Nothing to stop me killing you?" The goddess lifted her hands and gave a hiss of victory. "Has anyone got anything cute they'd like to say?"

*Yes.*

The voice came from behind. Lolth whirled, horror in her eyes, and a jet of blue fluid blasted into her chest. The goddess screamed, flesh boiling away, the blue water eating like acid into her face and arms.

Cinders lay on the floor before her, the magic horn gripped in his teeth, grinning like a mad thing as he hosed holy water all over his enemy. He humped through the flame barrier like a caterpillar, gleefully charging to the attack.

The blue water ran out. Cinders looked at his friends, wagged his tail, and champed the magic horn in his fangs.

*Cinders fetch!*

The Justicar ripped free of the webs that held him, Benelux brilliant white in his hand, just as Lolth teleported away. Escalla dived, snatched Cinders and the portable hole, and swarmed onto

Morag. She shook the tanar'ri until her teeth rattled, and suddenly Morag came to her senses.

"Lolth!"

"She's trying to leave the plane." Escalla clambered onto Morag's back, dragging Cinders behind her. "She's headed for the door into the Demonwebs!"

Morag surged up from the floor. As she began to teleport, Escalla yelled back at the Justicar.

"We'll take her!"

Recca had torn free from the black tentacles spell and was already screaming.

"Kill Recca! Take out his heart! It's not his! It's like his foot and hand!" Escalla's voice hung in the air even as she teleported away. *"His heart . . . !"*

With a flash, Morag, Escalla, and Cinders vanished. Wiping blood from his face, the Justicar turned, looking across the corpse of his friend the sphinx. He flexed huge shoulders and strode slowly toward Recca to deal Justice.

The cadaver held its red sword, dropped into its fighting stance, and hissed like a serpent.

The Justicar never slowed. His stride sped into a hard march, then a run that ended in a sword blow against Recca's sword that drove the cadaver to the floor. Jus spun and kicked, sending the corpse flying like a puppet.

Recca smashed into a broken furnace, and the Justicar bellowed in fury as he relentlessly closed on his foe. Recca staggered and came back into the attack, lightning fast. The red blade flashed in a mad web of attack, severing pipes and levers as Benelux hammered it aside. Steel rang on steel. Sparks flew.

Henry groaned. Polk stirred. Both of them stared as the Justicar strode past them, driving Recca back in fury.

Recca fought exactly as he always had—his showmanship immaculate, his acrobatics dazzling. He leaped over his foe—

exactly as Jus knew he must. Jus abandoned swordsmanship and grappled, and the fight suddenly became a battle of pure rage against rage. The Justicar's helmet smashed into Recca's face. He hit three times, then roared and punched his fist through the rough-stitched hole in Recca's ribs. Roaring, the Justicar clamped his hand and ripped the stolen, bloody heart out of his enemy. Recca screamed, green troll blood spurting from the wound. Jus shoved Recca back. Green blood drained from Recca's head and upper body, spattering the floor.

Recca staggered, took a two handed grip on his vampire blade, then made a wild swing at the Justicar. Jus blurred sideways, Benelux slicing a deep wound into Recca's thigh. Green blood drained from the wound. The cut flashed and healed, but Recca's upper torso was now drained of troll blood.

The monster attacked, leaping, whirling, screaming, slicing. Jus met the blade in three lightning-fast parries, spun, and severed Recca's arm. The limb flew free, green blood closed the wound, but this time the arm did not grow back. Yammering in rage, Recca blundered away, cocked his long sword clumsily in one hand, and charged straight at the Justicar.

Jus turned, caught the sword, and shattered Recca's elbow. The vampire sword flew out of Recca's hand. The undead warrior slashed with clawed fingers, and Jus twirled into the blow, caught, tripped, and shoved, ramming Recca backward to smash the cadaver's spine over his bent knee.

Recca screamed.

The undead swordmaster thrashed like a broken toy as the Justicar lifted him up over his head. Recca shrieked as the Justicar walked to the furnace, his huge strength holding the living corpse over his shoulders. The Justicar gripped, wrenched, and bowed Recca's body, bending it like a green stick. Bones split, flesh tore. With a hideous crack, Recca split in two, top ripping from bottom and troll blood spraying onto the walls. The Justicar tossed the monster's thrashing legs into the furnace where they instantly caught fire. The upper body still fought and screamed. Jus held Recca by the neck, looked at Enid's corpse, and said— "Here's Justice"—then flung Recca's body to the flames.

Recca wailed as he burned. The Justicar held Recca's stolen heart in his hand and pulped it, hurtling the remains into the flames. Recca's stolen troll blood boiled, and his flesh blazed like paper. The blazing skull howled once more then split in the ferocious heat. Bones and teeth scattered as the monster crashed dead into the fires.

The Justicar turned and retrieved Benelux from where she lay. The sword seemed strangely subdued.

*Well done, Justicar.*

"Not well done. It cost a friend."

He strode over to Polk and Henry, both now stirring—both smothered in dead spiders and splashed with blue fluid. Dazed, Polk stared over at the furnace where Recca burned.

"Son . . . ?"

"You're all right. It's done." The big man set the badger on his feet then helped Henry to stand. "We're leaving."

The whole palace suddenly gave a titanic shudder. The floor split open, and blank, empty space appeared in the gap. Whatever will had held this plane together, it was now breaking apart.

Henry tried to lift Enid and drag her away, but she was too heavy. Stricken, the boy looked up at the Justicar. The big ranger sank to his knees and rested a hand upon Enid's braided hair— still soft, still warm and fragrant. He surged to his feet, pushed Henry on his way—and with one stroke of his sword, cut off Enid's tail. Henry cried out, but the Justicar already had the bloody fragment through his belt. The ceiling ripped open, and blank nothingness flooded into the hall.

The Justicar grabbed Polk and Henry and ran hard and fast for the stairs.

"Go! Back to the bronze gates! We're leaving!"

The spider palace tilted as its legs gave way. Fighting through the crash and fall of wreckage, the Justicar hauled his friends outside, leaving Enid's corpse to the flames.

❈   ❈   ❈   ❈   ❈

Lolth lurched down the trail, blind from the pain. Her entire body was a raging ocean of fire. Flesh still hissed and dripped from her bones. She promised eternal torture to every one of her enemies.

The bronze gates that led into the Demonweb were just ahead. Once there, she could hide, heal, and abandon this damaged body for a new one. On any plane but here, she was immortal. Anywhere but here, she could come back to fight another day. Feeling each step tearing her flesh, Lolth lurched into a run.

That damned Justicar and his worthless faerie! Lolth turned, saw her huge spider palace through a haze of agony, and then croaked out words of command. Explosions rocked the palace and it began to dissolve, breaking apart as Lolth abandoned the magics that held it together. She betrayed her palace staff, her handmaidens, and her followers as she left the palace behind, certain of killing her enemies in the wreckage.

The gates were only a dozen steps away, when a voice snapped out at her from the rocks.

"Hey, bug bitch! Here's a present from Enid!"

Escalla!

Lolth dived, and a jet of blue holy water crashed into the ground behind her. A tiny splash of it seared her flesh. Lolth blindly fired a lightning bolt, shattering rock and dirt, but the faerie had gone. Looking wildly about, Lolth prepared a spell—then decided to turn and run. She saw the bronze gates ahead, laughed wildly, and ran through the shadows as she sped along the path.

The Demon Queen focused all her attention on her goal. She was only four steps away from salvation when the ground fell away beneath her. A cry of agonized despair escaped her as she looked down and saw the yawning portable hole, filled with shiny blue liquid.

\*    \*    \*    \*    \*

There was a splash and a scream. Morag slithered up the path, over a boulder, and stopped at the big brass gates. She stared as she saw Cinders the hell hound lying splayed over a rock, his nose pointing down and his tail all a-wag. Escalla—filthy, tired, and worn—was wiping her face. She looked up at Morag, then stooped to pick up the portable hole that lay spread out across the trail.

Expecting a savage fight with Lolth, Morag readied her blades. She looked sharply about the shadows and the rocks.

"Well, is she here? Did you find her?"

There was a snigger, and a thump-thump-thumping of a hell hound's tail.

*Spider lady take B-A-T-H!*

Escalla silently closed up the portable hole, sealing away the open well of blue liquid. On the ridge above them, Lolth's spider palace exploded, crashing in fragments to the sands. With Henry under one arm and Polk under the other, the Justicar sped out of the mouth of the palace just as it collapsed. The big man turned, watched the palace fall, and then looked over at Morag, Cinders, and Escalla. Cinders lit a flame to guide his friends.

They came together by the gates. Jus held Escalla, burying his face in her hair, while Henry looked desolately at the palace ruins. Morag heaved a sigh of release and opened up the gates into the Demonweb, quietly ushering the adventurers home.

*    *    *    *    *

In the fields of the Flanaess, an army stalled.

There were long columns of spiders, gargoyles, and trolls. Demons had been marching, surrounded by stinking legions of undead. The whole mass had been poised like a spear aimed at the cities of the Nyr Dyv, the great inland sea. The army now numbered almost a million strong.

And then a presence—a purpose—lifted from their minds.

The insensate carnivores staggered. The multitudes of scorpions and spiders suddenly animated, their will their own again, and they found themselves hostile, hungry, and surrounded by prey. Giant spiders flung themselves on screaming trolls. Gargoyles turned and ripped into packs of flapping varrangoin. Demons raved and tore each other into fragments, while the undead fell apart or simply wandered away.

A million strong, then a hundred thousand. A hundred thousand, and then a few small bands gorging themselves on carrion. The armies of Lolth dissolved like mist upon the winds. Lolth's spells were broken, her realm destroyed, and Keggle Bend was avenged.

## 26

In a strange, warm land of sand and palms, the skies shone a clear metallic blue. No clouds broke the smooth arc of the heavens. No storms or winds were allowed to spoil the careful order of each day. It rained at appointed times, heralded by the appropriate deities riding chariots through the air. The crocodiles basked, the ibises strutted importantly across the shores, and all seemed well with the outer planes.

The river Lethe flowed slow and solemn here. Every day, a fanfare of trumpets sounded just after dawn. The denizens of this place—clean, white beings with the bodies of humans and the heads of ibises—strode to the banks, and with formal gestures bid the reborn to arise. Dripping with the waters of forgetfulness, worshipers of Thoth who had deceased on the material plane arose blinking from the waters. Their ibis heads were new and unfamiliar, and they walked clumsily with their new bodies. The attendants wrapped them in white robes and led them to the temples where they would be instructed how to serve their benevolent, wise god.

The temple itself was without parallel. A vast stone statue of white marble reared a thousand feet into the sky—Thoth the Ibis in his crown, with his shepherd's crook in one claw and a khopesh sword in the other. Stone wings shadowed and protected an avenue lined with two thousand armed and armored guards. The hawk-headed soldiers stood rigid and silent. Behind them were ranked stone golems, crouching like leopards and with the heads of crocodiles.

An avenue ran from broad docks upon the river, up the guarded road, and into the Library of the Ages. Here, a titanic white building held untold millions of books. Here, the reborn servitors of Thoth collected scrolls and parchments, stone slabs, and clay sheets of cuneiform. There were the metal disks of modron script, iron cubes from Acheron, and clipped feathers from the bird realms of Hadir. Here, written works from every world on every plane were catalogued and stored. Thoth, god of wisdom, kept this place sacrosanct, protecting his horde, for knowledge gave power, and power was the divine right of gods.

This realm was where Thoth's faithful were rewarded. Most of the lucky residents had been given the privilege of working in the fields of the afterlife. In hundreds of thousands, they lifted water from irrigation canals. They threshed; they planted. Day after day, world without end. They had been raised blank from the Lethe and taught just enough to be content with their lot. The benevolent god allowed them the noble bliss of toil, while trading the results of their labors with other gods and demons from other planes.

Some of the wealthiest dead had provided themselves with little sculpted models designed to perform their work for them. These lucky citizens were given more lordly duties. They served as accountants, scribes, or guards. A group of these lofty beings sat behind an alabaster table at the library's golden doors, watching as a barge disgorged a strange trio of passengers at the far end of the avenue.

A huge, muscular slave carried a roll of carpet. Beside him stalked one of the ibis-headed minions of Thoth, a being that looked anxiously from side to side as it walked. Ahead of them floated a weird ball of light—a beautiful, scintillating flash and dance of rays that shone with a benevolence so pure that it lit their hearts with smiles.

The three newcomers walked directly up the great, broad road, passing under the stares of thousands of guardians. Giant statues glowered down at them as they passed. They mounted the steps—one hundred of them in pure pink marble—and approached the mighty portal to the Library of Thoth.

Two guards, huge stone monsters with the heads of hippopotami, stood before the door. In front of the portal, the ibis-headed clerks awaited. One rose, poised and beautiful, and made a lordly gesture toward the visitors.

"Travelers from beyond the blessed realm! Know that the knowledge here is only for the children of true wisdom. Why have you traveled here, where the blessed dead bask in the glories of Lord Thoth?"

In reply, the ball of light flashed and glowed like pure, angelic sun. It shone with a warmth, a simplicity and truth that made the world seem fresh and new.

"Children of Thoth! I am an amazingly benevolent energy being from far beyond your realms! Long ago, my people evolved far beyond mere physical form. Our endless lives are spent contemplating pure goodness and philosophies of truth. I have been sent to travel to your universe to experience the lives and truths that may be found here." Gentle rays of sunshine caressed the ibis-headed men. "You are fellow cherishers of wisdom. I therefore will present you with this manuscript of quintessential truths—written here, upon this sacred hell hound skin."

The huge human servant sniffed. Built with muscles upon muscles, the dark, glowering servant held a rolled pelt across its shoulders—a pelt with a hell hound head that grinned like an insane crocodile. Beside the pelt, the second attendant stood holding a water jar, his ibis beak a little pale, his feathers ruffled.

The energy being drifted to hover over the rolled black pelt.

"The knowledge upon this scroll is so pure, so perfect, that it is dangerous for the simple minds found in this reality. Only the children of Thoth have intellects broad and deep enough to encompass the beauty of this gift. Please, may we have an escort to the, uh, the whichever place you catalogue your treasures of the mind, so that we may place this holy document in your safe-keeping?"

The scribes beamed, looked at one another, and one of the creatures bowed. It took a stately staff of office from a rack and led the way to the doors of the library.

"Then follow, O benevolent energy being. Truly you have been led to the one place of purity in all the cosmos! Here your scroll will be read by minds wise enough to cherish it. Allow me to lead you into the submissions hall."

They moved through the Portal of Purity and along the Corridor of Concepts, hung a left at the Halls of Holiness, then drifted past the File Card Index of Indescribable Illumination—five stories high and perhaps a mile long. Cool wide halls were filled with ibis-headed beings. There were emissaries from other gods and silent, unmoving guards. The air smelled of sandalwood, and the residents of the afterlife hurried to carry out all the tasks appointed to them. The energy being's guide inclined its beak to various luminaries as they passed. It gave its visitors the grand tour, explaining the glories and the mysteries for their receptive minds.

"Here is the hall of Thoth. Your gift can be made before the god himself, for here his light of truth blasts the deceitful, destroys illusions, and brings bliss to the good."

"Ah." The energy being pocketed a golden doorknob behind its back. "And, ah, this is where great and mighty Thoth inducts his new arrivals?"

"Indeed! At the far side of this hall is our cataloguing area, where new gifts are identified and filed. Such duties are the reward of the greatest in life—priests, sphinxes, and kings!" The long corridors came to an end. "But come! The god awaits your magnificent gift!" The guide ushered them through a mighty portal. "Now, look in wonder, for here is the Throne of Verity! In its presence, only truth may be told, so that all may revel in its purity."

In a hall so high that flocks of sacred birds circled the highest column tops, in a room created by the tireless labor of souls allowed nothing but the wish to serve, was a throne of gold a hundred feet high. Enshrined upon it, sat a titanic being—ibis-headed, crowned, sceptered, and armed. Ranked before him were untold thousands of worshipers, all paying homage in perfectly coordinated bows. The energy being stopped dead and seemed a little bit diminished, while behind it, the two companions stalled.

The energy being wriggled its little pseudopods in alarm.

"Oh, frot."

"Frot?" The ibis-headed guide frowned, then shook the comment away. "Now we shall approach the throne. There is a line of supplicants bearing tribute. You shall be number five thousand and eleven—a very significant number, as you will doubtless realize." The ibis-being clearly expected a reply, but received none. "In any case, how would you like your gift announced? What sort of secrets are written on this scroll?"

"None!" The energy being spoke in a screech, unable to help itself. "It's a pyromaniac sentient hell hound skin with delusions of humor!"

The ibis stared at the hell hound skin, which grinned back and happily wagged its tail.

*Hello!*

Blubbering, its preconditioned mind none too agile, the ibis-being looked at the visitors in absolute confusion. "B-but why? Why are you giving a hell hound skin to the great god Thoth?"

"We're not!" The energy being thrashed in panic, trying to stop itself from speaking. "It's a ruse! We're here to do an abduction!"

"An abduction?" The ibis recoiled in fright. "You? A benevolent energy being?"

"I'm not an energy being! I'm a skinny faerie with the universe's most perfect butt!" The energy being thrashed in panic. "Jus! Little help here!"

Still holding Cinders rolled on his shoulder, the Justicar punched their guide with enough force to slide the creature out of sight amongst the curtains.

"Boring conversation anyway."

"Come on!" Escalla changed back into her usual form. "Let's move!"

Nine-foot-tall guardians made of solid stone heard the noise, turned in puzzlement, then started forward to investigate. Escalla waved happily at them and pointed to Henry, who still looked like an idiot in his polymorphed disguise of ibis head and kilt. She tried to feed the guards another lie.

"Hey! We're interlopers here to expose your sham of an afterlife!" Escalla stamped and cursed. "Damn it! This tell-only-the-truth thing is screwing up my best fast talk!"

"Escalla!" Henry's feathers flapped in panic. "It's not working! Change me back! Change me back!"

"Relax, they'll fall for it!" Escalla gave an easy shrug, apparently oblivious to the two stone behemoths stomping toward them. "Trust me! I'm a faerie!"

Jus dragged his sword out from inside Cinders's rolled hide and crashed Benelux into the guts of a charging stone guardian. Benelux sheared through solid stone, spraying chips and gravel as she blasted out through the juggernaut's back. The stone being fell in two, both halves thrashing madly in rage. Jus swirled, hacked the hand off the second statue, whipped about twice more and smashed off its leg and head. He grabbed Escalla as she whooped and applauded him, breaking into a lumbering run as they crossed the hall of Thoth.

On the huge throne, the great god Thoth stirred. The disturbance at the far end of the hall had reached his notice. Guards ran for the little group of fugitives and were left in parts on the floor as the intruders escaped. The god Thoth pointed a finger in command, and as one, all ten thousand supplicants turned, roared, and chased after the blasphemous infidels.

Thoth stood and roared, shooting bolts of light that blasted huge craters in the floor.

With a wave of enraged inhumanity hot on her tail, Escalla looked over the Justicar's shoulder as he ran through the hall.

"Wow! These people are pissed!"

A blast of light splintered a titanic column mere inches away. Hundreds of tons of stonework thundered through the air, and the ceiling began to collapse. Column after column tilted and smashed into each other, one after another. A wall of dust and debris hid the onrushing crowd from Jus, Escalla, and Henry. The Justicar pelted around a corner, ducked a sword wielded by a jabbering ibis-man, and felled the creature with a blow of his hand.

"*Escalla!* Do you have any idea where we're going?"

"Sure! Trust me! I'm a faerie!" Escalla opened the portable hole on Jus's belt and stuck her head inside. "Hey, Polk? Polk! Check the thingie!"

"I'm doin' it! I'm doin' it! But you can't rush art. I've tried to teach that fact to so many, but they just don't listen. Art's from the soul, girl! Soul! You don't rush soul. You do that, you get bad—"

"Polk! We're a little stressed for time here!" Escalla fired off a lightning bolt that blasted through a dozen crocodile-headed guards. "Could you just—you know—do it?"

Grumbling away, Polk sat beside a big bowl of enchanted water. Floating on the water was a wooden disk, and upon the disk was Enid's tail. The tail swung about, settled, and ended up pointing in a steady line. Polk sniffed and, cocking one eye, looked up at the faerie.

"That way!" He pointed in the direction indicated by the tuft of Enid's fluffy tail. "Is the boy still dawdling? Are we there yet?"

Leaning through the hole, the sound of sword fighting loud behind her, Escalla gave the tail a scowl.

"How do you know it's not the other way? You know—maybe the wet end points the way?"

"Do you want art, or do you want argument?" Polk pointed an imperious paw. "I'm a quadruped. I know tails! Now get goin'. We've got real work to do elsewhere!"

"Fine!" The faerie cast a cloud of choking fog to block the passageway behind her. "Sheesh! Badgers are so grouchy before their mid-morning nap!"

Folding his paws and muttering, Polk looked over to the tanar'ri who sheltered at the far side of the portable hole. She was gnawing all six sets of nails. Polk sniffed and shook his head.

"No gumption! Young folks today just have no gumption! Stop frettin', woman! It's only the halls of the gods!"

With her scales a horrid shade of grey, Morag rocked back and forth in panic.

"Oh, we are going to be killed." The demon heard a fireball detonate overhead, accompanied by the battle cry of thousands of Thoth's followers. "What am I doing here?"

Escalla popped her head in through the lip of the hole.

"I told you! You do the teleport thing for us, and dad will have your dream castle made, furnished—he'll even put in gardens! Peace and quiet—a love nest where the Blood Wars never go." The faerie gave an airy little wave. "So chill already! You're in a portable hole. What could possibly go wrong? Trust me! I'm a faerie!"

Escalla disappeared. Seething, Morag thrashed her tail and said, "I do wish she would stop saying that."

Outside the portable hole, the battle raged. They were deep amidst vast mazes of book-laden shelves that towered a hundred feet high. Librarians atop spindly ladders clutched for dear life as Jus and Escalla rampaged below, knocking into shelves and toppling ladders behind them. Still carrying a heavy brass urn of water, still with his ibis head and beak, Henry gave an apologetic bob and nod as he passed the librarians and hurried after his friends. Polk called out from down in the portable hole, and Escalla halted hovering at the next intersection and shoved her friends into a new row of shelves.

"That way! Hurry!"

The sound of the pursuing multitudes was like an onrushing tidal wave. The Justicar led the way, Cinders's smoke trailing behind him as he ran. The big man turned a corner, there was a thunderous roar, and the bookshelf just above him blasted apart as a huge lion paw came crashing through the air.

A titanic being loomed over the intruders. The creature was monstrous—a huge statue of black marble thirty feet high. Part hippopotamus, part crocodile, part lion, it roared and smashed down with a paw. Shelves splintered and tumbled in all directions. Escalla went tumbling in midair and landed hard upon her backside, bruising it fiercely. She shot to her feet, chittering in rage.

"You cut-price bag of golem puke!" She flew at the monster in an insane rage. "I'll get you for that!"

Jus stamped in anger as he saw her shoot by.

"Escalla! No!"

The faerie flew at the monster like an enraged gnat attacking a bear. She whacked the creature on its backside with her newly recharged lich staff. Stone chips flew, cracks began to work their way through the behemoth, and the monster whirled awkwardly around and about like a monstrous dog chasing its own tail. It crashed into shelves five stories high, which tilted, crashed, and fell into more shelves, then more, then more . . .

A crash and jumble came as the wisdom of the ages hit the floor and was trampled underfoot. The multitudes pursuing the interlopers were buried under the shelves. Somewhere in the distance, the god Thoth could be heard roaring in anger. All hell was breaking loose. The Justicar stopped in place, opened his hands and formed magic between his palms. The wooden shelves of the nearest library racks suddenly burst to life, shooting out leaves, branches, and tendrils. The vines snatched at the huge monster, forcing it to blunder clumsily about. Taking Benelux in his hand, the Justicar ran straight for the behemoth's nearest paw.

"Henry! Charge!"

Benelux crashed into black marble, showering chunks of stone across the floor. Henry carefully set down his sealed brass jar. He was just in time to hear the thud and see Jus knocked off his feet by a blow of the monster's foot. Jus flew one way—Cinders fluttered in another. They both hit the ground rolling, the Justicar coming up with his sword flashing in a parry and a massive stroke that severed the statue's paw. Roaring, the titan reared—still with Escalla battering its backside into rubble. As Henry charged, he heard her voice jabbering away in a frenzy of hate.

"I wear a thong! *Do you know what this is going to look like in a thong?* Do you have any respect for art? Do you? No! Well, respect *that!* And *that!* And *that!* And *that!*" The power charge of the lich staff had run out again, and now Escalla was just hitting a huge stone statue with a stick. "Oh, you're gonna play dumb? Well, take this!"

The top of the monster's head was wreathed in a fireball—not the most effective spell against blank stone. The Justicar cursed, shook his head, and surged back into action again. He dived, rolled to end up between the monster's hind feet, and hewed at the creature's legs, his sword ringing like a bell.

Jus tossed his magic rope to Henry. Henry whip-cracked the rope and swung up onto the statue's head, smashing his own sword down onto the monster's eye, making it shake its head and rear in anger. Henry was thrown clear, crashing through a bookshelf to land beside Cinders, who lay grinning atop a pile of magical scrolls.

*Hello!*

"Hey, Cinders." Henry blinked. His brass jar was a dozen yards away, still miraculously intact. "Having fun?"

*Fun!*

Escalla finally jumped free and whirred down to ground level. Jus pointed at the monster's flank, meeting Cinders's eye, and the hell hound enjoyed his friend's clever idea. As the monster came close, Cinders wriggled forward, reared, and blasted his flames. Hot enough to melt steel, Cinders's fire sent ripples chasing all through the marble along the monster's side, and the dozens of cracks from Escalla's lich staff glowed white-hot.

The Justicar disengaged, and his huge voice bellowed at Escalla through the smoke. "Escalla! Frost! *Go!*"

The faerie unshipped her frost wand and opened fire. Extreme heat followed by ice cold did the trick. The cracked stone burst, and the statue splintered like glass.

The Justicar parried falling rubble with his sword, too angry and too dangerous to dodge. As the dust settled, he strode through the ruins, collected Escalla, then signaled Henry and Cinders to regroup. The hell hound rippled over the wreckage, moving like a huge furry caterpillar, and behind him, hundreds of Thoth's followers came charging down the paths between the shelves. Some of the larger creatures forsook the paths altogether and scrambled over the mounds of scrolls, books, broken shelves, and stone.

Escalla watched Cinders pass her by and waved an astonished hand.

"Does anyone else find that amazingly disturbing?"

"You *had* to teach him to fetch." The Justicar parried an arrow shot from somewhere amongst the shelves. "Polk, which way?"

"Left, son! Go left!"

"Henry, Cinders, move!"

Galloping along to rejoin the Justicar, Cinders stopped, looked down a row of shelves, then humped out of sight and disappeared. An instant later, he came charging madly back, row after row of bookshelves exploding into flames behind him. The hell hound sniggered, and Escalla wagged her finger angrily at him as he passed.

"Cinders! Bad dog!"

*F-U-N-N-Y! Funny!*

"Damn it, Cinders! Steal that stuff! Don't just burn it!"

Henry snatched a glimpse over his shoulder at the fires and said, "I feel a bit guilty about this."

"Hey!" Escalla scoffed. "We asked them to let Enid go, and they said to go take a hike! So they can look on this as a lesson in not pissing off faeries by using my best pals as slave labor!" The girl had retrieved some wisps of clothing from Jus's belt and was pulling on new gloves of fine black elven mail. "Henry? Still got the jug?"

"Yes."

"Hoopy!"

Jus snatched up the hell hound and tossed him over his shoulder. Behind them, the fires spread. Winged guardians could be heard screeching as the soldiers of Horus were called upon to destroy the interlopers.

The group charged out from between the shelves and into a

great quiet hall where hundreds of figures lifted scrolls, books, and tablets from great untidy piles and sorted them at tables made from ebony. The workers never once looked up as the adventurers pelted past them, until suddenly a screech came from the portable hole.

"Back! Back, boy! You're runnin' too fast!" Polk blustered down in the depths of the hole. "Turn right, son! Right! Stop! Now go straight! Straight! Back!" There was a scrabble, and Polk's head emerged from the hole as Morag lifted him on high. "That's it! She must be right here!"

At a nearby table sat a silent figure dusting off a manuscript. Ibis-headed, androgynous, dressed in a kilt, and wearing a sad expression, the creature sighed as it worked. Escalla and Henry both stared at the creature for a long, quiet moment. The faerie slapped Jus on the shoulder and sent him on his way.

"Here we go! Jus, hold the fort! We'll be with you in a minute."

Enemies were thundering down the corridor that led into the room. The Justicar tied Cinders tight about his helm then strode forward, swinging Benelux in his hand. The sword was definitely not happy.

*Sir Justicar, I must protest! Can we not try reasoning with these creatures? These are worshipers of truth and knowledge!*

"If they're so knowledgeable, they should know when to shut up and run."

*Sir, I really must ask you to consider limiting the scale of this conflict!*

The Justicar planted his back against a huge shelf and heaved. His muscles bunched as his enormous bulk slowly pushed the shelf with its great load of books over, and the whole mass came crashing down to block the corridor. The first enemies tried jamming their way through the gaps, and Jus shoved them backward using a huge shelf board as a battering ram.

Over at the work tables, Henry and Escalla softly approached the ibis creature that was cleaning its book. Escalla took the

polymorph spell off Henry and returned him to his usual self.
They both edged up to the table, watching the sad creature at its
work.

"Enid?"

The ibis-headed being blinked and looked up at them. It had
Enid's eyes—honest and always a little shy, but no spark of recog-
nition came until her gaze lingered on Henry. She hesitated, then
nervously turned away.

"I'm not allowed to help you. You have to see a supervisor.
We're not allowed to help people."

"No. *We're* here to help *you*." Escalla spoke with infinite kind-
ness. "Do you know us at all? Have you seen us before?"

"No." The creature shrugged then looked down unhappily at
the table. "I . . . perhaps. We're not allowed to remember."

"I know." Escalla uncorked the big brass jar. "Here. We
brought you something."

"Oh! Oh, no." The ibis head looked away. "I am not allowed
to drink now. No food or drink until I make my quota."

"No-no-no! It's hoopy! This time you're allowed." The faerie
gently turned the ibis's beak toward her. "Listen. Thoth said his
afterlife arrangements suck and that we should come here and deal
with it. So we have a drink for you."

The creature looked anxiously at the brass jar. Henry's hands
shook, and his face was sick with love. The ibis head looked from
Henry to the faerie to the jar of water.

"I could get into trouble. How do I know I'm really supposed
to drink this?"

"Trust me!" Escalla opened her hands, the very image of pure
innocence. "I'm a faerie!"

The words made the creature jerk. It stared at Escalla in
wonder, then slowly held out its hands. Henry passed her his brass
jug. The contents smelled unpleasantly of river water.

The ibis creature hesitated. Henry kept his hands hovering

anxiously beneath the jug, and then the ibis head drank. It dipped its beak, drank slowly and deeply, and withdrew its dripping bill and stared into the air.

"Water from the river Mnemos," Escalla said. They had been gathered at vast expense and danger and effort from the wildest places of the outer planes—all to be brought here, for this perfect moment.

Enid turned her ibis beak and looked at her friends, her heart hammering. Her eyes seemed to clear. She saw Escalla sitting beside her and started to cry.

"Escalla . . ." Enid held the faerie against her heart and closed her eyes. "Oh, Escalla!"

"Hey! We've got a wedding. Can't have a wedding without my bridesmaid." Escalla cried wiping her own eyes. "It's all right. We got here. It's all right now.

Enid saw Henry and found herself in his arms.

"Henry! Henry!"

They cried. They kissed as best human and ibis could. Escalla sat a little distance away and let the lovers have their moment, and she wept like a babe. With a great wet sniff, she turned.

The Justicar and Cinders had set their barricade on fire and were striding to meet their friends. Enid held Jus tight, closed fingers in Cinders's fur as the hell hound jumped about and wagged his tail.

"Cinders!"

*Hello, cat lady!*

Polk waved.

"How?" Enid looked at them all in lost wonder, unable to stop her tears. "Why did you do it? Why?"

The Justicar took Enid by the hand and lifted her from slavery. "Because you never leave your people behind. *Ever.*"

A deep boom came from the barricade as Thoth's minions broke down the shelves. Enid looked longingly at her friends, then bowed her head and turned away.

"I can't leave. I'm part of this place now."

"Ha! No way." Escalla perched atop her friend's feathery head. "We made you a new body! Cloned it off your tail. We've got it in the portable hole. All we have to do is get you in there, read the spell, and you're back as good as new! So let's blow this joint!"

"A clone?" Enid was agog. "Just how much trouble have I put you to?"

"None! Nothing we minded!" The faerie happily shoveled priceless scrolls into the portable hole. "Well, we had to steal the clone spell from this wizard guy in Greyhawk, then make you a new body at Dad's place, then find the river Mnemos, fight a few evil denizens, avoid a few rampaging armies, then find this place and bust in. Simple!" Escalla finished looting. "Morag! Teleport time! Do your stuff, snake-babe. I think these locals are working into a real rage!"

Morag was there under protest. Escalla had tempted her with booklets of swatches and a roll of plans for Morag's dream home, but the tanar'ri was regretting the deal. Annoyed, the secretary peeked her thin face up into the light.

"Why are you all crying? I don't see what there is to cry about."

"Oh, yes you do." Escalla clicked her fingers. "All right! So now we get into the hole, and you teleport us to our getaway boat a few dozen planes away!"

Morag thrashed her tail.

"No."

The entire party stared.

"No?" Escalla placed a hand on the frost wand tucked beneath her belt.

"I can't. Not in here." Morag sniffed at the air as though it were poison. "This is Thoth's home temple. My magic won't work here. You have to get outside into open air. A garden or a field."

The Justicar grumbled, grabbed Enid by the hand, and led a charge to the far end of the hall. Behind them, the barricades collapsed. The group found a door into a colonnade and raced for the promise of open sky.

As they ran down a vast cascade of marble stairs, Escalla flew happily beside Enid's ear, so happy to have her girlfriend back that she couldn't let her go.

"So how's the food here? What do you afterlife guys eat?"

Enid ran awkwardly, holding up her kilt.

"Pulse."

"Is that a kind of sandwich?"

"Not really." Enid looked back over her shoulder. "Oh, dear."

Striding over the rooftops came Thoth himself, heading straight for the fugitives. As the colossal figure stepped over the colonnade onto the stairs, Escalla looked back and cast one of her oldest, simplest spells.

"Grease!"

"Hey Morag!" The faerie flew merrily onward. "How's that teleport thing coming?"

The tanar'ri grumbled from deep down in the portable hole.

"I'm working on it. Must you always be so pushy?"

From overhead, Thoth sang the song of avenging glory. With his sword in one hand and his scepter of life in the other, the god over-stepped the roofs and planted his foot right in the middle of a greasy patch that had suddenly spread over the stairs. Hundreds of feet tall, golden and magnificent, Thoth fell over like a jester treading on a banana peel. Escalla whooped and leaped high into the air.

"The faerie scores!"

Half the temple collapsed in the shockwave as Thoth fell. His scepter crashed to the ground beside the fleeing adventurers. Escalla immediately plucked out the hoopiest looking gem and threw it into the portable hole. Polk gave a screech of pain.

"Ow!"

"Sorry!" The girl looked around. "So can we do any more damage here? I think we're done!"

The Justicar had already pushed everyone else into the portable hole. He grabbed hold of Escalla while Morag stood waiting impatiently on the pavement. Jus leaped into the hole, Morag rolled it up and tucked it under her arm, and they teleported away.

# A Perfect Ending

A thousand miles away, the river Lethe crashed and tumbled into a maze of rapids. Grumbling, Morag slid across a fallen log to a hidden isle, passing through the unseen veil into another plane. The tanar'ri teleported again, and then again, muddling their trail as best as she could. Finally, she reappeared on the hind deck of a disreputable old boat and shook out the portable hole to let her employers clamber into the light.

They were on an alien river in a land haunted by pyramids and pteranadons. Coiling her long tail, the tanar'ri heaved a sigh and pushed off from the shore. They would have to cross into another plane by following the river before she could teleport again, making the leaps and jumps that would finally take everyone home.

They sailed onward, scooting into the river mists. Enid emerged from the hole—a sphinx once again, and with one of Lolth's best jewels hanging at her breast. The big cat settled quietly at the prow between Henry, Escalla, and the Justicar while Morag grumbled and propelled the boat from behind.

Enid looked at her dear, familiar paws, then out at the river as it crossed into another plane of reality. The riverbanks were now inhabited by dinosaurs dancing in feather headdresses.

"Um, where are we now?"

The Justicar shot a glance at Escalla, then gave a heavy sigh.

"Apparently those details are supposed to fix themselves."

"Ah." Enid neatly curled her tail about her hind feet, folding Henry beneath her wing. "Do you have any idea where you're going at all?"

Escalla threw a length of sausage to a velociraptor that danced along the riverbank.

"Sure I do! Trust me! I'm a faerie!"

"Yes." Enid purred quietly. "And no one touches the faerie."

Thoth's Kingdom was far behind. The nightmare of the after-life was fading to memory. Enid looked back and felt a little twinge of sadness in her heart.

"You saved me, but it will happen again one day. One day, we'll all have to part again."

Sitting happily in Jus's lap, Escalla polished her new engage-ment ring.

"Hell no! You guys are with me!"

Enid sighed. "We'll get old."

"Um, no." Escalla looked at her friends as if they were incred-ibly thick, then rapped her knuckles against their heads. "Hello? Has it not sunk in that you guys hang with a faerie? You won't get old! No one ages around faeries. Why do you think we're so popular?"

The Justicar raised one brow.

"I'd wondered."

The boat floated onward. Escalla rummaged through loot taken from the temple of Thoth. There were schemes to make, a wedding to plan, and Henry and Enid's romance to encourage—all that any interfering faerie could desire. Escalla plucked out magic scrolls, magic tomes, and scraps of parchment, delighted by each and every find.

"Hey! A shrinking spell! This is going to save me a fortune in potions."

"How?"

Escalla whispered into her friend's ear, and Enid blushed.

"Oh, I see."

"Hey," Escalla whispered again in Enid's soft fuzzy ear, "I'll promise you a thousand uses of my polymorph spell as an engagement present."

Morag slithered cautiously out of hiding, looked nervously about, then found that the Justicar had made a space for her at his side. She nestled down, unsure whether she was welcome, and then Henry handed her a piece of fairy cake.

Morag looked along the river and asked, "So do we have somewhere to go?"

Eveyone looked to Escalla. The faerie rolled here eyes.

"All right! All right! I got rid of the Hommlet deeds! I swapped them for a mansion. A *real* mansion! There's a whole private tower for Morag and her boyfriend. We can each have a wing of rooms, gardens, and even a hoopy little village nearby! It's .perfect!"

This was the first Jus had heard of it. He looked at Escalla in puzzlement.

"When did you swap the deeds?"

"When we went through Greyhawk! Some guy called Rump gave it to me." Escalla proudly unrolled the new deed and a map. "It's even got a name, see? Tegel!" Escala waved her hands to gather in all of her companons. "A few minor vermin to clear out, and the place is ours! Morag, welcome to the team!"

The reformed demon looked a little pained.

"Vermin?"

"It'll be nothing! Don't worry about it!" Escalla patted the woman's scales. "Trust me. I'm a faerie!"

It was a perfect ending: the river, faerie cakes, and a new adventure to begin. Escalla nestled against Jus and sighed.

"Adventure complete. And this time we even got treasure!" The girl scrabbled in her pile of loot. "See? I have this jewel from

Thoth! It must be a truth jewel!" Escalla planted the gem against her forehead. "Hey, Jus! Who has the fairest butt in all the lands?"

The big ranger leaned on his sword in the prows. He looked back at Escalla and smiled.

"You do."

"Hoopy!" Escalla gave a sudden frown. "Hey! Are you under my spell, or are you just saying that?"

The Justicar came and sat by his betrothed's side, spreading Cinders out to make a seat.

"Completely under your spell."

The boat floated past metallic swamps and fields of flowers. No one knew where the river went, or even where it stopped. All in all, the journey was the thing.

Enter the magical world of the
# DUNGEONS & DRAGONS®
setting in these novels based on
classic D&D adventures!

## THE TEMPLE OF ELEMENTAL EVIL
### Thomas M. Reid

Years ago, the foul Temple of Elemental Evil was cleansed of the evil that
dwelled there. Or was it? The Temple has brooded in quiet decay as the
seasons passed, but once again, dark forces are stirring in the land. In a
quest to avenge his slain master, a tormented elven wizard must lead
a band of rugged heroes into the very heart of evil itself.

## QUEEN OF THE DEMONWEB PITS
### Paul Kidd

*For one man, fighting in the Greyhawk Wars wasn't hell.*
*It was practice.*

When Lolth, Demon Queen of Spiders, seeks revenge against the Justicar and
his companions, it may well be the last mistake she ever makes.

## KEEP ON THE BORDERLANDS
### Ru Emerson

In recent days, the Keep has been increasingly hassled by elusive bandits and
vicious monsters, but the Castellan can't spare any guards to deal with the
problem. An odd mix of heroes-for-hire ventures outside the Keep to deal
with the troubles, but they find more than they bargained for—and maybe
more than any of them can handle—when they venture into the dreaded
Caves of Chaos.

*November 2001*

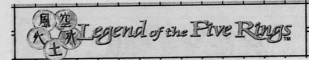
# The Phoenix
## Stephen D. Sullivan

The five Elemental Masters—
the greatest magic-wielders of
Rokugan—seek to turn back the
demons of the Shadowlands. To do
so, they must harness the power of
the Black Scrolls, and perhaps
become demons themselves.

March 2001

# The Dragon
## Ree Soesbee

The most mysterious of all the clans
of Rokugan, the Dragon had long
stayed elusive in their mountain
stronghold. When at last they
emerge into the Clan War, they
unleash a power that could well save
the empire . . . or doom it.

September 2001

# The Crab
## Stan Brown

For a thousand years, the Crab have
guarded the Emerald Empire against
demon hordes—but when the greatest
threat comes from within, the Crab
must ally with their fiendish foes and
march to take the capital city.

June 2001

# The Lion
## Stephen D. Sullivan

Since the Scorpion Coup, the Clans
of Rokugan have made war upon
each other. Now, in the face of Fu
Leng and his endless armies of
demons, the Seven Thunders must
band together to battle their
immortal foe . . . or die!

November 2001

A world begins anew...

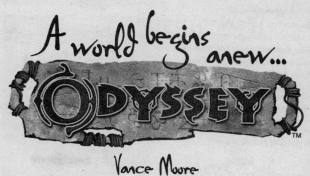

Vance Moore

**A hundred years has passed since the invasion.
Dominaria is still in ruins.**

**Only the strongest manage to survive in this
brutal post-apocalyptic world. Experience the glory and
agony of champion pit fighters as they enter the arena
to do combat for treasure.**

**In September 2001,**
begin a journey into the depths of this reborn
and frighteningly hostile world.